UMM DAWA . . . MOTHER OF MEDICINE

"You must leave this tent, immediately," Chelsea said in a voice much stronger than she felt.

"I will stay with my son."

"Impossible." She shook her head. "Perhaps, if your wife, his mother, wishes to join him . . ." she trailed off, wondering which of the women from the vast *hareem* claimed the affections of this man.

"He has no mother and I no wife."

"I'm sorry," she blurted, yet the joy she experienced to learn the child was an orphan suggested anything but. Her selfish feelings were quite shameless. Nonetheless, she couldn't squelch them, and couldn't stop wondering who all those women were if not wives. Slaves and concubines, perhaps?

Khalil merely shrugged and demanded, "Do you think a father less capable than a mother of caring?"

She stared at him nonplussed. Well, did she? Chelsea wondered, turning her criticism inward.

"Of course not," she denied. "But you still cannot go in there. You have to understand—"

"Understand this, woman." He stepped forward and grabbed her arm so quickly that she didn't have time to escape. "Muhammad's life is in your hands." He looked down at her. "And yours," he said, staring straight into her eyes, "is in mine."

EVERY DAY WILL FEEL LIKE FEBRUARY 14TH!

Zebra Historical Romances
by Terri Valentine

TERRI VALENTINE

SANDS OF TIME

ZEBRA BOOKS
KENSINGTON PUBLISHING CORP.

ZEBRA BOOKS are published by

Kensington Publishing Corp.
475 Park Avenue South
New York, NY 10016

Zebra, the Z logo, and the Lovegram logo are trademarks of Kensington Publishing Corp.

First Printing: December, 1993

Printed in the United States of America

To Marci Huff, my sister of the soul.
Thank you for your time,
your strength, your spontaneity,
but mostly for
the unconditional friendship we share.

Prologue

Dir'iyyah, Arabia
The Islamic year of the Prophet, 1002 AH

The *clackety-clack* of date palm fronds above the cluster of low-slung, black hair tents issued a noisy warning. Death lurked inside the largest dwelling, the air heavy with the pungent odor of camphor, coffee, cardamon, and burning dung. But the potent smells, even the winter wind howling beyond the camel-hair walls, were not enough to chase away the demons, nor to ease the discomfort of the boy lying on the pallet beside the stone-ringed fire.

Sheikh Khalil ibn Mani al Muraidi stared down at his small son, who was barely old enough to have left the confines of the *hareem* less than a month ago. He listened to the unbridled moans of pain and feared the worst. Bereavement was not something new to the Bedouin sheikh, but Muhammad was the child of his heart as well as his loins. He could not bear to give him up.

"I am sorry, *ya ràyyis,* there is nothing more I can do for the boy. His fate is now in the hands of Allah."

7

Khalil's dark eyes, steady and dry, lifted from his son and settled on the old man prostrate before him, whose frail body trembled with dread and anticipation. Of its own accord his hand moved to the hilt of his scimitar. To take the life of an incompetent physician was his right, in fact, his duty as the chosen leader of his people. What good was a healer who could not heal?

"Wait, *ya ràyyis.* Yusaf is wrong. Perhaps there is something that can be done to save Muhammad." The weather-etched face of the woman who dared to enter his private quarters uninvited was uncovered, her eyes as dark as his own and just as determined.

"Go back to your quarters, Umm Taif. This does not concern you," Khalil ordered. Nonetheless his sword, already pulled and placed against the back of the old man's exposed neck, hesitated.

"No, Khalil, you will listen first." Shiny amulets, shaped like hands to ward off evil, decorated her necklace, and large, hooped earrings tinkled with defiance. The silver row of bracelets on her wrists as she propped her tattooed hands on her hips repeated the rebellious sound. "Otherwise your son will surely die, and you will only have yourself to blame. Do you plan then to cut off your own head?"

Umm Taif, Mother of Taif, his cousin, was well past her child-bearing years, but she still commanded respect among the people of Dir'iyyah for her talent as a *kulhan,* an oracle. With a disgruntled sigh of capitulation, Khalil sheathed his sword and mimicked her stance, satisfied that he appeared much more intimidating with his towering height and broad shoulders.

"Allah bless you, *ya ràyyis,* for sparing my wretched, unworthy life." The whining voice of the old man filled the tent. His gray beard, as coarse as thistle, rubbed against Khalil's sandaled feet, an annoyance that he chose to ignore.

"So speak, woman, if you have something to say."

"There is a physician in Ad Dawadimi, a part of a traveling clinic from Persia, who can save Muhammad."

"How do you know?" Khalil lifted a dark brow in skepticism, for he could not remember the last time any of his people had visited the settlement a good day's ride to the west.

"I have seen this in a dream."

"Bah, foolish female musing. There are no *dukturs* in that hovel the Rashaad covet as if it were a prime oasis." Stepping over the prostrate man at his feet, he turned away. Even if he had heard of the famed men of medicine from Jundishapur who on occasion brought their knowledge and skills to the dwellers of the desert, how could he be certain they could help his son? That Muhammad would not die before he could return from such a long trip?

It was then that the emotions he had kept contained for so long chose to challenge his self-control. His eyes clouded; his throat began to ache as he struggled to conquer the unmanly display of emotion. He loved his son with all of his heart and was not ashamed of the feelings, only of his inability to accept that death was the inevitable conclusion to life.

"It is not foolish." Umm Taif's hand, as tough and calloused as his own, knowingly plucked at the coarse woolen sleeve of his *thobe*. "In my dream Ad Dawadimi is not as we know it. The Rashaad are no longer a threat to us. The sons of your sons and beyond—they are greater than even you or I can imagine."

9

"You speak of things none of us can ever be sure of, old woman, as if it is in our power to grasp the future in our hands and mold it to our liking." Making a fist, he shook his head. *"Wallahi,* by Allah! That is impossible."

"No, it is not. There is a way to defy fate. It is dangerous, but my magic and your determination can make it happen."

"And have you seen that success in your dreams, as well?" he asked, his misgivings unassuaged.

"You can save Muhammad, *ya* Khalil," she insisted, "but only if you are willing to make certain sacrifices and are willing to believe." She shrugged her shoulders. "Unless you are afraid."

"I am not a coward." Khalil whirled, brushing off the woman's disturbing touch, her words—and his own susceptiblities. There wasn't anything he wouldn't do—or attempt to do—to save his son. He would willingly face and defy Allah, Himself, surrender his own life, even his Bedouin pride if that was what it took.

"Then, you must do as I say. My visions of both past and future have never proven false before, have they?" she asked in a way to soften the fact she was telling him, the sheikh, what to do. Taking up his hand, she pressed a piece of parchment into its leathery center.

"What is this?" He frowned down at the offering.

"Baraka. A talisman to protect you, the passwords to accomplish your daring feat." Then she smiled mysteriously, revealing her old and broken teeth, and he sensed she was not telling him everything that she knew. "Just as important, it is the key to your future, *ya ibn-uxt,"* she said, this time addressing him as nephew.

10

Khalil opened the precious scrap to read the beautifully scripted message.

"The brown shell of the sea," he murmured, then looked up, his dark eyes dry, his emotions under control once more. "What does it mean, *ya amma?*" Only rarely did he call her aunt, only in times of concession to her unfathomable powers to see into the depths of another's soul.

"Follow your heart, *ya ràyyis.*" Taking the parchment from his hand, she placed it inside a leather pouch and tied it about his neck. "You will know its true meaning when the time is right."

Her answer, typically female, as only women were given such luxuries, did little to alleviate his remaining doubts. Nonetheless, he made his preparations to depart as quickly as possible.

Mounted on his black war mare, Khalil glanced down at the two old people there to see him on his way. Yusaf, whose traditional medicine had failed to save his son, could not hide his nervousness, but seemed only too glad that the burden of responsibility had been lifted from his frail shoulders. Umm Taif, whose mystery and magic offered the last shred of hope, conveyed an air of calm assurance. The chilly wind, already growing in strength, as if it knew his mission and thought to stop him, whipped the hem of his *mishlah,* a warm outer cloak, about his ankles and the tails of his *keffiyeh,* a cloth head covering, about his face. In the distance one of the camp saluki dogs howled its restlessness and was answered by another farther down the line.

"Ride west, *ya ràyyis,* against the wind, and do not

give pause to anything," the old woman instructed, her hand lifted to shade her eyes from the moonlight so bright in the night sky that it gave the skin of her weathered face an alabaster sheen of youth.

Unable to stop himself, Khalil stared at the lunar-created illusion of creamy white skin. He could only dream of touching such real perfection. The women of the desert, although beautiful, were dark-complexioned—never fair and soft. Khalil shook himself to be rid of the distracting vision.

"May Allah ride with you," the old man offered, his gaze adoring, as it always should be from that day forward. Had not his sheikh, more generous and just than any other in Arabia, spared his life?

"I will return by this time tomorrow," Khalil assured, keeping his nervous mare in check with the firm hand of experience.

The old woman simply nodded her head once. "Otherwise you will not return at all."

Grasping the woolen rope by which he led his fastest racing camel, Khalil started off across the drifting red sand dunes, immediately alert for the signs of passage Umm Taif insisted he would find in the desert on his way to Ad Dawadimi. It seemed she had seen those, too, in her vision.

The brown shell of the sea.

As Khalil urged his mare to greater speed, he couldn't imagine what those words could possibly mean. Was he simply chasing an illusive phantom across the endless desert? In the meantime, would his beloved son die in his absence?

Even if it were so, he would not give up. This was the

only chance he had to save Muhammad's life. He would take it, even if he regretted his action later.

And then he saw it, just as Umm Taif had described it, a startling light in the distance as if a star in all its fiery glory had fallen from the sky to burn brightly in the sea of sand.

Grasping the little pouch attached to the leather thong around his neck that contained the magic talisman, Khalil took up the chant as Umm Taif had instructed him to do.

"The brown shell of the sea. The brown shell of the sea."

Urging his mare to top speed, he raced toward the glowing lights on the horizon, uncertain just what he might face.

He would go through hell if he must.

One

Ad Dawadimi, Saudi Arabia
December 17, 1993

Once again, the holiday season promised to be a bleak affair.

With a sigh, Dr. Chelsea Browne stripped off one of her disposable latex gloves and tossed it into the wastebasket beside the makeshift examination table, and acknowledged she was being a Scrooge if ever there was one, but her circumstances warranted it.

The Saudi government allowed no Christian celebration, no colorful lights, not even a Christmas tree. However, in truth, even if she could have had such holiday trimmings, she probably wouldn't have bothered. What good was Christmas when she would spend it all alone?

Oh, sure, her mother and father would call her from their home just outside Atlanta, Georgia, just as they had last year. They would wish her well and ask her if she had received the packages. No doubt she wouldn't because their contents would be considered contraband and confiscated before they could ever reach her. Why couldn't

15

her parents understand that certain things—most things to be perfectly honest—were taboo here in Saudi Arabia? Even something as innocent as the technical medical book they had sent her last year was deemed pornographic because it dealt with genital disease.

Yes, her father would call, demand to know if she'd had enough of being treated like a second-class citizen in a third world country. Wasn't it time for her to come home and take up her cushy life where she'd left off nearly two years ago?

Perhaps he was right. There was still plenty of opportunity—almost three years—to pursue her equestrian dream of riding in the Olympics. And to think they would be held right there at home, in Atlanta.

Or better still. Maybe she should give the whole thing up and marry Michael. Now that would please her father to no end.

Capitulation was tempting, very tempting, especially when confronted with frustrating days' like today.

"What is the use?" Chelsea muttered, pulling off the remaining glove and pitching it in the trash. Then she marched through the open door and threaded her way along the maze of corridors. These Arabs were impossible to say the least—just like the woman she had finished examining.

Mawia was very pretty, probably no more than eighteen. Chelsea couldn't be exact, not with the way the Middle Easterners reckoned time and dates. Regardless, the girl was married to a well-to-do merchant of Ad Dawadimi. Three months ago Chelsea had warned her that to risk having children could possibly cost her her life. It seemed the little fool had gone home that very night and conceived a child.

16

Well, all she could do now was watch, and wait, and hope that Mawia's resilience and youth would see her through the next six months. That was the same approach she planned to take with Christmas as well.

Entering the small room of the ancient mud house she used as an office, Chelsea dropped down on the over-stuffed chair with the hideous green upholstery held to-gether with clashing duct tape that constantly came undone and stuck to the back of her white jacket. What she wouldn't give for a good, stiff drink about now. She laughed. Even that pleasure was forbidden in this country.

Finishing up her notes on Mawia's file, she pushed it to the side. Monday she would talk to Dr. Huff, her col-league at the mobile clinic, about that particular case. Joe was much more qualified to handle obstetrics. To be perfectly honest, as a man he was better equipped to cope with the entire Middle East mentality.

Yes, home was beginning to look better and better even if her father did try constantly to tell her what to do. What did it matter if she was giving up and running away? On days like today she couldn't imagine what had gotten into her when she'd decided to pass up the oppor-tunity to go into pediatric practice with her father back in Atlanta. Oh, no, nothing so ordinary for her. She had wanted to save the world single-handedly.

Succumbing to the feelings of regret, she closed her eyes and rubbed her temples hoping to ease the throbbing pain in her head. The faces of the many Bedouin children whose lives she had saved or enriched over the last year and a half ran through her mind like an old movie. Maybe she'd not healed the ailments of the entire world, but she had done her fair share. She knew then not only why she had come to the Middle East, but why she stayed battling government red tape and male prejudices as well as the insufferable weather conditions.

"Ya Duktur?"

"Yes, what is it?" Chelsea mumbled in English. Arabic still confounded her. Not that it was an especially difficult language to learn, but she found so little time to improve her skills beyond the tourist basics. Maybe this holiday she would make it a project to increase her vocabulary. She didn't bother to look up at Jamal, her young, male Arab assistant, interpreter, and chauffeur. Driving was one more restriction imposed upon her because of her sex—perhaps the most irritating of them all.

"There is a man in the outer room demanding to see a doctor immediately," he informed her in his heavily accented English.

Did men in this country know how to do anything but demand?

"Tell him to come back on Monday," she replied emphatically, her massaging fingers stilling as she shot Jamal an angry look. "The clinic is closed." She glanced back down at her desk in dismissal.

"I've already tried that. He threatened to cut off my head if I didn't bring him what he wanted right away."

Surely she had misunderstood Jamal. His English was abominable at times. She glanced back up at the young man. His normally dark face looked pale as if indeed he had been terrorized.

"He did what?"

"Threatened to cut off my head," he repeated as he took his finger and slid it across his throat, leaving no question that she had indeed understood him correctly the first time.

Unblinking, she stared at Jamal. What did these insuf-

18

ferable Saudis think? That everyone was at their beck and call? The physician, the scholar, even Allah, Himself?

She slapped the palms of her hands against the cracked leather of the chair's arms so suddenly that the Arab jumped back.

"What is it, *ya Duktur?*"

"The last straw," she muttered aloud. Combing her short-nailed fingers through her shoulder-length blond hair to push it out of her eyes, she stood, prepared to do battle if she had to. She was the one in charge here, after all. She was doing this . . . towel head a favor to even see him this late at night. And if he made even one comment about her being a woman . . . well, she would simply send him packing.

She marched from the office, brushing Jamal out of her way. To her surprise, he clutched at the sleeve of her jacket, forcing her to halt.

"I do not know what you mean by this one straw, but you cannot go charging out there, Chelsea," he warned with uncharacteristic familiarity. Her name came out more like *Shel*-sea as the *ch* sound was difficult for him to pronounce.

"Can't I? Do you think he might actually threaten me?" She laughed, but the short, nervous sound did little to conceal her rising concern. Quite frankly, she had never seen Jamal so shaken up, and they had been through several hair-raising experiences together traveling among the villages of the mobile unit's territory.

"Maybe. He is well equipped to do it." He swallowed hard. "I have not seen a sword like the one he is carrying since I visited the museum of antiquity in Riyadh."

"What? No submachine gun, no cartridge belts crisscrossing his hairy chest?" After all, she had seen them

19

come into her office dressed in just that way. Never once had she been threatened. "Ha! Doesn't sound all that ominous to me."

"You must not go out there alone. I am serious."

"So am I, Jamal." She deftly removed his fingers from her jacket. "I am quite capable of handling some desert bucko with a Zorro complex."

By the perplexed look on his face, she could tell Jamal hadn't the foggiest notion what she meant.

"You know . . ." To the accompaniment of a guttural sibilance in the back of her throat, she slid her finger across her neck in imitation of his earlier action.

His confusion only deepened.

"Oh, never mind." She waved her hand to indicate that he should take the lead. "Protect me if you feel the need."

He hesitated, for that didn't seem to be what he wanted either. Instead he glanced toward the back door, as if he thought to run. Maybe it wasn't such a bad idea.

A loud commotion, the sound of breaking glass, followed quickly by a shriek, nixed such cowardly notions. Chelsea reached the front room of the clinic first. She couldn't believe what she saw.

There was Jamal's slasher, just as he had described him, his curved sword—every bit as sharp and frightening as the young Arab had indicated—raised in both hands over his head. At his feet, which were spread wide and braced, crouched poor Fatima, the old woman who came each night to clean up the clinic. Close to tears, she was babbling incoherently.

"Hey, you there. Stop!" Chelsea cried in English, rushing forward and throwing herself between the old woman and her attacker. "Just what do you think you are doing?"

she demanded of the Bedouin, who seemed to have gone stark raving mad.

The sword continued its arced descent—coming right toward her. There wasn't time to move, not even to scream. Even as she threw up her hand to shield her face, she knew the gesture was in vain.

Somewhere she had read that a person continued to think, feel, and even see for many seconds after their head was severed from their body. The thought did not comfort her, for she was still thinking, feeling, and seeing. Her heart pounded so hard with fear she couldn't catch her breath, or was that because her lungs were no longer attached?

As if a razor blade pressed against her flesh, not actually cutting, she could feel the cold steel causing the hair on her arm to bristle. She realized then she was still in one piece, the glistening scimitar caressing her raised arm, the dark, unfathomable eyes of the Bedouin who held it steady assessing her as any man did a woman.

He said something in a voice rich and resonant, in Arabic, in a dialect she couldn't quite grasp—something about the doctor.

She stared at him mutely, noting every detail about him—odd what caught one's attention in crises. His face was hawklike yet extremely handsome, his clothing richly made, not ragged like so many who came to see her. And yet there was something different about them, about him, but what it was she couldn't quite decide. Then she glanced at the sword, encrusted with gems of every color and size, about to sever her right hand. She couldn't have spoken even if she had understood him. Jamal had been right. That weapon *did* look as if it belonged in a museum.

He repeated his demand. Without a doubt it was just that. She could tell by the masterful tone of his voice, by the hard, uncompromising way he continued to stare at her as if she were chattel to be appraised and bartered for.

Pointing at her, Jamal responded in a thin, frightened voice, his words just as garbled as the stranger's.

"Jamal, what is going on? What is he saying?" she asked, never taking her eyes off the Bedouin or his sword.

"Samt."

His brusque order defied misunderstanding. She uncharacteristically obeyed without protest, clamping her mouth shut. However, she refused to be further intimidated, by him or his glittering sword. She glared back at this man who dared to threaten her as if he had every right. Even when his powerful hand gripped the scimitar tighter as if he intended to raise it for the final blow, she refused to look away.

His dark eyes glistened, and one corner of his sensuous mouth lifted, almost as if he found her show of defiance amusing. She suspected his expression was more of a sneer she'd misinterpreted, for there was nothing friendly about him.

He asked a question. Although it wasn't directed *to* her, she sensed it was *about* her. To her surprise, he reached out and grasped a strand of her hair and rubbed it between his brown, calloused fingers.

"Jamal, what does he want?" Her defiance was no match for the terror that was beginning to take hold of her. Unblinking, she held perfectly still as he twirled the lock round and round. But then, when he stroked the side of her face with the back of his hand, she jerked back and couldn't stop the tremor that shook her.

Like a raptor circling prey, the Bedouin reacted to the

change in her attitude. This time his smile was undeniable, but still there was nothing reassuring about it.

"He just offered me twenty camels to buy you."

"He what?" she squeaked, unable to believe that something so ridiculous was actually happening to her. "What did you tell him?"

"I told him you were worth much more than that."

In the few seconds it took to glance at Jamal to see if he was serious, she found herself spun about and clasped against a hard, masculine chest.

"Jamal!" she cried.

Poor Jamal was talking fast, so fast she couldn't catch a word he said, but there was no denying the desperation in his voice, nor the determination in her captor's when he responded with equal excitement.

For the first time in her life, Chelsea was so scared she didn't have the slightest idea what she should do. She struggled, she even threatened to call the police, but it did her no good. It was as if she were clasped in an arm of steel, her worth reduced to the value of a few lousy camels.

"Tell the doctor to show his cowardly face, or he will forfeit his woman." Khalil stared at his opponent, a *hadhar,* a town dweller. Slightly built, the younger man was not used to manual labor. There were no calluses on his hands, no hardship reflected on his countenance, no *muruah,* manliness, in his demeanor.

"I told you. She is not the doctor's woman, nor is she for sale," the *hadhar* repeated. "She is the *woman* doctor."

"You lie, *hadhar,*" Khalil answered with the contempt all Bedouin felt for town dwellers. To better make his point he lifted his sword and pressed the curved blade against his captive's alabaster throat. He heard her shallow gasp of fear, but she didn't cry out or beg for mercy. Her bravery was admirable.

His, however, was deplorable, just as his threat was a hollow one. He could no more slit the throat of the beautiful female than his own son's. Not only because of the Bedouin code of honor that protected all women from harm, but because she was the *houri,* the beautiful nymph from Paradise, who haunted his dreams—the woman with hair and skin as light as the sands of *al rubba al khali,* the barren lands.

However, the *hadhar's* refusal to cooperate made his position difficult, for he would not leave without the doctor he had come so far to get; but he would not beg for his help, either.

"I tell you, sir, that is Dr. Chelsea Browne. She belongs to no man." The young man's worried eyes fastened on the sword. "Believe me, if you need a doctor, she is the best there is—the only one available tonight."

At the sound of her name Khalil felt his captive stir against his chest.

A woman doctor? He had never heard of such an abomination. But then, he had seen a lot of things in the last few hours that he'd have thought impossible—great carts that thundered and roared along without a donkey to pull them, captured stars hung along posts on the streets giving off their bright illumination until it seemed more like daylight. He glanced about the room in which he stood. Even here in the familiar mud houses of Ad Dawadimi the stars were strung about everywhere. How had they ever been harvested from the sky?

"Duktur?"

At the sudden sound of the woman's voice, saying something he could understand, Khalil glanced down at her. Even so, his doubts and suspicions were not alleviated. But then he found himself staring into eyes as blue as the wild desert anemones. He had never seen eyes like hers in his life. Whether it was their unusual color or something in the way she was looking up at him, her gaze spoke of knowledge and skill—and genuine concern.

"You . . . need . . . *duktur?*" Among her slowly and strangely spoken Arabic, even harder to comprehend than the *hadhar's,* he picked out enough to understand her question.

"My son." He couldn't believe he responded, but he did, enunciating just as slowly and deliberately as she, trying to convey what was wrong with the boy.

Confusion clouded her lovely blue orbs.

Frustrated, he clamped his mouth shut. What was the point of trying to explain when she apparently couldn't understand him.

Then the *hadhar* said something to her in a language nothing like the garbled Arabic that everyone here seemed to speak. No doubt an interpretation, or so he could only hope, that continued back and forth between them for a moment.

He didn't like not knowing what was going on, what was being said and plotted. Long ago he had learned never to trust the settled people, and the woman was one of them. Tightening his grip upon his sword in warning, he felt her stiffen against him.

"Your son, is he warm to the touch?" the youth asked.

Glancing down at his captive, Khalil realized she was waiting for his answer. He thought for a moment, remembering Muhammad on the pallet just before he had departed, moaning, his boyish face flushed. His hand when Khalil had touched it had seemed hotter than the fire beside which he lay. He nodded.

Again she spoke to the interpreter, then looked up at him in expectation.

"Is he . . . is he . . ." The young man made a rolling motion in front of his face and said something unfamiliar.

Watching the charade, Kalil tried to make sense out of it. Not understanding, he shook his head and shrugged his shoulders.

Then the woman took up the strange action, making the most awful sounds in the back of her throat, as if she were retching. Immediately he let her go. If she was going to be sick. . . .

From a safe distance he watched the two of them gag and heave. And then it struck him. They wanted to know if Muhammad suffered from the malady.

"My son," he said, then repeated their gesture and sounds.

As suddenly as it had all started, the charade stopped. The woman—the doctor—looked satisfied. And then she asked him another question. To his surprise she jabbed him in the side with one slender finger that was amazingly strong.

Was this some form of attack? Clutching his lowered scimitar tighter, he backed up.

She followed, prodding him again, a little to the left, and then again.

"She wants to know if your son has pain in any of those places."

"He hurts," he acknowledged, remembering how the boy had clutched his stomach, but he couldn't say exactly where.

Then she spread her hand and made a circle all about her chest. Gladly he allowed his eyes to be led to her most intriguing feminine attributes. He wondered if they were as creamy white as the rest of her.

The moment she realized what he was looking at, she dropped her hand and blushed.

"She wants to know if the boy has . . . red spots on his chest."

He flashed the *hadhar* a belittling look. How would he know? He hadn't looked beneath Muhammad's clothing. He shrugged, and to his surprise the woman stared at him with condemnation. Enough of this. He was not here to be judged for what he knew or didn't know about medicine. Instead, he came here to take the doctor back with him, and she could answer all these questions for herself.

Herself?

Savoring each curve of her body, he once again scrutinized the beauty standing so impertinently before him. Umm Taif had said nothing about the doctor being female. What had the world come to when women could be so . . . unrestricted.

Then a thought struck him. Perhaps she wasn't the doctor he had come for, and he remembered the talisman his aunt had given him.

"The brown shell of the sea," he said, palming the pouch around his neck and looking from face to face to see if the magic words caused a reaction.

The woman stared at him blankly, the *hadhar,* as well. They exchanged a few words, and then as if he had said nothing at all, they turned as if to go.

"The brown shell of the sea." Grasping his scimitar, Khalil stepped in front of them, blocking their retreat.

The woman considered him briefly, then brushed past him.

Not to be daunted, he followed. Never had he met a more infuriating female, especially now, waving her hand at him and shaking her head as if trying to tell him to stay back. He wasn't about to be told by her what he, a leader of men, was to do. But just as important, he wasn't about to let her out of his sight.

"What does his son have, *ya Duktur?*"

"I'm not sure, Jamal," Chelsea answered evasively, glaring at the infuriating Bedouin, who seemed intent on dogging her every step, even into the supply room, but she had narrowed it down to three possibilities. None of them were reassuring, and all could well be deadly. "We must hurry and pack."

"Surely you do not mean to go with him. You know the rules. We cannot leave Ad Dawadimi without making contact with one of the other doctors first."

"How do you propose we do that? Joe is in Riyadh and won't be back until Monday. The others are with the mobile unit making rounds. If it is what I think it is, I have to go. I, not we, Jamal. You stay here and make contact." But Chelsea knew her young assistant would never accept such a decision. She sighed. "How can you be sure we'll be leaving the city?"

"Just look at him." Jamal cast a dubious look at the stranger, who was poking around in the supplies like a stray dog did the garbage, without concern that it didn't belong to him.

She wondered if he was stealing anything and began to watch him more closely.

28

"He does not dress like anyone from the city, at least no one I know," her assistant continued.

Chelsea agreed, but made no comment.

"He is Bedouin, *badawiyin*," Jamal insisted. He used the purest form of the Arabic word that indicated the remaining few true nomads who resisted all governmental efforts to bring them in and settle them in shanty towns. They were a difficult, unpredictable lot. Chelsea had already had several unpleasant run-ins with them. "*Wallahi*, I have never heard a dialect like his. He probably hasn't been this far out of the desert in years."

There was no denying that Jamal was right. The Bedouin was dusty and travel worn, almost primitive and yet proud. He had come a long way—and he was definitely a breed apart from any of the other people who visited the clinic. Even when she and Jamal had taken their turn in the mobile unit, they had never run across anyone quite like him. But it didn't matter what he looked like, or what he was. He needed a doctor. Under the circumstances she had to go.

The illness they dealt with might be nothing—but then it might be everything she had ever been trained to dread. With so little to go on, she couldn't be sure. Grabbing up a satchel, she glanced around at the carefully organized shelves of supplies.

"Let me go with him," Jamal offered upon seeing that his plea had had no effect on her. "I will bring the child back here to you—"

"No, that's a risk we can't take." Her mind made up, Chelsea began stuffing supplies and instruments into the bag, making a mental list of everything she could possibly need. If it was appendicitis, then she couldn't forget the appendix inverter and in case of rupture . . . "Jamal, where are the Penrose drains, rubber tubes and suction apparatus?"

"Appendicitis?" He crossed to a cabinet on the other side of the room and returned with the equipment she was searching for.

"Maybe, but I can't be sure until I examine the patient." Taking the sealed packet, she started to insert it in the bag, but an ironlike grip clamped about her wrist, forcing her to stop.

The Bedouin. In her haste, she had almost forgotten him. He said something she didn't understand, but staring up at him, his dark eyes assessing the objects in her hand as if they were instruments of torture, she knew what he was asking.

"Tell him, Jamal. I don't have time to explain what everything is for. If we don't hurry, his son could very well die." Her warning translated, she sucked in her breath and waited, fearing he might not capitulate.

His steady gaze never altered, not even upon hearing that his son's life was at stake. Finally he dropped her hand and stepped back.

"Hurry. Get a couple of the ice packs." She rushed toward the refrigerator where they kept the antibiotics and other medicines that needed to be kept cold. Scanning the labeled vials, she carefully made her selections. Once again she turned to the Bedouin, sensing his reservations about her. At least he said nothing derogatory. If he had, Jamal had tactfully not translated it.

"Ask him how many people are in his encampment."

The question conveyed and answered, Jamal turned to her, his youthful face contorted with alarm.

"He says over a hundred, maybe two."

"So many?" Chelsea paled with fear. They didn't have

nearly enough vaccination or antibiotics on hand to take care of so large of number.

"Ya Duktur, you do not think it is really appendicitis, do you? What is it?"

She shook her head.

Jamal was not to be thwarted. His obvious agitation made the Bedouin restless, as well, and she didn't need that. She packed up the few precious vials in the cold packs, zipped them up, and handed them to her assistant.

"An outbreak of salmonella, if we're lucky," she said, arranging her features to conceal the fear that gnawed at her insides. So she didn't have to continue to face him, she took up a prescription pad and turned it over, jotting down a quick note to let the others know what she was up to. She would stickpin it to the door of her office as they left, confident that someone would find it should she not get back by Monday morning.

"And if we are not lucky?" Jamal took the satchels and slung them over his shoulder with the other bags she had already completed packing.

Unsure she should tell him, she gathered up the portable sterilizer and adaptors, praying that wherever they were going there would be some source of electrical power. If worse came to worst, there was always the power hookup in the Land Rover. When she turned around to leave, she found Jamal still waiting for an answer. She glanced at the Bedouin, wondering just how much he understood, how much he surmised—how much was better left unspoken.

"If we're not lucky," she replied with a resigned sigh, "we could very well be dealing with an outbreak of typhoid fever."

Jamal's look of horror said it all.

Two

If Jamal experienced second thoughts about going with her, he said nothing. However, she couldn't blame her most trusted assistant if he did. For all her medical training, Chelsea herself hesitated at the very idea of what they rushed blindly toward. Not that she feared either of them might catch the dreaded disease. They had both been vaccinated. The overwhelming prospect of facing a multitude of people infected with the bacteria made her uncertain, mostly of her own abilities to handle such an emergency. Dear God, the situation could well escalate into an epidemic. The ramifications were beyond imagining.

But she made assumptions, something a professional did not do. She must assess the situation firsthand, make a diagnosis based on facts not hearsay symptoms. There would be plenty of time later to panic.

Leaving the clinic by the back door, Chelsea led the way to the Land Rover parked in the narrow alley that ran behind the building. She deposited her armload of equipment in the rear, careful not to put anything on top of the portable lab, and turned to help Jamal stash the assortment of bags that contained everything else she could possibly need—or so she hoped.

To her surprise she discovered the Bedouin standing at a distance just staring at the vehicle as if it were truly a sight to behold. What a strange man, this regal desert nomad with his dark, intelligent eyes that seemed to read right into the most protected corners of her soul. In all likelihood, she should display the utmost caution when dealing with him. No telling what he might be capable of doing or what his true intentions were. Instead, against all logic, she found herself drawn to him, wondering why so forceful a man intrigued her. She sensed that a vulnerability she couldn't quite put her finger on ran deep below the surface of his formidable silence.

"Ask him where he parked his truck." Chelsea glanced around, looking for the inevitable red pickup these Bedouins always drove. Loaded down with tents and household goods in the back, women and children all piled on, sometimes even sheep and goats, such vehicles commonly sailed down the remote roads at neck-breaking speeds. Yes, indeed, these Arabs loved to drive fast

Then she noticed Jamal was having a difficult time trying to make his question understood. He pointed at the Land Rover, then the Bedouin, but the man merely shook his head and jabbed a finger at the air.

"What is he saying?" Chelsea demanded.

"I don't think he came by vehicle. He keeps pointing and saying something about his war mare. I've tried to convince him to get in the Rover, but he refuses."

"War mare? Are you telling me that he came here by horse?" She glanced over Jamal's shoulder at the enigmatic Bedouin, wondering just who he was—what he was.

What he was, was walking away. No, he couldn't leave. If in truth an epidemic of typhoid fever had broken out somewhere close by, even in some remote village, she had to find the location quickly, before the disease could spread to other encampments and towns.

"Hey you, wait," she cried, but the Bedouin never paused, never even looked back at her. "Follow him, Jamal." She scrambled into the passenger's side of the Rover, willing her assistant to hurry.

But Jamal was the exception to her rule regarding Arab motorists. All the others might drive like bats out of hell. Not Jamal. Slow and meticulous in merely inserting the key into the ignition and starting the engine, her driver took his sweet time backing up and even making up his mind to follow the Bedouin, who had struck out across the empty lot on the other side of the street from the clinic with long, quick strides.

"Don't go around the block. Stick with him," she insisted, her heart sinking when their guide cut down another narrow alleyway between two buildings and disappeared.

Wheels spinning in the sand of the empty lot, the Rover forged ahead, bouncing and rocking like a ship in high seas as they navigated the rubble, bricks and stones and chunks of mortar. At the street corner where the Bedouin had disappeared, Jamal braked, revving the accelerator when the still-cold engine threatened to die.

The alleyway was empty. Where had he gone?

"We have to find him," Chelsea cried, frustrated, seriously considering pushing Jamal out of her way and taking control of the steering wheel herself.

As if he sensed her mutinous intentions, Jamal suddenly pressed his foot on the gas. Chelsea clutched the dashboard to keep from being thrown backward. They cut around crates and parked produce carts that constituted a *souq,* a marketplace, during daylight hours. The narrow, winding lane made several sharp turns, and Chelsea strained forward at each curve, hoping to catch a glimpse of her target. There was no sign of the Bedouin, as if, like some ancient jinni, he had disappeared into thin air.

Finally they wound their way to the center of the marketplace, the shops deserted and closed for the night. Several narrow streets converged at that point like a multilegged spider, each leading in a different direction. Jamal brought the vehicle to a halt. Which way should they go?

"We've lost him," she murmured, sitting back and closing her eyes in defeat.

Jamal was not so fatalistic.

She did not question how he went about making his decision. Gratefully, she accepted and trusted his judgment. In no time they had wound their way out of the *souq,* headed out of town.

Once they reached the edge of the settlement, the narrow street widened, turning into a paved highway that led east out of the village. Buildings gave way to unpopulated steppe littered with the discards of humanity—a rusting abandoned car, a broken pallet that must have fallen off the back of a produce truck headed to market, a jumbled mass of used chicken wire—as if civilization didn't want to give way to the desert.

That was when she saw him, or so she assumed it must be her Bedouin, perched on a small rise off to the left in the distance. It didn't surprise her to find him astride a coal black Arabian horse every bit as magnificent as its rider; in fact, such a duo seemed only natural.

"Look. There he is," she cried, pointing at her discovery.

The Rover hit a bump in the road, catching her off guard and pitching her forward in the seat. She managed to right herself, but then the vehicle came to a sudden halt. Once more she clung to the dashboard.

Like a carelessly flung ribbon the empty road stretched out before them across the landscape now empty and very still. The unnatural silence except for the steady hum of the Land Rover's engine sent a shiver down her spine. She glanced at Jamal to find him staring intently toward the rise where she had thought she had spotted the Bedouin.

"What is it, Jamal?" she demanded, furling her brows. Whatever bothered him, she felt it, too. She glanced down, noting that the hair on her arms stood out straight, just as it did on the backs of Jamal's hands gripping the steering wheel. Static electricity, she rationalized, but why would it be so prevalent here and now? The lack of an answer unnerved her even more.

"I think we should go back." Although he spoke softly to her, his gaze never lifted from the distant rise.

Turning her head, she caught sight of what held the young Arab enraptured. With a loud gasp, she caught her breath.

The Bedouin had returned, a magnificent desert prince straight out of the magical tales, *Thousand and One Nights*. Chelsea couldn't take her eyes off his arrow-straight figure, and as hard as she tried, she couldn't control the way her heart began to knock. A breeze lifted the hem of his black cloak, billowing it around him. Then the wind invaded the thick mane and tail of his mount, whipping the long hairs about like strands of black fili-

36

gree. Neither horse nor rider moved a muscle as they stared back down at the lone vehicle.

"He's waiting for us, isn't he?" she wondered aloud, her breath rasping in and out of her lungs so painfully she clutched at her throat.

"No doubt." Jamal swallowed loudly, confirming he shared her fear, or perhaps they experienced a natural excitement for the unknown? "I still think we should go back."

Go back? Some inner sense of self-preservation readily agreed with what he suggested, yet her heart insisted otherwise. The last thing she needed was to get involved with some desert Lawrence of Arabia, but to leave, to abandon someone—especially a child in need of medical attention—well, she just couldn't do that. She took her responsibilities as a physician much too seriously. No way would she turn her back on a golden opportunity to save the world—something she had been waiting for for so long. This had nothing whatsoever to do with her heart, she told herself. Professional dedication motivated her, nothing more. By God, she had what it took to be a great doctor, not just a mediocre one.

"Follow him," she said softly.

"I do not think—"

She raised her hand and silenced the young man's protest. "If you don't wish to go, I'll understand, truly I will, but I know what I must do." Her mouth set, she stared at him with as much determination as he presented.

After a long pause, Jamal looked away, shifted the Rover into low gear, and revved the engine, ending the confrontation, much to Chelsea's relief. Her threat to continue on her own had been just that—simply a threat. How would she have ever accomplished such a feat?

"I pray to Allah for both of our sakes, you know what you are doing, *ya Duktur*," he grumbled. Then he turned the steering wheel, and the vehicle took out across the desert.

Her sentiments exactly. Although she had won this one small battle, she didn't feel victorious. The real war had yet to be faced. In spite of her brave words and convictions, fear gripped her with icy fingers. When the time came, when the real test of fortitude confronted her, she could only hope she would know what to do.

Khalil watched the noisy metal monster slowly climb its way up the rise with the surefootedness of his finest camel. Had it swallowed up the *duktur* and the *hadhar?* Did it now come after him? Two white eyes lighting up the red sand like beacons in the dusk, the war machine, greater than even the fabled ones of his forefathers who had fought the invading infidels from the north, seemed unstoppable. His mare stiffened beneath him and snorted, her apprehension mirroring his own. To say the least, the future and the strange people who inhabited it were nothing like he'd anticipated.

All of the terrible, frightening unknowns—they had been the main reason he had left his mount in the desert outside Ad Dawadimi. Shiha was a brave creature, the finest war mare he had ever mastered. Still, he knew better than to expect a courage from her that he couldn't be sure he, himself, possessed.

"Easy, mare," he murmured, stroking her long, agile

38

neck wet with the sweat of anxiety, not exertion. The same perspiration rolled down the back of his own neck.

Although the horse continued to dance about, she held her ground bravely. Considering his own uncertain state, what more could he demand from her?

He wished he could say the same for the pack camel he had brought with him. The *dhalul* was being most unruly and stubborn as camels were apt to be, pulling on its lead line, bellowing and belching in protest, its great gazelle eyes wide in terror. It took all his strength and concentration to keep the frightened animal under control.

Like a stalking jackal, the great metal beast came to a grinding halt at the bottom of the rise, its two luminous eyes unblinking, its gleaming metal teeth clenched. Khalil felt the same overwhelming urge to run as that which quivered in the horseflesh beneath him.

But he dared not be so cowardly, especially since the woman had shown no such fear. Then he saw the golden-crowned head of the *duktur-houri* stick out of an opening on the side of the monster where its ear should be. She was speaking to him in that strange language of hers. It made no sense. Was she begging him to save her? No, nothing in her voice suggested a plea, nothing at all. In fact, to the contrary, her tone sounded demanding—most irritating, and very unbecoming in a woman.

If she belonged to him, he would be tempted to cut out that wagging tongue of hers or to teach it ways to pleasure a man, not torture him.

But he did not own her, and it was doubtful he ever would, if for no other reason than she struck him as the kind of female who refused to be anyone's property. What had the world come to when women could be so independent? What had become of the honor and pride of the men bound by God to protect them?

His questions unanswered, Khalil turned his horse's head in the direction of home, confident the woman and her tamed monster would follow.

Just why he was so sure of her actions, he couldn't say. He reached up and clutched the talisman on the thong about his neck. Perhaps the magic of the *baraka* would see to it; perhaps it was destiny. More likely, the will of Allah decreed that he, a powerful prince of the desert, must be humbled and made to pay dearly to save the life of his son.

"Oh-h-h!" Gritting her teeth, Chelsea expressed her frustration with the only means available. It was impossible to communicate with the Bedouin. So why did she bother to try? She drew her head back through the window into the vehicle and dropped down on the seat. As she watched, he turned his unwilling horse about with an experienced hand she couldn't help but admire. Then he urged the mare forward with a barely perceptible tightening of his legs, the camel he led with a leather thong bawling in protest as the trio moved off at a surprisingly rapid pace. In no time they descended the far side of the rise.

"Follow him, Jamal. Whatever you do, don't lose him now," she ordered, fearing once again the Bedouin might disappear—this time for good. She still didn't have an inkling where they were headed. Her futile, frustrating attempts to find out their destination had gone unanswered. As unreasonable as her anger might be, she still couldn't help but feel nonplussed by his lack of response.

Without protest her assistant did as instructed, throwing the vehicle in low gear in order to take the steep incline. Once they cleared the top of the rise, Chelsea sat back in her seat and released her breath. Just ahead, spotlighted in the headlight beams, the Bedouin moved along at a pace easy to keep up with, one that would not unduly tire his magnificent mount.

Again she had to admire his faultless horsemanship. However, she refused to be so generous in her opinion of the rest of him. His arrogance, even when he just looked at her, infuriated her to say the least.

Why did his typical, chauvinistic attitude bother her so much? All Arab men acted that way. She found it easy enough to ignore them. Men everywhere did the same thing, she concluded. But coming from this enigmatic stranger, such behavior inflamed that something inside of her that made her constantly struggle to prove herself an equal.

It had been that way in college, then even more so in medical school where even today a woman must work twice as hard to be successful. But getting her degree with honors hadn't been enough. She had still felt the need to prove herself as a top-notch physician.

Perhaps that was why she had taken this impossible job in Saudi Arabia. No, it had been more like she had coveted the position, gone after it with a vengeance. The fact that Michael had wanted it so badly had only made her more determined to snatch it from beneath his very nose.

Michael. What audacity. He had accused her of some romantic nonsense about looking for a macho hero to rescue her from a life of discontent. Her only dissatisfaction had been his inability to accept her for herself.

Brushing away the memories of both him and his ridiculous theories, she refused to dredge up any more of so painful a part of her past. Not now. Not ever. Michael would always be a chapter in her life best closed forever.

The Land Rover bottomed out in a small ravine, so hard that Chelsea hit her head on the roof of the vehicle and couldn't help but cry out. Jamal brought them once more to a halt. Frowning, he turned to make sure she was okay.

"Chel-sea . . ."

"It's all right." Rubbing the bump that already began to swell, she impatiently waved him on. "Whatever you do, don't let him get out of sight."

Did she read pity on Jamal's youthful face? Before she could decide, he looked away and concentrated on his driving.

For what seemed a lifetime they followed that undaunted horseman, up and down hills that at some indeterminate point turned into sand dunes of monumental proportions. Even when the tires of the four-wheel drive Land Rover spun and fought to dig in and inch forward up an especially steep slope—and each one got steeper and steeper—the feet of the untiring horse and camel never faltered.

It seemed as though the Bedouin magically sprouted wings. But no, such fancies could only be a moonlit illusion created by the hem of his black robes flapping in the wind . . . a wind that began to whirl the sand like spun sugar.

And then they were stuck once more. The wheel beneath Chelsea's feet whined, the Land Rover bucked, but still they didn't move except when the rear end skidded sideways. Helplessly she watched their guide, never once bothering to look back, slip over the rise and disappear.

"Please, Chel-sea, surely you can see this is impossible. We have to go back." Even as Jamal made his announcement, the Land Rover rolled backward down the hill.

Her throat tight with determination, Chelsea couldn't explain why she found it so difficult to accept the validity, the inevitability, of what Jamal was telling her. A force beyond any driving need to contain a possible outbreak of typhoid fever, more than some high-flown, egotistical compulsion on her part to save a faceless, nameless child of the desert, seized her. It was as if something vital inside of her refused to give up, as if . . . as if . . .

As if an unavoidable destiny called to her. Destiny. Could hers truly be out there somewhere in that vast desert just waiting for her?

Chelsea glanced out the side window to hide the fact that her eyes filled with tears that were absolutely ridiculous. Perhaps she had been in the Middle East too long and Islamic beliefs and philosophies had finally worn her down—taking control of her life. Perhaps Michael had been right about her.

Impossible. She, Chelsea Browne, was in charge of her own life, she always had been, she always would be. She would choose whether she continued this pursuit or returned to the clinic, not some unknown . . . something out there beyond the whirling sands, beyond the next dune.

"All right. Go back, damn it." By God, she made her decision, but not without regret.

Glittering eddies danced by the window. They reminded her of wind spirits alive and calling to her, surrounding the Land Rover like the desert children who often crowded about the vehicle when she made her monthly rounds to the remote villages. Those children. How could she ever forget them shoving their innocent, pleading faces against the window to worship her as if she were some kind of goddess? What did they call her? She thought for a moment conjuring up a vision of their brown, dirty faces. Umm Dawa. Umm Dawa, their youthful voices chanted. Mother of Medicine.

Her heart lurched in remembrance and filled with a need to find her individual place, her calling. The children offered her that kind of fulfillment, the only kind she needed, she swore vehemently to herself. She reached out toward those helpless souls calling to her, her palm coming to rest on the windowpane. Then she realized the wind, the swirling sand beyond the window, sounded like young voices crying. Her own fertile imagination had created the illusion.

How uncharacteristic of her to act so illogical, so ill-prepared, especially when it came to her profession. What had gotten into her? What had made her rush pell-mell into an impossible situation with so little information to go on? Returning to Ad Dawadimi was the best thing to do. This senseless race across the desert would accomplish nothing.

Even as she validated her decision to retreat, Jamal turned the vehicle around. They started back the way they had come. In spite of it all, her heart cried out a denial that even her most forceful logic could not stifle.

The winds outside responded to the silent struggle inside of her, whipping the sands into a frenzy visible only in the headlights. Soon it turned into a blinding wall of glittering confetti that pounded on the hood, roof, and windshield.

"Jamal!" She glanced at her driver seeking reassurance that such storms were not unusual, even though she had never experienced one during her many months in the desert.

"I-I-I don't know. I have never seen anything like this." His uncertainty only alarmed her further.

Yet they continued on, so slowly that it took them several minutes to start up the next rise. The tracks of the tires that led up and over offered reassurance that they would eventually make it back safely to civilization as long as they followed the trail, the only thing visible in the headlights other than the flying sand. Chelsea settled down on her seat, confident that the return trek, although a bit hair-raising in such a violent storm, would go smoothly.

Reaching the top, the nose of the Land Rover angled down, and they started to descend the other side. The headlights cut across the undulating sand, the surface smooth and undisturbed. There wasn't a tire track to be seen.

"Where did they go?" she cried, sitting up once more to stare out across the vast, virgin land, seeking any kind of clue that they had come this way earlier.

"Blown away," Jamal murmured.

"Hurry, take the next rise. There must be tracks on the other side," she insisted.

He never argued. Neither did he agree. Without a word, he drove forward. On top of the next dune, he brought the vehicle to rest once more.

Nothing. Not a hoof print, a tire track, not a single

sign indicated they had traveled this path only moments before.

Chelsea's heart faltered. Then she spied the radio, their contact to the world beyond this ever-increasing nightmare. They might be stranded, but only temporarily. She grabbed up the hand-held microphone and pressed the switch on the side.

"Mobile unit three calling base. Over." She clicked the switch, waiting for a reply.

Static, more than normal, but no human voice spoke back to her.

"Mobile unit three calling base," she repeated.

Still no response.

"Have you forgotten there is no one at the clinic until Monday morning?"

No, damn it, she hadn't forgotten! She had simply hoped.

"Besides, we are probably too far away to make radio contact," Jamal continued in a calm voice, too calm to her way of thinking. "With this storm . . ."

"So what do you suggest we do?" Pinning the driver with an angry glare, a look meant to cover up her own misgivings more than to blame him, she slammed the microphone back into its cradle. How would they ever find their way back in such a raging storm? She couldn't be sure how far they had come, or even in which direction. Hoping Jamal had been more observant, she waited for him to speak.

"*Shamaal*," he said with studied reverence, staring out the front windshield. Granules of sand pinged against the glass with an ever-increasing tempo.

Shamaal, the legendary windstorm of the desert reputed to have swallowed up many an unwary traveler.

46

She had heard of it, but she had only thought such high drama a plot device crafty storytellers in the old marketplace used to make their tales more exciting.

"What are you saying?" In the face of Jamal's uncertainty, genuine panic sprouted and took root in Chelsea's heart.

"I am saying . . ." Turning off the engine, he looked at her, the terror in his dark Arab eyes foreshadowing his words. "Sandstorms like this can go on for days and days. In the last few hours we have zigzagged in so many different directions, I cannot be sure where we are at the moment. In our haste to get out of Ad Dawadimi, I bet we didn't bother to pack one canteen of water much less some food."

Although he said "we," she suspected he really meant "you." Why was such neglect her responsibility any more than his? As the desert expert he should have thought of those things, too. She had never thought that they might get stranded in some . . . larger-than-life sandstorm.

"If we try to go on, we are likely to get farther lost than we already are, and our fuel won't last forever, you know. Yet if we just stay here to wait out the storm, there is the chance that sand may well find its way into the engine. We might never get it started again." He laughed, but it was a bitter sound. "Sorry, *Duktur* Browne. Only a miracle or someone who knows the desert far better than I can save us now."

In other words, there was only death to look forward to? A slow, horrible death?

Chelsea sat back, stunned. How could this be happening to her, a woman, a giver of life? To die here, the victim of impulsiveness, especially her own—well, she just couldn't accept that fate. With disbelief she watched

47

the swirling sand grow thicker and thicker in the beam of lights outside the impregnable Land Rover. Would it soon cover them up completely, make them just another dune in the sea of thousands that no one would come across for days, or weeks, or even years?

She looked down, her worst fears confirmed. There at her feet the grit already began to accumulate, the tiny granules finding nooks and crevices in the floorboard to seep through just as Jamal predicted. As if on cue the headlights dimmed for a moment that seemed eternal before returning to normal. Only a flicker, perhaps, but a warning of what to expect.

What were they going to do? The idea that they would just sit there and wait to die was inconceivable to Chelsea. Her fingers curled about the door handle, and she turned, placing the flat of her free hand against the window already pitted by the sand. She would not stay here and be buried alive.

Beyond her fingertips, a face appeared in the window, covered from the nose down like some bandit of old.

Startled, she screamed and jerked back.

The black eyes considered her through the dirty glass—piercing, unafraid and quite curious. Was it death come to claim her so soon?

Spurred by childhood terror of demons ogling her as their next hapless victim, she shielded her eyes with her hands.

Gathering her courage, she peeked between her fingers. The face was gone.

"Look."

Following Jamal's pointing finger, she lowered her hands and glanced out in front of the Land Rover where the waning headlights still illuminated the whirls of sand.

The black horse took on the sheen of wrought iron, only the silken strands of its mane and tail mingling with the dancing desert eddies. Its rider sat unerringly in the saddle, nothing but his dark eyes peering from the folds of his robes and headdress. She caught her breath, her heart thundering in her ears, as she stared at the handsome Bedouin.

A miracle occurred—or did her perception change? Now he resembled a courageous knight, without armor, but of storybook perfection, a man like she had only dreamed about and thought impossible to find. Then she narrowed her eyes, chiding herself for such foolish notions, thoughts that Michael had planted in her head. What she saw, what she imagined, could only be a mirage, one that suddenly came to life, moving out of the beams of light.

"Where did he go?" She angled in her seat to look behind them, wanting more than anything not to lose him, even if her discovery was merely a delusion. The red glow of the taillights revealed nothing, her heart everything.

Something thumped against Jamal's side window.

They both turned at the same time.

The Bedouin's covered face peered back at them. He shouted something over the shrieking of the storm, something she didn't understand, but apparently Jamal did.

After several false starts and none-too-gentle coaxing, he cranked up the reluctant engine. There on the top of that precarious hill of sand he turned the vehicle around and started back slowly in the direction they had originally traveled. The motor sputtered a couple of times. On each occasion Jamal revved the engine to keep it running, and Chelsea mumbled silent prayers that it wouldn't die.

Opening her eyes, she stared out across the sand spotlighted in the headlights. Already their second set of tracks had been covered up—obliterated by the storm— leaving them marooned as surely as if an ocean surrounded them.

Nestled in the dip between the dunes, the raging winds calmed somewhat, howling overhead, a reminder that the danger still wasn't over. Without him saying it, Chelsea sensed Jamal wasn't sure of his direction. Then the Land Rover gave a mighty heave, and the engine coughed and died despite her assistant's attempts to keep it running.

A silent yet momentous understanding passed between them. Wordlessly he attempted to restart the vehicle, without success. Again and once more. The *dah-da-da, dah-da-da* rhythm of the uncooperative engine began to slow down. The headlights dimmed, taking on a soft yellow glow. In no time they would be gone. The Land Rover would never start now.

Once again, horse and rider stepped in front of the waning headlights, a reassuring beacon.

He signaled them.

"What do you think he wants?" Chelsea asked.

"He wants us to get out of the vehicle."

Get out? Impossible. Yet the Bedouin survived out there regardless of the blowing, biting sands.

If asked, she couldn't have begun to explain why she felt so inclined to follow a stranger's orders. Wordlessly she opened the glove box and took out the emergency flashlight stored there. Then she pushed open her door, confident the Bedouin had no intentions of harming her, at least not at that moment. As if a great vacuum had been released, the handle tore from her fingers. She let it go, concentrating on placing her steps carefully in the sand that enveloped her sturdy leather boots clear over the ankles.

Jamal called for her to return to the Land Rover, his voice taking on a note of near panic, but the raging wind carried off his cries.

Whether she navigated the few feet separating them of her own accord or the Bedouin rode forward to meet her, she couldn't be sure, but suddenly she stood before him, the flashlight revealing the regal figure astride the horse and swathed in billowing, black robes.

He said nothing. What was the point? She couldn't have understood him anyway. And yet it was as if she could read his every thought. He reached down, offering her his hand.

She stared at the outstretched appendage, aiming the flashlight at it to get a better look. It was a very large hand, much larger than her own slender one—brown and strong. Ancient warriors must have had hands much like his, she mused. The tendons in his wrists and fingers stood out in clear definition. She noted the calluses, the fine lines crisscrossing the wide palm, the scar that ran down the extraordinary length of one finger.

Oh, how she wished to give herself up to that hand, to trust it as well as the rest of the man, to just forget who and what she was. Lifting the flashlight once more, she stared up into his face, only his eyes visible. They were dark, unreadable, haunting. An uncontrollable shiver slithered down her spine, stirring an excitement she had never felt before. But even if she wanted to take him up on his offer, she couldn't.

"The supplies. Jamal. I cannot leave them behind."

51

He couldn't have possibly understood her words, for she had mumbled them in English. Nonetheless, his hand withdrew, his gaze lifted and focused over her head.

She turned, her white coat ballooning, the flashlight beam locating its target. Dear Jamal. He was already out of the Land Rover attempting to open up the rear door. He, too, must have read her mind. Did he even realize their guide was more than willing to abandon him to fate?

And then the Bedouin rode past her, totally disregarding the fact that she would have to trudge her own way back to the stalled vehicle. Then, if that wasn't enough, his cantankerous camel, bawling a noisy protest, nearly stepped on her as it shuffled past.

Irate, she made her way to the rear of the Land Rover, but the situation only got worse. The next few moments were some of the most frustrating in all of Chelsea's short career.

Every medical item she had packed in the vehicle was absolutely vital; otherwise, she wouldn't have bothered to bring it. She didn't dare leave even one single thing behind. She wouldn't. At her insistence, Jamal was busy handing the Bedouin the different packs and arguing over each and every one. The pile on the kneeling camel's back grew higher and higher, the Bedouin's glare harder and harder. Finally it came down to the portable generator . . .

"Ya Duktur," Jamal turned to her in defeat after another somewhat lengthy argument. "It seems it's either the generator or me. He refuses to take both."

She looked up at the Bedouin. Damn his unyielding male jackassery. Who did he think he was to put her in the position to make such a choice? Of course there could be no question of which one would be left behind, but, oh, she found it so hard to slam the back door of the Land Rover closed and abandon that precious generator. Nonetheless, she did exactly that.

Wielding her flashlight, she watched in silence as the Bedouin ordered an unhappy Jamal to climb atop the camel. Odd, she had always assumed camels and Arabs went together like bread and butter, but it seemed Jamal didn't like the idea of riding one any more than she did.

And then with little guttural grunts, the surly beast rose first on its hind legs and then its front, its great splayed feet reminding her of the fuzzy bunny house slippers she was so fond of wearing in the privacy of her small apartment back in Ad Dawadimi. Poor Jamal, tossed about like so much baggage, apparently found nothing in the situation the least bit amusing. His face, normally so dark, was quite ashen as he hung on to the ropes that secured the supplies to animal's humped back.

"Duktur."

Chelsea glanced over her shoulder. Only she remained on the ground as the Bedouin had remounted his mare and again extended his hand to her.

She couldn't bring herself to reach up and put her hand, her trust, into his. Obviously he meant for her to join him astride his spirited mare, so delicate in build. And yet, from experience, Chelsea knew the Arabian horse to be a sturdy breed, so concern for the animal wasn't what made her hesitate. Her uncertainty stemmed from something much harder to cope with, something much more personal.

Did he intend for her to ride behind him, to wrap her arms about his waist? Did he surmise that she would be

53

only too willing to cling to him in order to keep from falling off?

Clearly, he thought himself in charge of the situation. Well, he was in for a few surprises.

She would much rather walk than humble herself so in front of him or any man for that matter.

Ignoring his offer, she curled her lip in disdain and lurched forward with determined strides, the flashlight illuminating the way. She managed to take only a few steps before a muscled arm wrapped about her waist, dragged her upward and deposited her with a hard, painful thud on the mare's back.

The total look of disapproval in the eyes of her abductor stung almost as much as the flying sand. He didn't bother to conceal his contempt for her, a feeling that had been evident from the first time he had laid eyes on her.

A contempt she felt threefold for him. With a toss of her head she twisted about and swung her leg over the horse's withers to sit astride. His hand, the one he had offered to her and she had refused, snaked in front of her and grasped at a handful of mane.

"Yigbid gabd," he said, shaking the tuft of horsehair.

Chelsea continued to stare straight ahead, ignoring him, his bullying tone and manners.

"Yigbid gabd," he ordered once more, his voice muffled by the covering on his face. This time he grabbed her unwilling hand and placed it on the mane. His fingers remained firmly wrapped about hers, shaking them until they unfurled, her palm pressing against the horse's neck.

She turned to scowl up at him and found him doing the same as if he thought her truly stupid. She didn't need to hang on like a novice. Jerking her hands away, she buried them both beneath her armpits. A cloth descended, encasing her flying hair and protecting her face. Then, just to show him how little she thought of him and his smelly rag, she haughtily flipped her head around, her back ramrod straight.

Horseflesh tensed beneath her, and she prepared for the jolt that would come.

But that shock didn't begin to compare to the one she experienced when his arm wrapped about her, his hand cupping her breast as he pulled her back against his rock-solid chest.

Three

Insolent female. He should have let her do exactly what she wanted to do—walk, follow behind him like the subordinate Allah intended all women to be. Anger bubbled up from the simmering cauldron of emotions deep within Khalil. He should have *let* her? Oh, no, he should have *demanded* it. After all, trailing behind was a woman's place, afoot or at best astraddle a contemptible donkey, and a man usually bestowed that honor only on his favorite wife.

Then to allow her—no, to invite her, a mere woman—to ride with him on his most valued war mare, well, what had he been thinking? To make matters worse she had rejected his generosity. He would not ignore such an insult.

Tightening his arm about her, he pulled her closer. He couldn't ignore the swell of her breast filling his palm, befuddling his mind, tearing down the barriers of his self-control. First his pride and now his honor sacrificed. Just as Allah warned. These were the very reasons why women should be restricted to the *hareem,* for they could not help who and what they were, wanton one and all.

She entered his world now, one he ruled as lord and master. In time she would learn what was expected of her—what *he* expected of her—not only as a healer who must prove her worth, but as a woman under his care and protection.

His arm which had adjusted to encircle her waist, as slender as the sleekest gazelle, made it most difficult to maintain the necessary attitude of superiority. She rode with the skill of the finest warrior in his tribe, as well as he did himself, he admitted with reluctance. What kind of fool would give a woman such freedom by teaching her to ride so boldly? She constantly urged Shiha, his most willing mare, to greater speed. If not for the howling wind, the biting sand, his own hand firmly controlling the reins, the horse would have obliged and set a reckless pace that Maha, the camel, would have tried valiantly to match.

The problem wasn't the camel's lack of speed, but the worthless *hadhar* she carried on her hump. The last time he had looked back to check on them, the rider, bouncing about like an uprooted reed in a fast-moving river, had looked green about the mouth, like so many of his kind, sick from the constant swaying.

Khalil curled his mouth in utter disgust. In his opinion a man, even one from the settlements, who didn't know how to ride a camel was not much of a man. The *duktur-houri* had made a poor choice in picking the *hadhar* over that strange contraption she had left behind. But who could say for sure what influenced female decision-making. Certainly not the logic that guided a man's.

He dared not allow any one of them, the *hadhar,* the camel, even the woman, as distracting as she was, to be the main focus of his concern. Instead he must concentrate on the storm. It was much more violent than during his first encounter. Would he find the raging winds, the intense light, the eventual blazing fire, impossible to penetrate? The thought that he might forever be condemned to a world he knew nothing about, an age of unnatural wonders and customs, filled him with a private terror that he would never show openly. Then he remembered the talisman around his neck.

"Il-bunniya asdaaf min il-abhur." The brown shell of the sea. Over the shrieking of the storm which reminded him of a wounded beast in the throes of death, Khalil took up the magic chant that had carried him safely through the spinning vortex once before. He had to believe in its power to return him to his own world. Otherwise, death would claim his son, and only Allah knew what would happen to them.

He still had no idea what the strange words meant. The brown shell of the sea. His journey had taken him nowhere near the mighty waters that he had heard about from his father's father but in all of his life had never seen. Perhaps the will of Allah never intended for magic to be seen or understood, only revered and accepted; nor the power a woman's charms challenged, even by so mighty a sheikh as himself.

Chelsea had never experienced such a storm, though she could remember one spring when a devastating tornado had ripped through the countryside near her childhood home outside Atlanta when she was just a little girl. Just how the valiant mare pressed forward through winds that made even the slowest progress a struggle seemed impossible to her. Even now the labored breath-

58

ing of the tired horse rasped in her ears. If they didn't stop soon, the animal would surely collapse, its lungs bursting, probably filled with the debilitating sand that had already defeated the supposedly indestructible Land Rover.

However, that storm was nothing compared with the one raging through her, tearing at her insides, destroying the resistance she had so carefully constructed around her most feminine heart. He had touched her, a fleeting caress, so subtle that she couldn't even be sure he had been aware of it. But her flesh would never forget the feel of his strong fingers molding around her breast. The experience had been over as quickly as it had occurred, leaving her to wonder if it had happened at all. Perhaps she had merely wished he would touch her so. Oh, God, Michael had been right about her all along. Beneath her feministic armor she was nothing but a fainthearted female dreaming of being swept away by passion. It just took the right man pushing the right buttons.

Aware that her once rigid spine now willingly contoured to the masculine chest behind her, she straightened. She forced her thoughts back to the real danger. The storm. *Shamaal.* Rudolph Valentino or not, didn't he realize that if they lost their mount, they would then be at the mercy of the desert, and the child, his son, who desperately needed medical attention, would be sacrificed as well?

Somehow she must make the Bedouin see the logic in stopping here and now to wait out the storm. She turned, determined to make herself understood, but his strange, incomprehensible mumbling stopped her and sent an uncontrollable shiver down her spine.

What was it he said over and over to himself? she

wondered. Even if she couldn't decipher his actual words, his tone revealed the courage and strength of will with which he spoke. He chanted the phrase so many times she found herself parroting the syllables under her breath until she knew them by heart. She would have to ask Jamal to interpret them for her when they arrived at their destination—if they ever got there.

Success seemed more dubious than ever to her.

Still the Bedouin urged his mount on. How cruel and inhumane, Chelsea decided, to use so beautiful and willing a creature with such ill regard. But then she imagined he treated everything under his dominion that way. If only she were in charge. If she held the mare's reins in her capable, more compassionate hands, she could end the poor beast's agony. There would be no need to convince its torturer to do otherwise.

The obvious solution struck her. All she had to do was reach out and take control, just as she had learned to do in every other aspect of her life, the deed done before her captor could react. Her face bundled up to her eyes with the bit of cloth he had wrapped about her head, she peered up at his equally covered countenance. As if searching for something—but what?—he stared out across the blowing sands, totally unaware of her. She wouldn't have a better opportunity.

Did she dare be so bold? Without a doubt he would be furious with her interference. Heaven knew what punishment he would inflict upon her. He might even be capable of killing her. Then the exhausted mare stumbled, reenforcing her need to do something quickly. Reprisal or not, she simply must take the risk.

No more than the ends of a length of rope looped about and knotted beneath the Arabian's small muzzle, the reins jiggled just inches from her reach. Releasing the handful of mane, she grabbed at them, her fingers entwining in the rough hemp, and she pulled back.

The mare's response to the pressure came as a total surprise, but Chelsea had been astride plenty of horses when they reared. As unnerving an experience as it could be, a cool head, a steady hand, would eventually master a mount gone out of control. However, the horse presented the least of her problems.

"Humagga' mar'a!"

Not sure what the Bedouin said, she could well imagine he cursed her, especially when he brushed her hands away none too gently, almost knocking her from her seat.

"No," she cried in retaliation, fighting to maintain control of the horse and, if the truth be known, of her own destiny. Her weight shifted one way, and his the other, when the mare, as quickly as it had reared up, dropped back down on all fours with a jarring thud. Confused by the mixed signals created by the fight taking place over control of the reins, the animal rose again much more terrified than the first time, its front hooves pawing the air, its shrill shrieks of protest harmonizing with the howling wind. Horse and riders hung there in midair for what seemed like eternity.

The mare apparently lost its balance or perhaps its footing and began to topple over. To Chelsea, hanging on for dear life, nothing compared to the helpless feeling of falling backward. She wrapped her strong, capable legs about the horse, determined to stay put. The Bedouin, too, maintained his seat; in fact, she could swear the arrogant bastard was enjoying himself. Didn't he realize that if the horse fell on them. . . .

Horror coursed through Chelsea. Several years ago she had witnessed just such a freak accident where one of the finest horsemen she had ever competed against had been crippled for life. And the thoroughbred, one of the most talented jumpers on the Grand Prix circuit, had been destroyed. Releasing her grip on the mare, she tried to dismount and managed only to minimally break her fall.

Chelsea hit the ground with such force she suspected the palms of her hands, her cheekbone as well, would be scratched and bruised. The heavy weight of the horse slammed against the backs of her knees, trapping her, and if it hadn't been for the sand beneath them, her legs would have been crushed. She screamed, and since she couldn't roll out of the way, she squeezed her eyes closed, preparing for the inevitable blow from a flying hoof. The Bedouin's fate remained a mystery. He could be injured, even dead for all that she could see. What would become of them all if, God forbid, that should happen?

Odd, but she felt nothing, only numbness, could see nothing, for every time she attempted to look up bits of flying sand slashed at her unprotected eyes. With only sounds to go by, she strained to listen, to pick up any clues to the fate of her companions. She heard only the unabated wail of the storm and a strange, unexplained crackling that came from somewhere overhead. Giving up, she lowered her face, allowing the spinning sensation in her head to take control. Sweat trickled between her shoulder blades. How hot she felt, so hot. . . .

The pressure against her legs relented, yet she didn't know quite what to do with her freedom. Before she could make up her mind, a hand, or so she surmised, grabbed her around one ankle and, ignoring her feeble protests, dragged her across the sand as if she were no more than a sack of rags. Her hip brushed against something warm and furry, and automatically she reached out and grasped what she recognized even in her blindness to be the thick, coarse mane of the horse.

Clinging to that last bit of security, Chelsea glanced upward, protecting her eyes as best as she could. She gasped. What she saw had to be an illusion of her grit-filled vision, of her befuddled mind. Otherwise, death was only moments away.

The sky, in spite of the blowing sand, glowed brightly, an enormous ring of fire falling directly toward the spot where she huddled. There was nowhere to run, nowhere to hide. Terrified, she buried her face against the neck of the mare to shield her eyes from the flames, from the unbearable heat that accompanied them.

Lying there, helpless and exposed, Chelsea knew in a matter of moments the raging inferno, whatever it was, wherever it had come from, would consume everything within a hundred yards around her. How ironic. When she had driven away from the clinic only a few hours ago, the last thing she had thought to face was her own mortality.

In life a person was only allowed to make each decision regarding their fate once, or so she had been taught. Knowing what she must face, would she have still been so rash in choosing to dash off into the desert ill-prepared?

* * *

"Asfal, Maha. Down." Khalil mercilessly slapped the camel's flank, ordering it to its knobby knees. At the moment he envied the animals natural defense against the biting sand, the ability to close up its nose, mouth, and eyes. He could only ignore the grit, keeping his face covered as best as possible.

Finally the stubborn beast obeyed, dropping down on bent forelegs even as it continued to bawl in protest. Before the animal settled all of the way or the foolish *hadhar* could utter a word, Khalil pulled him from the saddle and shoved him into the protective shelter the large, hairy body offered.

"Stay. Do not move," he shouted at the frightened man and turned away.

The fires of destiny rained down upon them, giving him no time to prepare or explain. Bowing before the blowing sand and the intense heat, he staggered toward the spot where he had left the woman. He supposed he should be grateful for her outrageous disobedience. What had she been thinking when she had fought to snatch the reins from him? Her foolishness could have cost them their lives and the mare's as well. At the same time he had to admit it may well have saved them all.

He glanced up. The familiar glow of the flames they must traverse to reach his world descended much faster than he first anticipated. The edges of the fiery ring concerned him. The *hadhar* and camel would be too close to the fire, but he could do nothing more for them. His only thought was that he must protect her, the beautiful *houri.* No, he must not think of her in those terms, only as the *duktur* who would save Muhammad's precious life.

The fire drew nearer, so close he could smell the acrid odor. He flung himself down, covering the woman huddled against the withers of the mare with his own body. Feeling her fear as it mingled with his own, he could do nothing except prepare for the inevitable.

When he had gone through the ring of flames the first time alone, he had thought he world surely die from the unbearable heat. But the animals had shielded him from the worst of it, and amazingly they had come through the ordeal unharmed as well. However, the storm, the blinding light, the fire, none of it had been as intense as this second time. He thought once more about the camel and the *hadhar* so far away. Had he condemned them to certain death in his haste to save himself?

The woman stirred beneath him, reminding him of his one and only goal—to save his son. At first her movement brushed against his chest like delicate butterfly wings, and he recoiled as his body responded to it. At all cost, her safety must come first, he reminded himself.

He wrapped his arms tightly about her, tucking her head crowned with gold into the hollow of his shoulder, thinking only to protect her. A fire more consuming and intense than the one that licked at his flesh swept through his heart as her struggle intensified. He could well imagine what she must think as her fists pounded against his unshielded chest, the meaning of her cries—if not the actual words—only too clear. How could she think he, an honored sheikh, would harm her?

Pinning her with his weight, he grabbed her flailing hands in his more powerful ones and pressed them in the sand beside her head to still them, to try and gain her attention, her trust. Staring down at her, he read the defiance as well as the terror in her eyes.

"Shh. Shh. My beautiful one," he whispered, attempting to calm her as if she were one of his spirited mares.

Did she not know of the desert code that forbade a man from taking a woman against her will? Did such respect no longer exist in her world? Had man with all of his progress stooped so low as to violate mothers, daughters, sisters and wives?

When at last she stilled, he pushed aside the *keffiyeh* he had wrapped about her face. Against his will he felt himself drawn into the mystery of her eyes, so blue, they must surely possess a magic like none other. Suddenly he found it harder and harder to remember his all-important honor and to control his natural urges—urges he had suppressed for so long, ever since the death of Tuëma, his one and only beloved wife, Muhammad's mother.

The desire to sample those untried lips, soft and pliant, unravaged by the cruel elements, set his heart to racing, unleashing his blood to surge helter-skelter through his virile body. That inner storm, much more violent and devastating than the one descending from the heavens, swept away his noble ideas like so much debris. Brushing aside his own *keffiyeh,* he lowered his head, bringing his aching lips so close to hers he could feel her sweet breath fan across his face. Then her mouth began to tremble. Was it with anticipation . . . or fear?

Pulling back, he sensed it was the latter. Some day he would have her, but for now, at all costs, he must shield her from harm—be it from the inferno about to engulf them or from the more dangerous one raging within himself.

Until that moment when his mouth moved so close to hers, Chelsea struggled quite admirably against both him and her conflicting emotions. Until then she had considered the Bedouin only as another of those chauvinistic Arabs, the enemy to best, there only to make her life impossible.

But thoughts traveled strange paths when confronted by the prospects of dying. Her senses seemed to have developed a mind of their own, coming suddenly to life and giving new meaning to everything about her, especially the stranger who lay on top of her, his handsome face filling her line of vision.

Somehow her chameleonic heart turned traitor. She saw him now truly as a man, whole and complete and as mortal as herself, yet willing to protect her. His dark, penetrating eyes held her entranced against her will. The lines of seriousness between his equally dark brows added to his mystique. What burdens and responsibilities had etched his face with so much character? she wondered, wanting to reach up and smooth the wrinkles away. It was only curiosity, she assured herself, restraining her impulsiveness. Nothing more.

Her attention was drawn downward, noting the small leather pouch encircling his neck on a thong. What did it hold? Relics of his past perhaps? Treasures?

She glanced back up at his face. Studying the rest of his features, she found herself comparing him to other men who had made impressions, not necessarily favorable ones, upon her life. His nose was straight and noble, his cheekbones high, accenting the hollows beneath them. His mouth—although thin-lipped and outlined by the dark, closely trimmed beard and mustache—was a generous slash across his face. When it spoke as it did now, so softly that the sound never reached her, she found it impossible not to focus on those lips, to feel comforted, yet at the same time utterly confused.

Good God, she faced certain death, yet she calmly contemplated a man's mouth as if it were the most important revelation to come her way in a long time. Self-consciously, she licked her own dry lips with the tip of her tongue. The full implication of her action registered when his eyes, the unmistakable desire fringed in dark, thick lashes, swept downward to watch the innocent gesture as if it were the most flagrant sexual display. As if he, too, found her overwhelmingly hypnotic; as if he, too, forgot the ring of fire about to consume them.

Against her better judgment, she stared back, her eyes once more drawn to that leather pouch around his neck. Something told her to touch it, that the answers to her questions lay in its depths. In spite of the overwhelming urge, she couldn't bring herself to be so bold, fearing he would misinterpret her actions.

Once she had read that the sum total of a person's life flashed before one's eyes at the moment of death. Did that include thinking about those things never experienced, those things most wished for and fantasized about in the deepest recesses of the mind?

She started at the unexpected turn of her thoughts, lustful thoughts, and groped to make sense of them. Lust was nothing new to her. Michael had taught her plenty about the baser nature of the male species, and innocent fool she had been at that time, she had readily succumbed to his seduction. But somehow in this desert lord, desire became something very different, very noble—and very exciting.

He displayed a reservedness, even as he lay on top of her pinning her to the ground with his large, all male body. He did not move against her as she would expect a man to do—as Michael had done. Didn't all men think it was their God-given right?

His hands trapped her wrists with a gentleness, as if he feared to crush the delicate bones he mastered. Regardless of his unassuming manner, she didn't doubt for a moment that this nameless stranger controlled the situation. He could do whatever he pleased with her. She would not stop him.

To discover a willingness within herself to make the same old mistakes caught her by surprise. She refused to accept she might be like so many women—weak, in need of a man to make her life complete. Not Chelsea Browne, proud of her independence and self-sufficiency.

Tearing her eyes away, she began to struggle once more, as much with herself as with him. She assured herself that only the prospect of immediate death caused her to act so out of character, not the fear that she would never have the opportunity to experience the man-woman thing everybody talked about as a conscious participant not just an unresponsive receptacle.

Where had that ludicrous notion about unadulterated sex come from? Surely not from her, she who had been stung so viciously in her first serious relationship. Hadn't she learned her lesson? All men were the same—self-absorbed and arrogant about their own importance. Yet when she gazed up at this man who made her aware of things about herself she didn't want to acknowledge, his expression remained unchanged. So did his domination, although he did not take advantage of it or of her, even when he could have. She found it hard to believe he might be different.

Realizing the futility of her struggle, both inner and

69

outer, she gave up the fight, wishing he would do something, anything other than continue to stare at her as if she were some mindless creature who needed soothing.

Oh, why didn't he just kiss her?

Instead, the circle of flames descended, crackling and hot. She buried her face against his shoulder. The leather pouch lay against her cheek. At last she found the courage to reach up and grasp it in her hand.

Nothing happened, but unfulfillment was par for the course. A tear of frustration trickled down her cheek.

Oh, God, how she wished that if she must die, it wouldn't be alone with a nameless stranger, but with someone who loved her, someone with whom she shared an affinity. As selfish as the thought might be, she couldn't quite push it out of her mind.

As if the eye of the storm swept over them, the sands stilled and settled, the wind grew silent, the acrid smell of burning sulfur filled the air, but the flames never touched them. The heat became so intense she could feel it behind her closed eyelids, blinding her, scorching her throat.

Fire and brimstone. A childhood vision of hell only added to the chaos in her mind.

Love me. Love me, she thought, clutching that pouch with all of her strength. *Oh, Chelsea. How foolish to wish that this man, so different, so totally alien to everything familiar, could possibly love you.*

Like an answer to her prayer, the strong arm curled tighter about her, holding her close, shielding her as she had never been before except as a small child by her mother. Without hesitation she burrowed deeper into the protective shelter of that most masculine shoulder smelling of leather, sage, and man. She inhaled deeply, savor-

70

ing the sweet perfume that assaulted her senses, intoxicating her.

Gladly she clung to that nameless shoulder, turned herself over to its promise of safekeeping, allowed herself for the first time in a long time to be willingly dependent upon another, to acknowledge her helplessness to do otherwise.

"I only wish I knew your name," she murmured, more to herself than to him, for she knew he couldn't possibly understand what she said.

"Khalil. What is yours, beautiful woman?" The whispered response came as a shock.

"What?" She lifted her face and found him staring down at her with total comprehension.

"Your name?" he asked again. "The *hadhar* told me, but it was so unusual I cannot remember how to say it." His mouth, so close, parted slightly.

"Chelsea. Chelsea Browne," she whispered, gravitating toward those lips, allowing her own just to graze them.

She didn't question how they understood each other; she only knew they had entered some strange place where their minds lay exposed, where language presented no barriers, where only hearts spoke. An excitement coursed through her, one she couldn't explain, for it was more than bodily pleasure. A kiss, somehow it would seal that special something between them. Make it irreversible. But it must be mutual. Lowering her lashes, she waited for him to complete the act.

"Shel-sea Brown," he repeated with the same inflections Jamal used when he pronounced her name, his mouth moving against her, teasing yet not completely committed.

71

Hurry, please hurry, before it escapes.

"Shell, sea, brown. The brown shell of the sea?" he demanded. His mouth lifted.

She strained toward it, trying to reclaim it and the moment she feared was lost.

"You are the brown shell of the sea?" He gripped her wrists tightly.

"What? I don't know what you mean." Surprised at the intensity in his voice, she let go of the leather pouch and began to struggle.

A loud sound erupted, like a clap of thunder right over their heads. As if someone flipped a switch, it grew dark, the burning heat gone along with the light. Terribly cold, Chelsea shivered. She couldn't explain it, but she felt suddenly alone once more. It was such a wretched feeling she wondered how she had managed to live with it so long. She peeked over Khalil's broad shoulder, not sure what she would discover.

To her surprise the sky glimmered with star clusters brighter than any she had ever seen before, as if they were closer, larger, less obscured.

"What happened?" she asked, looking to Khalil for an answer.

But the Bedouin stared at her as if he no longer understood her, his eyes hard, unreadable. He released one of her wrists, and pushed himself up.

"Yiguwm giyaam!" he ordered, pulling at her other arm. Although she no longer understood his words, his meaning was quite clear.

Suppressing the urge to cry, she stood, hugging herself to keep warm. He turned and began to walk away. Blinking back tears, she realized the moment of comprehension was over. Perhaps, it had never happened and had only been her wishful imagination. No, she had asked him his name in English, and he had replied, hadn't he? There was only one way to find out for sure.

"Khalil?"

At the sound of his name, the Bedouin whirled back around and stared at her as if she had spoken a sacrilege.

"Il-bunniya asdaaf min il-abhur," he replied.

That phrase again. The one he had whispered over and over during the storm, the one she could repeat by heart, but didn't know the meaning of. She would ask Jamal to interpret it. . . .

Jamal! A new and even more devastating fear coursed through her. What had happened to her assistant?

A short distance away she spied the camel he had been riding, lying on its side, unmoving, but there was no sign of the young Arab. With quick, determined strides Khalil, if that was truly his name, moved toward the beast that looked as if it might be dead. Forgetting her own problems, including the cold, she scurried after him, falling once in the deep sand and scrambling to get up again. Her heart raced with dread, fearing what she would discover.

On the other side of the dead camel they found her driver huddled against the still, silent beast. Lying face-down, his inert body was raised unnaturally off the ground, enough that his back had not been protected by the bulk of the animal. The stench of burnt flesh made her nauseated.

"Jamal," she cried, choking back the sick feeling. She stumbled over the feet of the burned corpse of the camel, realizing it was dead. Those fuzzy house slippers. She would never wear hers again. She brushed Khalil out of her way and knelt beside her friend, noting the burns along his spine and fearing the worst. No, no, Jamal couldn't be dead as well.

Immediately the physician in her took over. First, she checked her patient's pulse. Thank God, she found it beating strongly. Then she made sure he was still breathing. A bit shallow perhaps, but his ribs swelled and receded against her probing hand with consistency. However, he appeared to be unconscious, and the burns on his back didn't look good.

"Jamal?" she called softly, brushing granules of sand from the side of his youthful face. When she didn't get a response, she began looking for something to cover him with, as much to keep him warm as to protect several of his worse burns from contamination.

She realized then what her assistant had been trying to protect with his own body. The supplies, or at least most of them. Somehow he had managed to strip the baggage from the camel's back and shield it from the fire, even though it had probably meant sacrificing himself.

"Oh, Jamal, you brave fool," she murmured. Spying her traditional black medical bag, she pulled it from the stack and quickly sorted through it, extracting several packages of bandages. Carefully she picked the burnt edges of Jamal's shirt from the wounds which appeared clean and dirt free and covered them with the sterile dressing. She glanced around, discovering a piece of canvas that had been used to hold the bags together on the back of the camel. Although it wasn't that clean, it was all she had, and she draped it over the unconscious man to keep him warm and hopefully from going into shock.

Frustrated at her lack of resources, she sat back on

74

her haunches. Out of the corner of her eye a flicker of light caught her attention.

The fire? She glanced up, fully expecting to find the frightening, unexplained phenomenon had returned, this time to claim them all. But it was only the morning sun climbing its way up over the eastern horizon, a golden ball of fire, perhaps, but not the dreaded flames.

Had the ordeal existed only in her imagination? No. The dead camel and Jamal's singed hair and blistered face sticking out from under the canvas covering proved otherwise. What did it all mean? But more important, what were they going to do now?

She glanced up to find the Bedouin standing over her, just watching her, his face unreadable. Realizing that he had not once attempted to help her, she turned on him determined to tell him just what she thought of his insensitivity, even if he didn't understand her. If nothing else, expressing her frustration would make her feel a whole lot better. The tirade erupted and she just let it go.

To her frustration he ignored her, signaling her to come to him as if she were a disobedient dog. A few feet away the horse stood as unscathed as its master, the Bedouin. And indeed, she had not been injured either. Why? Why had the fire spared them but not Jamal or the unfortunate camel?

It was something he seemed not to question. Instead he mounted the horse and stuck out his hand.

She could understand his urgency, truly she could; there was still his ailing son who needed her help. Regardless of his insistence, she refused to leave Jamal behind. She shook her head, pointing at her assistant and then at the supplies. Didn't the man realize their importance as well, not only to her, but to saving the life of his son?

That miraculous moment of communication between them might never be repeated. Just like during the sandstorm, she realized she would have to fight for everything she wanted to take with them, and their inability to understand each other only made the process that much more difficult.

He grabbed her arm and pointed over the horizon. She stubbornly shook her head and sat down once more in the sand beside Jamal, sorting through her black bag. Then, to her utter surprise, the Bedouin jumped off the back of his horse and dragged her to her feet.

They struggled. She even managed to hit him with her medical bag before he overpowered her, snatching the satchel from her hands before tying them behind her back. Then he bent down and threw her over his shoulder as if she were booty from a raid, her medical bag clasped in his other hand.

"Put me down." She wiggled and bucked, but to no avail.

The humiliation didn't begin to compare to her anger when he remounted the horse with her still in tow and took off, never once looking back.

Her cries unheeded, he reined the mare toward the rising sun.

The last thing she saw as they crested the dune and started down the other side was the sight of Jamal's still figure lying beside the precious supplies and the dead body of the sacrificial camel.

More than ever she believed the Bedouin to be the cruelest, most ignorant man she had ever been forced to deal with. It didn't matter that he had saved her life. The fact that he had callously abandoned an injured man to face the elements of the desert without a chance of survival negated his heroism.

What about her precious supplies? How could she be expected to deal effectively with an epidemic of typhoid fever without the necessary equipment and medicines?

Oh, how could the situation possibly be any worse?

Four

A few moments later they reached the outskirts of Dir'iyyah, just as Khalil knew that they would, but there had been no point in trying to explain that to the stubborn *duktur-houri*. He did not expect her to trust him, at least not until she could see for herself that he had no intentions of sentencing even one as unworthy as the *hadhar* to die in the desert. But with no way to transport three people as well as the supplies with only the one horse, he had had no choice but to leave all but her behind temporarily.

From the rise above, the encampment, bathed in the golden morning light and bordered on the north by the *wadi* swollen with the runoff of winter rain, looked just the same as when he had left the night before. Black, low-slung tents dotted the sea of sand, like islands dispersed among stately date palms as graceful as dancers that continuously swayed and clacked in the cool winter breeze. Khalil approached his domain with a jumbled mixture of hope and trepidation. Muhammad, his beloved son. Did he still live, or had the daring raid into the future only been in vain?

The woman asked him something, blue eyes narrowed in indignation. Since he couldn't understand her, he chose to ignore her, clutching her and that black bag of hers tightly. Urging the mare forward, he picked a trail through the hodgepodge of tents, flaps securely fastened down to keep out the cold.

At every turn he sought clues to answer his greatest concern—the welfare of his son. To his relief those who emerged to greet their leader, although bundled up, were clear-eyed, their faces unmarked with the painted signs of mourning. Undoubtedly Muhammad still lived. Khalil's parental heart gave thanks. Still he wanted to see the boy for himself.

Soon a crowd followed them as he continued toward his own tent near the center of the encampment. No one spoke to him directly, but more than once he overheard comments about the strange woman he brought with him.

"Who is she?"

"She must be a prisoner."

"Most assuredly, for her hands are bound."

"If that is so, why does she ride in a place of honor instead of walk?"

"Does this mean retaliation against our own women and children?"

Evidently, the nature of his mission remained a mystery. He preferred to keep it that way. In his haste to depart yesterday, there had been no opportunity to present his plans to the tribal council, much less discuss them at length. Nor had there been time to explain that there would be no reprisal against the tribe, but then he had not known he would return with a woman. Later he would share with them his great adventure, but only after ascertaining the condition of his son. Even then, he doubted he would tell them everything. Some things were best left unspoken.

In front of his own tent he dismounted and handed Shiha's reins to a servant, who emerged to welcome home the master. Confident the tired mare would be well cared for after its long, grueling trip, he faced the anxious crowd.

"Go, be gone with you," he ordered, shooing them off with the wave of one hand. Let them think what they wanted. Their speculation and gossip could never come close to the truth. Selecting two of his best warriors, he told them where he had left the *hadhar,* supplies, and dead camel. Without explanation, he sent them on a mission of retrieval, threatening them with death if they should fail to bring back even one item left behind.

After the men rode away, he once more focused on the woman, who amazingly enough had remained quietly seated on the mare. He scowled up at her, disliking her superior position. She glowered back with equal arrogance. His first impulse was to drag her from that horse, to make her kneel before him. After all, he deserved such homage. Something stopped him, something other than the unapproachable, yet vulnerable, expression on her beautiful face.

Since sharing the mystical ring of fire with her, after that much too brief moment of intimacy—the likes of which he had experienced with no woman before, not even Tuëma his once beloved wife—he found himself unable to think of the *duktur-houri* as merely a female. And yet her femininity was all that he could think about. She was the brown shell of the sea, his talisman, the one who possessed the skill to not only save his son, but more disturbing, if old Umm Taif had spoken truthfully, held the key to his future in her small but capable hands. Did she perhaps know that?

No woman should wield such power over a man. Lack of control weakened a free *Bedu,* left him open to attack from both his enemies and brothers and could well be his undoing. Although he recognized the danger, all she had to do was look at him as she did now. . . .

The overwhelming need to prove his domination over both her and the situation brought his determination full circle. He reached up, grasped her about her supple waist and, ignoring her show of resistance, jerked her to the ground to stand before him as he untied her wrists. Forced to throw her head back to look up at him, she railed at him, using words he could not understand. However, her meaning was only too clear, not only to him, but to those brave few who watched from a distance.

Such humiliation before his people could not, would not be tolerated. Clamping his hand over her mouth, he dragged her toward the tent, no easy task with her feet and fists flying.

Once inside, he glanced about, relieved to find the spacious pavilion empty. The central fire burned brightly, its warmth beckoning, but he avoided it, the uncomfortable memory of another fire still fresh in his mind.

What was he to do with her? He didn't wish to just thrust her upon his young son, not until she calmed down, until the boy could be prepared to accept her. Until then, he could think of only one place to leave her.

Brushing aside the curtain separating the women's section from the main room of the tent, he dumped his noisy, uncooperative burden before the cluster of occupants— sister, aunts, and nieces—who stared in surprise at his sudden appearance among them carting a strange, unruly female.

He offered no explanation. He didn't have to. Instead he dropped the black bag in which she had put so much stock at her feet and turned away. Umm Taif would take the situation in hand. If in truth the old sorceress possessed a third eye, then the arrival of this impossible woman would be no more than she expected.

Even now, did she laugh at him behind her expressionless face, secretly hoping he had met his match? Probably he had, but he refused to let her see that. He glared at his aunt when she calmly rose to confront him, casting a curious glance at the bound prisoner.

"So, *ya ibn-uxt,* you found her, I see."

"My son?" he asked, ignoring the knowing—much too knowing—look in the old woman's dark eyes.

"Yusaf moved the boy to your private sleeping quarters when the council arrived demanding an explanation for your disappearance. Such a public return will only make matters worse. What were you thinking?"

At the moment he was thinking he would like to cut out Umm Taif's wagging old tongue, but she spoke the truth. The council would have to be dealt with soon. First, he would see to the welfare of his son.

"Calm her." He pointed at the *duktur-houri,* who was making quite a spectacle of herself. "I will send for her as soon as I see to Muhammad." He sighed with the thought of the monumental task to be confronted. "As soon as I prepare both him and Yusaf . . . for her presence."

Yusaf would do as ordered under threat of death, but Khalil would prefer that the tribal physician willingly cooperate with the woman doctor, even though her very

82

existence, much less her authority, would be degrading to his status and standing among the tribe. And status meant everything to Yusaf, ever since his arrival years ago with the young princess who had become Khalil's bride. After Tuëma's death, he had stayed with the Durra. At first Khalil had watched him suspiciously, but in time he had come to depend on the physician. No matter that he had been unable to save Muhammad with his own skills, Khalil trusted the old man's opinion and needed to retain his loyalty, in case the woman proved unworthy.

"I won't be long, Umm Taif," he warned. With a nod of his head he swept out of the women's quarters.

His aunt would make every effort to obey his command. How she would go about such a difficult task did not concern him. It was the responsibility of the women in a family to make another of their kind adjust to new surroundings. Oddly enough, he found it hard to believe that the *duktur-houri* would truly accept her circumstances, just as he doubted he would ever bow to the cruel joke fate played in his life.

Sheikh Khalil ibn Mani al Muraidi dependent upon the skills and whims of a woman?

He ground his teeth in frustration. There was nothing he wouldn't do or endure, for the moment at least, to protect his son's life—including suffer a little private humiliation.

Reaching the curtained section he claimed as his private quarters, Khalil swept inside, savoring the familiarity, like a wolf in its den. He spied the camel saddles stashed about, horse blankets and other gear—just the way he had left them. Then he dropped to one knee before the pallet where he often slept when he sought moments of solitude, as impossible as that was in a house with only curtains for walls. The small, still figure of his most precious son occupied the bed now.

"Muhammad," he whispered, running his cold hands, over the small forehead. He found the difference in temperature between his flesh and the boy's, and the child's obvious incoherence, discernible and most alarming.

A rustling sound caught his attention. He looked up, frowning, expecting to find. . . .

But it was Yusaf, as timid and quiet as a jerboa, a small desert rodent.

"You have brought the physician, *ya ràyyis?*" The old man fell to his brittle knees before him.

Khalil nodded, his concern for his son increasing. "How has the boy fared?" he demanded.

"I cannot be sure. Where is the *duktur?*" The old man glanced about nervously, his confusion adding even more wrinkles to his wizened face.

"In the women's quarters." Khalil stared him straight in the eyes.

"The women's quarters?" the old man echoed. "I-I-I do not understand."

Khalil knew what the old man must be thinking. The women's quarters was taboo to even one so ancient and respected in the tribe. Now another, a stranger, had been given privileges denied to him.

"There is much I do not understand, either, *ya* Yusaf," Khalil confessed with a frown, but he did not look away. "I have seen the future. It was nothing like you or I could ever expect. Nothing remains as it should be, not even the sacredness of a man's position. It seems the *duktur* . . . is a woman."

"A woman? Impossible!" Yusaf declared in open surprise, turning away before Khalil could be certain of what

84

the look meant. When he made no comment, the old man looked back at him incredulously. "You accept this, *ya ràyyis?*"

"I have no other choice at the moment. Otherwise my son will die."

Yusaf studied him for a long moment, perhaps seeing things Khalil had never meant to reveal, but the opportunity to conceal them had passed.

"Then, until you tell me otherwise, master," the old man conceded softly, "I will accept this also." He bowed his head in submission.

"Very good. Inform Umm Taif we are ready for . . . the brown shell of the sea."

Like something out of a dream, no, more like her worst nightmare, Chelsea took in her surroundings and shuddered. All around her strange women, some old, some young, painted with tattoos and henna, pointed at her as if *she* were some kind of sideshow freak. Who were they, these women? All of the Bedouin's wives and concubines? His harem? Didn't all Arab men have one?

Wide-eyed, she looked from face to face. So many of them, Chelsea counted at least two dozen, some exotically beautiful with their huge, dark, kohl-accented eyes, long ebony hair, their feminine figures clothed in clinging costumes that accented their lush curves—figures made to please male sensuality. How could any man so blatantly and openly cater to his baser needs? Chelsea found the situation utterly disgusting. It shook her to the very core of her own femininity.

Clamping her mouth shut, she glanced down at her once white jacket, long gray skirt, and serviceable shoes—

the uniform required for all women physicians in Saudi Arabia—and felt extremely dowdy in comparison. What would she look like with her eyes painted, her much more willowy figure so displayed? She tried to imagine herself dancing with veils to the strange music of the Middle East.

Where did that Freudian slip come from? she wondered.

Before she could formulate an answer, one of the braver women, an old one with amulets in her ears and on her wrists, reached out to touch her. Automatically she shrank back to avoid being prodded and poked, but one dark finger twisted an errant lock of her blond hair as if it were precious strands of gold.

"Dhahabiyy," the woman murmured.

Chelsea had no idea what the old witch said, but she suspected she was trying to decide if she wished to lay claim to her find as if it were only the matter of removing it from her competitor's head. Scalping was an American tradition not Arab, Chelsea reminded herself. Even so, she reached up and snatched her personal and firmly attached property from the woman's leathery paw.

Another tried to feel one of the big white buttons on the front of her jacket. Backing up, Chelsea slapped the hand away as it came toward her breasts.

Like a pack of starving dogs, the women pursued, all suddenly reaching out, grabbing at her sleeves, the folds of her skirt both front and rear, pulling her hair, unlacing her shoestrings, chattering and yapping, some uttering that strange little trill that Arab women were famous for making. It was impossible to stave them off for long. They simply didn't stop and grew louder and more insistent by the moment.

To her horror she noticed that one of the younger ones had discovered her medical bag. The contents lay scattered on the ground, and the culprit was in the process of tearing apart the packets of gauze, streaming them out like lengths of ribbon as she giggled and postured, contaminating and rendering useless the once sterile contents.

"No!" Chelsea cried. "Leave that alone." She rushed forward to reclaim her possessions and tripped over one of the older women.

Like a cat that had just had its tail stepped on, the woman flexed her henna-painted claws and hissed. Chelsea prepared for the inevitable attack, wondering just what that pack of she-devils planned to do with her.

The masculine voice coming from the other side of the thin partition sounded as sweet to her ears as a cavalry call to charge. Whoever spoke, it was not Khalil—the tone and pitch was too high and frail—and yet the women paused in their harassment to listen to what the person had to say.

They looked at her, their eyes shooting daggers, or so it seemed to Chelsea. The old woman with the amulets pointed toward the exit, grunting something at her, a dismissal most likely.

Chelsea didn't need to be told twice. She was more than willing to leave that room full of vicious predators. Gathering up her belongings and stuffing them back into her medical bag, she gave the group a haughty glare and swept forward, pushing the woolen flap aside.

There in the communal section of the tent, she halted to catch her breath. That had been close. Much too close. Then she spied the old man. For all that she could tell, he could have been fifty, or a hundred, or even older judging by his rounded shoulders and wizened face. Yet his eyes, behind the oddest-looking pair of glasses she had ever seen, sparkled with an undeniable energy and intelligence. She couldn't explain it, but she felt an instant affinity to this stranger. Relieved to at last find someone somewhat normal in a world gone insane, she smiled.

In turn he studied her as if she were some kind of strange bacteria under a microscope.

Her mouth tightened. Too many times she had been scrutinized with that same sort of disapproval, by her father, in medical school by male instructors who thought a woman had no business wasting their precious time, by male students who had found her ability to best them a threat. So she returned his rudeness with her own challenging stare. After a few moments of impasse he signaled for her to follow him, which she did, but not without making it clear that she did so by her own volition.

He led the way across the main room of the tent to another cloth divider. She could only imagine what she would have to face on the other side. Could it be anything worse than the harem?

Ushered in, she spied the Bedouin kneeling in the middle of the tiny space, his back turned to her. Oddly enough, she experienced a rush of relief to see him again. What she felt was more than relief, she admitted with confusion, something much more disturbing. She didn't like it, not one bit.

"Look here," she began, taking up where she had left off when he had so rudely tossed her to that pack of she-wolves. She started forward, then paused when he didn't bother to glance up at her.

Her heart tripped all over itself like an awkward child with untied shoestrings. She could see his face in profile, his noble aquiline nose, his strong chin and sensuous mouth. That mouth. How could she forget it? Her lips yearned for the feel of it. She realized then what was different about him. He had removed his *keffiyeh* and outer robe. His dark hair, longer than her own shoulder-length style, gave his undeniable masculinity an untame-able look. Like the difference between a sleek thoroughbred and a wild Arabian stallion. The first belonged under saddle; the latter would never submit.

He could have been praying for all she could tell, and she fell silent, thinking she should avert her eyes and give him privacy; but she couldn't look away even when she tried.

Then she heard faint moans. At first she thought they came from the old man, his face blocked from her view when he had moved around in front of Khalil, but the sounds were too high-pitched and childlike even for him.

If not the old man, then who? Tearing her gaze from the handsome Bedouin, she clutched her medical bag. Of course. It had to be the sick boy. Years of training took over, and she rushed forward without invitation, making her way to stand beside Khalil, bending down herself. When her shoulder brushed his, she fought the urge to turn and touch him, to reassure him that she would do all she could for his son, but something about the way he held himself aloof checked her impulse.

The boy lay there, a truly beautiful child, his face high-cheeked and sculpted just like his father's. His eyes, those of a wild, little thing, were dark, and although feverish, they honed in on her, steadily watching, just as his father had many times before. His lips were full, bow-shaped, nothing like Khalil's. Did he have his mother's mouth? His mother. Khalil's wife. Something akin to agony twisted her insides.

She envisioned the group of women she had just escaped. Which of them was this boy's mother? The pretty one with the great doe eyes? No, she was too young. The older one with the amulets perhaps? Whichever one she might be, why was she not here with her son, as she should be, doing things only a mother could do to make her sick child feel better?

Chelsea risked a sideways glance at the man who held such power over them all. Had Khalil in his infinite ability to be insensitive forbade the poor woman access? Handsome or not, she wouldn't put it past the brute.

Reaching into her bag, she pulled out a pre-packed thermometer, unwrapped it, shook it down, then hesitated, staring into the wide, frightened eyes of her patient. How was she ever going to make the child open his mouth and cooperate when she couldn't even tell him what she wanted him to do? She slid another look at the boy's father. He studied her in that predatory way he possessed, suggesting he didn't particularly trust her either.

How she missed Jamal. As interpreter and diplomat on these medical forays, he always reassured not only the sick but their anxious families that she wouldn't do anything harmful. Poor Jamal. What had happened to him? How frightened he must have felt waking up and discovering he had been burned and callously left to die. Did he blame her? She would if the situation was reversed.

If only she could escape and make her way back to him. Helpless frustration gnawed at her. Even if she did manage to get away, how would she ever find her way back to the spot where they had left him? The desert all looked the same to her.

With a sigh, she glanced back down at the boy, assessing her immediate problem. There was only one way to accomplish the task at hand. Perhaps not the most efficient means medically, but she could well imagine the resistance she would get, not just from the boy, if she tried to roll him over and take his temperature with more accuracy. Quickly she unbuttoned the front of his tunic, exposing his torso. His skin was clear, without a rash. That could be a good sign or not, depending on how long he had been ill. She slipped the thermometer under the boy's arm and, placing her hand against his shoulder, held it in place with firm but gentle pressure.

"Laa latkha aat."

She looked up to find Khalil spoke to her. Did he question her action? Would he insist that she stop?

His large fingers splayed across his own chest, tufts of dark hair spilling from the casually unbuttoned *thobe*. Against her will, her gaze settled on that wide expanse of masculinity, remembering how it had felt pressing against her own body, dominating her—yet shielding her. With a supreme effort she dragged her errant eyes away. Chiding herself for her unprofessionalism, she focused on his other hand which clasped his son's much smaller one with a caring she had only glimpsed once before, during the fiery ordeal.

She glanced back up at his handsome and hawklike face, his eyes, the exact color as his hair, dark and mesmerizing as they assessed her, waiting . . . waiting. She swallowed down the rising excitement. What did he want from her? What did she expect from him?

A raging tidal wave of conflicting emotions buffeted

91

the line of defenses with which she had so carefully sur-rounded her heart. Who was this man, this arrogant des-ert prince who dared to treat her as if he owned her? What forces had brought him to her door, as if he had sought her out? Her eyes widened with realization. With-out a doubt, that was exactly what he had done—come looking for her specifically. Why?

Once again she glanced down at the clasped hands, father and son, scrambling to make sense of it all. She could be certain of only one thing. Even if she couldn't understand anything he might say, or that he was such an oddity by all the standards she had to judge him by, foremost he was a doting father. He had come to her for help and, as all concerned parents did, expected her to perform miracles. Such humanness from this enigma touched her as nothing else could.

She realized then what he was asking her.

"No, no spots," she affirmed, shaking her head, at-tempting to smile with a confidence she didn't quite feel. "Not yet, anyway," she murmured more to herself, lifting the boy's arm and removing the thermometer. Only then, in order to determine his temperature, did she finally look away.

One hundred and four point three. High for appendi-citis, but she still couldn't rule out that diagnosis.

If only she could ask a few simple questions. Several well-placed probes into the patient's somewhat distended abdomen elicited no pronounced reaction, nor was there any rigidity in the lower right rectus muscle. Still, she couldn't eliminate the possibility of appendicitis. But if it was, she didn't think the appendix had ruptured—not yet.

Frustrated, she sat back on her heels, only to be bombarded with a barrage of unanswered questions. How long had the boy had a fever? Was he vomiting, had he eaten, did he have diarrhea, constipation? She desperately needed so much information in order to come to a proper conclusion, but she had no way to get the facts, at least not quickly.

She could only sit there and observe, her hands symbolically tied. In the meantime, if something should happen. . . . No, she couldn't blame herself. She did all that she could. A helplessness bubbled up within her. Oh, how she needed Jamal and the precious supplies and equipment she had been forced to leave behind.

She looked up to find the two men waiting for her analysis of the situation and, of course, an immediate cure, as all family members did. The burden of that responsibility weighed heavily upon her, and she yearned to shake it off. Even if she could be certain of what ailed the child, with so little information to work with and no way to communicate, she couldn't explain to them what she'd found anyway. Her frustration came full circle.

Stifling the feeling of incompetence, she checked the boy's pulse, finding it slow—not a good sign. To her surprise the old man picked up the boy's other wrist and mimicked her procedure. He grunted as if satisfied, but with what she couldn't be sure. Her actions or his own findings?

Could he be some kind of tribal medicine man? Even as the possibility zipped through her mind, he reached across the boy, grabbed the thermometer and, twirling it round and round in his fingers, held it up to inspect it with a critical eye—as if he suspected its use but had never seen one. Odd. How was it possible that so large a band of Bedouins had never been exposed to one of the many mobile medical units, no matter how remote and off the beaten track their community might be?

The settlement, even though it had appeared to be only a temporary one when they had entered it, still had been vast, interspersed among the huge date grove beside the wide, running river. Such a well-developed oasis had to have a name, had to be on some map, had to have been visited at some time or other by outsiders.

She realized then what she was doing. Stalling. Trying to put off making a diagnosis, right or wrong, and deciding how she must handle the situation. But why? Why would she act so incompetent?

The answer was simple enough. She had nothing to work with, no equipment and therefore no conclusive facts with which to make a decision. Under normal circumstances she would have drawn blood and run tests with the portable lab in the back of the Land Rover, looking for signs of specific bacterial infection. Then she could have turned to the well-stocked cold pack and started the boy on the proper medication. That was what being a doctor was all about . . . wasn't it?

The art of medicine is an exacting process of elimination, a function of the mind not the heart, gentlemen . . . and ladies. The majority of us cannot depend on gut feeling. Our decisions must be based purely on the facts at hand. That way we are less likely to make mistakes, mistakes that could well cost our patients dearly—the loss of life, limb or abilities.

That lecture. She remembered it as if she had heard it only yesterday. It had caused the first real rift between her and Michael. She had believed what the lecturer had said, taken his warning to heart, determined to apply it— to become the very best doctor that she could. Michael had scoffed at Dr. Lawson, calling him an old fuddy-duddy, out of touch with the real world of modern medicine.

What she wouldn't give for a little of Michael's shoot-from-the-hip self-confidence about now.

She stared down at her young patient and found him watching her with a look that made her think of a wise old man. Once again she probed at his abdomen, seeking a tender spot, but found nothing conclusive. Gut instincts told her she dealt not with appendicitis—the child either had a case of salmonella poisoning, if they were lucky, or more likely suffered with typhoid fever.

God help her. She glanced up. God help them all, for she had absolutely nothing with which to battle the disease.

She turned, and rummaged in her medical bag once more, hoping beyond hope she would find what she knew wouldn't be there. Antibiotics. Pausing in her fruitless search, she sat back on her heels.

What she needed were the supplies that had been left in the desert. She must have them, now. With a sweeping look of determination, she studied Khalil, who stared at her just as intently. Somehow she had to gain his cooperation. She must make him understand.

She stood.

Like a shadow Khalil rose also, placing himself between her and the exit. Whether his actions were conscious or not, Chelsea couldn't be certain, but she decided then and there not to be intimidated any further by him or her lack of communication skills.

"Jamal," she stated, propping her fists upon her hips and drilling the Bedouin with her most commanding look, as if that might get across her meaning. "We must go back and get him." When she attempted to brush past him, Khalil reached out and stopped her as if he had every right. She stared down at his restraining hand and back up into his impassive face.

"Look," she warned, shoving at his hand which refused to budge, "if you want me to save your darling son, then you must do what I tell you."

Making him understand was like trying to stave off a band of marauders with a popgun. As impossible as the task seemed, she refused to give up.

"Jamal. You know." She held out her hand to indicate the small Arab's approximate height.

Khalil's gaze took in her action, then once more settled, unchanged, on her face.

"Ja-mal," she repeated slowly as she mimed the act of driving a car, her hands on the imaginary steering wheel. "Veroom. Veroom." She gave her best impression of the sounds an automobile made.

"Veroom. Veroom," he mimicked, his dark eyes lighting up with what appeared to her to be condescension. He shook his head in lack of understanding or refusal to comply, she wasn't sure which, but he seemed to be waiting to see just what strange thing she would do next.

Feeling utterly defeated, she threw up her hands. What was the use? He was incapable of understanding anything. Then she remembered that he had called Jamal something. But what? She racked her brain to recall. Hattie? Adder?

"Hadhar," she murmured.

"Hadhar, laa. Muhammad." A contemptuous sneer accompanied his rapid-fire response, and he increased the pressure on her already numb arm.

"Bring me the *hadhar* first, or no Muhammad," she insisted, sensing she had at last gotten through to him.

"Muhammad." Eyes narrowing, he shook first his head and then her with so little effort it surprised her. He pointed at his son, his free hand moving to his scimitar, daring her to defy him any further.

Just where the courage came from, she couldn't be certain, but she had had enough of his overt sexism. She began to fight, wondering if this would be her final show of defiance, and she gave her struggle all that she had. At one point she knew she caught his cheek with a fingernail, for he grunted and grabbed her wrist with such anger that she thought he would snap the bones.

The pain he inflicted didn't stop her. Nor did the sword he carried. Even someone stubborn and thick-witted wouldn't be so foolish as to cut off the head of the only person who could save the life of his son. Or would he?

In spite of her logic the weapon cleared its scabbard with a *whoosh* and swung high into the air over her head. Appalled as much as frightened, she swung at him again. Her fingers curled about the pouch around his neck.

The moment she touched that bit of leather the strangest feeling washed over her, one that seemed to flow through him as well, for he paused as if he had been physically struck, his sword hovering above them both. Staring deep into his dark eyes, she experienced his frustrations as if they were her own. She swallowed down her own confusion. Perhaps what she felt wasn't all that different.

"Khalil, think about what will happen to your son if you kill me." Her softly spoken words were as much a warning as a plea.

His hand wavered with understanding, but his hard, accusing gaze gave no ground.

"Then, nothing must happen to my son or those responsible, all of those responsible, will die."

Hearing a most pitiful sound, she darted a glance across the room to discover the old man prostrate on the floor, his arms stretched upward in supplication. He spoke with a rapid desperation, and strangely enough, she understood everything that he said.

"Oh, great one, I am loyal to you. Only you. Spare me. Spare me," the old man groveled, degrading himself. Why? His head was not the one about to roll.

Perhaps she'd underestimated this Arab's unbalanced sense of right and wrong. First Jamal, then her, and last the innocent old man. His callous disregard for life, and not just her own, hacked away at her notions of fair play. His lack of sensitivity shouldn't surprise her. Treachery, deceit, selfish disregard—they were no more or less than she expected from any man.

Strange, how very calm she felt watching that unwavering blade descend toward her. A most fitting end after all that had happened to her today.

The most ridiculous urge to laugh overwhelmed her. It seemed she had been right in her original assessment of her life. Christmas, indeed, promised to be a bleak affair, if not a lethal one to boot.

Five

"Reconsider, *ya ràyyis*," Yusaf begged. "Remember, she is merely an ignorant female who knows not of her offense to the great Khalil ibn Mani al Muraidi, sheikh of all the Durra tribe. Did you not, in all of your infinite wisdom, tell me that the future and those who inhabit it are nothing but fools, unlike our world?"

"Wait a minute," the woman protested. "What right do any of you have to . . . What do you mean by the future?"

Khalil grasped her arm, shaking her into silence, displeased with what she had to say. How he could understand her words made no sense to him, but he could. Likewise, she comprehended the old man's observations. He wasn't so sure if he liked that either.

"Why do you defend her, Yusaf? To save your own worthless neck?" Khalil brought his descending sword to a halt just inches from the woman's collarbone. Surprised that she never once flinched, never once softened her most unbecoming glare, almost as if she were daring him to carry through with his threat, he turned his attention to the groveling physician whose servitude better appealed to his sense of superiority.

"To save the most precious life of your son, oh, leader." Even though the old man trembled, his gaze held steady as did his logic.

"Then, you think she can save him." He didn't look at her. Khalil found the woman's unfailing arrogance maddening. Even a man's favorite wife would not dare such a display of defiance and expect to get away with it. More than expect it, she thrived on it. A peculiar sense of pride intermingled with the irritation she stirred within him, and he found himself watching her out of the corner of his eye for signs of weakening, no matter how subtle. He found none.

"Just who do the two of you think you are to discuss me as if I'm not even here?" At last she came to life, clawing at his restraining fingers. "And what did he mean when he said I came from the future?"

"Silence, woman."

Amazingly enough, she obeyed, but he couldn't be sure for how long.

"Answer my question, old man," he insisted, turning his attention once more to Yusaf.

"Yes, *ya ràyyis,* I do believe she can save the boy . . . if you give her what she asks for."

"She *asks* for nothing." His hand tightened on the hilt of his sword. To his satisfaction, her beautiful blue eyes took notice of his action, but then they swept upward again, colliding with his in an undeniable challenge. "Instead she dares to make demands."

"I didn't ask to come here, you big arrogant slug, or have you forgotten that?"

"Must I cut out your tongue to silence you, woman?"

They stood there, just staring at each other. Nothing he did made her look away. Then he spied the talisman she clutched in her hand. His *baraka*. How had she gotten her thieving little hands on it? Letting go of her arm, he reached out and snatched his property from her fingers.

"Appease her, oh, wise one," Yusaf appealed, "for the moment anyway." He shrugged his thin, stooped shoulders. "After she cures Muhammad of his malady, then you may cut off her head if it so pleases you."

At that, Khalil threw back his head and laughed, noting that the woman looked with confusion from his face to Yusaf's, as if she could no longer follow their conversation. Good. That was what he wanted. That was. . . .

Abruptly he stopped laughing and critically examined the pouch. The magic talisman? Did it give her the powers? If so, why didn't it do the same for him? He didn't like being passed over. Not one bit. He pinned the old man with his most superior look. Yusaf and Umm Taif, they were as thick as thieves. What did Yusaf know that he wasn't telling?

"Then, it *is* your wretched hide you think to protect, you sly old jackal," he accused.

"Please, master. I wish only to choose my own time and path to Paradise. I am loyal to you, and only you," he repeated.

"Very well, Yusaf." Somewhat appeased, Khalil lowered his weapon, noting with further satisfaction the relief on the lovely face of the brown shell of the sea. "Your honesty and logic has convinced me—for the moment. But know this, if you are wrong about her and her abilities, it will be your head that rolls along with hers." Still clutching the talisman, he eyed her with suspicion, wondering if he was right about its magic or if she only pretended to have lost the ability to understand.

She inspected him with equal intensity as if accusing him of snatching the power from her. The power. He knew all about power, and she knew all about willfulness. A willfulness he was determined to master. At the moment he could think of just one way to accomplish his goal. His gaze settled on her mouth which failed to tremble even under his intense scrutiny.

"You are too generous, my lord. How can I thank you?" Yusaf's whine intruded into his lurid thoughts. "As to her . . . requests?"

"The *hadhar* she *asks* for is probably already in camp," Khalil confessed, suddenly finding it impossible to lift his gaze from her beautiful lips. Did they taste as sweet as he imagined? "Abdul and Turki went after him and all of her baggage soon after our arrival," he managed to murmur through the debilitating fog clouding his logic.

"Medical supplies?" Yusaf asked.

At last willing himself to look away, Khalil nodded.

"She obviously does not know of your wisdom and generosity."

"It is hard to say what she knows or does not know." He found himself watching her with fascination once more, wondering just what she thought of him. She acted so fearless, so unaffected, yet he suspected it was all a facade. Did she find him attractive? Did she think of him in ways he thought of her? It had been a long time— too long—since any woman had affected him so. A rush of mixed emotions coursed through him.

"You must bring the supplies here right away, *ya ràyyis,* the moment that they arrive."

102

Khalil shot the old man a squelching look. This tendency toward arrogance must surely be a disease, for it seemed Yusaf showed symptoms of having caught it from the woman.

"That is, if it pleases you to do so, oh, lord." The old man prostrated himself once more.

"It pleases me, Yusaf." He wished he could be so confident about his feelings toward the *duktur-houri*.

He sheathed his sword and gave her a none-too-gentle shove, as much to prove to himself as to show her that he had not given in to her demands for the wrong reasons. Then he swept out of the small room, his private sanctuary that would never be the same again. His hand tightened on the hilt of his sword once more. *Wallahi*, by Allah, Turki and Abdul better not fail him. He had a need to see heads roll, any head since it could not be the one that deserved to be severed from its most delectable body.

Then he sighed, acknowledging that decapitation was the last thing he wanted to do to her. What he would really like to do to her. . .

No wonder Allah, in all of his heavenly wisdom, had decreed that women, all women, remain secluded in the protection of the *hareem*. Otherwise, they were distracting, too much so it seemed, even to a man of character and stature like himself.

He marched on. The soft patter of feet picked up speed behind him. Without looking he knew who followed him, felt the reins of civility within him stretched to their limit, realizing she would dog his steps, without regard to his position or Bedouin pride, unless he took firm control of the situation. Emerging through the front entrance to the tent, he selected two of his most trusted warriors, stationing them in the doorway.

"Let no one pass in or out of this tent, or it will be *your* heads that roll," he warned, meaning it. If he found it so hard to resist her, he suspected only the threat of death would keep his soldiers, even his most trusted ones, in line.

Unsheathing their swords, the men unquestioningly crossed the curved blades in front of the opening to make an impenetrable barrier. To his satisfaction he heard her unbridled protests trail him like a yapping she-dog.

It felt good to have thwarted her, to have shown her who was master. Picking up his pace, he had taken a few swaggering steps when his smirk dissolved into a frown. Had he truly won? She would still get what she demanded, and he had no choice except to give it to her.

Unclenching the hand that held the talisman, he stared down at the unimpressive leather pouch, wondering just what was the extent of its powers. He would have to ask Umm Taif—demand the truth, the whole truth, from that most difficult woman.

It seemed of late he encountered no other kind. Woe to the world that catered to a woman's lack of reason. Woe to the man who initiated the first fatal step. He carefully retied the talisman about his own neck, wondering if he did indeed possess the power to understand, or if it sought to possess him.

Khalil ibn—she couldn't begin to remember the rest of his ridiculously long name. How infuriating, enough to make any woman swear off men, all men forever.

"Coward!" Chelsea shook her fist at his retreating

back; but he did not bother to look at her, so her action and accusation went unnoted even by the guards he had had the audacity to post to keep her from following him. As unruffled as Buckingham Palace guards, they completely ignored her as if she didn't exist. Like a caged wild animal, which was exactly how she felt, she hunkered down so that she could peer through the crossed scimitars that blocked her escape, two sharp half moons she dared not grasp. Helplessly she watched the arrogant Bedouin walk away. He had the talisman. When he had snatched it from her hand. . . .

Not that she believed in Middle Eastern magic, in outrageous fairy tales like Aladdin's lamp, a jinni, and flying carpets. Even as a little girl she had known such things were impossible. But all evidence pointed to the fact that the leather pouch had been responsible for her ability to suddenly understand what everyone said, and they understood her as well. That was no illusion. The old man, Yusaf, had said she had come from the future. However, *that* went too far.

Perhaps she was dead. If this was hell—and what woman wouldn't think to be treated like chattel was hell—then Khalil must be Satan. Remembering the scathing fire and brimstone that had taken the life of the camel and probably Jamal's as well, the netherworld seemed the logical explanation. That storm had not been a natural phenomenon even for the desert. Her mind scrambled to remember just what terrible deeds she might have committed during her short lifetime to deserve such a fate.

Tears were not something Chelsea normally resorted to, even in the worst of crises and never when it involved a man. Living in a male-dominated world had taught her that crying never got the results she wanted—respect instead of condescending sympathy. But he wasn't a man, she reminded herself, and this wasn't the world. Her eyes filled and blurred. She sniffed impatiently. Her own weakness only made her more angry.

"Damn him!" she cried, but he already claimed that status. Did she?

She stood and marched back across the tent. There had to be some way out of this predicament, some way to prove she didn't deserve such a horrible fate. Some way. . . .

She paused in the doorway of the sickroom, noting that the child had grown silent and still. The boy? Was he the solution to her problem? If she could only save him, would she get a second chance to redeem herself? But how could she possibly accomplish such a miracle, without her medical supplies and equipment?

Then Yusaf, from his vigilance at the boy's side, looked up at her expectantly. What was he trying to tell her? Oh, if only she still had that talisman.

If only she had her supplies. And Jamal. She glanced toward the top of the tent. God grant her one small request. Give her Jamal.

But God had turned a deaf ear to her. Apparently she was on her own.

"It's not my fault if something happens to that poor child. What do you expect me to do?" she cried out.

The old man continued to regard her as if he thought she had lost her mind. Maybe she had, but it was more than mental capacities she lacked. All those years of training in medical school had taught her nothing, nothing at least that would help her now when forced to rely strictly on her own abilities.

Still she refused to give up. To do so went against every fiber in her physical and mental makeup. By damn, Chelsea Browne would never accept defeat and her own mortality without putting up one heck of a fight.

Hell and its master had a thing or two to learn about female tenacity.

She glanced back down at the sleeping boy, wondering if in truth he was the devil's spawn. How could that be? He looked so young, so innocent—so helpless. In her heart she knew she had been sent there to save him as well as herself.

If the standard ways to cure him had been blocked, then she would at least make him more comfortable and hope that the illness, even if it did turn out to be typhoid fever, ran its course and spared him. In addition she could see to it that the disease didn't spread.

Now that sounded more like a skilled physician. She racked her brain to remember everything she'd learned about typhoid. Typically the bacteria was transmitted by unsanitary conditions—contaminated water, food, sewage. Somehow she must find out from Yusaf if the boy suffered alone or if there were others in the village who had similar symptoms. In the meantime she would assume she dealt with an isolated case and take every precaution to keep it from spreading. Quarantine was her first priority.

Whether Khalil realized it or not, he had done them all a favor by posting a guard outside the tent. Since he wouldn't allow her out, she wouldn't allow him or anyone else in. That little bit of control made her feel much better.

She set about tackling the sanitation problems, deciding to clean up, sterilize, or incinerate everything in the sickroom, including the boy's bedding and clothing—anything that might carry the infection. With a purpose, and perhaps a streak of vindictiveness, she set to work.

From her medical bag she extracted two packages of latex gloves. Quickly donning one pair, she offered the other to the old man, who looked at her rather strangely before accepting them. He found the see-through gloves utterly fascinating, turning them around in his hands, even peering down into the openings as if he thought to discover something hidden inside.

"You must put them on," Chelsea instructed, holding up her own hands, snapping the cuffs of the gloves, and wiggling her fingers for emphasis. "And keep them on."

Apparently he understood her instructions, for he complied, fluttering his fingers back at her once he completed the task.

That had been accomplished easily enough, she decided. What they needed now was something in which to boil water and a pot big enough to sterilize clothing, dishes, and any paraphernalia she might need to use or that the boy might have soiled.

An image of a blackened brass kettle sitting beside the fire in the central room of the tent popped into her mind. Perfect, even if a bit small, but she also remembered seeing a large cauldron in the women's section. The thought of entering that den of she-devils again made her shiver, but she needed that pot. She would just have to bolster her courage and go after it.

With no qualms about confiscating either of the utensils for her needs, she stood, signaling to Yusaf to wait there for her. Since he was still engrossed with his gloves, she felt confident he would go nowhere. She marched across the main section of the tent and, with only a moment's hesitation, swept into the women's quarters.

All those exotic eyes turned toward her like cocked pistols ready to fire in rapid succession. Off to one side she spied the black pot, a lot bigger than she remembered, and no doubt much heavier. Ignoring the pointed stares, she moved toward her objective, staking her claim to it.

Taking that cauldron was like trying to snatch a bone from a pack of ravenous dogs. The women instantly leapt upon her as if she were a market thief. Amidst the din of screeching, someone pulled her hair, another pinched her arm, and she swore she felt teeth sink into her forearm before she managed to tear herself away. Determined to win, she fought back, grasping and wrestling with the best of them. She wanted that cooking pot, and she would have it.

"Yuwagguf!" The sharp command rang out.

Her attackers pulled back, snarling and gnashing their teeth like the uncivilized pack of scavengers they were.

Making good use of her advantage, Chelsea wrapped her arms about her newly claimed possession, noting the toothmarks on her arm. She would wash the wounds out right away. They could all be rabid for all she knew.

Huffing and puffing with the weight of her burden, her hair straggling into her eyes, she turned to find the old crone with the amulets standing before her, hands perched on her hips.

"I need this for Muhammad," Chelsea declared, pulling herself up to stand as tall as she could, determined not to give up what she'd paid dearly for with her own blood. There was no doubt in her mind that the old witch was in complete charge of the others; she had been the one to call them off. If she could only get past her. . . .

"Yighaadir." Her bracelets jingling, the woman pointed toward the exit.

A barrage of protests erupted from the others behind the leader. The matriarch turned and, waving her hands about, broke into a long tirade, none of which Chelsea understood. But she did grasp this much—she could have the cauldron; no one would attempt to stop her again.

She struggled with her acquisition, dragging it beyond the dividing curtain, and finally resorted to rolling the cumbersome pot along on its side. Although round, it had a tendency to pull to the left, and she had a terrible time getting it across the large, open space to the sickroom on the opposite side of the tent without mowing down everything in her path.

On her way she grabbed up the brass kettle she had spied earlier and threw it into the empty pot, so that she would have both hands free to steer. The racket created as the metal kettle scraped against the walls of the tumbling cast-iron pot set her teeth on edge, but that didn't slow her down.

Finally she managed to wheel her booty through the dividing curtain that separated the sickroom from the rest of the tent and paused there to get her breath.

The old man simply watched her while she battled to right the container as if he found her antics most amusing. But when she pulled out that beat-up old kettle, he jumped to his feet, babbling, gesturing wildly, a look of terror on his wrinkled face as he began pulling at the sparse tufts of hair on his head. She couldn't understand what he was saying, but she knew it had to be something like "Woe is me."

110

"It's only a kettle, Yusaf." She thumbed the lever and made the lid flip up and down. *Clink, clink, clink*. The sound reminded her of snapping jaws. "It's not going to bite you." Chelsea stared down at the utensil in her hand, the pungent odor of cardamom and coffee rising up to greet her.

What was it about a dented coffeepot that would make the old Arab go stark raving mad, his eyes practically rolling back in his head, his entire body trembling? If she didn't know better, she would swear he was pleading with her, but to do what, she couldn't imagine.

She chose to ignore him and went about the business at hand, positioning the cauldron in one corner of the sickroom. There. She dusted her hands, then propped them on her hips, admiring her handiwork. Now what she needed was some water.

Not that she expected to find any kind of modern conveniences, but everyone—rich, poor, sophisticated or backward—had to have a supply of water. She glanced about looking for a source, but didn't find one. Her only choice was to try prying the location out of the old man, who had now fallen to his knees and was babbling on without once taking a breath.

Bending down, she tapped him on the shoulder, ever so gently, to get his attention.

Although his caterwauling continued, he looked up at her.

"I need water," she demanded, the moment she had his attention. Raising her curled hand to her mouth, she made exaggerated sipping sounds.

After several repeat performances, he seemed to grasp her meaning. Rising to his feet, his eyes still watching

111

her warily, he slipped by her, disappearing behind the dividing curtain.

During his absence, she kept busy. First she disinfected her own wounds. Then she changed her patient's bedding, replacing the pallet the child lay upon with an assortment of small, colorful blankets she found folded and piled in a corner. Already he appeared more comfortable, and noting what felt like a draft to her, she took up a rather ornate robe from the top of a stack she found in a basket and covered the boy up. Although it had golden threads running through it, it was the warmest thing she could find, so she didn't hesitate to use it. Once she covered the boy clear to his chin, she sat back, observing her patient as he nestled down contentedly.

When Yusaf returned with the water, she decided, the next thing she planned to get out of him was a fresh change of clothing for the boy, something warmer than that scratchy nightshirtlike thing he'd been wearing. Surely the boy had more appropriate clothing.

Back to the task at hand, decontaminating the sickroom. She took up the extracted pallet. It smelled of wild sage, and well-oiled leather, very familiar, but she couldn't decide exactly why. Careful not to let it brush against her clothing, she dropped it in the cauldron.

At that point the old man returned, toting the most dubious-looking object she had ever seen outside a biology lab. Some internal part of an animal she cared not to name, it obviously doubled as a water bag. Why so squeamish when she had dealt with internal organs before? It wasn't that she must touch the entrails of some beast, but when she eventually got thirsty, chances were *she* would have to drink water from it. She would have to be awfully thirsty, she vowed.

For now she planned to use the water only for sterilization, not consume it herself. Resolving to cross that bridge when she came to it, she turned and filled up the kettle.

The old man broke out in a tirade again. She paused, held that beat-up coffeepot to inspect it more closely and could find nothing extraordinary about it, and set it on the coals to heat up. Who could figure what set the crazy, old bedbug off so easily?

With single-minded purpose she began gathering up everything in the room that might have been soiled by the boy and separated it into piles to either be burned or dumped into the pot—rugs, linen, clothing, an assortment of saddles and tack, some of which looked familiar, some that didn't. Thinking of her own precious riding equipment back in Georgia, it seemed such a shame to destroy such well-made and no doubt expensive gear, but she couldn't take the risk of it passing on germs to others. It had to be either burned or sterilized. Without a qualm she tossed what she thought might survive the hot water into the cauldron. The rest must be incinerated.

She knelt and checked the contents of the coffeepot to see if it was boiling. Not yet. She sighed. At this rate it would take forever to fill up that huge cauldron. Deep in her own thoughts, she heard a commotion erupt from the other side of the dividing curtain. She lifted her head. The quarantine. Whoever entered would simply have to leave.

Then she picked out a familiar voice among the many, one she thought never to hear again. Could she be hallucinating, or was it truly Jamal who spoke?

She cast her grateful gaze heavenward. God granted

small favors. Scrambling to her feet, she changed her gloves and hurried out to investigate.

"Jamal," she cried, relieved to discover her young assistant, not only alive, but on his feet, even if he appeared a bit worse for wear with one side of his face as red as if he had fallen asleep beneath a tanning lamp. Aware of no one but him, she rushed to his side, anxious to check his burns. Pulling off the cloth wrapped about his head, she inspected the burns there, turning it this way and that. A couple of spots on his scalp worried her. She would dress them with silver nitrate. Although serious, the burns were not as severe as she had first thought, and the hair would eventually grow back.

Next she examined the injuries on his back, finding them worse than those on his head, but still not as critical as she remembered them to be. Carefully she tended them, Jamal the model patient, but she was still baffled by her initial inaccurate assessment of his injuries. How could she have made such mistakes? Putting it down to the confusion of the moment, she finished up. Satisfied she had done all that she needed to do, she left to check on her boiling water.

She returned to discover that Jamal had discarded the remainder of his Western clothing and had donned one of those long, nightshirtlike garments all the other men were wearing. Just what did he have on underneath it? she wondered. Nothing? It was a mystery just like what Scotsmen wore under their kilts. One she wasn't about to solve by taking a peek.

She realized then, except for his short, Western-cut hair, he looked like all the other Bedouin, just like Khalil, who stood beside him, only a lot shorter and not nearly as commanding or handsome. Like a little boy playing cowboys and Indians, her once meek assistant seemed to be enjoying his desert make-believe. Some macho thing, apparently. Male bonding, maybe. Men *were* the same everywhere, she decided.

"Where are the supplies?" she asked Jamal, tearing her gaze from the real desert overlord, unwilling to get caught up herself in some little girl romantic notion that she might possibly find that kind of man exciting.

"Being unloaded now."

"Thank goodness," she said with relief.

Even as she spoke the first of the boxes and satchels were brought in. Spying the cold packs among the other medical supplies, she fell to her knees before them, unzipping one of the insulated bags, praying that the antibiotics had remained at an even temperature despite the fire. To her relief the many vials had not been broken throughout the long ordeal and everything seemed satisfactory.

"Jamal, I need your help. Do you feel up to it?"

He nodded.

Gathering up the precious packs, she led the way to the sickroom. At the door, she realized they were being followed, so she turned, using her own body as a barrier.

Her gaze collided with Khalil's dark one.

"Tell him he can't come in," she said to Jamal. She found it impossible to tear her gaze from his.

"I cannot tell him that. He's the sheikh."

"Well, I'm the doctor," she replied, her dander up, the spell broken. "This tent is officially under quarantine. Tell him *I* said he can't come in. In fact, I want him and all his cronies"—she glanced about the crowded main room—"to get out." She pointed toward the exit. "And tell him I said to take his precious wives with him or he won't be seeing them for a while, either."

Even if Jamal refused to translate her order, her imperial gesture could not be mistaken. Before Khalil could reciprocate with his typical arrogance, she turned, leaving her unfortunate assistant to deal with the impossible Bedouin.

"He and all of his wives," she muttered under her breath, realizing she had just experienced her first wave of jealousy. Jealous? Of him?

"Never," she said aloud. What did she care how many women he had in his life?

Returning to her young patient's side, she knelt down, forcing her thoughts to things that were truly important. Extracting a sterile needle and syringe, she prepared an antibiotic injection from the limited supply. As she flicked the side of the syringe to rid it of any air bubbles, she heard the chirp of the coffeepot. True to the laws of nature, the moment she turned her back on it, the water must have started to boil. She rolled up the boy's sleeve and pinched his arm. Just as soon as she finished giving the injection she would change—

Knocked over backward, she found her arm pinned down by the weight of the old man. She realized then what he was trying to do—wrench the needle from her hand.

He must think she was trying to hurt the boy.

"Jamal," she cried out, struggling to maintain her grip on the syringe.

He arrived in the nick of time, just as Yusaf was about to toss the vital medicine into the fire.

"Tell him it's only good spirits," she said, lunging for

the syringe, without success. "Tell him it won't harm the child."

He began his interpretation before she could finish.

The old man spoke just as rapidly, but at least he didn't throw the drug to the flames, just dangled it over the fire in warning.

"Good spirits or not, he says you must do to yourself first anything you plan to do to the sheikh's son."

"Jamal, tell him there is only so much medicine. I cannot waste even a little." She gave the old man a pleading look, hoping to convey her sincerity.

"Not good enough. He refuses to let you do anything to Muhammad that you will not do to yourself."

"Okay. Tell him okay." Turning, she rummaged in the bags, looking for a bottle of sterile saline solution. She would simply give herself a placebo, a trick she had learned in residency. Often patients after surgery would demand more painkiller than was safe to give them. A shot of an inert substance often would quiet them down, never the wiser, and safe from overdose. Yusaf would never know what she put in the syringe. She lifted out the vial and began to make up the harmless injection.

The old man renewed his objection.

"Now what?" she demanded, pausing.

"The top of the bottle. He says the one you used for the boy was blue. That one is red."

Damn. She hadn't thought he would notice such a small difference. Refusing to waste even one drop of the limited supply of medicine, she stared down into the satchel. What was she to do? All of the bottles had red tops except the antibiotic . . .

And one vial of tranquilizer.

Hesitating, she weighed her options. No doubt, the

drug would make her sleepy, but if she added it to the saline solution already in the syringe, perhaps it would be well diluted and ineffectual.

She would simply have to take that chance.

"Blue," she said, lifting up the vial and showing it to the old man before adding a little to the syringe.

Satisfied, he nodded his head.

It only took her a second to give herself the injection and then the boy his. God, she prayed she didn't have to go through this with every injection she gave the boy.

For the moment she felt fine. With any luck she would remain in that condition. Perhaps if she stood and walked around a bit.

"Chelsea, what is it?" Jamal asked.

"Nothing." She smiled bravely, feeling somewhat woozy. "I think I'll just take a little walk." She slipped out of the sickroom into the main part of the tent.

To her amazement it was still crowded with an assortment of strange men, all Arab, all diabolical to look upon, led of course by none other than the almighty devil himself. They stared at her as if she were some kind of apparition and a most unpleasant one at that.

"Jamal," she called over her shoulder, wondering if her perception was already being altered by the tranquilizer. "I thought you got rid of them," she said when her assistant joined her.

"I did. It just takes time to move out all of the women and their possessions."

"No, you don't understand. Nothing must leave this tent, not unless it's to be burned."

"Chelsea, you must understand. You are talking about everything they own."

"We are talking about their lives."

118

God help her, her head was beginning to spin. She gripped it, closing her eyes. Adding to her confusion, she could hear the women complaining in the background on the other side of the curtain, undoubtedly about the sudden move.

Soon she realized the men protested even louder.

Fighting down the waves of dizziness, she glanced at them. Dumbfounded, they stood around the central fire, just staring down at the ring of stones, as if that pile of rocks had become the focus of their lives.

To top it all off, Yusaf, whom she had left in the sickroom, squeezed past her, nearly knocking her down. Holding up what appeared to be that old, brass coffeepot in his surgical gloves as if it were an icon, he threw himself at his master's feet, babbling. The pot smacked against a rock, the handle snapping off in his hand. Horrified, he began speaking rapidly, pointing every now and then at her.

Unable to clear her hazy mind, Chelsea frowned. Just what did he accuse her of? It had to have something to do with that all-important kettle that *he* had just broken.

She suppressed the urge to giggle at the absurdity of the situation. Then, just as she was about to dismiss the entire situation as irrelevant and ridiculous, Jamal grabbed her arm, forcing her to face him and his incredulous look.

"Wallahi, Chel-sea. What have you done?" he demanded.

"What have *I* done?" she defended, finding it harder and harder to concentrate on what it was she had to do. Oh, yes, the quarantine. "We have to get all of these people out of here. This tent is off-limits to everyone,"

119

she reminded him, wondering if her words sounded indistinct or if she just imagined it.

"Chel-sea, you don't understand, these people—"

"These people cannot be here," she cut him off, suddenly finding she didn't particularly like the familiar way he spoke to her, something that had come about since leaving the clinic only yesterday. "And that's Dr. Browne to you," she added in a drunken slur.

"Well, *Duktur* Browne, I hope you have a good explanation for absconding with the sheikh's most prized possession."

Most prized possession? She slid a wavering glare at Khalil. What would a demon like him claim as most important? A woman, a child? The urge to giggle struck her once more. Oh, surely not a coffeepot?

She watched in fascination as his hand moved down and gripped the hilt of his scimitar. At last the giggle emerged. She quickly, or so it seemed to her, bit it back. Oh, no, not again. She had never met a man so prone to threaten violence at the slightest provocation.

"You know the fate of a thief, don't you?" Jamal asked, shaking her lightly.

"A thief? That's ridiculous. I'm not a thief," she protested through the rising fog, even as Khalil grabbed her by the wrist, forcing her to either move closer to him or stretch out her arm. When her feet refused to move, she chose the latter, still quite confident he wouldn't harm her, not over a coffeepot.

Then she paled, vaguely recalling the literature she had read before coming to the Middle East—something about antiquated customs that were still occasionally enforced. The ancient punishment for stealing even something trivial. . . .

She tried to recoil her arm, but her muscles refused to cooperate. Did the arrogant Arab actually consider chopping off her right hand? He wouldn't dare. Or would he?

"Let go of me," she cried. All thoughts of quarantine forgotten, she began to struggle in earnest even as Jamal launched into rapid dialogue.

He sounded far away. Dear God, let him be able to defend her from so barbaric a fate.

A gut-wrenching feeling balled in the pit of her stomach. The room began to spin so fast she had to close her eyes. Her knees felt like rubber, bending, bending. . . .

Her last thought before she hit the ground—this time the Bedouin's threat was for real.

Six

"You should have seen it, Umm Taif. Wanton destruction everywhere. My saddles, my blankets, my bed." Pausing, Khalil lifted his hands to emphasize his frustration. "Even my best ceremonial *mishlah. Wallahi!* But at least the council didn't see any of that, only the coffeepot that she had stolen—that was all that seemed to matter to them. Bah! I tire of old men and their equally antiquated traditions." He resumed his pacing. "What am I to do?"

Once before Khalil had asked that question of someone else. That time he had rejected the advice to ignore tradition and rued the day he had turned a deaf ear to wisdom. Now he asked again, unsure if it was the sagacious thing to do or not.

Why did impossible situations and women always go together? This female, Allah help him, stirred his blood and ire beyond mortal tolerance. She didn't know her proper place or, more likely, refused to stay in it just to spite him.

Little fool. Her repeated defiance had them both immersed in a cauldron of hot water. He doubted either of

122

them would fare much better than his ruined saddles and tack. She faced accusations of stealing while his ability to lead had been questioned. For all that he cared, she could have the cursed coffeepot, but such charges, made before the council of elders, could not be ignored. That gaggle of old men had seemed stunned that he hadn't cut off her hand then and there as the law decreed.

Allah only knew he had been surprised himself. Never before had he hesitated to follow Bedouin justice, but when it came to the *duktur-houri* he found himself doing and feeling many things that were not traditional.

Turmoil ruled his household and his mind. If he did not put a stop to the chaos immediately, would it be long before it overtook the entire tribe? He could not begin to imagine how one woman could manage to create such havoc in so short a period of time, but without a doubt, that was exactly what had happened. Never had he met a female so apt at putting herself in the middle of trouble, then stirring it up like a brooding ostrich hen in desert dust.

"I should have punished her and been done with it," he muttered, whipping about to stalk in the opposite direction, forgetting where he was or before whom he paced.

His idea of punishment didn't include cutting off her hand. No indeed. He could think of much more refined and satisfying ways to teach such an impudent female who was master. However, such satisfaction would be for his own benefit, not the council's.

Overwhelmed by the power of his frustration, Khalil sighed, the sound more like a growl than a suspiration. Men, wiser and more powerful than he, fought battles over women like Chelsea Browne. He had heard the great

123

tales of the enchantresses beyond the sea whose beauty ruled the minds of even the greatest rulers, destroying empires as vast and unconquerable as the Persians in distant Baghdad. Ah, but he would gladly wage war for this particular golden-haired beauty, with his worst enemy the Rashaad, even with the almighty sharifs in Mecca, he morosely confessed, if only he could tame her—claim her for himself—be sure that she would be faithful only to him.

He had never felt so strongly for any woman, not even Tuëma, Muhammad's mother, whom he had loved with an untainted heart.

"The first thing you must do, oh, nephew," Umm Taif at last offered her advice with a touch of impatience, "is to stop your self-flagellation and mindless pacing. It serves no purpose to torture yourself so or to wear a path in my finest rug."

"It was only a coffeepot," he exclaimed, as much to himself as to his aunt. "Why cannot that group of impotent old jackals see that?" He paused, clasping his hands behind his back. "A well-used coffeepot. It can easily be replaced."

"Its theft represents much more. You know that, Khalil. She has defied you, made you look weak before the council. How can a man who fails to keep peace in his own household think to lead and protect an entire tribe? Bah, she is only a woman, and well used herself. She is no protected virgin, I can assure you."

"Old woman, curb your tongue if you wish to keep it." Khalil glared down at his aunt comfortably arranged on her pillows in her cramped quarters of the new tent in which he had installed the women of his household. Chelsea had demanded that he move everyone out of his old one. The woman ordered and he obeyed. Did she think her restriction applied to him as well? He was Sheikh Khalil ibn Mani al Muraidi. He went wherever he pleased, slept wherever he chose. No woman dared tell him what to do.

At least not without his consent. He realized then his aunt watched him with a waggish glint in her dark eyes, that she found him and his predicament amusing. She baited him with her outspokenness, and he had fallen much too eagerly into her trap.

"What do I care if she is a virgin or not," he snapped and resumed his pacing, if only to irritate her. "I care only that she save my son's life."

"Of course, *ya ràyyis*," she answered simply, her startling declaration regarding the state of the *duktur-houri's* innocence left unexplained.

Her ensuing silence served only to rub raw the emotional wound she had so skillfully inflicted. He could not stand it another moment.

"How do you know she is not a virgin?" he demanded, attempting to sound only curious.

"Know?" she murmured. Then ignoring him, she turned her attention to rearranging the dark blue skirt of her dress to her best advantage. "I thought you said it did not matter to you," she finally stated.

"It does not," he snapped in return. He stared at her, daring her to press the matter any further, daring her to defy him another moment.

Still fussing with her clothing, the old sorceress smiled knowingly, but knew better than to look up at him standing over her. Difficult hag. She knew no master but her own whims, and he had let her get away with it for much too long.

At times like this he regretted ever taking such a she-wolf into his household. Probably would not have if it had not been for Tuëma's insistent pleading when his uncle and cousin, the old woman's husband and son, had been killed in a blood feud with the Rashaad. By taking in Umm Taif he had saved not only her life but her two daughters as well.

Tuëma. There had been nothing he would not do for his one and only wife. Although their marriage had been a political one, an attempt to unite two warring tribes, he had loved her, although warned not to, with a heart pure and unscarred. He would have cherished her for a lifetime and treated her with the highest respect a man could bestow upon a woman, especially the mother of his heir, if only she had remained faithful.

When she betrayed him, Bedouin law decreed that he divorce her and return her to her own family for punishment. Otherwise he would have lost his honor and respect among his own people. The penalty for adultery was death. Tuëma's father had killed her with his own two hands.

All he had left of her and that faithless passion was a stern lesson learned about loving too much, Muhammad, his beloved son, and a blood feud with the Rashaad that most likely would never be resolved.

During that terrible ordeal, a very special relationship had developed between him and his crafty old aunt. She had become his unacknowledged counselor in all matters, especially personal ones. She knew of his unrequited love, of his pain, of his unerring devotion to his son, of his determination to never show such weakness again when it came to a woman.

But most of all, no matter what she might say to him

in private, she had never betrayed him, and in turn, he protected her. Umm Taif, regardless of her unorthodox ways, was the only person he could completely trust.

All this they shared in that moment of silent communication. He turned away, presenting his rigid back, unwilling to let her see more, to see him falter.

It was not love that tore him asunder, he told himself, at least not the love of a woman, especially one whose honor was questionable. He would never fall victim to that kind of jealous passion again. Instead it was concern for his son that drove him to make his choices with reckless abandonment. Muhammad's life over all else.

"Your uncle, my husband, once said he could tell if a woman had lain with a man by the way she walked," Umm Taif at last offered teasingly in explanation.

Khalil continued his pacing. Against his will, he conjured up an image of the *duktur-houri,* trying to remember how she walked, if it was distinctive. He had no trouble picturing her swaying hips, her proud, straight shoulders, her defiant chin.

"But I say, it is not in the way a woman moves that reveals her secret self, but her eyes. The golden-haired one watches you, oh, nephew, with a longing that only one who has knowledge of such earthly pleasure can express."

"You are mistaken." Only during the fire had he seen her look at him with anything close to passion, and he attributed that to the magic. He turned to walk away, unwilling to hear more, unwilling to envision her beautiful body entwined with anyone else's, unwilling to think of her with himself, either. At the doorway, he faced the old woman once more. "Besides, when have you seen us together?"

"Just because I am confined to the women's quarters does not mean that I cannot see beyond life's dividing curtain, that I do not know the true uncertainty that nags at your wary heart."

"Silence." She probed too close to the truth, a truth he refused to acknowledge. "What could you, a female, know of a man's heart?"

"Or lack of one?"

"You overstep your boundaries, old witch." He stepped toward her menacingly.

"And you are unwilling to confront the ones you place upon yourself," she declared with defiance. Then her tone and eyes softened. "Love need not be artless and conditional, Khalil. True love can easily be experienced with the eyes open."

"I prefer not to love at all."

"I prefer never to die." She sighed with patient resignation. "We both know that is impossible."

"Bah! You are only a foolish old woman."

"And you, my nephew, are a foolish young man if you refuse to listen to me once again."

"Enough. You have tampered with my life long enough for one day. My patience wears thin. My mind is made up. The woman must pay for her crimes." He swept toward the exit, his many questions still unanswered perhaps, but his heart filled with an unyielding resolve.

"What is her crime, *ya ràyyis?* Is it that she dared to prick your pain and make it bleed? Should you betray yourself, is she at fault? Why do men always blame women for their human failings?"

If anyone but Umm Taif had said that to him. . . .

In silence he brushed the curtain out of his way. It

128

seemed he had just waged his first battle—that all-important inner one—and lost it.

"The talisman. Don't forget the talisman," she said. "It is the key to open every door including the heart, the mind."

"What are you saying, old woman?" He paused and looked back at her over his shoulder.

"Only what you came to hear. Open it, Khalil. Look inside of it."

Reaching up, he untied the leather thong about his neck, loosening it so that he could see what the pouch held. A seashell, a brown one, and curled about it a lock of golden hair. The soft hair of a horse's forelock, he told himself. It couldn't be a woman's, for such hair didn't exist in all of Arabia. He looked back at the woman on the cushion, his eyes narrowing with disbelief. How had she known?

"Give it to her if you have the courage. But I warn you now. The magic of the *baraka* is intertwined with the power of the fire. Tamper with the one, evoke the other."

His hand curved possessively about that bit of leather. It belonged to him. To give it up to the woman would be the same as ripping open his *thobe* and exposing his heart to her discretion.

He had no heart, he reminded himself. A long time ago he had carved it from his own chest and buried it along with his unfaithful wife. There was no chance of restoring it, not now. Not ever.

Ignoring the cold, the welcome winter rain beginning to fall softly on the parched land beneath his feet, he turned away and strode from the tent with a purpose.

The council be damned. And damn his prying old aunt. He would deal with the woman in his own way.

Chelsea awoke in the darkness, an unnerving blackness so complete that the silence became unbearably loud. For a moment she thought she was back in her own bed, in her own apartment in Ad Dawadimi. Comforted to think it had only been a bad dream, yet oddly enough left with a feeling of unfulfillment, she reached out, groping in her night blindness, seeking out the alarm clock she kept on the bedside stand to check the time.

She could find no clock, no table. Instead she discovered the edge of a coarsely woven woolen rug. Beneath it was the cold, hard ground.

Just as cold and hard, reality came tumbling down on her. The fear, the frustrations. Exactly where she was. How she had gotten there. The child. The man. She frowned. Especially the arrogant Bedouin who had forced her to come here and now forced her to stay.

She slid her hand along the side of her own body, encountering a second rug that had been thrown over her for warmth. She wondered at the thoughtfulness, who might care one way or the other if she were chilled. She drew in a deep, uncertain breath. The acrid smell of a fire, long gone cold, tickled her nostrils. Then she focused once more on the only thing still not explained— what she could hear.

What she thought at first to be the ticking of a clock, she realized now was much too erratic. What made the noise? Lifting her face, she listened hard to the steady *tap, tap, tap*. Could it truly be rain pattering on the tent roof over her head? It had been a long time since she had heard such a wonderful sound.

Brushing aside the cover, she scrambled to her knees, hoping to make her way outside so that she could see the rain, feel it against her dry skin, even taste it, for she was terribly thirsty. When she tried to stand up, a wave of dizziness overtook her, and she dropped to all fours to steady herself. More memories, terrible ones, crowded out the gentle rhythm overhead. The broken coffeepot, the accusations, the sword descending—down, down, down. Shivering, she drew all of her limbs close to her body and lay back down, pulling up the rug and drawing it tightly about herself.

The significance of her automatic gestures struck her. She had covered herself with her own two hands. She still had both of her hands. Whimpering with relief, she pressed those precious appendages to her heart, vowing never, never to do anything that might jeopardize them again.

Closing her eyes, she listened to the rain once more, soothed by its patter overhead. The sound reminded her of her thirst.

Envisioning the water bag not far away, she no longer cared what it used to be. She had to have a drink. In the darkness she made her way on hands and knees to the spot where it hung near the pile of medical supplies. Taking it down, she took a swig and then another. It tasted good.

Sated, she crawled back to her bed. Lying there she heard all kinds of unidentified sounds. Little scratchings, creakings. Night noises, she assured herself. Nothing more.

A light flashed behind her. Chelsea rolled over to see

what had caused it, but the brightness vanished as quickly as it had occurred. The rumble of thunder, right overhead, seemed to go on for an eternity drowning out all other sound. Then it was dark and silent once more.

She felt the tears rise up and could think of no reason to suppress them. Alone, a prisoner abandoned in a strange place, she couldn't be certain of her circumstances. Would she ever get home again, she wondered, not Ad Dawadimi, but back to Georgia? Suddenly home and family, even her overbearing father, looked good, and she would give anything if she could see them all again.

Then she heard another small sound, a creak like that of leather or of an ankle beneath live flesh and bone. Her self-pity instantly dried up. That was no ordinary night noise. She was no longer alone.

"Who's there?" she called out. Her voice trembled as much with her still-rampant emotions as with the after-effects of the tranquilizer.

She couldn't be certain how she knew; the presence approached her as silently as a cat. It was nothing that she could hear or see, merely a feeling. She struck out at the darkness, finding only emptiness. Her heart slammed against her ribcage with an anticipation closer to excitement than fear.

Another unidentified sound, this time right behind her. She turned to face it.

Red embers glowed in the stone-surrounded fire she had assumed was dead. A streak of sparks shot upward, making little popping noises, as a pair of hands stirred the dormant coals. They were a man's hands, large, workworn, yet slender and unadorned. The sensitive hands of an artist or a musician, perhaps—masterful hands.

From a safe distance, she watched those amazing fingers coax the sleeping flames to life, little by little, until the fire crackled and hissed contentedly. The golden light it cast fell on the face of its reviver.

Khalil's craggy countenance, shaded by the edge of his *keffiyeh,* was a patchwork of dark and light, revealing not a single emotion. He said nothing crouched there before the fire watching her with those dark, hooded eyes of his, just as she studied him in silence. The urge to say something, anything, to break the intensity of his stare was canceled out by her inability to be understood. Besides, she could think of nothing to say.

"Ya'tiy." He pointed to the empty spot before the fire across from him. *"Yijlis."*

It was a command, of that she had no doubt. She obeyed, making her way cautiously to the place opposite him and sitting down. The fire emitted a warmth impossible to resist. She held out her hands, palms up, to absorb it, suddenly conscious of how translucent her fingers appeared and how they shook.

He watched them, too. She thought for a moment he was going to reach out, grab her, drag her through the coals, then . . . then. . . .

Uncertain of what he might do, she darted a look back up at him, her gaze colliding with a determination she found impossible to counteract.

His hand lifted. With a start and a gasp, she recoiled. Then she realized he held something out toward her.

It was the talisman dangling from its thong wrapped about his strong, brown fingers. The flickering firelight glistened on the smooth leather. A gift? Or a lure, more like it.

Did she dare attempt to take the offering? Trap or not,

133

how could she refuse when it possessed the power of communication?

Like a wary cur, she snatched at the pendant, hooking the thong about one finger and pulling the prize toward her. With the talisman pressed against her heart she stared at him, waiting for him to speak, fearing that she wouldn't understand a word he said, that what had occurred earlier between them had been some kind of cruel hoax her mind had played upon her.

Finally she couldn't stand it another moment.

"What do you want from me?" she asked, her voice raw and broken with emotion. She tucked her hands under her arms to protect them.

"What do you want me to want?" He studied her face as if looking for clues to some mystery.

"What kind of a damn fool question is that?" she demanded. The moment she asked it, she wished she could take back her impulsive query.

As quickly as a desert scorpion, he struck, snagging her by the elbows and lifting her up and over the fire as if she were no more than a light-weight rag doll.

"I do not understand this any more than you do, Chelsea Browne, but I do know this much. You will act and speak as befits a woman of my household." His hands tightened upon her arms, pulling her closer. "You will show deference to me and my position." His face swooped down, filling her line of vision. "You will yield when I decree it." His mouth, those undeniable sensuous lips, descended, their intent only too clear.

"I yield to no man," she cried out. "Least of all to you." Angling her face away, she began to struggle, her feet swinging freely. The toe of one of her shoes caught him on the shin.

134

Upon hearing his grunt of pain, she anticipated him letting her go, wondering if he would simply drop her into the fire and watch her burn. She wouldn't put such a brutish act past him. To her surprise he instead gripped her tighter, if that were possible, swung her about, and settled her on her feet before him, a tent post against her back.

Like the dark side of the moon, his face lay hidden in the shadows. Even that close she could see nothing that might give her a clue as to what he planned to do to her. On the other hand, her expressions had to be fully revealed by the flickering firelight. Too late to hide them now. Still she turned her face away. Too late to quell the whirlwind of abhorrent feelings ripping through her. She fairly quivered with them, and his hands upon her arms must surely detect what she fought so hard to deny even to herself.

Oh, how she wished to yield to his open, simple demands. Yearned to denounce every sentiment and belief with which she had so carefully protected herself, especially the idea that no man could be honest except in his selfishness.

Therein lay the difference. Men like her father, like Michael, cajoled, deceived, gave and withheld to get whatever they wanted, unmindful of whom it might hurt, as long as they got their way. Men like Khalil merely demanded it as if it were their God-given right.

She looked up at him, this tall desert lord, trying hard to pierce the shell of darkness that surrounded him. Perhaps in so harsh an environment it was his duty to make such demands—just as it was hers to give in to them.

His face moved closer—she could feel his warm breath dance across her cheek, the desire as crisp as static electricity. She lowered her lashes in anticipation, straining forward ever so slightly.

"Chel-sea, are you all right?"

"Jamal," she murmured, startled at the sudden, unexpected intrusion, and oh, so thankful for it. Disengaging herself from the overpowering embrace—amazingly the Bedouin allowed her to escape—she squeezed past her robed seducer. She brushed the hair from her face, the moment of weakness from her heart, and hurried to join her assistant, who stood silhouetted in front of a curtain. To think that she had almost turned into one of those fluttery-eyed females in a Rudolph Valentino flick, just begging to be swept away by the hypnotic gaze and strong arms of some desert lord.

She realized then she was in the quarantined tent. Her patient—how could she have forgotten him?—lay just on the other side of the curtain.

"Wh-hat time is it?" she asked, hurrying to reach the boy, or more accurately to get away from his father. Her head spun, her hands shook, she was stuttering. "He should have received another antibiotic injection by now and—"

"Chel-sea, it's already taken care of. Are you sure you're all right?" Jamal stopped her with a gentle hand upon her arm. Frowning, he stared out over her shoulder—at Khalil, of that she was positive.

The last thing she wanted or needed was some kind of confrontation.

"I'm fine. Really, I'm just fine." She gained the young Arab's attention by grasping his sleeve and smiling widely. "Just a little disoriented by the tranquilizer, that's all. God, I hope I don't have to go through that every time I give a shot to the boy." She flung her disobedient hair out of her eyes once more.

"I've taken care of that, too." Although Jamal spoke to her, he shot another quizzical look across the darkened tent. "The old man understands and trusts me now. As far as the boy's treatment, I followed your verbal instructions throughout the night—every two to three hours I gave him another injection. He's resting easier, and his fever is down considerably. In fact . . ." Spying the leather pouch suspended from her clenched hand that clasped his arm, he paused mid-sentence. "What's that?" he asked, pointing.

Her eyes followed his finger, and her heart lurched. She'd forgotten all about the magic talisman. Glancing with uncertainty toward the shadowy figure on the other side of the room, she tightened her grip on the leather thong. Would the Bedouin demand his property back? If he did, would she return it? If she didn't, would he then claim she had stolen it and threaten her once more with dismemberment, only this time follow through with it?

"Leave us, *hadhar*." As if he knew her thoughts, Khalil stepped forward into the light.

"No, Jamal. Stay," she countered in desperation, finding her opponent incredibly handsome, but she wouldn't give in to him. Not over this or anything else.

Poor Jamal. He didn't know what he should do. She could tell by the uncertainty radiating from his dark eyes as he looked from one to the other. But then his fear—or was it loyalty she glimpsed whenever he glanced at his fellow Arab—overrode his concern for her. Bowing slightly with deference, he flinched as if in pain from the burns on his back. Then he slipped away before she could stop him.

She could have followed her assistant's lead, but that would have been cowardly. Tucking the talisman behind her back, she bravely faced the barrage of apprehensions and the fearsome source of them all.

"You must leave this tent, immediately," she said in a voice much stronger than she felt.

"I will stay with my son."

"Impossible." She shook her head. "Perhaps, if your wife, his mother, wishes to join him . . ." she trailed off, wondering which of the women from the vast *hareem* claimed the affections of this man.

"He has no mother and I no wife."

"I'm sorry," she blurted, yet the joy she experienced to learn the child was an orphan suggested anything but. Her selfish feelings were quite shameless. Nonetheless, she couldn't squelch them, and couldn't stop wondering who all those women were if not wives. Slaves and concubines, perhaps?

He merely shrugged and then demanded, "Do you think a father less capable than a mother of caring?"

She stared at him nonplussed. Well, did she? she wondered, turning her criticism inward.

"Of course not," she denied. "But you still cannot go in there. You have to understand—"

"Understand this, woman." He stepped forward so quickly, and grabbed the arm that she had tucked behind her back to hide the talisman, she didn't have time to escape. "Muhammad's life is in your hands." He stared down at the bit of leather, but did not attempt to take it. "And yours," he said, staring her straight in the eyes, "is in mine."

With that he spun and stalked away, slipping out of the tent before she could formulate a decent retort.

But at least she had the talisman.

Just as important, she still had her dignity.

She started to tie the leather thong about her own neck, then thought better of it. Perhaps there was a down side to its unexplained power. So instead, she slipped it into the pocket of her jacket, pausing to finger the folded piece of paper she found there.

Pulling out the Post-em note, she opened it. Oh, God. It was the short message she had written to the others at the clinic letting them know what she was up to. In her haste she had forgotten to stick it on the door on her way out. Now no one had any idea what had happened to her. As far as they knew, she and Jamal had simply disappeared into thin air.

What was she to do? Fighting down the rising panic, she did the only thing she could, what she had trained an entire lifetime to do. She turned and entered the sickroom to tend her patient.

Stuffing the note back into the pocket along with the talisman, she fought down a rising sense of fatalism.

How much more would she have to give up before this ordeal was over?

Seven

Several days—long days and longer nights—passed within the confines of that tent, stripped bare of everything that could be deemed a touch of comfort. Even the guards had disappeared, not that Chelsea planned to go anywhere during the quarantine. It would have to be something awfully important to make her disregard her own orders.

Concerning those rigid instructions, she worried about what had happened to all of the stuff she had ordered burned. Had it been destroyed or only carted away? She supposed she was being a bit overcautious, but when possibly dealing with a deadly disease like typhoid only a fool took chances.

She couldn't be absolutely certain that the boy suffered from typhoid fever, without the proper blood tests she never would be sure, but the prescribed treatment seemed to be effective. Thank God for the antibiotics; otherwise they might not have been so lucky.

Throughout the isolation, her mind dwelled on many things, much of which she didn't understand, mysteries she had no way of solving. But what came back to haunt her, especially in the dark, quiet hours of the night, were Khalil's last words to her. He held her life in his hands, the insinuation that her fate depended upon what became of his son. Such threats were a lot of hot air, she told herself whenever assaulted by a vivid image of that terrible curved sword the desert sheikh wore at his side, descending toward her. That aspect of her predicament really was nothing to worry about. If she was to be concerned, it would be because no one would have any idea where to begin looking for her.

Then she discovered the boy suffered with intestinal hemorrhaging which, in itself, often proved fatal. She could only hope there was no perforation which could result in peritonitis. Ill-prepared to deal with such a complication, she faced a thirty percent chance of losing him.

If only she could get him back to the clinic, and civilization, maybe then she had a better chance of saving him. But Khalil in all of his stubbornness had refused to even listen to her repeated pleas.

"Impossible," had been the message he had sent back to her.

Under the circumstances she did all that she could do, only too aware it might not be enough. What upset her the most, and it was selfish she supposed, was the thought of personal failure. She hated losing patients, even though it was an inevitable part of being a physician. Death made her face her own limitations.

Exhausted from night after night of little or no sleep, she refused to give up hope or to give in to her fears, not only of the helplessness of her situation, but of the man who had taken away her control. Although her fertile imagination conjured up all kinds of crazy explanations of who he was, what he was, where she was and even how she had gotten there, her analytical mind refused to accept such nonsense.

By now her friends and colleagues had to be aware that she was missing and even without a clue would search for her until they found her. All she had to do was to keep her head and hang on a little longer. The undaunted cavalry would arrive—eventually. She only hoped it wouldn't be too late for both her and the boy.

However, one small, inexplicable factor plucked at the fabric of her otherwise infallible logic. The talisman and the strange power it seemed to possess. Seemed, she reminded herself. She had absolutely no proof that it was any more than a little leather pouch on a thong.

Without really thinking about it, she slid her hand into her pocket and fingered it; then realizing just what she had done, she quickly withdrew her hand. Until she could fully understand what it was and how it worked, she dared not use it, not after the strange dream she had had that very first night after it had fallen into her possession.

Who hadn't read the epic tale of *The Lord of the Rings?* The story of hobbits, elves, dwarfs, and a magic ring that could overpower the mind of those who wore it. The talisman? Could it and the man to whom it rightfully belonged in turn possess her and steal her soul if she gave into them? It was a chance she refused to take.

Not that she'd had much need of a translator of late, magic or not. Since Khalil had moved his household, not once had he come in person to check on the welfare of his precious son. She wasn't certain whether to feel relieved or to think him callous when queries arrived several times a day through messengers.

Without being asked, Jamal spoke to them, apparently satisfying all of their questions without telling them the whole truth of the situation, and sent them away. She wasn't too sure if she liked her assistant's take-charge attitude or not, but then she wasn't certain about much of anything she felt of late. She'd even been tempted to test the power of the talisman, but so far she'd managed to resist the urge.

The only person she found the need to communicate with was the Arab physician, Yusaf, who refused to leave the boy's side and demanded to know everything she did and why. Sometimes he even offered her bits of advice; but she considered his limited knowledge and herbal remedies nothing but mumbo jumbo, and she ignored them.

Jamal continued to act as interpreter, again much of it on his own initiative. The old man took a terrible risk of being infected, but he appeared not to care, even when it was explained to him. Instead, he fashioned himself a necklace hung with latex gloves. Amulets to ward off the evil spirits, he informed Jamal, hand-shaped, the very best kind. She couldn't help but admire his dedication if not his homespun philosophy even if she didn't understand his reasoning. One didn't ward off disease. Nonetheless Yusaf remained, calm and ever observant, and always underfoot, often giving his approval—as if she needed it or even wanted it. Just like his advice.

He looked at her now with that same annoying stare. As usual she chose to ignore him. In the process of sorting through the vials, something she did every day as if she might discover a cache she had overlooked, she remained silent, listening to Jamal once more painstakingly explain the reasons why they must always wear latex gloves on their hands, not just around their necks whenever they handled anything Muhammad touched.

Amazingly enough, over the last few days she had begun to pick up a limited vocabulary of Arabic on her own. Credit went to necessity and repetition, she supposed, but she was glad of it. At least *something* positive had come out of this most trying situation.

Smirking, she shook her head in disbelief when the old man said something back to Jamal about the power of *baraka* being the strongest medicine of all, then grew alarmed when he became agitated and attempted to place that filthy voodoo cure about the neck of her patient.

"No, no!" she cried, pushing his frail body aside and placing herself between his ignorance and her patient.

She only caught a little of what he said back to her, something about life and death. She sensed it was a warning of some kind, but she couldn't be absolutely sure.

"What did he say, Jamal?" she demanded, still shielding the boy with her own body, thinking wistfully about the talisman just within her reach.

"You don't want to know, Chel-sea." Jamal gave her the strangest look, almost one of terror. "It was nothing important."

"I don't care. Tell me what he said."

But before he could comply or she could succumb to temptation, a loud commotion erupted beyond the dividing curtain.

"See what's going on now, Jamal," she said, not wishing to give ground to that stubborn old man, confident the intrusion was just another messenger sent by Khalil. She glanced down at her wristwatch. Odd, it was a little on the early side for another intrusion. Whoever it was, her assistant could handle them.

144

A few seconds later when Jamal returned, she and the old physician were still in deadlock.

"Duktur, I think you best come in here."

"I'm a bit busy here. What is it?" she replied somewhat exasperated.

Jamal said something very quietly to the old man, something that made him back up and glance around wildly. A sense of dread coursed through Chelsea. And then Yusaf rushed out of the sickroom.

It was the first time he had left Muhammad's side except for necessities in days. Where was he going? she wondered in mild curiosity. Setting aside the pack she still clutched in her arms, she scrambled to her feet and followed her assistant back through the curtain.

Chaos greeted her. An Arab man, not much older than Jamal, stood in the front room, a boy, obviously ill, in his arms. An entourage of dark-cloaked women followed him, all talking at once behind their veils. One of them was crying, trying to grasp the child in her own arms and hold it to her breast.

Chelsea didn't panic. It was inevitable, she supposed, that others would bring her their sick and infirm. With gentle persuasion, she took charge of the lad, laying him on the rug she used as her personal bed. The woman, she couldn't be much older than seventeen or eighteen, hovered over them. The child's mother, no doubt, yet so young to be one. At seventeen all Chelsea had had to think about was high school and getting to the barn to ride her favorite horse. She hadn't thought much about boys and sex and definitely not about motherhood.

Chelsea smiled reassuringly at the woman, wondering just what her childhood had been like. Then she turned her attention to the task at hand, and with efficient, capable hands she checked over her new patient.

Her hands began to tremble, her heart to hammer in her chest. The child suffered from the same symptoms as Muhammad. And if it was typhoid. . . .

True, two cases didn't necessarily make an epidemic, but she did find it noteworthy that the boy was about the same age as the sheikh's son. Was there some kind of connection?

"Jamal, I want you to send these people back to their own tent. Make it clear that it is imperative that they immediately burn this child's bedding, and any other personal effects you can convince them to part with," she instructed, uncertain just how worried she should be, but she refused to take any chances, even a slim one.

Before her assistant could do as she ordered, another group of anxious parents arrived with yet another sick child. Again it was a boy approximately the same age as the others. He, too, displayed the identical chills and fever, the cramping, slow pulse and lethargy.

What was the common thread here? What did the sick all share other than their sex and approximate age?

Chelsea sat back on her heels and stared at her two new patients. She listened as Jamal gave their parents instructions, and from the little she could decipher, she was fairly confident her orders would be followed.

Once the families were convinced that their children were in good hands and left, she set to work, making up two initial doses of antibiotic injections. She gave them with such quick efficiency that the boys only cried for a few seconds. Then suddenly she realized she didn't have the ever-present critical watchdog standing over her hindering her movements.

"Yusaf? Where's the old man?" she asked, glancing about.

"I don't know." Jamal began to search the stark tent, checking behind the curtain that had once been the women's quarters and returning with a worried look on his face. "He's simply disappeared."

"That's just what we need." Utterly exasperated, she groaned, carefully covering her new wards with blankets and stoking the fire by which they lay. "In his stupidity he could very well be running around contaminating the rest of the camp."

"I don't think so."

"What do you mean?" She paused, the stick she used to stir up the coals resting against her raised knee.

"Most likely he has gone directly to the sheikh."

"Why would he go to Khalil? To try and hang amulets around his head?" she asked sarcastically, resuming the task of stoking the fire to keep the two boys as warm as possible.

When he didn't answer, she glanced up at her trusted assistant. Her heart slammed to a halt at the way he looked back at her, and she knew then whatever Yusaf had said to her earlier had indeed been very important even if Jamal had denied it at the time.

"Yusaf? What did he say to me earlier? What does he plan to tell Khalil?"

"You know, Chel-sea, our limited supply of antibiotics will only go so far," he replied evasively. "If any more sick arrive, we will run short. Maybe you should let the old man practice his style of medicine on these other boys." He shrugged. "It could solve a lot of problems. Who knows. Maybe it will even help."

Even as he spoke, another commotion erupted outside the tent.

"I could go after him. Tell him you have agreed to take his advice. That way I could set aside the vials of antibiotics just for Muhammad . . ."

"Are you suggesting that I should allow that quack to hang filthy amulets around these boys heads? That I should show preference for one patient over another?" Without hesitation she accepted the new patient, another boy about the same age as the others, and prepared an injection for him as well, the last dose in that vial.

"We must never forget that Muhammad *is* the sheikh's son and Yusaf the sheikh's physician. He wields a lot of power here."

"Sheikh's physician or not," she declared, giving the child the shot and covering him up with a warm blanket once he had quieted down, "all life is equal."

"Including your own?"

"What do you mean by that, Jamal?" she demanded, clamping her lips together.

"I didn't want to tell you. I didn't want you to worry." His gaze which had held hers up until that moment shifted uncomfortably. "All along Yusaf has accused you of trying to put the evil eye on the entire encampment. Every time you have thwarted him or ignored his suggestion he has sworn you will kill them all, if not with ignorance, then on purpose. Now that more children have fallen ill, he might well be able to convince the sheikh that you are to blame."

"How absurd." Irritation laced with a touch of panic took hold of her with cruel, icy fingers. Such allegations were abominable and unjust. So far she had done everything in her power to save Muhammad, and she would continue to do so with her new patients. "Surely Khalil won't believe such nonsense," she insisted. Or would he? Her hands shook; her voice trembled as well. She stood. "So you think he has gone directly to Khalil with his lies."

"I do. We can only hope our sheikh cannot be easily swayed by the words of his trusted physician."

"Our sheikh? Hah. He may be yours." She choked on the injustice of it all. To think that Jamal might actually be falling under the spell of this place shook her confidence.

"He may even be Yusaf's master," she added. No wonder the old man had scrutinized everything she did so closely. He had been looking for evidence with which to sabotage her efforts. Whether motivated by jealousy or fear of displacement, if he should misinform Khalil and sway his opinion of her. . . .

Her hand had somehow slipped into her pocket and now made a decisive fist about the amulet. She had no other choice.

"But he will never be mine." With that she whirled and started toward the door.

"Wait, Chel-sea. Where do you think you are going?"

She halted only when Jamal's determined hand grabbed her arm and forced her to turn around. In silence she glared at him. An answer wasn't really necessary. They both knew her intent, to reach Khalil before the old man could tell his slanted version of the facts.

"Don't do this. If you overstep your place and try to confront him . . . it might only make matters worse."

"Worse? How much worse could they be?" she demanded. "What do you mean, overstep my place?"

149

"Let *me* go," he coaxed. "Perhaps I can try and make him understand . . ."

"No." Tired of all of this kowtowing to an arrogant, ignorant Arab who, at least in her opinion, didn't deserve such deference, she pulled her arm away. "I'm the doctor. I'll handle this."

"Chel-sea, you are being irrational."

But she was already headed out the door. "If I'm not back in a couple of hours, you must continue to give *all* of the boys the prescribed injection every three hours. Do you understand? That's an order."

Outside the tent, she was surprised to discover a black-clad figure huddled next to the doorway. It looked up, dark, worried eyes probing hers for news. One of the young mothers. She immediately recognized her, and for some strange reason felt an affinity to her. Her medically oriented mind refuted what her woman's heart considered. It was a foolish thing to do.

"Go on," Chelsea instructed, the amulet clutched in her hand as she brushed aside the tent flap as well as her reservations and waved the girl inside. "He'll no doubt recover much quicker with you there."

"Bless you, great one." With comprehension and adoration shining in the dark eyes, the only part of the woman Chelsea could actually see, the black-clad figure slipped inside. Chelsea wondered if the girl even realized the danger she put herself in. She doubted it would matter.

Pulling the collar of her jacket about her throat to protect it from the unexpected cold wind that whipped all around her, she once more focused on the task at hand and trudged forward.

Perhaps Jamal was right. She might only make matters

150

worse, but she preferred to tackle her problems—as well as the cause of them—head on, not sit around and wait for them or him to catch up with her.

With the wariness of a tethered falcon Khalil watched his sworn enemies across the fire, hoping his eyes remained hooded and unreadable. Why were the Rashaad here? What did they want? No matter what their motives were, by Bedouin law he had no choice but to restrain his overwhelming urge to draw his scimitar and challenge them to a duel to the death. He could do nothing, at least for three days.

"Master, I must speak with you right away." The summons, whispered in his ear, caught him off guard.

"Not now, Yusaf," he responded to the old man, whose sudden appearance and obvious agitation presented a nuisance at the moment.

Once more he studied the five men who sat with him about his fire, drinking his coffee, and expecting to be fed. Three days could be a very long while. Still watching his guests, he sipped the contents of his own cup, then smiled. The expression never reached his eyes or his heart. Much could happen in that length of time. Much indeed. Look at how drastically his life had changed in that many.

"Please, master," Yusaf pleaded. "It's about . . . the woman and your son," he whispered the last part of his sentence.

"Be quiet, fool." A barely perceptible nod from Khalil sent a hovering servant scurrying about the perimeters of the group of seated men, none of whom seemed to have heard what the old physician had said, and yet he

151

wondered. As the eldest Rashaad held up his empty cup to be refilled by the serving boy, his foxlike gaze settled on Yusaf, only for a moment before returning to the man who sat beside him.

The woman. The sweet smell of cardamom-laced coffee filled the air, stirring up memories better left dormant. Khalil glanced at the pot, with the twist of date palm coir in the spout to strain its contents, held in the boy's hand, wondering where Umm Taif had come up with a replacement on such short notice. Only too well he recalled the circumstances by which he had lost its predecessor.

A flashing picture of Chelsea Browne, delicate yet capable hands on hips, her head tossing in gold-crowned defiance, made him frown. As quickly as his lips arced downward, he settled them once more into a straight, unemotional line. It would not do to allow his foe to read him too easily. No. It would not do at all.

Unrestrained, his thoughts continued down their dangerous path, conjuring up yet another image of the disturbing witch-woman. This time she was bending over Muhammad, her magic a strong influence over his son. His son. He fervently prayed for his recovery.

He missed the boy—terribly. Would have liked his heir by his side now to teach him the finer points to being a wise leader. Someday Muhammad would make a good sheikh, even better than his father, for he possessed a streak of his grandfather's undeviating shrewdness. Someday, Khalil vowed. If his son survived.

"And so, my friend, I see your herds fare well on their green winter pasture," the rival sheikh made conversation.

Khalil glanced up from contemplating his cup of coffee gone cold. Aziz ibn Sha'la was not a man to make small talk. What did the Rashaad chieftain care about the condition of another man's herds unless he planned to steal them?

"Well enough," he replied, lifting his cup and waggling it, an indication for it to be taken away.

"And that grandson of mine." The hawk-nosed Bedouin glanced about the unimpressive tent, no doubt taking in every detail, every lack of comfort with satisfaction. "I do not see him about."

"He's about." Khalil shrugged noncommittally, shifting back against the curve of his favorite *shedad,* a silver-mounted camel saddle of acacia wood, which he had barely saved from destruction.

To think his precious son shared the same blood as the despised Rashaad made him shudder inwardly. He glanced down at the old man's hands curled about the handleless coffee cup. He wondered if Tuëma had pleaded for mercy from her father before those cruel fingers had slowly strangled the life out of her.

Tuëma. The blood feud between Rashaad and Durra went much deeper than the death of a deceptive woman, much deeper even than the demise of his uncle and cousins. Years ago when his father had brought his clan, by invitation, to settle beside the *wadi* to raise their superior breed of camels and horses, the warlike Bedouins on the northern borders had at first objected to the invasion. Then, slinking hyenas that they were, they had quickly recognized that they had more to gain by raiding the encroachers than running them off.

But Khalil's father was not a man to be bested. *Ghazzu,* the raid, ruled all of their lives, becoming a personal vendetta between two men, Mani al Muraidi and

Aziz ibn Sha'la. No one went unaffected, not even the women or children. How well Khalil remembered his first raid as a young boy not much older than his own son. He had been knocked from the back of his horse and, standing unprotected in the melee, had been struck down by a blade that had nearly taken his young life. He still carried the scars of that cowardly attack and would never forget the face of the man who had tried to kill him that day.

A man who had eventually become his father-in-law.

The feud had nearly wiped out both tribes, and to end it, to preserve the last shreds of *ird,* honor and avoidance of shame, on both sides the two elderly sheikhs had struck a deal, a marriage that would unite them and hopefully end the terrible fighting.

Old men's hopes had been in vain, for no one could have foreseen that Tuëma would resent her role or that she had given her heart to another, one of her own tribesmen. In his blind innocence of youth, Khalil had never known or even suspected her unhappiness, for she had played the part of obedient, loving wife with the shrewdness of her father. Only months after the birth of their son and his shaky rise to position of sheikh had she betrayed them all and proudly proclaimed she had no regrets. In the end he still had loved her, yearned to forgive her, to protect her, but he had had no choice except to return her to her father to meet her preordained fate. To do otherwise would have cost him his power and no doubt caused much suffering for his people. Oddly enough, he wondered if he would make the same decision today if given the opportunity. Today he was a much more astute leader.

"I would like to see my grandson now."

Tensing, Khalil focused on his unwelcome guest and his demands. Why did Aziz wish to see Muhammad? What scheme was his foxlike brain devising? To honor the request was impossible, but that did not stop him from calmly calling over the servant and whispering in the young man's ear.

"Go out as if you search for my son. Say nothing to anyone, but I want you to see how many Rashaad are in camp, where they are positioned, and report back to me. When you return say that Muhammad will arrive shortly."

"Thy will be done, oh, master," the boy replied, never questioning his instructions. Bowing, he backed up and slipped out of the tent.

"At your request, Aziz, Muhammad will join us soon," he announced, his gaze unwavering as he once more leaned back against the saddle.

What he needed was a diversion, something to distract his enemy—for three days. But what? He could think of nothing at the moment, but he had time before the servant returned.

In the meantime it was his duty to feed his unwanted guests. Yes, food. Mounds of it would sate the Rashaads' voracious appetites and give him the time to figure out just what it was they had come for.

He clapped his hands. Platters arrived, heaped high with roasted camel meat, rice, barley and flat sheets of unleavened bread, enhanced with dates and herbs. A virtual feast to impress even the most critical guest.

Accepting a heaping bowl, he stared down into the steaming food. His gut tightened at the succulent smells and the thought that whatever his enemies had planned might very well have something to do with the welfare of his only son.

Her hands still buried in the pockets of her white jacket, Chelsea clutched the leather pouch even tighter. She would give in to the temptation only this once, she vowed. Her shoulders hunched against the surprisingly biting cold of the desert. She hurried along, more determined than ever to confront Khalil, to chastise him for his barbaric manners, his foolishness if he listened to Yusaf's lies. She had no time for them if he wanted her to save the life of not only his son, but the others as well. She refused to forget about those children. How could she with the way that woman had looked at her?

If he refused, she would simply insist to his face that he take them all back to the clinic, would remind him that her disappearance would not go unnoticed and soon the authorities would begin a search for her, if the hunt wasn't already underway.

Surely not even so arrogant an outlaw would care to face the wrath of the all-powerful Saudi government.

She noticed the gathered cluster of men and horses as she rushed by them, thought they seemed rather restless, and found their unrelenting stares most annoying, actually frightening. Determined to get by them as quickly as possible, she continued on her way, brushing past them as if they had not even caught her attention. However, when she reached the small, secluded pavilion down by the *wadi* where she had learned Khalil had moved his household, she was surprised to find it likewise surrounded by armed and dangerous-looking Arabs.

Something wasn't right, but just what it was, she

couldn't be certain. And, then her heart nearly tripped over itself and the obvious answer. Perhaps these were soldiers sent to find her.

She was saved, rescued, at last.

"Thank God you have found me," she said, rushing up to the closest man and plucking at the dark billowing sleeve of his *thobe*.

"Be gone with you, woman." He stared down his beak of a nose at her, lifting his arm to shake her off as if she were no more than a pesky mutt. The ferocity of his action and words sent her reeling backward.

But it didn't stop her, not for a moment.

At the mouth of the tent she ran headlong into an emerging servant who seemed as intent upon his urgent errand as she on hers. Wide-eyed, he elbowed past her, and then before she could think to stop and question him, he raced off, heading in the direction from which she had just come.

Driven by the same level of determination, she burst through the tent entrance and, suddenly daunted, paused there on the threshold to assess what she saw. The winter wind rushed in around her like an unconcerned imp, skittering across the flames of the central fire, causing them to pulsate with life. The flickering yellow light reflected on the faces of the men who stared up at her, mouths opened, conversation pausing mid-sentence. Stone replicas of each other, they sat on rugs about the fire, one leg beneath them, the other raised to rest their left arm as they ate only with their right hand according to Bedouin custom.

There among them sat Khalil, his expression revealing his anger and surprise to find her standing before him. He was so regally handsome that she struggled to catch her breath and to keep from crying out his name. All the spiteful things she had come to say to him stuck in her throat, refusing to emerge. Oh, how she wanted to believe in him, to trust him. Then she was assaulted by an overwhelming need to get away from him before . . . before. . . .

"There. There is the witch-woman! I swear to you, oh *ràyyis,* she plots to murder your son in his sleep. I beg of you, do not blame me for what she does." Old Yusaf might have looked quite comical standing there, that amulet necklace of rubber gloves hung about his turkey-like neck, if his accusations hadn't been so serious.

A restless murmur filled the room, and all those dark, chauvinistic eyes settled on her. Chelsea shook off the intimacy that left her feeling so vulnerable.

"You lie, old man, and you know it." Gathering her wits about her, she stood to her full height, which wasn't all that tall, and planted one fist on her hip. The other hand, about which the talisman hung, pointed at Yusaf in its own denouncement. "I am the only one who can cure the boy." She glanced about the room not recognizing any of the other men, but assuming they were tribesmen and that they might have children of their own. "I'm the only one who can save all of your sons. Three more, as ill as Muhammad, were just brought to me."

It was with a giddy sense of power she cast a superior glance over the group, knowing that what she had said had definitely been understood and caused them great agitation.

"Who is this woman, Khalil? Another rebellious wife?"

She couldn't believe that the mighty, arrogant sheikh took such a razzing from another, even if the older man looked important. And just what had he meant by another rebellious wife?

"I'm no man's wife, and if I wish to rebel—"

That was all she managed to get out before the unseen, unkind palm descended over her mouth and nose, stilling her tongue and stealing her ability to breathe.

The hands that pulled her from the tent displayed not even a hint of gentleness. The biting wind was just as ruthless as it stung her cheeks and lashes wet with tears of frustration and defeat.

She had every right to say whatever she pleased, every right, she railed against the cruel restraint and an even harsher country. She was Dr. Chelsea Browne, of Atlanta, Georgia, a free and equal citizen of the United States of America.

But it seemed there was not one person in that entire male-oriented world gone insane who agreed with her.

Eight

"Chel-sea, what happened?" Jamal's concerned face hovered over her.

"Happened?" Chelsea pushed herself up from her degrading position on the ground where her escort had unceremoniously dumped her. She laughed bitterly, knowing she must look a fright, wild-eyed and disheveled, her jacket torn at one shoulder where she had tried to get away—without success. Ridiculous tears spiked her lashes, but she refused to let even one more escape. The absurd situation did nothing to diminish the sense of unfair futility that pierced her heart.

It was then she made up her mind about the talisman, and she tied it around her neck. Whether it would eventually possess her soul or not, for now, she needed it, needed to be able to communicate. Perhaps if she'd not been so foolish from the beginning and worn it, the situation might not have gotten out of hand.

Khalil had refused to even hear her out. He who had thrown his own body over hers during the mysterious fire to protect her. He whose son she had labored so hard to save. In return, he wouldn't even listen to what she had to say in her own defense.

If he should decide to believe Yusaf's ravings, there was nothing she could do to stop him. She was at the total mercy of a cold, barbaric man driven by compulsions she couldn't even begin to comprehend. Oddly enough, she wanted to understand him, and that in itself made no sense. It had to be some crazy Valentino complex that she suffered from, the need to be carried off into the night by a take-charge kind of lover who would protect her with his life if necessary from a world full of pain and disappointment. *The last thing you need, Chelsea, is another man trying to run your life.*

"Chel-sea? What did he do to you?"

Damming her burgeoning emotions, she welcomed the human contact and didn't resist as Jamal shook her with restrained insistence. Still, she couldn't bring herself to respond, afraid of what might actually slip past her trembling lips.

"Perhaps I can help, oh, master." The gentle voice that spoke quivered with hesitancy, yet the arms that cradled her radiated warmth and an inner strength Chelsea could only wish she possessed.

Looking up, she discovered a young woman kneeling beside her, the dark, almond-shaped eyes old for so youthful a face that was full of wisdom and compassion for her.

"Who are you?" she asked.

"Umm Nuri." She pointed at one of the sleeping children.

Ah, yes, the young mother she had so foolishly allowed into the quarantine tent.

"It is comforting to know that even the great ones have tears."

"I am not crying." Chelsea sniffed back the truth.

"Of course not, Umm Dawa."

Umm Dawa. Mother of Medicine. It was a familiar name, one she had acquired among the villages she visited on her regular weekly rounds.

"Then, you have heard of me." She clutched at the hope that all was not lost as fervently as she clung to the young woman's arm.

"Of course. We have all heard of you. How our great sheikh brought you here with Umm Taif's magic, a magic that will save my son."

How simply put. How misconceived. Chelsea's gaze swept upward with curiosity. Who was this Umm Taif the woman spoke of?

"You confuse brute force with something loftier." She made a scornful face.

"Perhaps, but by the will of Allah you are still here."

"Don't give God all the credit. I'm here because it is my job to be here," she scoffed. By the way, just where was *here?* she started to ask, but before she could get her question out Jamal's excited voice cut her off.

"Duktur! Duktur! Hurry." The impassioned plea came from the curtained-off section where Muhammad rested.

Muhammad. The sheikh's precious son.

"Oh, no. Now what is it?" Chelsea muttered, scrambling to her feet, certain the worst had at last come crashing down on them, that something terrible had happened to the boy during her brief absence.

"Umm Dawa," the young woman reiterated as Chelsea hurried away.

She looked back, a small smile of appreciation making

its way to her lips. How nice to hear such a vote of confidence from another even if unfounded. If the woman only knew the truth of their circumstances, that the great Umm Dawa flew by the seat of her nonexistent pants, she might not be so generous with her praise.

Pushing back the colorful divider, Chelsea entered the curtained-off section not sure what she would find. She prepared herself for anything.

Anything, that is, except for what she found.

"Muhammad," she cried softly.

At the sound of his name the boy, who was sitting up, turned in her direction.

"Saba? Where is Saba?" he demanded, rummaging in his bedding as if looking for something or someone. "You must find him now."

A quick glance at Jamal, who shrugged, offered no clue to what it was the boy wanted.

"Saba? Who is Saba?" she asked.

"If Saba has died of hunger, I shall cut off your head." There could be no doubt of Muhammad's lineage. He'd perfected that same superior look that his father boasted when demanding his way and making his ridiculous threats, as if he thought she should fall to her knees before him and be grateful for the opportunity to serve him and this Saba, whoever he was.

"You will be cutting off no one's head. Not today or any day," she stated matter-of-factly. She had no intention of jumping when a mere child cried "hop," but his arrogance and tantrum were signs of health she couldn't ignore. In fact, at the moment she was only too thankful for the bratty way he acted, even if she did have to restrain herself from swatting his exalted behind. Issuing a sigh of relief, she lifted her gaze to the ceiling, blessing the forces much higher than any of them for the timely intervention.

When she looked back down at the boy he sat with his arms crossed over his puffed-out chest. Jeez, did father and son sit around together all day perfecting that posture? Then she realized he assessed her in a way no child of eight or nine should, almost as if he stripped her with his youthful eyes. Shocked, she wasn't quite sure how to react.

"Are you one of my father's women?" he asked with a confident air uncharacteristic for one so young.

"What?" Her mouth remained fixed in surprise. "Just how many women does your father have?" She clamped her jaws shut. Now, how had that question managed to pop out?

"Many." He continued his unabashed inspection of her, those dark orbs of his big and round and lashed like one of those Precious Moments statuettes her mother so loved to collect. "All that he could want and more," he boasted.

"Well, I'm not one of his many conquests." Donning an air of professionalism, she dropped down beside her impudent patient, palming his forehead, checking the glands behind his ears and pushing aside his long shirt to palpate the ones under his arms as well.

He didn't object to her probing; in fact, he seemed quite subdued by it. She glanced down her nose at him, smiling to herself. Or could it be that he was taken aback by her denouncement of his infallible sire?

"You do not like my father?" His youthful voice seemed on the verge of tears.

Surprised at his sudden mood swing, reluctantly touched by it, Chelsea paused in her examination and stared down at him. Perhaps she had spoken a bit harshly. After all, Muhammad was only a little boy and a sick one at that.

"I like him, I suppose," she conceded, but only to calm him, not because there was even a remote chance that it might be true. She returned to her examination.

"And what do you think of me?" His little face beamed, his heart-melting gaze taking on that superior air once more.

"I think you are one lucky little boy," she replied, pulling his shirt back down and straightening it across his slender shoulders. And then with the way he continued to look up at her, she couldn't help but smile at him. "I think you need to lie back down and rest some more."

Amazingly he complied, scooting back under the covers. Instinctively she pulled the hand-woven blanket up to his chin, so like his father's, set with determination and pride.

"What is your name?" he asked in a voice quickly becoming strained with exhaustion.

"Chelsea Browne. *Duktur* Chelsea Browne," she added with the authoritative air of an adult. Poor kid. He'd been through an awful lot.

"Chelsea Browne," he repeated, a small frown furling his youthful brows. Then he gave her one of those all-male looks, the ones that so exasperated her. "No. That name does not fit you. I will call you the Golden One."

"You will call me *Duktur,* and you will go to sleep, young man," she insisted, tweaking his chin, confident that in his weakened condition he couldn't last much longer.

"I am not sleepy," he balked even as he rubbed his eyes and yawned.

Chelsea rose, relief coursing through her—not only a physician's sense of accomplishment that her patient would recover, but a personal one that Khalil's son would live. Alarmed by such strange feelings and the tears that clouded her vision, she turned away, unable to even meet Jamal's dark eyes which she sensed following her across the room.

"Chel-sea?"

"Continue with the injection schedule, Jamal," she instructed, waving off her assistant's inquiry. "I must see to the others now."

"Chelsea?"

She paused at the sound of her name on the little boy's lips.

"I shall ask my father the next time I see him if I am old enough for my own *hareem*. If so, I shall ask him for you."

She turned and started to set the impudent, little scamp straight, then realized the futility of her intention. The boy was incapable of understanding that she, or any woman for that matter, might not wish to be a part of some man's demented sex fantasy, not his—God, she was no cradle robber—and definitely not his father's.

"We'll talk about this later, young man," she scolded as any adult would do, wagging her finger at him, then dismissing his overactive imagination as not so unusual in a boy even if it did upset her. He probably didn't even know what he was talking about.

"I *am* a man, Chelsea," he boasted with all honesty. "And you shall be my number one wife."

"Your wife?" Flabbergasted, she threw up her hands and swept out of the much-too-confining space, but the more she thought about it, she couldn't help but find the little charmer adorable. He had managed to snap her out of her strange mood.

The sound of Jamal's unabashed laughter trailed after her like a pesky shadow. She did her best to ignore it.

Sated, the despised Rashaad slept. Finally. Khalil sighed with relief. He had thought they would continue talking throughout the night when all he wanted to do was escape and check to make sure his precious son was safe.

His dark brows furled as he rose, then paused to study the scattered prone forms in the tent. Even after the long hours of carefully worded conversation and innuendos he still had no idea why the Rashaad chieftain was there, a mystery only time would solve. At the moment there were more pressing questions that required his attention. Those answers he could demand, no matter the time.

With the stealth of a desert lion he slipped out of the tent, leaving his enemies to slumber by the warmth of the fire. As he made his way through the chilly night toward the cluster of tents set farther back from the *wadi*, he let those worrisome questions run through his mind. Why had Yusaf accused the woman of trying to kill his son? Up until this evening the old physician had accepted her presence, never complaining. What had happened to change his mind?

At the entrance to the tent he had once called his own, Khalil paused, feeling quite foolish for his hesitation, yet he couldn't help himself. There were many things he didn't understand about sickness, invisible evil spirits that invaded the body. But it seemed that the woman was not afraid of them.

He straightened. Nor was he afraid of what he could not see.

He swept into the tent.

The rock-lined central fire burned low, a red glow in the middle of the enclosure. He could make out several pallets stationed around it where before there had been only one. Hers.

Easing forward, he bent, inspecting each bundle. Surprised to discover children, Abdul's son, and Bandar's and Turki's, as well. What were these boys doing here in a tent designated for the sick?

Then it dawned on him. They, too, must have been struck down by the evil spirits. Was that what Yusaf had been talking about? Quickly he dropped the blanket back over the sleeping child and stepped back.

"Ya ràyyis, what are you doing here?"

He whirled to discover the *hadhar* stationed in the doorway that led to where his son lay. He felt like a thief in the night, here in his own tent, and didn't like the sensation, not at all. Nevertheless, he could not shake it.

"Muhammad," he demanded.

If the *hadhar* found his presence and demands in the middle of the night disturbing, he said nothing. Instead, he stepped to the side with deference, making way for his superior to enter the curtained-off section of the tent.

Entering, Khalil glanced about the familiar quarters finding this place that had once been warm and personal anything but. Nothing of his mark was left, except for the boy who slept peacefully beside the fire.

"My son," he murmured, dropping to one knee beside the small figure and pushing aside the covers to get a better look at him. All he could think of was the Rashaad and the carefully worded inquiries about the boy. What did they want from him? He reached out and stroked Muhammad's soft cheek, so like his mother's.

It was cool to the touch.

Overcome by a sense of relief, yet not sure he should feel that way, he looked up to find the *hadhar* watching him from a respectful distance away.

"The fever broke earlier today," the younger man offered. "By the will of Allah, your son will live, *ya ràyyis.*"

Allah's will and the woman's healing touch. Old Yusaf was wrong about her.

"Chelsea." Satisfied, Khalil brushed the boy's cheek once more with affection, then rose. "Where is she?"

They stood there, two men of equal determination facing each other. It was almost as if the *hadhar,* who had claimed she was under no man's safekeeping, thought to protect the *duktur-houri.*

"Asleep. Alone," Jamal finally yielded, nodding toward the empty women's quarters.

Asleep. Alone. Khalil could see her now in his mind, that golden hair of hers spilling across a cushion, her eyes, the color of a spring sky, curtained with a fringe of long lashes. As tempting a vision as it was, he shook himself to be rid of it. Now was not the time to think of the woman and the tempting pleasure for which Allah had so well designed her. For now it was enough to know that she was there.

"Come. I wish to speak with you," he announced abruptly, reluctantly turning his back on the women's quarters.

This time the *hadhar* didn't conceal his surprise.

"To me? What about?"

"Walk with me. There is a generous moon to light our path." Khalil moved toward the tent door.

Once outside, he took up a leisurely pace, one the younger man matched in timid silence. They walked for a while, and just as he had promised, a full moon cast its radiance across the gently undulating water of the *wadi*. Khalil frowned. It now seemed as if the heavenly beacon tagged along, a curious observer eavesdropping on what they said. At the edge of the water he paused, clasped his hands behind his back, and glanced out over the water through which the moon's reflection cut a glimmering zigzag path.

"I have many questions," Khalil began. So many, he wasn't sure where to start, or if he should even ask them, but he had to know. He turned to face his companion, wondering just how much the younger man had figured out. "The woman. Where does she come from?"

"Dr. Browne?" Standing beside Khalil, Jamal studied him with guarded interest. "She is an American."

"A-mer-i-can." He repeated the unfamiliar word slowly, rolling it around on his tongue, then took up his pace once more, skirting along the sandy bank. The name meant nothing to him. It must have shown on his face.

"The United States. Across the ocean," Jamal added, matching him step for step.

Still he did not respond.

"Have you never heard of the United States of America, *ya ràyyis?*"

"Of course I have heard of it. A country of insignificant infidels," Khalil snapped, stopping once more to make his point. But it was a wild guess based on the descriptions his grandfather had used when talking of the barbaric, light-haired warriors from the north who

170

had come to the desert to claim the ancient town of Jerusalem as their holy city years before. How mistaken those metal-clad men with their crosses and crusades had been then. Only Mecca was holy, and the *Qu'ran* the written words of Allah. They were the foundation of mankind and the true religion, and always would be. His point made, he moved on, his confidence renewed.

"Infidels. Yes, I suppose you could call them that." The *hadhar*, nearly running to keep up with him, craned his neck and looked at him quite strangely. "Insignificant. Never. Everyone knows the Americans are the most powerful people in the world."

"Impossible. No empire could be more powerful than the Osmanli." The simple-minded town dweller must have confused the barbarians with the invincible Turks to the north, Khalil decided, but did not correct the misinformed fool in his ignorance. For generations that great empire had ruled, and no matter how many more generations passed, he could not foresee their downfall. Allah forbid that the world might ever embrace the infidels and their erroneous beliefs.

"These A-A-merican women." He stumbled over the unfamiliar word once more, saying it several times in his mind so as to not forget it. "What do they . . . like?" This time when he halted, he turned his back to the silvery water and stared out over the sea of tents that housed his people.

How would all of their lives be changed now that he had so recklessly and thoughtlessly rushed into things he knew so little about? Perhaps it was best he not know. What kind of leader was he to not consider the consequences for those who looked up to him?

Nonetheless, the woman intrigued him, and he had to

171

know, even if he never acted on the information. He kept his face angled away, not wanting the other man to see how important the answer was to him.

"Like?" the younger man echoed.

"Yes," he said with impatience. "What do they find . . . attractive in a man?"

If the lowly *hadhar* found his inquiry unusual or belittling, he did not react. For the sake of his wretched neck he had better not.

"I suppose they like what every woman likes about a man, *ya ràyyis.*"

It was the kind of guarded reply Khalil might expect from a cautious servant, but, by Allah, it wasn't what he wanted. Exasperated, he turned to confront the *hadhar.* What he wanted and would have was the truth.

"Please, great one." Upon seeing the fury reflected on the sheikh's face, Jamal clasped his hands together and slid to his knees in the wet sand. "Why must you ask these difficult questions of me?"

"Because you are the only one who can answer them." *You are the only one who is familiar with the future and knows what it holds for all of us.* He stared down at the shaken *hadhar,* wondering just what his reply would be. At moments like this, oh, how he wished he were not a sheikh, but merely a man like any other. While the common man took truth for granted, it often evaded the great.

"Jamal, you are the only one I can turn to, whose opinion I can trust."

It took a great effort on Khalil's part to reach down and lay his hand upon the other man's shoulder, a gesture to encourage him to rise, to be an equal, a feeling he had not openly expressed since his youth, before he had become the leader of his people. And then he smiled, from the heart, or at least he hoped that was how it appeared, something else he had not done for a very long time.

Hesitantly, the younger man straightened. Neither spoke, but after a shared moment of intense sizing up, they began to walk once more in silence, side by side in camaraderie.

"*Ya ràyyis,* you must understand, I know only a little about Americans. I have never been there."

"I see. This A-merica. Is it very far away, then?"

"Across oceans."

Surely the *hadhar* must mean the great sea that lay to the northwest, the Mediterranean. That would confirm his assumption that the *duktur-houri* was an infidel and account for the strangeness of her language. Still there was so much he did not know about her. The lack of knowledge about the future made him even more uneasy, but he was too proud or perhaps too wise to ask for further clarification.

"The women there, in America. They are treated much differently than here in Arabia," the young man began.

Just as he had suspected.

"How differently?" he pressed, trying hard not to sound too interested.

"They can do and be whatever they please." Even as he said it, he sounded perplexed.

"Are you sure? Seems impractical to me, even foolish." Just as amazed, Khalil came to another halt. "Who protects them?"

"I do not know." Jamal shrugged. "Their government, I suppose."

"Government. Ha! What fools. That is what the family is for."

"They wear whatever they please." Warming to his subject, Jamal continued. "Even marry whomever they choose."

"Are you sure of this? What of the father's rights?"

"Apparently he has none."

"Then, what of honor?"

"Apparently they have none of that, either."

"So, if a man seeks to claim a woman, how does he go about it, if not through the father?"

Jamal mulled that over for what seemed a very long time.

"It seems they talk to the woman directly," he finally said. "They even can see her alone without causing anyone shame."

"Go to the woman? How can that be? A man can't just go barging into another man's *hareem* . . ."

The *hadhar* shot him a guarded, but condescending look.

"Ah, of course, there are no *hareems,* are there?"

Jamal shook his head.

"So the man is alone with the woman. What does he do then?" He knew only too well what he would do if left alone with so brazen a woman, but he suspected that the *duktur-houri* would never accept that.

The question must have been another difficult one, for the younger man walked on for a few moments before answering.

"First, he brings her flowers and sweetmeats."

"Flowers and sweetmeats?" Khalil frowned. That was the last thing he had expected to be told. What an odd custom. He glanced then at the other man, wondering if perhaps he was lying. "How do you know this?" he de-

174

manded skeptically, turning with a look of superiority and planting his fists on his hips.

"I-I-I have seen it in movies, oh, great one. I swear it is the truth."

"Movies?"

"You know, moving pictures." Jamal did a strange little back and forth shuffle that added nothing to his explanation.

How a picture could move was beyond Khalil, but the *hadhar* seemed much too frightened to lie. Besides, if carts and wagons could move without the aid of a horse or donkey—and they could, he had seen this with his own two eyes—why question how a picture could move?

Then and there Khalil decided he never wanted to see the future again.

"So then what? After the flowers and sweetmeats?" Sweetened dates were easy, but where was he going to find flowers this time of year?

"Then . . ." Jamal paused, his gaze casting about as if he were ashamed to look Khalil in the eyes. "Then he must go down on his knees and . . . ask her . . . for her hand."

"What would I want with her hand? Hang it around my neck like a *baraka?*"

At that outburst, Jamal gaped at him thoroughly shaken.

"I mean this man, what does he want with a woman's hand. Surely he does not wish to cut it off?"

Jamal shrugged. "I am not sure, but afterward," he rushed on, as if relieved to be finished with his story, "when she consents to give it to him, they always kiss."

"Do they?" His dark brows furled in confusion. "On the mouth?"

The younger man nodded.

"Bah. I will not go down on my knees before any woman, even for something more than a kiss." Khalil picked up his speed, intent on the vision of Chelsea Browne standing over him, gloating, dangling her disembodied hand in front of his face. "I will simply *take* her hand and anything else, if I decide I want it."

"Ya ràyyis?"

He turned to confront the other man, realizing the game was up. They both knew what he planned to do.

"Be careful." Jamal smiled cautiously. "The *duktur* is accustomed to getting her way and can be quite . . . impossible when crossed."

"Well, then, my friend, the *duktur* and I have something in common." Khalil straightened, standing proudly, defiantly. "I am used to always getting my way as well. We shall see whose will is stronger."

Even as he said it, even as he turned to stroll away with great dignity and confidence, he wondered once again, where in the name of Allah was he ever going to find flowers?

Nine

Chelsea awoke feeling totally, terrifyingly alone. And that was strange, for as long as she could remember, she had always relished her solitude.

Not so tonight.

Perhaps the unfamiliarity, the insecurity, of her surroundings gave her a case of the willies. Whatever the reason, she glanced around warily and jumped when the crude woven tent snapped in the incessant wind like a sheet hung out to dry. Her hand pressed to her heart, she collected herself. The jitters were caused by more than just flapping tents. Perhaps it was the isolation of this settlement that seemed to have been lifted up and dropped back down in some far-off time and place.

That was it. Her imagination simply ran away with her. One didn't just turn back the clock as easily as crossing over a threshold. Illogical or not, an overwhelming fear that she would be stuck there for the rest of her life trailed icy fingers of dread down her spine. She shivered uncontrollably.

"Get a grip, Dr. Browne," she chastised herself. Her situation wasn't as bad as all that. Just as soon as she got the medical crisis in this remote, but present-day village under control, all she had to do was insist, and she would be returned to the clinic, posthaste. She was more than confident that none of them, not even the most arrogant among them, wanted another Middle East hostage situation on their hands.

There's no place like home. There's no place like home. An absurd image of her standing in a void, her eyes closed, clicking her heels filled her mind. She giggled to think she might suffer from a Dorothy complex, but she highly doubted she had made her way to the other side of the rainbow. More like the underside of hell.

Ah, it was always darkest just before reaching the light at the end of the tunnel, she reminded herself. Not sure where she had heard that particular adage, probably one of her mother's unusual twists, she prayed that it held a grain of truth. At the moment she was in the deepest, darkest pit in her life. An end and a little light would be most welcomed.

Then remembering just why she'd awakened—her three new patients needed another injection of antibiotics—she brushed aside her gloomy thoughts, labeling them just as insignificant as the tangle of blond hair that hung in her eyes.

Reluctantly, she dragged herself out of the warm cocoon of blankets, and slipping on her white jacket out of habit, she made her way to the main section of the tent, now the infirmary. She glanced around, then frowned, trying to figure out what looked different.

The children were all sleeping on their pallets just as she had left them a few hours ago, except that one of them, Nuri, had kicked off his blankets, thrashing about in his restlessness. She hurried across the room to cover him back up. His little hands and feet were icy cold, his forehead ember hot, his fever raging regardless of her attempts to lower it. She realized then what was amiss.

Not only old Yusaf, but Jamal, they were both absent. And the boy's mother. Glancing about, she searched the darkness for the persistent woman, to whom she was beginning to feel an attachment, but the young mother was nowhere to be found. Odd that she would leave her son alone after going to such extremes to worm her way in.

Chelsea sighed. Another breech of quarantine, and there wasn't a damn thing she could do about it. Nothing she did or said got through to these people, it seemed. Quite frankly, that didn't surprise her, as nothing these unpredictable nomads did. In fact, nothing about this entire forsaken country amazed her, not anymore, not after all she had been forced to endure.

Suppressing her frustration, but not the yawn that overtook her, she groped her way sleepily to the supplies piled in one corner of the tent. Knowing exactly what she was looking for, she dug down through the packs and satchels to the one where she kept the syringes.

She paused, thinking she heard something, a little scuttling sound not unlike what she'd imagined she'd heard before over the last few days. But every time she tried to find out what made the unidentified noises, she discovered nothing. So for once, too tired, she didn't bother to investigate.

Blindly, she slipped her hand into the familiar depths of the supply pack . . . and froze.

Something had brushed against the back of her hand. Whatever it was, it was furry, and it wasn't her imagination.

Wide awake, she emitted a little screech, jerked back

her arm, and scrambled to her feet. She shuddered uncontrollably, wiping at the knuckles of her right hand
where the sensation of something crawling over them refused to go away. She could stand many things, but not
little furry things, especially in the dark.

Her first instinct was to retreat, her second to track
down the disgusting intruder and dispose of it, but she
didn't consider either solution practical at the moment.
It stood to reason that whatever she had touched had to
have been as frightened as she had been and would be
far away by now. That logic, as sound as it was, did
nothing to alleviate her aversion or her hesitation to reach
back down into the supplies.

No matter how she felt, she needed those syringes.
Glancing about once more, she sought assistance. None
came. She would simply have to get what she wanted on
her own.

Just to be on the safe side, she kicked at the pile of
packs, then waited a few moments, but heard nothing.
Telling herself she had only imagined the incident in the
first place, she knelt back down. This time, however, she
cautiously slid her hand between the satchels. Snagging
the pack she needed by the handles, she jerked it out
and scooted back several feet before finally venturing to
stick her hand inside of it again.

To her relief she found nothing there except what was
supposed to be there, a supply of sterile bandages and
syringes. After taking out what she needed for the rest
of the night, she zipped up the bag and took it with her.

Thank goodness she kept the cold pack separate from
the others, in a spot close to the front entrance where
the room was coolest. That's where she would keep the
syringes from now on as well, at least until that . . . that

. . . admit it, Chelsea, old girl . . . until that rodent, that rat, could be gotten rid of. She shuddered at the thought of what had run across her hand, knowing she was lucky it hadn't bitten her.

In no time at all she prepared the necessary injections, and putting them in the pocket of her jacket, she knelt down beside the closest child.

"Wake up, Nuri," she said, shaking the boy lightly, hating to disturb his sleep, but having no other choice.

His eyes snapped open with the alertness of a warrior, wild and primitive. When they focused on her she could read the distrust.

She smiled at him, hoping to reassure him, but then he spied the dreaded needle and like all children began to whimper and resist. Oh, what she wouldn't give for one of the colorful balloons she usually kept in her pockets to offer as a reward for cooperation from her young patients, but in her rush to get out of the clinic she had failed to pack any. But then she remembered that they had been out of balloons anyway. A delivery had been expected sometime before Christmas.

Oh, my God, Christmas, she thought with a jolt, even as she tried to gently restrain the struggling child. What was today? She tried to recall how many days had passed since she had left the clinic. Three? No, more like four, but she couldn't be absolutely certain. How could she have lost track of time so easily?

No more successful in subduing the rising sense of panic than the child who began to scream and kick, she felt her own self-control begin to falter. How was she supposed to do this all by herself? Damn it, where was Jamal? It seemed whenever she needed him, he was nowhere to be found.

As if he heard her mental condemnation, her young assistant appeared, suddenly sweeping in through the doorway, allowing a gust of frigid air in with him. There was something about him, something different, more than just the way he had wrapped his *keffiyeh* about his face as if he were becoming like all the rest of these impossible people, but she couldn't decide exactly what that something was.

"Where have you been?" she demanded, not hiding her irritation. "And secure that flap tighter. You're letting in a cold draft." She looked back at the child, whose struggle had intensified with her distraction, forcing her to once more concentrate on holding him down. At least his show of resistance could be considered a healthy sign, she thought, trying to look for the positive in a situation gone completely awry.

To make matters worse, she received no answer from her normally cooperative assistant. Instead he ignored her pointed question, even as he knelt to aid her in her attempt to calm the frightened, wide-eyed child. All he used were soothing words of encouragement.

She sat back on her heels and crossed her arms. Not that he said anything so differently than she had, but apparently coming from . . . from . . . from what?

Overwhelmed by the injustice of it all, she shot Jamal a look of resentment. Another Arab, a man, perhaps? Whatever the unfair advantage he had over her, it set her teeth to grinding to watch the child grow still, even if it did make it possible for her to push up his sleeve and give him the necessary injection.

"See, it wasn't all that bad, now was it?" she murmured, rubbing the spot on Nuri's thin, little arm where she had pricked him. Then, truly not liking to hurt any child, she brushed an errant tear from the boy's cheek still raging red with fever.

On a whim, she stripped off one of her latex gloves—she would have to dispose of it anyway—and blew it up like a balloon, a trick she'd learned in medical school. The inflated fingers stuck out like antennae on a satellite. Although it wasn't as colorful as a real balloon, it still captured the child's interest. It was as if he'd never seen such a thing. Dismissing that as impossible, she tied a knot in the hand hole and tapped it into his outstretched hands.

"So where were you?" she asked Jamal again, sitting back on her heels to sneak a look at her young assistant from the corner of her eye. Nuri returned her volley and actually giggled with delight. Without thinking, she swatted the toy back to him.

"Out." Jamal didn't bother to glance at her, instead seemed quite fascinated with watching them play with the sputnik balloon.

Now, wasn't that just like something a man would say and do? She took out her frustrations by smacking the balloon. It floated calmly back to the child, a mockery to how hard she had hit it.

"Well, don't go *out* again without telling me beforehand." She stood up, and made her way to the next child, already awake and regarding Nuri's acquisition with curiosity. She only had one glove left, but there were more in the pack. She frowned. Ah, yes, the packs and the mystery invader.

"There's some kind of furry creature living in the supplies. Get rid of it, Jamal," she ordered.

She didn't particularly like his smug silence, or his bemused look, not that she could do much about either one, but it seemed the longer they remained here in this hellhole of a backward community, the more . . . Arabic Jamal acted.

God, what she wouldn't give for a long, hot bath, clean underwear—and the familiar pinch on the backs of her knees from the torn upholstery of her office chair back in Ad Dawadimi—and a good, old-fashioned mousetrap. But wishing never made anything happen.

The injection given, she tucked the amazingly cooperative second boy under his covers, and giving him his reward, she turned her attention to her third patient. In silence Jamal helped her administer the last injection.

As he blew up the glove he'd retrieved from the supplies without incident, she could swear that he was looking at her quite strangely.

"What?" She glanced up, her inquisitiveness hardened by her anger.

All he did was shrug, but she detected a definite glitter in his dark, devious eyes. Odd, she had never noticed how condescending his expression could be—until now. Disturbed by what she saw, by the strange feeling of uncertainty clawing at her insides, she snatched the balloon out of his hand and tied the end in a knot.

"Chel-sea. Do not be so . . ."

Even as she handed the last child his prize, she looked over to find Jamal still staring at her. His face was contorted with concentration as if he searched for just the right word to use.

Bitchy? she supplied, but didn't say it aloud.

"Do not be so difficult with yourself."

It was a very American expression he tried to convey, and she found his twist to it most endearing.

"You mean, don't be so hard on myself," she corrected.

Smiling, he nodded.

For a moment she considered his advice, then rejected it just as quickly. Only by being hard on herself had she managed to get as far as she had. It was the only way she would get through this crisis like every other she'd faced.

"Life is what it is, Chel-sea. To fight what Fate has decreed for each of us is a path only a fool takes."

"Ah, Jamal. That is where your culture and mine clash. Life is only what you make it, what you squeeze out of it." She lifted her hand and demonstrated. "Otherwise, what is the purpose for being here?"

It was an argument they had engaged in many times in the past, and as always, they resolved nothing by it, only reinforced the chasm of differences between East and West.

A loud pop broke the moment of impasse. Nuri began to cry. Chelsea turned to discover his balloon had floated too close to the fire, and bursting into flames, the remnants melted away as if it had never existed.

Patting his head in a comforting gesture, she experienced a startling revelation, one that set her to thinking. Perhaps Jamal was right after all. Maybe her life reflected the insignificance of that balloon, destined to burn brightly for a moment, then disappear just as quickly into nothingness, no matter what she did or didn't do. But, oh, how she wanted to make a difference in this world.

"Okay, Jamal," she conceded quietly. "I'll try." Looking up through the film of unshed tears, she smiled bravely at him.

She couldn't explain what passed between them, a silent understanding, or perhaps an acknowledgment that they had much left to face before this ordeal was behind them.

"It will be all right, Chel-sea. I promise you."

She didn't question his motives when he put his arm about her slumped shoulders and held her rather awkwardly. She found his actions endearing, so she didn't hold back on her own response. They had been through so much over the last year together, it only seemed natural to share this as well. Still savoring the feeling of being protected, she heard the sound behind them, felt the overpowering presence, and knew who it was even before she could turn to confirm what she already suspected.

She pulled from Jamal's embrace and whirled around.

Khalil. He stared at them with condemnation, revealing an inexplicable pain like nothing she had ever witnessed before on any man's face. Then, just as suddenly as he'd appeared, he spun on his heels and swept out of the tent.

Fate. She swayed in her indecision. Impossible to fight or control? No. She would never accept that she was nothing more than a shifting sand dune in the desert of life.

Unable to explain or even fully comprehend her actions, Chelsea raced after that arrogant, yet somehow vulnerable man. She couldn't stop herself, even if she wanted to.

Oddly enough, she didn't want to.

"Khalil, wait."

He heard her call and ignored it. And what of the pain

that cut through him like the sharpest scimitar? He chose to deny that, as well.

She grasped his arm. There was nothing hesitant, soft, or meek about her overture. The heat of her touch which promised paradise on earth penetrated through the thickness of the sleeve of his *thobe*. He shook off both her hand, strong and sure, and the raging temptation, even more powerful.

No woman would ever affect him in that way again.

Alas, the ache, the unreasonable disappointment in the weakness of a woman's true nature, cleaved its way through the pain, leaving behind its residue of poison. She was no different than Tuëma had been. His heart hardened, a victim of the bitter effects of life's venom.

He paused, collected himself, and posed for the benefit of the *duktur-houri,* only too aware of the image he made with the icy winter wind whipping at his *thobe* and *keffiyeh*. It was a regal vision that would make even the bravest, most fierce warrior tremble in fear. Perhaps if he had used such tactics with his wife instead of acting like a love-sick pup, he might have saved her. Yes, this was definitely the best way to handle a woman.

He prepared himself for her arms to wrap about his legs at any moment. She would plead for his forgiveness. Beg him to spare her.

He held perfectly still, arms akimbo, legs braced wide apart, patiently weighing his princely choice of life and death over an insignificant female too weak to protect her own honor. Even after he made up his most generous mind, he still stood there . . . waiting.

Well, what took her so long to throw herself at his feet?

The urge to look over his shoulder tugged at his self-assuredness. No, he would never give any woman that kind of satisfaction again, to allow her to see how much she affected him. Shrugging his broad shoulders, he settled once more into a purposeful, imposing stance to demonstrate his superior strength of mind.

She would come to him. By Allah, she would beseech him to show compassion and mercy, promise to be faithful. After a while—after a *long* while—he would grant her requests.

Still he stood there in spite of his affirmations. His patience, never his strong point anyway, began to wear thin. Then a terrible, inconceivable thought struck him. His arms dropped to his sides. What if she had no intention of throwing herself at his feet? Instead, what if she used this opportunity to try and escape?

Alarmed, he spun about. To his surprise he found her just standing there, quietly, almost regally, a few paces away, so he quickly struck his imperial pose once more. Then they simply stared at each other. It didn't matter that he glared at her from his superior height. Even when he purposefully gripped the hilt of his scimitar, a warning to her that had worked in the past, that didn't evoke the reaction he wanted from her either.

He looked her up and down like a hawk sizing up prey. She stood as straight as a fortress parapet against attack, defying the cold wind, the blowing sands—defying him and the fact that he was only doing what was best for her. Not even an army of true believers could breech such a well-constructed fortification. It would take time, patience, and a relentless siege to rival even the longest in history to tear it down.

War games. He knew well how to wage them. What were her weaknesses? Her strengths? Where was the mortar in her wall of obstinacy and misconception? Those clothes she wore, he decided. Very unfeminine. Already there was a tear on one shoulder. Who had done that? His gaze skimmed over the slope of her arm. He would find out who had dared to man-handle her and deal with them accordingly.

Yes, it was her strange clothing. His gaze riveted on the round fasteners on the front of her white coat. Therein lay the line of his attack. He did not like what she wore and had every right to strip her of it. Every right as the man.

He stepped toward her with a purpose. To his satisfaction a tremor coursed through her, but it passed quickly and was not repeated. Instead her delicate face lifted. Was that a challenge she issued? A challenge to him?

This was not going at all the way he planned it. However, he, Sheikh Kahlil ibn Mani al Muraidi, would never again be bested by any woman, especially by this one.

Once more he struck a princely pose. If she would not willingly play her role of weak dependent, then he would remind her of it.

"Woman, I have decided to forgive you." He prepared himself to be showered with feminine gratitude.

"Forgive me?" Her posture mirrored his—except that she was so much smaller, and she was laughing instead of scowling. "You forgive me for what?"

Unbelievable. Was she truly that dim-witted? His brows knitted in consternation. Or did she think to toy with him?

"For your indiscretions, little fool, what do you think? A less generous man would not be so tolerant of your . . . shameful behavior." Generosity. Yes, that was the

189

trait the *hadhar* had suggested American women found attractive in a man. But could he be generous and commanding at the same time? He could if it was required.

Then he tried to recall what else the man had said. The recollection caused him to frown. Something about going on one's knees and asking. Jamal must be mistaken, for no man would do that.

"Tolerant? Hah! Do you really think of yourself as tolerant or generous? And what was so shameful about my behavior?" She stepped toward him aggressively, wagging a finger at him. "Just who do you think you are to judge me or to tell me what I can or cannot do?"

It took an amazing amount of willpower not to retreat before her yapping female attack.

"I am your protector, Brown Shell of the Sea." His chivalrous statement sprang from his heart, from the core of his beliefs. Surely she must respect that.

So when she began to laugh, he could not understand what she found so amusing. Confused, humiliated, he could not combat the sense of dishonor that swept over him with the fury of a sandstorm.

By the power of Allah, no woman dared to scorn him again, publicly or privately.

Determined to silence her, to rid her of this obstinate streak of disobedience, to make her see reason—his reason—he grabbed her arms and shook her, a bit roughly perhaps. Oh, the ridicule abated all right, only to be replaced with indignant, incoherent screeching. One would think he was killing her by the names she called him, some of which he did not know the meaning.

He could only think of one way to shut her up and get her attention at the same time.

His mouth descended to cover hers, dampening her

Muhammad. She shot Khalil a determined glower. "But I want him back in an hour," she insisted.

Khalil never blinked or gave any indication that he would cooperate.

"He is still very weak, and will tire quickly. He needs his rest," she went on to explain in what sounded to him a little more like the plea it should have been in the first place.

"Very well. I agree to return my son to your care before sunset," he compromised.

"Sunset? But that's hours away and—"

"Sunset or not at all," he cut her off.

Although she lifted her face in defiance, she held her tongue.

Satisfied, he took his son by the hand once more and led him toward the door, but his victory was short-lived.

"You, sir, do not deserve the title of sheikh." Her voice rang out with clarity, yet shook with defiance. "What kind of leader are you to intentionally keep people in darkness and ignorance? To trick them into doing what you want them to do? Perhaps I should call you what you truly are. Devious, unprincipled, a . . . a tyrant."

What in the name of Allah was she talking about? He prided himself on his principles and fairness. Bristling, he paused before the exit of the tent and angrily turned to confront her and her false accusations.

"Bah! You know nothing, foolish woman. I do not lead my people except where they wish to go."

"Then, if you are so wise and fair, release me from the curse this charm holds over me." She stood there clutching in her fist the talisman Umm Taif had given him that he, in turn, had so generously passed on to her. Red marks encircled her slender neck. From his hand?

No, they were from the leather thong, as if she had struggled to be rid of his most precious gift.

Why would she wish to throw away such magic?

Before he could insist on an explanation, could comply with or deny her demand, a strange, almost inhuman sound erupted. And before he could even determine the source, she spun about.

"Oh, my God, Nuri." All else forgotten, she dropped the basket she held and rushed toward one of the pallets that seemed to have acquired a life of its own.

Perplexed by the commotion, he watched as the woman dropped to her knees and pulled back the blanket, revealing a young boy in the throes of some kind of fit.

"Father? What is wrong with Nuri?" Muhammad also watched, his trembling fingers clutching Khalil's. "Is my friend going to die?"

"No. No. The *duktur-houri's* magic is too strong," Khalil said, unsure of the answer himself. Even as he said it, the woman looked up at him, her eyes filled with doubt.

"Get Muhammad out of here, Khalil," she whispered as she held the convulsing boy's head in her hands, attempting to smooth back the rumpled hair.

Although his body continued to jerk and twist, the child did not seem to be breathing, and his face was turning blue. The color of death. He had seen it before, had been powerless to do anything about it, to stop the dark angel from descending and claiming its victim. The boy grew still.

There was nothing she could do, either. But to his surprise, she lowered her head and placed her mouth over the lifeless one. Hers was truly an act of Allah as she breathed the spirit back into the dying child. He wanted

226

angry accusations. Yet the moment he lifted his face, her rage intensified. So he did the only thing he could think of—he kissed her again, long and hard, until her struggle ceased, her muffled protests abated, until she merely trembled in his embrace.

Although the deed sprung not from passion but desperation, soon the shifting dune of desire overwhelmed him, making him forget the justification for such dishonorable actions. Her mouth softened against his own. But it was the sound, somewhere between a sigh and a helpless moan of defeat, that erupted from her throat that left him shaken and wanting more. It was conquest at its highest, or so he told himself, nothing more. She was under his protectorship. He had every right to claim her if that was what he wanted.

To claim her. To tame her. It was all he could think of for the moment.

Submerged in his need, he renewed his domination, pulling her closer, feeling the press of her breasts against his ribcage, his groin in her belly.

It had been a long time since he had known a woman. Too long. He wondered if she had ever known a man, then rejected the notion as unreasonable jealousy that could easily consume him if he let it.

His hand found the familiar curve of a breast, cupping it, warming to it, exploring it, responding to it even as it blossomed beneath his bold caress.

All he needed were a few precious moments alone with her, and she would be his, totally, completely, irrevocably. Tearing his mouth from hers, he glanced about the desolate village. Where could he take her? His own tent was filled to capacity with the dreaded Rashaad, sleeping off their over-filled bellies. Even so, he could not risk them seeing her again. Besides, Umm Taif was there. It was none of the old woman's business what he did.

He looked longingly at the large chieftain tent where she resided. It too was overrun—with sick children. He did not want to remind her of her duties, just for a little while, just as he didn't want to think about his own. Then he remembered the small pavilion near the edge of the *wadi* that the women used in warmer weather to congregate and bathe. It would be deserted now; of late he had taken advantage of that to be alone. It was a perfect spot.

In silent determination he swept her up into his arms, forgetting all else but the need to unite them in a way that would bond them forever and always. He had taken only a few steps when she stiffened, her hands moving up to push against his chest.

"Where are you taking me?" she asked with a gentle hesitation he'd not heard before.

"Someplace where we can be alone." Pleased with the change in her, he kissed her forehead.

"And why would you think I wish to be alone with you?"

Why? He stood there, blinking down at the sudden change in her attitude, unable to fully comprehend the venom in her voice. Why else? Because her body had given every indication? Because she had kissed him back with equal fervor? Because he was the sheikh, and it was what he had decided was best for them both.

But it seemed she still possessed a mind of her own. Her defiance still lived and beat as strongly as his out-of-control heart beneath her teasing fingertips.

When she began to struggle, he had no choice but to put her down, to push away the raging, physical need. It was either that or sacrifice his *ird*. No Bedouin dared forsake his pride and honor, a vital part of who and what he was. And yet, it took all of his strength of mind to do the honorable thing according to his understanding of her culture, not to give in to the desire to carry her off.

At the same time he had no intention of giving her free rein to do whatever she wanted.

Even as she protested, he took her by the arm and led her back toward her tent. His tent, he reminded himself. In his generosity, he allowed her to stay there, to eat, to sleep, to keep warm and dry. To live. So much for generosity. Apparently it meant nothing to her.

At the tent entrance, he forced her to face him, which she did with an anger to match his own. That defiance. It was too much to ask him to bear for even another moment. The only thing of substance he could pin it on was the clothing she wore. How he hated those clothes and all they stood for. Her abilities far greater than his, her will no woman should possess.

He reached out and ripped the despised white jacket from her body, that symbol of her authority, amazed at how easily it stripped away.

Still she continued to defy him.

It seemed a shame to destroy the unusual shirt she wore with the odd but efficient fasteners, but it couldn't be helped. Nonetheless, his task was not an easy one. She fought him with all she had, the shirt of superior construction holding steadfast, only giving way after several unsuccessful attempts to tear it. Holding the shredded garment in his hand, he was surprised to find the even stranger one she wore beneath it.

Her generous breasts rose and fell against what he could only surmise was some kind of armor. The talisman, the link between them, nestled in the valley of flesh, a blatant reminder of just how fragile was the bond between them. He stared, fascinated as much by the whiteness of her naked skin contrasted by the brown leather pouch, as by her slender fragility. Perhaps his conquest, so hard won, yet so little gained by it, was not such an honorable thing after all.

Ashamed, he watched as her bare arms moved up, crisscrossing her lovely chest, but couldn't stop the raging desire that ripped through him with the same violence he had used against her. Even though she kept silent, he detected a glistening in her beautiful blue eyes that could only be unshed tears. He had not meant to make her cry.

So noble. As noble as his bravest, most spirited war mare. When she shivered, as much with defeat as the cold of the night air, a terrible twinge of guilt tore through him. What had he done?

"I will see that you are given adequate clothing." This time his generosity sprang from sincerity.

If she heard his remorse, if she knew of his self-flagellation, she failed to show it, or perhaps she did not care. Who could blame her?

"I don't want your clothing. I would rather face hell naked than depend on your . . . charity." Prouder than ever, she spat out the last word as if it were poison. Before he could formulate a response, she spun about and disappeared into the tent.

The first rays of sunrise edged their way over the distant hills as annoying as an unwelcomed guest. He stood there, forced to face the revealing light and the fact that once more he cared for a woman possessed of unconscionable defiance. How could this be happening to him again? It was then as he bemoaned his personal dilemma

194

that he suddenly remembered the original purpose for his visit.

Muhammad. Had he completely forgotten about his precious son? All because of a woman—an impossible, unappreciative one at that. How could he have allowed such fatherly neglect to occur?

Well, it would not happen again.

His vow did nothing to lessen the terrible ache that stalked him like an unrelenting, merciless lioness on the hunt. An ache not just of the body but of the heart.

Fate. It seemed to be his curse to always deal with difficult women. What terrible affront to Allah could he have committed to cause himself such misery?

Misery. Yes. He was miserable. He held the power to alleviate his pain; the *hadhar* had given it to him, dangled it before him like a water bag before a thirsty beast.

He refused to give in, to give up, to prostrate himself before any woman. Only Allah could claim such humbleness. He would much rather suffer.

Determined never to give in, Khalil turned his back on the tent, the woman, his feelings, and marched away.

But it seemed suffering was exactly what fate had in store for him.

Ten

Chelsea couldn't begin to explain the unreasonable anger that swept through her like an out-of-control *shamaal,* twisting and turning, leaving behind bitter dregs of reproof. Her ire wasn't directed just at Khalil, even though the arrogant bastard richly deserved every taunt, every foul name she had called him both openly and in her mind. Mostly, she had to admit, she was mad at herself.

What had come over her? How could she have allowed that man to kiss her, touch her in ways she'd permitted no man, not since the disastrous affair with Michael. What did it take for her to learn her lesson? Lightning to strike her dead?

With a vengeance she tackled the pile of supplies, determined to ferret out and destroy the one enemy whose demise didn't cause her to question herself or her sanity.

"Chel-sea, what are you doing?"

"That rat." She whirled to face poor Jamal, unfortunate to be the first man she encountered after her confrontation with the most infuriating male she had ever known. She knew she had to look a fright wrapped in a camel-hair blanket, but it was all she had to cover herself with. "Did you get rid of it like I ordered?"

"Well, no. Not exactly. It's not what you think, Chelsea."

Ignoring his response, at best a flimsy excuse for his blatant disobedience, she returned to digging through the pile of supplies, muttering under her breath that it was no surprise that he probably hadn't. Tears sprang into her eyes, those ridiculous indications of female weakness of which she would have no part. With the back of her hand she dashed them away, refusing to give in to the feeling that she had lost control of every aspect of her life, not just her tear ducts.

Overwhelmed by the confusing rush of emotions that ranged from anger to fear, and yes, panic, she sat back on her heels. She struggled for air as if she were in a tank depleted of all oxygen. Dear God, even if she did manage to find the rat she sought with such a vengeance, she had no idea how she would deal with it.

But deal with it she must, just like she had every other unpleasant, seemingly insurmountable moment in her life. She narrowed her eyes and sniffed. Otherwise, she might as well lie down, roll over, and allow the "powers that be" to have their way with her.

"Here, little mousy, mousy," she beckoned in a singsong strained by the unshed tears. "Come out, come out, wherever you are." She carefully pushed aside another pack and gasped—mostly in surprise.

Two little black eyes stared back at her, unblinking, unafraid—almost intelligent.

"Look. I found it," she cried in a triumphant whisper, pointing. Then grabbing up the fire poker just within her reach, she planned her strategy to take out all of her frustrations on her hapless victim.

"Chel-sea, wait."

Whack! Whack!

The stick descended on the spot where the brazen animal hunkered. Unharmed, for her aim was lousy, it scurried beneath another satchel and disappeared.

"You won't get away from me, you low-down, diabolical beast." She was unsure whom she called such names, the rat or Khalil, but the fervor of the chase, the promise of victory, ignited her blood. Nothing would stay her from her chosen course now. God, she sounded like a mail truck plowing through a snowstorm.

Standing with feet braced wide apart, she bent at the waist and burrowed through the remaining packs.

"Chel-sea, have you gone crazy?"

Before she could respond to Jamal's ridiculous question, the little pest ran between her feet. Actually it was more like it pranced on long hind legs. What kind of rat was that?

She screamed and did her own high step from foot to foot.

As if it wasn't bad enough that she looked like some kind of gutless wonder dancing about, apparently she was having hallucinations as well. Even as she tried to rationalize just what she had seen, that it had truly been simply a rat, whatever it was hopped as big as you please underneath the dividing curtain that separated Muhammad from the rest of the children.

What if that filthy . . . thing decided to bite the unsuspecting little boy? God only knew what kind of disease it carried. At all cost, she must protect her helpless patient.

Brandishing her stick like a weapon of war, she charged into the small room.

"Chel-sea, you have to listen to me," called out Jamal.

Not now. She had to save Muhammad. As she reached the boy's side, she saw the enemy slip beneath the stirring child's blanket and disappear.

Horrified, she threw herself over the boy and tried to scoop him up into her arms, but he was amazingly heavy, and oddly enough seemed to be fighting her. The best she managed to do was scoot him off the edge of the pallet.

She raised her stick and began beating every square inch of that bedding. The beast, whose face had somehow taken on the same haughty attitude of that equally dangerous man that she would just love to beat with a stick, wouldn't escape her wrath now.

"No, *Duktur,* no."

Vaguely she heard Muhammad's childish plea, but she ignored him, too. There was only this need within her to be rid of the terrible insecurities that had somehow manifested themselves into a living, breathing entity—a disgusting rat that didn't deserve to live. When at last she completed the gruesome task, she sat back on her heels, exhausted. Then suddenly haunted by an image of how the beast's little body must look all beaten to a pulp, she hesitated to search for it.

As ridiculous as it was, she burst in tears, actually feeling sorry for the vile creature.

She turned to shower her feelings on the little boy, to hug him to her heart, to tell him everything would be all right now, she had saved him . . . and froze.

Two sets of black eyes—one pair large and luminous, the other small and beady—stared at her.

That brazen, indestructible rat. How could it be? Didn't Muhammad realize the vermin was sitting in his lap. She lunged forward, determined to knock it away.

"No." Muhammad turned his shoulder to her, deflecting her hand.

Why was he shielding it? She paused in the middle of another swing. Coddling it . . . as if it were some kind of pet?

The boy beamed up at her, his dark eyes so like his father's, radiant with joy as he picked up the little beastie and practically shoved it under her nose.

"This is Saba," he said with the same arrogant, irritating tone of voice his father loved to use.

"Saba," she murmured, staring cross-eyed at the creature, unsure exactly what Saba was.

Saba stared back, his tiny nose twitching. She could swear his buck teeth smiled at her. Sitting on his haunches, he raised his front paws and groomed his whiskers. Then he unfolded one extraordinarily long back leg and scratched behind one very ratlike ear. She noticed then his tail had a little black tuft on the end.

Before she could inspect the strange-looking rodent further, Muhammad pulled back his cupped hand and allowed it to climb onto his shoulder, which it did without hesitation, seemingly perfectly content to perch there like a bird.

"What is it? It's not like any kind of rat I've seen." Chelsea glanced up at Jamal for an answer.

"A jerboa," her assistant replied. "They burrow in the desert by the thousands."

"I see, kind of like a chipmunk. Ah-h-h." Hesitantly she reached out to stroke the furry, little head, feeling terribly guilty that she had tried to kill it. "And the children make pets of them," she expounded, filled with nostalgia at her own childhood memories of a baby squirrel that had fallen from its nest when she wasn't much older than Muhammad. She had raised it, loved it, but then her mother had insisted she let it go. That had been one of the hardest things she'd ever done in her life—letting go.

"Make them pets? No, not usually. Usually they roast and eat them."

"Eat them?" Chelsea jerked back her hand. Her stomach revolted at the thought of eating cute little cartoon characters like Chip and Dale.

"Well then, Muhammad, you must promise to keep Saba in his cage," she scolded in a motherly tone, generously willing to tolerate the animal as long as she didn't have to worry about tripping over it. God, she sounded just like her own mother.

Hugging the jerboa to his heart, the boy simply stared up at her blankly.

"Surely he has a cage." She glanced up at Jamal, looking for reassurance.

"These are Bedouins, Chel-sea. Nothing is confined here, not horse, camel, dog . . ."

"I see. Just the women are given such preferential treatment," she replied on a sour note. She began straightening the boy's pallet so that he could hopefully go back to sleep and she could, too.

"There is good reason for such customs, you know." Jamal bent to help her, but she brushed him off.

"What? Men and their petty jealousies?"

"No, not jealousy. It has to do with a man's honor. His worth is judged by the respectabilities of the women under his protection."

"What's honorable about treating women like subhumans?"

"Subhumans? I'm not sure what you mean by that. Women are revered and sheltered as the givers of life. To dishonor another's woman is an intolerable offense, one of the few that gives a man the right to kill the offender."

"If I didn't know better, Jamal, instead of chauvinism, I would swear you were spouting medieval chivalry. Knights in shining armor and all of that baloney."

"How do you think the barbaric infidels arrived at such noble sentiments? Surely you do not imagine that they invented them all by themselves?"

To be honest, she never thought much about the origins of knights and chivalry. Rescuing ladies in distress, battling fire-breathing dragons, she supposed they had always gone hand in hand with Christianity.

"The infidels took much besides lives during their unsuccessful attempts to invade our ancestral homes and holy places."

Invasion? She had never once considered the Crusades from the other viewpoint, but had always believed them to be a noble undertaking to spread Christian beliefs and civilization in the Middle East. Just like her presence in Saudi Arabia to offer her medical skills. Could it be that Jamal harbored resentment for her presence?

Invader. Was that all she was with her lofty ambitions to save the world? What if these people neither wanted nor needed to be saved? It was quite a sobering thought, at the least, one that made her truly feel like the ugly, self-absorbed American.

"I had no idea. . . . I-I-I'm sorry," she murmured, shaken as if someone had held up a mirror for her to see her true image for the very first time, not the one she carried in her mind.

"Do not be. Without the infidels, without the oil fields, without *Dukturs* like you, we would still be a poor people, nomads forever in the midst of civil war, dying like flies in our ignorance."

"Then, you don't think of me as just a woman?"

"You, just a woman?" He laughed as if he found her sudden insecurities ironic. Then his expression sobered. "Never. You are *Duktur* Chel-sea Browne. Umm Dawa. Mother of Medicine. You have a great destiny to fulfill."

He sounded as corny as some Gypsy fortune-teller out to make a quick buck by telling his marks what they wanted to hear, and she felt foolish for falling for such a ruse. Nonetheless, Chelsea flushed with pride, wanting desperately to believe him, to believe in her dream—in her own abilities.

It was then, with that Gypsy image very much alive in her mind, that she heard Muhammad's cry of joy.

"Umm Taif. Umm Taif. Look. The *Duktur* found Saba." He held up his pet for the benefit of someone behind her to see.

Chelsea turned to find a real life Gypsy standing over her, the domineering woman with the hand-shaped amulets in her ears and around her neck whom she had encountered in Khalil's *hareem*. Beside her stood Yusaf, that crazy old physician. What was the geezer up to now? Behind them hovered Nuri's mother, who worriedly plucked at the sleeve of the other woman, only to be ignored.

By the looks on Umm Taif's and Yusaf's faces and the fact the sun had barely crested the horizon, Chelsea assumed this was no social call.

It was an inquisition, at best—a prelude to battle, most likely.

"Out," she demanded, pointing toward the doorway as she rose to meet the challenge head on. After all, the tent was still under quarantine and under her command. She had every right to refuse them entry, even Umm Nuri, who had foolishly chosen to align herself with the enemy.

Instead of complying, the old woman tossed a bundle of strange clothing at Chelsea. Instinctively she caught them and wished instead she had let them fall on the ground.

"We are here to see that you dress and act properly from now on," Umm Taif declared.

By whose order, Chelsea did not have to ask. Khalil, who else? Well, she was not willing to be treated like chattel in a marketplace. She could care less about his honor or anything else. She flung the clothing back in the old woman's face. After all, she had a great destiny to fulfill, didn't she?

However, attempting unsuccessfully to stare down her opponent, she found Jamal's prophecy seemed of little consequence and even less comfort. The eve of conflict had at last arrived, and she felt ill-equipped to defend herself.

But defend herself she would, at all cost.

The traveling merchant's caravan had stopped for the night in the protection of the encampment. Maybe the man thought Khalil crazy when instructed to artfully arrange on a bed of woven palm fronds the sweetened dates and nuts he had just sold the persistent sheikh. Even when told to take them to the tent of the woman *duktur* along with the fistful of precious desert blossoms purchased from an old woman for a price well beyond their worth, he didn't dare question the sheikh's strange request.

"This is not the holy month of Ramadan. Is there to be a wedding, *ya ràyyis?*" the merchant asked.

"No wedding," Khalil replied, refusing to elaborate, even if the man was a guest in his encampment.

"What am I to say when I deliver them?"

"Say?" Khalil stared blankly at the merchant's brazen curiosity, battling an unfamiliar sense of panic that welled and threatened to consume him. Jamal had not mentioned if there were to be instructions sent along with the offering. He had just said to send flowers and sweetmeats, and the woman's hand was his to claim. Surely something so personal was not done by messenger. No matter what the custom, he decided there on the spot, he would not stoop to such barbarism, even to get what he wanted. "Say nothing."

"Even if asked?"

"Say nothing," Khalil repeated. "To no one. Disobey and it will cost you your head."

"As you wish, *ya ràyyis.*" The merchant salaamed and set about the assigned task with the nervousness of a frightened gazelle.

As he wished? Not at all. Khalil spun on his heels and hurried from the stranger's tent. If things were as he wished, there would be no need for him to make such a fool of himself.

They stubbornly refused to budge. Not until she changed her clothing. That Chelsea refused to do . . . at least not until they left.

And so they reached an impasse, neither side willing to yield.

Let them stay. She would simply ignore them.

Tossing aside the bundle of clothing, Chelsea continued her doctoring, practically tripping over Umm Taif and Yusaf, who followed her wherever she went. Would they tag along with her to bed that night? she wondered. Without a doubt they would, if given the opportunity, if something—or someone—didn't put a stop to this insanity and soon.

Was it really only last night that she had struggled with feelings of desolation? What she wouldn't do now for just a moment, if not a lifetime, of solitary confinement.

"Excuse me," she said, brushing past the old physician, who stood in the middle of the room making a total nuisance of himself as usual. She swore he deliberately stuck out his foot. Why else had she stumbled and nearly fallen flat on her face?

She pinned him with an accusing glare, unsure how much longer she could hold her tongue. So when the commotion erupted at the front entrance of the tent, Chelsea was in no frame of mind to deal with yet another intrusion. Enough was damn well enough.

"I don't care if it is the king of Siam, himself," she warned as Jamal hurried to intercept the strange Arab who seemed determined to push his way in, "just send him away. Not one more person is allowed to enter this tent," she added pointedly, engaging in a staring contest with Umm Taif, a war of wills that gave every indication of going on forever.

Obviously the old witch had no intentions of backing down. On the other hand, Chelsea had much more important things to attend to and refused to waste another moment on such foolishness.

Whirling about, she returned to her duties, stiffening her spine against the unceasing stares, closing her ears to the frenzy of excited babble taking place on the other side of the dividing curtain that Arab people always seemed to resort to whenever confronted with opposition.

She had too much to do to get involved. Besides the injections for each child, they also needed feeding, or at least encouragement to try and eat something. Muhammad needed bathing. Nuri's pallet demanded changing. Poor little mite. His fever continued to rage. Nothing she did seemed to bring it down for very long. She was extremely worried about the boy. However, worry never accomplished anything, and there was still all the discarded clothing and bedding to be boiled and disinfected. All thankless tasks, but they must be tended to without delay or interruption.

All of a sudden the growing list of chores seemed too much for her to manage single-handedly. What was wrong with her? Chelsea paused and rubbed her eyes with the heels of her palms.

Exhausted, frustrated, bombarded by a sense of hopelessness, she glanced about the tent. Jamal was still arguing with the stranger. Umm Taif and Yusaf continued to watch her every move, determined to exert their exasperating will on her.

Umm Nuri? She looked as if she wanted to help, but each time she gave any indication of rising and offering her assistance, that old witch stayed her with a warning hand which she obeyed.

The answer was obvious. No one really gave a damn whether she succeeded or failed, whether these children lived or died, or even if others came down with the dreaded disease. The way these people resigned themselves to such tragedy as commonplace, almost seemed to thrive on it, was nothing short of archaic. Why couldn't they understand that each and every task she performed was vital to their own safety? Why couldn't they . . . ?

Struck by a gut-wrenching revelation, Chelsea paused. What if the stranger she'd told Jamal to send away had only come seeking medical attention?

Hoping it wasn't too late, she swept aside the dividing curtain to rescind her thoughtless order and came to a sudden halt at what she saw.

Jamal stood right in front of her, the stupidest grin she had ever seen plastered on his dark face. Holding out what appeared to be a plate of hors d'oeuvres, he looked like a costumed waiter at a Middle East theme party.

"What is this?" she demanded, staring down blankly at the artfully arranged. . . .

For the life of her she couldn't decide what those little brown, shriveled-up things were that covered the woven palm fronds. Some kind of date perhaps, but prepared in no way she'd ever seen before.

"For you, I believe," Jamal replied, dumping the whole conglomeration into her unprepared hands.

"Oh," she murmured, nearly dropping the unusual platter and scrambling awkwardly to hang on to it. Then before she could voice an objection, he crowned the unidentified mess with a bouquet of . . . weeds. Or were they supposed to be flowers? Without thinking she licked the brown goo from her fingers. Sweet . . . like candy.

"For—for me?" she stuttered. "Are you sure?"

What a truly dumb thing to say. She sounded like some giddy school girl receiving her first flowers and candy. Well, actually, if they had been flowers and candy they would have been her first. She had just never been the kind of girl boys sent such . . . tokens of affection.

In fact, while in school she'd never had much at all to do with boys. There had only been time for her horses and her driving need to prove to her father she could become a doctor. In the end there had been room for only one of those ambitions. The need to prove her father wrong had won over her love to ride, over dreams of some day participating in the Olympics.

Then in medical school there had been Michael who had turned her head, causing her to temporarily lose sight of her life-long goal. Even so, Michael had never sent her flowers and candy.

Flowers and candy in the middle of the desert?

"Who?" she managed to get out.

"Who do you think?" Jamal replied, that silly grin of his widening.

"But why?" she persisted. The thought of Khalil sending her flowers and candy for the traditional reason, well, it was completely out of character for the man.

"Wallahi!" Her assistant rolled his dark eyes. "Must I explain everything to you?"

No, not everything, and absolutely nothing when it came to men.

"Was this your idea of a joke? Or his?" she demanded, looking for a place to discard the meaningless gifts. The closest receptacle was the empty hands of the old physician. "Here," she said, tossing them to Yusaf. "Enjoy yourself." She marched away.

Oh, how it hurt to be the brunt of so degrading a prank, especially a male prank. One would think she would have learned by now.

"Chel-sea, it wasn't like that." Jamal gripped her arm painfully, forcing her to halt.

"If not a bad joke, then what was it?" She pried his fingers from her flesh.

"He asked me what you would like and—"

"He asked? Hah! You mean he demanded, like always." Jamal wasn't much taller than she was, and she leaned into him, her face in his.

"He wanted to know what would please you. I told him. What does it matter how he went about asking?"

Jamal had told him that she wanted flowers and candy from a man? Where had he gotten such a ridiculous notion? And then an even more terrible thought struck her.

"What else did you tell him about me?" she demanded, pressing forward.

"Nothing. I swear." He stumbled backward to avoid being stepped on.

Satisfied he told the truth, she turned on her heels with the intent to retrieve her gifts, even if she had to take them by force. Just why did she want them? She couldn't begin to explain. But she did . . . for now.

Later she could throw them away.

Her change of heart came too late. As if vultures had descended, the palm leaf platter had been picked clean, only a pile of pits remaining. Both scavengers, Yusaf and Umm Taif, were licking their fingers clean of the last bit of sticky evidence.

How could anyone eat that fast? she wondered. Even someone starving? To look at them, they obviously were anything but.

Still she had no one to blame but herself. She had given them to the old man, told him to enjoy them. What a time he chose to listen without questioning her motive. Stooping, she began to gather up the scattered flowers that had been dropped on the floor and trampled beneath uncaring feet.

What was she doing picking desert weeds up off the ground as if they were long-stemmed roses? Worse, what kind of foolish romantic nonsense filled her mind? She shouldn't care if Khalil, that infuriatingly arrogant man, sent her traditional tokens of courtship. After what he had done to her last night, to think of him in such common, everyday terms was a mistake, a big one. He was a desert nomad, an unredeemable relic from the past like everyone else in this godforsaken country, and she an American—a doctor, for goodness sake. This was no Cinderella fantasy that would end with "they lived happily ever after."

Yet, in spite of her rationale, she found herself wondering, actually anticipating, what his next move would be.

And so she stood there in the middle of that tent, clutching those wilting, broken stems to her heart which so foolishly slammed against her ribcage as if it had never been awakened before. Her eyes, which must look as haunted as she felt, darted about. Everyone was staring at her. They knew. Umm Taif. Yusaf. Nuri's mother. Even Jamal. She could tell that they all sensed what she was feeling.

Somehow, she had to get away, had to sort out the confusion of her thoughts. Yet when she glanced down at the children, saw their needs, she knew she couldn't afford such personal luxury. As always, she had too many responsibilities to see to first.

"Look, Chel-sea." Jamal gently squeezed her shoulder. "Go change your clothes."

"No." She shrugged off his well-meaning hand. To do as he suggested would be the same as giving in, giving up, admitting defeat. "Have you looked at that stuff?" She glanced down at the colorful, discarded pile, feigning distaste to cover a nagging curiosity she refused to acknowledge.

"Could it be any worse than what you are wearing now."

Her gaze darted to herself, to the camel-hair rug she had thrown about her shoulders, then back down to the garments on the floor.

"No, I suppose not." Still she made no move to retrieve them.

So Jamal did it for her. Picking them up, he gently placed them in her hands. "Think of all you will accomplish with this one simple act of concession." He cocked his head toward Umm Taif and Yusaf. "We will be rid of them," he said conspiratorially, "and we can get on with our work, undisturbed."

His logic was infallible, which made her decision that much easier.

"Very well. I'll do anything to just get them out of here." As she swept through the tent to her private abode, the curtained-off section that had once been the women's quarters, her chin lifted in defiance, and she refrained from looking at the gawking Bedouins.

But she knew their inquisitive eyes followed her even as she disappeared from sight. So be it. Let them put that in their hookah and smoke it.

It could not be said that the Rashaad were anything but exemplary guests. Still, Khalil couldn't wait to be rid of them. He called for yet another precious camel calf to be butchered just to feed them another day. On the third day, tomorrow, he wouldn't hesitate to demand to know their reason for being there in his encampment. They would either have to tell him or leave. Personally, he hoped for the latter.

He glanced up at the young girl. Even veiled, he recognized one of his younger, prettier nieces. Concealing his irritation behind an expressionless mask, he directed a look toward the women's quarters. Where was Umm Taif? He had specifically requested that the older woman serve these men he considered most unsavory. He did not wish for one of his household to attract unwelcome attention. For as long as he remained the sheikh of the Durra tribe there would never be another union between his clan and the Rashaad.

"You slept well?" he asked, hoping to distract the older sheikh, whose eyes even now roamed over the heavily concealed figure of his niece.

"I cannot complain, even if my bed was lonely."

Before Khalil could take offense, the Rashaad chieftain delved with his hand into his morning meal consisting of a bowl of rice flavored with clarified butter and a loaf of unleavened bread.

He stared at the old man, who never once looked up from his overt preoccupation with food. As much as he'd like to think his only concern should be for the welfare of his women, Khalil knew better. But what it was the Rashaad wanted, what sinister plan they plotted behind their devious silence, he would simply have to wait until the proper time to find out.

Alas! The game of waiting had never been his strong point.

Umm Taif quietly entered, whispering something to her youngest daughter, who turned and quickly vanished behind the protection of the *hareem* curtain. His aunt appeared calm enough, yet there was something amiss. He could sense the old woman's agitation, something perhaps in the strange look she flashed him as she silently gathered up the empty bowls and cups from the circle of men.

Umm Taif knew something he didn't, but just what, he could not be sure. Whatever the secret she hid behind her darting eyes, he was certain he wouldn't like it.

"My grandson? Will I see him today?" the Rashaad chieftain asked.

Caught off guard by the unexpected question, Khalil looked at the other man. His enemy pinned him with a pointed glare, which he returned without hesitation. Again he sensed that whatever it was the Rashaad wanted, it had something to do with his most precious son, his one and only vulnerable spot. No doubt the old sheikh knew that as well.

"My son?" he replied, a none-too-subtle reminder of his higher claim to the boy. "Of course." A terrible fear coursed through him unchecked. Even so, he managed to calmly place his empty bowl in his aunt's waiting hands and rise. "I will bring the boy to you myself."

His offer was not made in generosity. Only under such

a controlled situation would he allow the other man near his one and only heir.

"No need to go to so much trouble, my friend. I will walk with you."

As much as he wanted to deny the old man that privilege, to insist that he sit and wait, to restrict the Rashaad movement in the encampment, he didn't dare. Such an act would be tantamount to a declaration of open hostility. Raiding each other's herds was one thing—outright war another. IIc could not in all consciousness put his people in such peril because of his own personal hatred and fears.

With a flash of unsettling intuition he realized that whatever the rival clan wanted, it wasn't just the boy who shared their blood. Muhammad was simply a means to get to what they really desired.

He should be relieved, he supposed. But then he envisioned the moment the old sheikh had first laid eyes on the *duktur-houri*. Chelsea Browne. The woman of the future. What secrets did she keep concealed behind the veil of her intelligent blue eyes. What powers did she possess that he knew nothing about?

Khalil narrowed his eyes as his mind scrambled to put the clues to this mystery all together. What could the Rashaad possibly suspect? Worse, what did they actually know?

His heart lurched with a strange, new fear. A very personal one. Chelsea, his treasured brown shell of the sea, was in danger.

How had a mere female gained such power and importance in his life? Filled with a helpless sense of doom, he realized that only a fool considered someone who pos-

215

sessed the knowledge of what the future held, even a woman, as insignificant.

Khalil ibn Mani al Muraidi, sheikh of all the Durra, perhaps he had his weaknesses, but he was no man's fool.

Eleven

Chelsea slid her bare arm into the gauzelike sleeve and marveled at how the exquisite red-and-green-striped material hung nearly to her hips when she spread her arms. Equally impressive was the precision of the hand stitching at the seams and hems of the flowing garment. She ran her fingertips along the scooped yet modest neckline. Modest or not, the lace of her bra almost showed. She considered taking it off, but just couldn't do it. Instead, she reached inside of the neckline and pushed it down to conceal it.

Her hand brushed against the tiny red and green beads. How carefully someone had sewn them in row after row until they created a sparkling band that accented the swell of her bosom.

Her grandmother would respect such beautiful needlework and appreciate the talent of the unknown seamstress. When she returned to the clinic in the next few days—and it would be in the next few days, she assured herself—she simply must take this gown back with her and send it to Granny Browne, a testimony to the artistry of the women of the Middle East.

Chelsea held out both arms like angel wings. Odd. She had found not a single button or any kind of fastener on the entire dress. The bodice, made of a red wool as soft as the finest cashmere, hung loosely from under the arms, flowing into the generous skirt. Then she put on the sleeveless overdress, made of a silklike green fabric. The costume ballooned even more.

Conjuring up an image of the other village women, she recalled the way they had wound a sash first about their waist and then their hips to give their clothing a more fitted shape. Picking up a length of red material, there for that purpose she surmised, she tried to emulate the style.

There. On the second try she knotted the sash at the point of one hip bone, the fringed ends hanging freely. Then she spied the bouquet of desert flowers she had carried in with her. Unable to stop herself, she bent and plucked one cluster of daisylike blossoms, and inhaling a sweet scent that reminded her of apples, she entwined the flowers in her hair.

Bedecked as she was, she felt like some noblewoman of old waiting for her knight in shining armor to come to her rescue. If the truth be known, she looked like a Christmas ornament, all red and green.

Christmas? Her heart skittered to a halt. Was today the twenty-fifth of December?

What did it matter? The holidays held no special meaning for her, she tried to convince herself. They were merely a time she spent in morose reflection counting all of her mistakes and failures. Well, those feelings seemed light years away at the moment, almost as if putting on this gown lifted the burden of shortcomings from her shoulders.

Uninhibitedly, Chelsea twirled about, wishing she had a mirror in which to view herself. Pausing to clear her spinning head, she glanced down and saw her shoes, those god-awful clodhoppers, so very unfeminine in comparison with the rest of her costume. Unexpected, almost childlike laughter rang out. It startled her, especially when she realized the irrepressible sounds had come from her own mouth.

After a few moments, the fit subsided. God, she couldn't remember the last time she had laughed like that, nor when she had felt so . . . happy with her own femininity.

Could a simple dress be responsible?

Her hand moved up to her throat and curled about the pouch around her neck. The talisman. She trembled at the feel of the soft leather. Could it be just as she'd predicted? The mysterious energy she feared it possessed finally had taken over, stealing her willpower. Did it control her very state of mind?

What did it matter that it gave her the ability to understand and be understood? Nothing, if it meant she lost her identity to its power.

Grasping the bit of leather, she jerked at it with all of her strength, but no amount of pulling and tugging could break the thong. With shaking fingers she reached behind her head and first picked at the knot, trying to remain calm so that she could accomplish the task. But when the strap stubbornly refused to come untied, she panicked and began to claw at it.

When that approach didn't work, she clutched the pouch once more and tried to pull it off over her head.

"Umm Dawa? I heard your laughter and then your screams. I thought you might need my help to . . ."

Chelsea whirled about to find Nuri's mother standing in the doorway, her almond-shaped eyes wide with curiosity. How utterly foolish she must look with that stupid thong entangled in the hair at the base of her skull, the loop too small to slip any farther than the jut of her chin.

"Help me get this off," she demanded, pulling the talisman back down and lifting up her hair to expose the troublesome knot.

The poor woman unquestioningly rushed forward to assist her, but the moment her fingers touched the leather thong, she whimpered and pulled back.

"Please, hurry. Untie it," Chelsea insisted, trying hard to conceal her rising impatience and the ridiculous feeling that wherever the leather touched her skin it burned.

"I dare not, Umm Dawa. You must forgive me."

Truly frightened, Chelsea turned to confront the other woman.

"Umm Nuri." Nuri's mother. In her opinion, a woman should have an identity beyond her relationship to a male. "Please, you must help me."

The woman shook her head. There could be no question that she would not be easily swayed from her refusal.

"Why?"

"That is the magic of Umm Taif."

"The old woman with the hand amulets?"

"Yes. She is the sheikh's aunt, my mother. Her powers are strong, very strong. Only she or the one for whom such *baraka* was intended can remove it."

The one for whom it was intended? But wasn't that herself? Chelsea wondered. If not, then whom?

The answer was only too obvious. The first time she had seen the cursed pouch, it encircled Khalil's neck. Like a flash flood she was helpless to stop, the memories

220

of that first frightening encounter with the talisman's powers raced through her mind—the terrible storm, the unexplained ring of fire, that first magical caress. What did it all mean? What was happening to her?

Could she handle the truth?

She couldn't be sure, but at the same time she refused to hide behind the veil of ignorance for another moment.

Then, as if forces greater than she granted her request, she heard a voice that was undeniably Khalil's.

He was here. Her heart began to hammer with the strength of her convictions. Nothing more, she assured herself, just a determination to know the truth. This time she would not let him get away without answering all of her questions.

To Khalil's relief he found his son sitting up on his pallet playing with that diabolical rodent of his. While he loved the boy dearly, he had to admit it disturbed him that a child of his might show a sensitivity unlike other boys.

"Father," Muhammad cried, bounding up when he discovered his sire standing in the doorway.

To see his son well and out of danger was truly a miracle of miracles. He had willingly made a sacrifice and would do so again, but at the same time it left him feeling uneasy.

Chelsea. His beautiful brown shell of the sea. After convincing the older sheikh to remain outside, he had entered the tent and looked for her, but she was nowhere to be seen, even though he knew she was there. He could sense her, smell the intoxicating scent that was uniquely hers. Now that she had fulfilled her obligation, by all that was fair, he should return her to her own world.

Oddly enough, he could not do that, not yet.

"I have come for you, my son." Glancing back down at Muhammad, he took the boy by the hand and led him into the central part of the tent where the other sick children lay. As long as there were those who needed her—and there would always be someone who required medical attention, of that he could be sure—perhaps the *duktur* would stay to heal them with her magic just as she had his own son. It was a solution, albeit a selfish one, but very effective.

Unwilling to show the true depths of his relief that her healing powers were so strong, he silently squeezed Muhammad's hand. "We go on a very important mission. You must leave your pet here."

"Important?" The boy's eyes widened with self-importance. "Where are we going, Father?"

"Yes, just where *do* you think you are going? And as far as that rodent, I refuse to have it running around this tent unrestrained."

Khalil looked up to find the *duktur-houri* standing in his way. She refused? Impertinent female. Who was she to refuse him anything? He eyed her up and down. His gaze, not nearly as disciplined as his convictions, settled on the gentle swell of her breasts highlighted by the gown she wore. He frowned. Where had he seen that dress before? He couldn't quite place it, although it dredged up restless feelings within him. Had it been Tuëma's?

It wasn't the gown that held him transfixed, he decided, but the flawless skin beneath it. Even with her fists propped on her hips and the offensive demands spilling from her lips, the woman was a vision of beauty in red and green, his dream of heaven on earth.

"I have come to take my son home." Not that this tent wasn't his as well. Never would he concede ownership to her. It just was not home at the moment.

"That is not your decision to make, Khalil. Only I am empowered to release a patient under my care."

"Power?" Dropping his son's hand, he took a step toward her. What woman dared speak of such manly things as power and refusing? "I am his father and I am the sheikh. I am the only one here with any kind of power."

"You're wrong. I am the *duktur*."

And it was true. She did possess powers, powers that went beyond her medical knowledge—power over him. He would never admit that, at least not to her. He encircled her slender neck with his hands, felt the fear pulsing against his palm. Or was it fear? Now that was real power.

"Father, no." Muhammad was only a child, but to Khalil's surprise the brave boy moved to stand between him and the woman, his small fists pressing against the solidness of his father's belly. Even his son rebelled against him, it seemed, all for the sake of a woman. A very special woman.

The wisest thing he could do would be to take this infuriating bundle of trouble back to where she belonged, now, at this very moment. He probably would have followed through with that most intelligent resolution if he hadn't spied the wilting camomile blossoms falling from her hair. Could they be some of the flowers he had sent her?

Releasing his grip on her throat, he caught the apple-scented cluster before it could fall. Even as he did so, her hand moved up, intercepting his as if startled that he had let her go, then lunged for her once more. Their fingers brushed, and to his surprise it was as if the shocking strength of a most turbulent desert storm swept through him. She gasped as if she, too, experienced the lightning. He would like to think that she did. Yet when he again offered his hand, to solidify the contact, she slapped it away and edged backward.

The fragile blossoms flew from his grasp and showered Muhammad, who was still between them.

"My flowers," she cried, snatching them up as if they were precious even as she shot him a pointed look of accusation.

What did she think? That he had tried to rip them from her hair? Why would he do that when he had been the one to give them to her? Maybe she didn't know they were from him. He frowned. But then, who else would she think had sent them?

They stood there staring. No, it was more like she dared him to make another move, so he reciprocated, remembering what it was they originally fought over— just who was in charge.

"Muhammad, how are you feeling?" she finally asked, never lifting her eyes from Khalil's unwavering glare.

"I feel good, Umm Dawa. Truly I do," the boy assured with strained urgency. "I would like very much to go with my father. And see . . . I have devised a way to keep Saba out of your way." He left Khalil's side and hurried over to a small, lidded basket and put the little rodent inside, securing the top. "See," he repeated, lifting the makeshift cage for her to view. "He cannot get out."

"Then, I suppose I can give my permission for a short outing," she conceded, taking the confined animal from

to ask if he would survive. She seemed much too busy to reply. It was as if she'd forgotten he was even there.

Feeling truly inadequate, he turned and propelled his reluctant son outside.

"Father?" The boy looked up at him, his eyes, so like his mother's, wide with panic. And trust. Yes, just like his mother's when he had led her to her death. "What will happen to Nuri?"

"I do not know, my son." He shoved away the most disturbing images from his thoughts. "I honestly do not know."

However, it was then that he realized just how powerful was the alluring magic of this woman of the future. Powerful even over him.

Although it had been just a febrile seizure from which Nuri had suffered, Chelsea knew it was just a matter of time. The boy was so sick, and nothing she did seemed to make a difference. His fever raged uncontrollably; he hemorrhaged internally, all the signs indicated as much. Powerless to halt the complications of the typhoid, simply said, she was going to lose him.

It wasn't her fault. If only his parents had brought him in earlier. With so little to work with. . . . It wasn't fair. Tears of frustration welled and hovered on the edge of her self-control.

She couldn't be certain how long she sat there, holding the child's head in her lap. At some point she realized Nuri's mother sat beside her, clutching her son's hand and rocking—just rocking in silent grief—as if she instinctively knew what would happen.

"I am sorry." Chelsea wanted to say more, but the

right words never formulated. No amount of apologizing would replace the woman's son or make up for the fact that she had failed at her given task.

And when the boy died, it was so quietly. He never opened his eyes, never spoke. A soft sigh of defeat passed through his pale lips, his last breath taken with a struggle, then released without a fight.

Knowing it was over, she gathered the courage to glance at the child's mother. Umm Nuri said nothing, never once accused Chelsea or demanded that she do something to bring him back. Gathering the empty shell of her son to her heart, the woman began to cry, softly at first, but then she abandoned all attempts to hold back.

"Umm Nuri," Chelsea said gently, touching her arm tentatively.

"No, you must not call me that anymore. I am merely Rakia. I am no one's mother now."

Unable to console—God, she'd never been very good at that—Chelsea rose, her eyes so blurred by tears that she could hardly see where she was going. She only knew she had to get out of that tent, away from the evidence of her inadequacies, even for a little while. Just long enough to collect her professional composure, she assured herself.

"Umm Dawa, you must not . . ."

Ignoring the protest, she darted out of the tent and ran, guided by nothing more than her instincts. Soon she found herself at the edge of the water of the *wadi,* staring down into the swirling depths, the village, her failure, all of it far away.

Brought to a halt by the barrier of the turbulent river, she could run no farther unless she had the power to walk on water. She threw back her head and railed bitterly at the irony of her thought. Wasn't that how all doctors envisioned themselves? Gods, balancing the forces of life and death. Out of habit she attempted to bury her hands in the big pockets of her medical jacket. Only then did she look down discovering how scantily she was dressed, especially by Arab standards.

She glanced around, taking in her surroundings. No doubt her lack of proper covering was why those men eyed her so strangely.

Looking was one thing, but now it seemed they were coming at her with determined strides. What did they want?

She didn't recognize them. They looked like all the rest of Khalil's men, overbearing and intrusive, their faces concealed beneath the drape of their *keffiyehs*. Thinking to avoid a confrontation, she turned away and retraced her steps back toward the encampment, knowing that was what they would have demanded of her—to return to confinement. She didn't want, nor did she particularly need, a scene. Not now. Without a doubt, they would report her to their sheikh. And that most arrogant Arab of all would think it was his duty to punish her.

Deep in her own thoughts, she didn't hear the muffled footsteps until they were upon her. She wheeled about to investigate, but before she could complete the maneuver, she was grasped by both elbows and lifted off her feet.

"Let go of me," she cried, indignant that they would touch her.

Her silent abductors ignored her outburst and whisked her along, even though her feet frantically churned the air.

"Did you hear me?" she demanded. "I said put me down. I will not be treated like so much baggage—"

Her verbal barrage was abruptly cut off by a dirty hand placed over her mouth and nose. Her struggle then became one of desperation, but it did her little good.

She couldn't understand the need for such brutality. Did Khalil condone this? Had he perhaps even ordered it upon learning that one of his "people" had died in her care? Would this be the end of her?

When they approached a pair of horses, it made no sense. Where were these men planning to take her?

Twisting about, she caught a glimpse of one man's face. She recognized him, but she couldn't quite remember where she had seen him. Had he been one of the guards Khalil had placed at the door of the tent? No, that didn't seem quite right, but he was definitely not the father of one of her patients. So where had she seen him? She couldn't be certain.

Tossed on the back of one of the horses, she tried to jump down on the other side, but the strong arm encircling her waist prevented such a reckless escape.

"No, no, pretty *duktur*. Your struggle is useless and quite foolish. It will only go that much harder on you, for the sheikh does not tolerate such willfulness."

The sheikh? Then, she had been right. These men had been sent by Khalil to punish her and carry her to her death.

They were off, the horses following the bend of the *wadi*, leaving the village and the last vestige of her hope and courage far behind.

Twelve

"And so, Grandfather, I can ride like the fastest wind and fling my lance with accuracy," Muhammad concluded with pride, his arm lifting to demonstrate his prowess with a weapon. He found it not in the least bit difficult to converse with a stranger, especially when asked to talk about himself. "I also have my own hunting falcon. Do I not, Father?" He turned to Khalil to corroborate his boast.

Khalil nodded in silent pride, noting with irritation that the Rashaad chieftain paid scant attention to what Muhammad was telling him. Instead he stared out over the horizon.

"Grandfather?" the boy demanded when he got no response to his lengthy oration.

"Of course, my grandson." The old man glanced down with a detached smile, patting the child's bare head. "You are indeed a fine, young combatant." His eyes scanned the distant dunes once more as if he expected to see something there.

What did the sly fox seek? Khalil's instincts were instantly alerted. Careful not to draw attention to himself, he searched the desert for signs of invasion. He wouldn't put it past his rival to attack under such dishonorable conditions.

The Durra herds were large, the horses and camels well-fed on the abundant winter grasses around the encampment, the water of the *wadi* plentiful. The summers more often than not left the riverbed dry and his people in need. Not so this year, he suspected. There would be more than enough for all. Therefore, to be envied by those less fortunate was to be expected; in fact, he considered it an honor.

He prepared for the ritual *ghazzu,* looked forward to such raids to begin soon. They provided a way to hone his leadership skills by protecting the property of the entire tribe.

Even in the distance, he saw nothing but the restive herds themselves and the shepherds sent out to watch over them. He relaxed, although his gaze continued to scan the steppe.

It was then that he spied the two horsemen atop the far-off ridge, galloping away from the encampment. At first, he wasn't sure there were riders, only a couple of rebellious mares that had escaped their shackles. He glanced at the Rashaad leader, and although there was nothing discernible in the other man's returned look, Khalil knew he had at last found what they had both been searching for. In a sense, he felt relieved.

"Are those your men, Aziz?" he asked, pointing toward his discovery.

"What men? I see no one." The Rashaad's gaze never wavered.

Not that Khalil expected honesty. Looking up, he found the hill crest empty, but the riders had been there.

Of that he was sure, for he had seen them with his own two eyes. At least now, he knew what to prepare for, and make ready he must.

"The boy has been ill. Now that I have honored your request to see him, he must return," he offered in explanation for his blunt discourtesy. Returned to where he didn't say, and he wasn't going to. Taking Muhammad by the hand, he began to walk away.

"Father, please. I am not tired. I wish to stay a little longer."

"Yes, Khalil, allow the boy to stay a little longer," the old man echoed. "Besides, I understand he has a very fine physician to keep him well. A woman, no less, of mysterious origins. Is what I hear true?"

Khalil paused and looked back, shrugging guardedly, anticipating where this new line of attack led.

"Did you plan to keep this . . . treasure all to yourself and not share it with the rest of us? Surely you didn't intend to act so niggardly."

"You are mistaken, Aziz." Khalil glared suspiciously at his rival. What did he know about Chelsea? How had he gotten his information?

"Am I mistaken?" Aziz aimed his question at Muhammad.

The boy glanced at his father uncertain how he should respond.

It had never been Khalil's nature to lie, but he willed his son to do just that. He knew he must protect Chelsea.

"You are mistaken, Grandfather," Muhammad finally murmured.

"The boy displays his heritage well," the old man said with a derisive chuckle. It was a direct affront to Khalil, one he must ignore or admit his dishonor.

"He will make a fine Durra chieftain one day," Khalil countered.

"Only time will tell." Aziz smiled slyly. "But neither of us will be here to find out for sure, will we, Khalil? But then there are many things we may never be made aware of, aren't there?"

He couldn't explain why, but his heartbeat accelerated, certain that somehow Chelsea had fit into the Rashaad's devious plans from the beginning. But how could that be? How could an encampment at least a day's ride away have known of her existence, much less her abilities, so quickly? And why did his rival reveal his knowledge now? Unless . . . unless . . .

Chelsea. Her safety was all he could think of. Thank Allah that she was tucked away in his tent in the middle of the encampment. It would be difficult if not impossible even for the sly Rashaad to attempt to harm her.

"Don't be so sure, old man," he threatened with no attempt to conceal his hostility. "Not all of us resign ourselves to fate. I expect you and the rest of your men to be gone within the hour."

With that unacceptable breach of Bedouin protocol, he departed, ushering his silent, wide-eyed son before him.

At any moment Chelsea expected the horsemen to halt and get on with the gruesome task assigned them. Would they just impale her on one of their wicked-looking swords? Her stomach knotted. Or perhaps they planned to cut off her head with one mighty swoop. At that grisly thought she found it impossible to swallow. To her surprise, although they were well beyond the encampment and anyone who might be a witness to the deed, her captors showed no sign of stopping. Instead they urged their mounts to even greater speed—as if they feared pursuit.

Who did they think would come after them? Jamal? Good God, her assistant didn't even know she was gone, for he had been resting at the time she had fled the tent. Even if he did awaken, and discover her absence, would he even think to question it for a while? He would have his hands full as it was taking care of the dead child and his mother.

So who else could they fear?

Khalil, came the unbidden answer. That was ridiculous. He had been the one to send these assassins on their errand in the first place.

Where did they plan to take her? Wasn't one place just as good as another to commit murder?

Why, oh, why didn't they just get it over with?

The untiring horses galloped on.

Her mind conjured up an even more horrible fate than a quick demise. They planned to carry her far away from the encampment and let her go. Her death would be a slow, terrible one as a victim of the hostile desert. There would be no evidence of violence, no one to point an accusing finger at, only an implication that it had been her stupidity for wandering away from the settlement and getting lost that had gotten her killed.

Still they rode on, the horses now lathered, never missing a stride.

Yes, she would die in the desert, a meal for predators and scavengers, soon to be no more than picked, bleached bones. Oh, how her mother would cry to never know what had happened to her foolish only daughter.

May Allah curse the cold heart of that arrogant Arab

who had done this to her for his cold heart. How could he be so cruel?

Amazingly enough, she remained dry-eyed, as if she had left her fear behind along the shore of the *wadi* with her courage and hope. All that remained was her impatience to be done with it all.

And an ever-growing hatred for the man who had brought her to this state, both of mind and body. Khalil.

Even now, she could see his dark, penetrating eyes and could feel the slow-burning fire that radiated from their depths, licking at her skin, teasing her, confusing her, stripping her of every vestige of dignity she had garnered over her short life span. At last she'd figured him out, even if the revelation did come too late. His ego meant everything to him. More than his people, more than her. How could she not have seen the man's true nature, if in reality that was all he was. God, she had almost fallen for his macho act.

Well, he may have fooled her, but she wouldn't concede the finale. She would not allow her death to be on his terms and timetable. If she was to die, then it would be where and how she chose.

Twisting and bucking with all of her strength, she struggled to free herself of the arm that held her anchored to the back of the running horse. When she began to fall, she prayed she might hit her head on a rock and be free of the power all men held over her. Involuntarily, her hand moved up to grasp the cursed talisman around her neck, that traitorous appendage clinging to the leather pouch an indication that her soul tenaciously cleaved to life.

She hit the ground so hard, surely she must be dead. She couldn't move, she couldn't catch her breath, nor could she open her eyes. It wasn't so terrible—this dying, she thought, graciously giving up the battle, waiting for whatever would come next.

But then, remembering the ordeal of fire she had passed through with Khalil, she came to a most distressing conclusion. Maybe she was already dead, and the last few days had been some cruel joke God played upon her. This was her own private hell. This was life after death, and from that there could be no escape.

Caught up in her own macabre thoughts, she wasn't prepared for the painful jolt, not just to her psyche but to her body.

"Get up, woman."

She lay there wondering if she didn't comply, if she didn't move a muscle, if her assassins would eventually go away and leave her alone.

"We must hurry, Ibrahim," said one of the men. "If we were seen and followed . . ."

"We are in worse trouble if the woman is dead."

Then, she wasn't already dead, she concluded with relief.

"Woman?" None too gently, a foot again nudged her in the side.

Frantically Chelsea digested all of what the men said. If she wasn't to be killed, then what was their purpose for dragging her from the Durra encampment? Only one possibility came to mind—not a very pleasant one.

Here she lay on the ground, an open invitation. If rape was their intent, she would not make it easy for them. She tensed for a fight, then thought better of it. Perhaps the best thing she could do was remain quiet and still until they made their move.

At her lack of response, one of the men squatted down and bent over to examine her. Even sightless she could detect his movement, for his bulk shaded her face from the heat and brightness of the late afternoon sun. It took all of her willpower to just lie there, trying not to breathe, to flutter an eyelid or to swallow, while he no doubt stared at her.

"Do you think to fool me, woman?" Something, a finger most likely, slithered along the column of her neck. In no time he would find her pulse and answer the question for himself. Besides, she couldn't hold her breath for another second.

Her eyes jerking open, Chelsea recoiled at the reptilian touch. "Stay away from me," she cried.

"Ah, good," the man next to her said, smiling down at her in a way that she dared not interpret as friendly. Yet he made no move of aggression toward her, and he seemed genuinely relieved to find her alive.

"Thank Allah," declared the man still standing, much shorter than the first. In obvious relief he templed his hands in front of his face and cast his gaze toward the heavens.

So, they didn't plan to kill her, or to molest her . . . then what? She studied their faces long and hard, and no longer could be sure they were Khalil's men. The only thing she was certain of was that they were in a great big hurry. Well then, she would just have to do everything in her power to slow them down.

The man beside her stood and attempted to pull her up with him. She groaned and went as limp as a corpse, refusing to cooperate.

"What is wrong with her?" the smaller man asked in a whiny voice.

"How should I know?" the other one replied, equally

exasperated. "Maybe she broke something when she jumped."

"Why do you not look, Ibrahim?" wheedled the little man she nicknamed Mutt in her mind, for he reminded her of that comic strip character.

"Why do *you* not look?" retaliated the larger man. This one she dubbed Jeff.

She suspected neither one of them even knew what to look for, and if they did, they wouldn't know what to do if they found something wrong. If the situation wasn't so serious it would almost be laughable.

"Pick her up," Jeff demanded.

"No. If she should die on me, then it is my head that will roll," came Mutt's refusal. "You pick her up."

It seemed neither one of them wished to be responsible for her. Well, they could bicker all day long as far as she was concerned, for it gave her time to think, to come up with a plan of action, to. . . .

A plan of action. Of course. If they had taken her off from the encampment for their own reasons, maybe she could convince them for their own good to take her back to the clinic. Then she frowned. That would mean leaving Jamal behind, but once she returned to Ad Dawadimi, she could seek out the authorities who could organize a search party. It wasn't as if she were actually deserting him; in fact, she would be doing everything in her power to rescue them both.

Her plan was a good one, she assured herself. Good or not, to be truthful, it was the only one she could come up with on the spur of the moment. Now all she had to do was figure out a way to implement it—successfully.

"Listen to me, you two buffoons." She pushed herself up on her elbows, noting the tender spot on her right

239

shoulder blade. Nothing was broken, but she would be sore tomorrow. If she could get home, then it would be well worth it. "You are fighting over nothing. If anything happens to me, you both will suffer the consequences," she warned. "And it's not just some petty sheikh that you need to be concerned about. I'm an American citizen. If anything happens to me, the government, both yours and mine, will come after you."

The two men glanced at each other as if they couldn't believe she had spoken so forcefully with them. Then they stared down at her as if they thought she'd lost her mind.

"Just who do you think you are calling ignorant, you crazy woman?" the tall man asked with a derisive snort, hauling her up by the arm as if he didn't care if it pulled from its socket. "Why the sheikh would want you, I cannot imagine, even if you are some kind of jinni." He began to drag her toward his horse. "He warned you might try something like this."

The plan wasn't going at all the way it should.

"No, you must listen to me," she cried, tugging at the man's painful grip on her wrist.

"Would you prefer we just left you here to die?"

Caving in to avoid her worst fear, she allowed him to put her back on the horse, a prisoner to male conceit that believed they always had everything under control and had that right. Only God knew where they were headed. And only God knew what would happen to her once they arrived.

Had the whole world gone mad or simply that part of it in which she now resided? Neither possibility was particularly reassuring.

* * *

240

The moment Khalil entered the tent, he knew something was terribly wrong. It was more than the wailing women gathered to console one of their own and prepare the boy's body for burial. More than the way the *hadhar* frantically attempted to disperse them. Grief was a natural part of life, or was that not the case in the future?

The fact that the child had died alarmed him considerably, knowing full well that it could have been his own son who had succumbed to the evil spirits. He glanced around, looking for Chelsea, wanting reassurance from the *duktur* that it was safe to leave his precious heir, but she was nowhere to be seen.

Her absence struck him as very odd.

"Hadhar, where is Chelsea?" he demanded.

Looking up, Jamal conveyed his relief as he hurried to join him.

"Thank Allah, you are here, *ya ràyyis.* I feared Yusaf would never convince you to come."

"Yusaf? What do you mean. I have not seen the old man all day. What is wrong?"

"Chel-sea. We cannot find her."

"What do you mean, you cannot find her? Where did she go?" A disturbing feeling formulated in the pit of Khalil's belly.

"She rushed out. After a while when she didn't come back, I went looking for her, but nobody has seen her since she was spotted making her way toward the *wadi* several hours ago. I searched the water's edge but found no sign of her. Then when I returned to the tent, hoping maybe she had come back during my absence, I discovered all of these women." Jamal glanced about worriedly. "The boy must be buried immediately."

"The illness?" Khalil asked, accepting Jamal's counsel as unquestionable. After all, he was Chelsea's assistant.

"Otherwise, it could spread very quickly."

Taking charge, Khalil cleared the tent in moments and made arrangements for the boy's body to be buried immediately. He saw the resentful looks the mourning women gave him even as they complied, taking the poor boy's distraught mother with them. Before the day was done, he knew that the council of elders would hear of his grievous, disrespectful act, his second one for the day. It would not go well for him.

He turned and placed the hand of his son into that of the *hadhar.*

"Is Muhammad safe here?" he demanded.

Jamal nodded. "He cannot catch the typhoid again. And Chel-sea?"

"I will find her."

"Father?"

Remembering his son and that he would grieve from the loss of his friend, he knelt and confronted the boy as if he were a man.

"You must not cry, Muhammad. But be brave. Show our people you will someday make them a fine leader."

It was a lot to ask from one so young, but it was necessary.

"I will not fail you, Father." Muhammad nodded, sniffing back unshed tears.

Relieved when the *hadhar* showed up with the caged jerboa and handed it to Muhammad, Khalil suppressed the urge to hug the child and hurried from the tent, knowing exactly where to begin his search.

In no time he saddled and mounted his favorite war mare, heading into the sun. Its black hooves flew over the steppe as if the animal possessed wings or at least the knowledge that their mission was a most important one to the master. On the rise above the encampment Khalil found what he was looking for—the prints of two horses.

He paused and dismounted only long enough to evaluate his find. From the depth of the prints he surmised that the animals carried riders, one heavier than the other, or perhaps it carried two. The way the prints veered as if the beast's load was unsteady confirmed his suspicion. Whoever they were, whatever their purpose, the raiders had taken Chelsea with them.

Gathering up his reins, he quickly remounted and reined the mare's nose in the direction the prints led. As long as the wind held steady and the sun gave him a few more hours of light, he would find them. He wouldn't give up until he did.

With that vow, he urged Shiha to give him all the speed her delicate legs could muster. It was a command she willingly obeyed.

The last rays of the setting sun turned the winter sky blood red. An omen, Chelsea decided. Not necessarily a good one. She shivered involuntarily beneath the sheerness of her gown. Despite the illusion of fire in the west, the air had grown cold, and as much as she despised her own weakness, she welcomed the bit of warmth her captor's body afforded her.

Long ago she'd given up wondering how much farther they had to travel, or even where they might be going. She had also abandoned all hope of rescue. The worst part was, this time she didn't even have Jamal to keep her company, to keep her sanity intact. For the first time in her life she was totally on her own, the only things to fall back on her own wits and abilities, and at the moment she didn't have much confidence in either of them.

Then her hand crept up to grasp the familiar warmth of the leather pouch nestled in the valley between her breasts. The one thing she had that she didn't have before was the talisman, and oddly enough it gave her comfort. Did it truly have powers, or did she only fool herself with such an outlandish notion? God, the next thing she would expect to pop up would be a flying carpet or a jinni in a lamp, or some such romantic nonsense.

Deep in her debate between delusions and cynicism, she couldn't explain what it was that caused her to look up, a subtle tightening of the arm about her waist perhaps, or the way her captor's breath sucked in against her ear.

She could swear she caught movement to the left of them, but she couldn't be certain.

Then her abductor brought his mount to a twisting halt.

There on a ridge traveling parallel with them Chelsea spied what caught his attention.

"By all that is sacred, we are doomed," the Arab muttered, terror evident in his voice and in the way he cruelly jerked the head of his mount back around.

In contrast her hopes soared.

Against the blood-colored sunset the black mare and its rider appeared the embodiment of a demonic silhouette, especially when the spirited beast reared, its front hooves pawing the air, a loud whinny reverberating across the desert. Perhaps the image wasn't so far from the truth.

"Khalil," she cried softly, her relief mingling with an excitement akin to awe at the magnificence of the picture horse and rider made.

"May Allah protect us," cried her captor, kicking his horse into action, demanding greater speed, but the animal was much too exhausted from its heavy load and refused to comply, even when he flayed its withers with the ends of the reins.

Chelsea tried to twist about to see if the distant rider would follow, to confirm that he was real and not a figment of her desperate imagination. The flapping tail of the Arab's *keffiyeh* blocked her view of the ridge, but the sweat trickling down the side of his face and the set of his jaw gave her the reassurance she sought. Indeed they were being pursued.

Could it be that this was not Khalil's doing? If so, she could only imagine what he would do to these men when he caught them.

She realized that the other man, the shorter of the two, was far in the lead, apparently quite willing to desert his partner in crime without compunction. Her captor must have known that as well. Shouting something that was carried off by the wind, he turned to look over his shoulder.

Chelsea, too, caught a glimpse of Khalil, who was only a few lengths behind them and gaining, his scimitar drawn and glistening with the same malice that radiated from his dark, determined eyes. Her captor would get off easily if the angry sheikh merely decapitated him. Even as that bloody thought crossed her mind, Khalil's sword lifted along with his cry for revenge.

Did she really want another death staining her hands? No, no, she was a giver of life, not a taker. Appalled that she would find satisfaction in violence, even if only in thought, she began to struggle. She must stop this madness before it was too late.

Unsure what happened, whether she caused her captor to lose his grip on her, or if he released her of his own volition, she suddenly felt herself pitch forward and to the side. Not that falling off particularly scared her, it was the manner in which she fell. This time she had no control over the situation or her landing. Hooves pounded dangerously close to her unprotected head. Dear God, she was going to be trampled.

She screamed. Then she hit the ground so hard the sound was abruptly cut off. Instinctively she curled and rolled, wondering as she did if she moved in the wrong direction, toward death not away from it.

As if to confirm her fear, something hard grazed her shoulder. A hoof? The pain that tore through her was sharp and blinding. Fighting down the fear, she waited for its counterpart to follow and finish her off.

Instead, what she felt was an overwhelming sense of stillness. She realized then that the thunder of hooves was fading. Looking up, she saw the cloud of dust kicked up by the horses constantly renewing itself in the distance.

At first, disbelief surged through her. The crisis had passed over her, and somehow she had managed to survive. Alarm quickly followed. She may be alive, but she was also alone, battered and sore, at the mercy of the desert.

How could Khalil just leave her? How could he be so callous and uncaring? How . . . ?

"Chelsea!"

The rough pressure of hands gripped her shoulders, attempting to turn her over. She cried out as much with relief as with pain where the fingers dug into her bruised flesh. Then she was in his arms, unmindful that she hurt. It only mattered that he was there, holding her, protecting her—picking her up in his strong arms, carrying her as if he planned never to let her go.

"You came for me," she murmured joyfully, throwing her arms about his neck and burrowing against his chest. Yes, it was nice to be held by a man.

"Did you doubt that I would, my brown shell of the sea?"

She looked up into his steady, dark eyes, so serious in their searching. The truth lodged in her throat.

"You did doubt me, didn't you?" He paused, still staring down at her, a frown marring his handsome face.

"I thought you had me taken away to be . . . to be . . ." She couldn't voice the awful accusation.

"You have given me no cause to treat you so harshly. Woman, accuse me of many things, but not of being unfair. You must trust in me to do what is best, just as I must trust in you to obey." He gripped her arm tighter and pulled her closer. "Never give me cause to doubt you, Chelsea. Promise me." When she didn't answer he shook her. "Promise me."

"Khalil, I . . . I . . ." The words came to a stuttering halt. How could she tell him that she found it difficult to put her faith in any man? Even now, as he held her so closely, she couldn't find it in herself to surrender to him completely, to do what he asked, to trust him, to obey, if even for the moment.

All her life she had thrown herself without reservation

into all kinds of situations as long as they didn't involve her woman's heart. She had taken every risk, and then some, when it came to her career. Just like seeking out the challenges of working in the Middle East. She had believed in her abilities as a physician and her rights as a woman.

Even to ride a horse and have confidence that so unpredictable a creature could and would carry her over fence after fence safely had not been so very difficult. But, then, no horse had ever failed her, not unless it had been her own miscalculation that had set it off course.

Not so with men. It had never been that easy. She'd trusted Michael, and he had disappointed her. But the problem went deeper than that. Much deeper. Even deeper than the male professors who had discouraged her, even mocked her determination to fulfill her ambitions. Where the true distrust lay was with the one man she should have been able to rely upon and trust above all others. Her father.

As always, when she brushed against the core of her insecurities, she just as quickly withdrew to a safer plane, unwilling to delve further into the pain. It was a rejection she just couldn't confront, not yet. Perhaps, not ever.

She found herself staring up into the face of this desert sheikh, a man nothing like any she had known in her life, a stranger whose existence epitomized all that she struggled to overcome, and yet, she could not tear her eyes away, could not turn her heart against him. She tried to figure out what it was about him that made her want to trust him, to fall beneath the spell of his unwavering eyes, to be what he willed her to be. As biased as his attitudes and prejudices were when it came to women— and God knew he was a textbook example of male chauvinism—she actually found herself understanding his motives which were as pure and basic as his beliefs.

A man's responsibility was to protect a woman. In return, a woman must accept the limitations the man set down for her, for in truth they reflected his own vulnerabilities.

Chelsea glanced around at the windswept steppe, desolate and harsh—as real a world as any she had ever known—and was thoroughly awed by it. As difficult as a subservient position was to accept, such was the law of the desert. God knew she hadn't managed to protect herself very well. She needed what he offered.

Here in the desert there seemed to be only a fine line of distinction between chauvinism and chivalry.

God, what was she thinking? She was not some simpering woman to meekly settle into some desert lord's *hareem*. Apparently she'd been in the sun too long.

"I promise you nothing," she replied at last with a vengeance. Unwilling to become a bit of fluff in any man's game, desert sheikh or wheeler-dealer, she began to struggle. She just wanted her feet on the ground, wanted to get away from the effect of this man so that she could think straight for a moment.

But he would have none of it. As if he claimed the right to her simply because he had saved her, he held her tightly, refusing to let her go.

Although she continued to fight him, he mounted his horse, and holding her firmly yet gently, he positioned her in front of him.

Then the wind was whipping at her face, tearing away the mask of her resolve, leaving nothing but the insecurities, exposed and raw. Or was it his touch upon her traitorous flesh that made her falter in her beliefs?

"Deception." He whispered the single word against her ear.

A shiver, frightening yet delicious at the same time, jolted her spine.

"A dangerous pastime you contemplate, my brown shell of the sea. Be very careful. I am no longer a man easily fooled by a woman's games."

What could he know of deception? Men like him only knew how to bully and cajole and hurt. Spurred on by righteous indignation, she struggled that much harder, but it was a battle she'd already lost, even if she didn't admit it.

Deception. The only person she'd ever successfully deceived had been herself. Now it seemed she was incapable of even doing that anymore.

Thirteen

Khalil knew the moment she gave up the struggle. It was the same moment she defeated him. The same moment he turned his back on every principle he held as fundamental, the moment he abandoned his *ird*.

He wanted her. He would have her. Afterward, he would face the consequences of so dishonorable an act. Somehow he would not allow the shame to touch her.

Urging his mare to greater speed, he rode with a purpose. That purpose? It was laughable, deplorable. He, the mighty Sheikh Khalil ibn Mani al Muraidi, lived only to possess a woman, a woman who most likely would deceive him in the end. Had she not so much as admitted that? At least, she had been honest about her intention. Even so, he could not wait to bare his heart and soul, to risk it all, to make the ultimate sacrifice and to claim her as his woman.

When at last they arrived at the encampment, he slowed and circled the fringes of the settlement as much to avoid being seen as to cool his exhausted mare. By the time they reached the small, isolated tent along the *wadi* he now claimed as his place of refuge, both tasks were accomplished. Just outside the doorway, he dismounted, reached up and dragged the woman down to stand beside him as he quickly striped the saddle from his horse and let it go. Shiha he could trust to make her way to the herd and stay there unshackled.

Of the woman he wasn't so sure. Never once did he release her. Even as he gathered up his tack in one hand to carry it inside, he kept his other arm anchored about her waist, fearing if he let her go she would bolt.

She said nothing. Neither did he. His claim to her didn't need to be discussed—it simply was.

Just inside the doorway, he flung his gear to the ground, glad to be free of it. Eagerly he turned his attention to the woman, staring down at her from his superior height. Even so, he found her a formidable opponent, exciting, more desirable than any female he had ever encountered, elusive in her promise of pleasure to come.

Houri. Yes. She was that and more. His vision of heaven on earth.

His hands trembled. To claim her physically was his due, and yet when he reached out for the sash wound about her waist and hips, he hesitated, unsure, wanting something from her other than that unblinking scrutiny, as if she wished to strip away his forehead and reveal his thoughts as much as he wanted to unveil her body.

But that was more intimacy than he had bargained for, more than he could give, more than she should have to bear. It was pleasure he wished to share with her, not the burden of buried pain.

Looping the sash about his wrist, he pulled her toward him, until there was no more than a breath between them.

252

Her eyes, so blue, bore into him, still probing, still seeking what was best she never have.

Encircling her waist with one arm, he meshed their bodies together, her breasts proud points of fire against his ribs, a heat that spread throughout his tortured body, and still she did not give up her quest of things best left concealed.

He claimed her mouth, his kiss hard, demanding, seeking to dominate. Bracing himself, he prepared for her physical resistance. Custom required that all women struggle to protect their virtue even from a husband, and he claimed not that right. In turn it was the man's place to end it as quickly as possible. But she never uttered a protest, never lifted a hand in objection to his none-too-gentle advances. Still, she fought him, but in a way he was ill-prepared to counter. There was no acquiescence in her surrender, only challenge, meeting his every action with one of her own.

Oddly enough, her manner heightened his desire to conquer, completely, not just her body, but her soul. This was no mock battle for custom's sake. This was man and woman on equal footing, striving for a rite of passage, but each for their own purpose. His conquest or hers, the outcome remained uncertain to the very end.

He wanted victory more than ever, could taste it on her lips, but victory, he suddenly realized, was all in the terms of the surrender, his as much as hers.

Gentle. No, merely constrained, and ever watchful to pick up her signals, as confusing as they might be. It was a feat to challenge even a man among men.

His arm against her back conveyed an unyielding

strength such as Chelsea had never sensed in any man, and yet there was restraint, almost a fear, but of what?

Of her?

How could she, an insignificant woman according to his Arab way of thinking, possibly frighten a man like Khalil?

Yet each time she met his passion head-on, matched it, challenged it, she felt his hesitation, even if it was only for a moment.

Never had she known such power over a man, and she had no idea what to call it or from where it came—only that it was magic, for suddenly it freed her. It made her giddy; it made her reckless.

As in her youth, before those years of rude awakening, first at home and then during medical school, she had ridden her Thoroughbred over jumps and through courses that had made the competition hesitate. But not her. Not the unstoppable Chelsea Browne of Atlanta. Such challenges had only made her more determined, a better rider, and finally a more collected one, one with Olympic potential. Could taming such a man as this one do the same for her as a woman?

There was only one way to find out. She pressed him, testing her theory, her hands skimming over the thick robes, boldly exploring the male physique beneath. Savoring each discovery along the way, she realized she had seen nothing of him but his face, his hands. The rest she could only imagine. And imagine she did.

His chest? She fanned her fingers over the wide expanse, watching them travel in twin arcs. Would it be smooth or hairy? The thickness of his clothing prevented her from telling. Then her hands met with the corded muscles of his arms, the breadth of his shoulders, and paused when they reached the edges of the *keffiyeh* covering his hair. She longed to once again see his dark hair. She glanced up, intent on brushing the bit of cloth out of her way.

Her gaze collided with his, dark and unwavering, always unwavering. His lips were pressed into a determined, sardonic line. There was nothing hesitant or fearful in his manner now. Had she only imagined it earlier?

"I know what you're about, witch-woman." His hands, big and powerful, snatched her by the wrists, holding her arms high over her head, his body so close to hers she could feel the contours of his manliness. "Are you sure this is what you seek?"

Her first instincts were to struggle against the manacles of his fingers, to proclaim her innocence with protest, both verbal and physical. No doubt such resistance was what he expected. Instead, possessed by a streak of stubbornness, she held steady, staring back at him.

"I seek only to please you." It was a line right out of a movie. A damn good one even if it was a lie.

"To please me or unman me?" He threw back his head and laughed.

How had he pegged her so easily? Her heart leapt into her throat, her anxiety quickly converting to irritation when he didn't stop laughing. He made fun of her, and that she didn't like.

"So you think it funny, do you? Well, this has gone just about far enough." She lifted her knee and caught him in the groin, just like she'd been taught to do in the women's defense class she had taken several years ago.

She wasn't exactly sure what she expected his reaction to be, most likely release her and fall to the ground cringing in agony. At least that was what her instructor had indicated would happen. However, she wasn't dealing with some ordinary street mugger, rather with a rugged man who had suffered much and was capable of inflicting far worse on her. Dear God, what had possessed her to do something so stupid?

True. His eyes clouded as much with surprise as pain, but he never let go of her. In fact, it seemed to her his grip clamped down stronger. Then after only a few moments, he began to back her up, step by step, his body guiding hers as if they danced.

"Khalil, please. I'm sorry."

Other than the smoldering expression on his face, his only response was silence, deadly, unrelenting silence.

She stiffened her legs. He kept her moving. She tried to collapse. He carried her along. Retreat, retreat. Stride after calculated stride until she stumbled over the edge of a thick carpet. Unprepared for him to at last release her, she fell to her knees before him and looked up. The hilt of his sheathed scimitar was only inches away from her face, a terrible reminder of just what kind of man she had so foolishly chosen to cross.

She had no idea what to expect then. He could just as easily decide to cut off her head as do anything else. Provoked by the uncertainty, by the way he just stood there, flexing and relaxing his hands, her breath whooshed in and out of her lungs in painful gasps. She was afraid, and she didn't bother to hide it, instead closing her eyes to avoid having to watch the inevitable conclusion.

How loud her breathing sounded in her ears. Oh, to think that he must be truly laughing now at how easily he'd beaten her. Tears of humiliation gathered behind her eyelids as there in her self-imposed darkness she waited to be smitten. How long would he make her wait? She counted the slow, cruel seconds one at a time. Until she begged him to get on with it?

She might be afraid, even humbled, but beg? Never. If she must die, it would be with dignity. If she had already forfeited her life, what more did she have to lose?

Thinking to confront him, to force his hand, she snapped her eyes open. To her surprise she found him on his knees beside her, his dark eyes only inches away, his breath the one so ragged and tortured to hear.

His head was bare. The dark, thick mantle of hair about his shoulders gave him a barbaric look she found utterly fascinating when combined with the short, carefully trimmed beard and mustache.

His face moved so close it blurred in her vision. She found his mouth irresistible as it covered hers with a kiss as untamed and exciting as the visual image that lingered behind her lowered eyelids.

Breath held, heart pounding, she gave herself up to his masterful direction. His hand moved behind her head, to cradle it, even as he pressed her down on the soft, thick carpet, his masculine weight against her feminine slenderness almost too much to bear. And yet, when he attempted to move away, even just a little, she found herself reaching out to clasp him to her.

Fearful her actions, as innocent as they were, would be misinterpreted, she dropped her hands, trying to hold on to him with only the power of their kiss. However, it seemed he would have none of her subjugation, no matter how subtle. To her disappointment he moved away, stretched out beside her, as deceptive as a sensuous desert cat. Lifting one knee, he propped his arm upon it, relaxing the hand that only moments before had held her.

Then he turned his dark, steady gaze upon her, studying her with undisguised passion that belied his show of disinterest.

"Khalil," she began, pushing up onto her elbows.

"Shh. Shh." He placed one finger upon her lips, his eyes narrowing as if he couldn't make up his mind. "Come here." He thumped the front of his *thobe*.

Unsure just what he expected from her, she rolled, dropping her head upon his chest. The top of his robe had come undone revealing a thick matting of dark chest hair between the loose lacing. Her hand ached to touch it, but she held the impulse in check.

"This . . . thing . . . you do with your tongue . . ."

"What?" Aghast, she lifted her head to stare at him. Surely she hadn't heard him correctly.

"When I put my mouth to yours." The intensity of his stare remained steady. With two fingertips he touched his own lips and then hers. "Is this some American ritual?"

"French kissing?" she murmured, sitting up. The heat of embarrassment flooded her face. God, had she really kissed him so brazenly and not realized it?

"Ah." He slowly nodded his head, then cocked it, his eyes never lifting from the intense scrutiny that made her squirm with discomfort. "The French crusaders. I know of those barbaric infidels." He frowned. "Then, it is not an American custom."

"Well, no. Yes. I don't know. It's just something people do."

"Not all people."

"I never thought about it much," she confessed. Thoroughly mortified, she glanced away.

"You find pleasure in this French kissing?" Grasping

258

her chin, he forced her to look at him once more. He would have none of her attempt to sidestep the issue.

She nodded, feeling a sense of guilty relief at her admission. He must think her wicked indeed now. She blushed and looked down, but only with her eyes, for he still held her chin in his hand.

How ridiculous that she, a medical doctor, was having trouble discussing something so simple as kissing. She had been asked direct questions before by patients. But that was the difference. She had been an authority figure, a source of information for budding adolescents. This time her own womanhood was involved.

Oh, God, she had never been any good at relationships and frank discussions. She and Michael had never talked much about what they liked or didn't like. But then, maybe that had been part of their problem. If she had just told him from the beginning how she felt, he wouldn't have accused her of being frigid, incapable of experiencing sexual gratification.

"Do it again."

"You aren't serious." Surprised, she darted a quick look at Khalil.

A hint of a smile molded his lips. Yes, it seemed he was quite serious in his demand. And it was a demand not a request. Draped against a pile of cushions, he eyed her with commanding candor. Apparently he expected her to do what he told her, then and there. He didn't seem the least bit uncomfortable with the unorthodox situation, nor did he seem particularly concerned with her awkwardness. He just sat there, waiting, staring at her.

"No." She couldn't just kiss a man like that, when ordered. Thinking about the mechanics of what she would have to do . . . like some sex manual. Well, it was just impossible. She started to get up.

His hand that seemed so relaxed snaked out and stopped her, pulled her atop him, his face inches from hers.

"I said kiss me, woman. Now." His mouth moved toward hers.

Shaking her head, she reared backward, but there was only so far that she could retreat within the confines of his powerful arms.

This time when his lips covered hers, she made it a point to keep hers solidly sealed.

"Teach me, Chelsea."

The whispered request against the corner of her mouth chipped away at the foundation of her determination.

"Please."

With that one simple word, the walls of her inhibitions came tumbling down.

When she opened her mouth, he imitated her action. At first, just thinking about it, she shyly flicked her tongue in and out. There, she had done what he'd asked. She made as if to end the kiss.

He would have none of it. His hand moved up her back, trapping her head, yet he made no attempt to take charge of the kiss.

"Again," he ordered, barely lifting his mouth from hers.

Such passive aggression. It confused her. It thrilled her. Sighing, she surrendered to the resulting tide of passion that washed over her, forgetting her reservations in the process.

Her tongue darted boldly forward, met with swordplay

resistance that took her breath away. The fight for dominance moved beyond the kiss.

Khalil rolled, covering her from head to foot. Then and only then did he end the kiss, on his terms.

"My, but you are a fast learner," she gasped, as his mouth laid claim to her jaw, the side of her neck, the bit of modest bosom that swelled against the front of her gown.

"Yes, I am, and you would be wise never to forget it."

Such an arrogant threat, yet she sensed the vulnerability that prompted it. She found the boast and the man who had made it endearingly amusing.

"I think you should give the instructress a little of the credit," she insisted, laughing softly. "Otherwise, I might not be so willing to teach you anything else."

"There are other things?" When he lifted his head his expression was quite serious in its concern.

"Perhaps," she teased. She allowed the amusement to settle in the curve of her lips. *"You* would be wise never to forget it, either."

The quip was no more out of her mouth, than she found herself quite efficiently pinned to the cushions and carpeting.

"Take your credit, woman. I care not. There are other, more rewarding things that I seek." A look of determination enhanced his handsome face as his hand moved down to untie the sash of her gown. Trusting him, she lifted up, just enough so that he could unwind the length of cloth from her body.

"Much more rewarding." Kneeling between her thighs, he slid his fingers beneath the unbound dress, pushing the skirts up, out of his way. Skimming her passion-heated skin, the roughness of his palms ignited every nerve, setting her aflame in a way she had never experienced before. His large, masculine hands made her feel petite in comparison, especially when they paused, encircling the indention of her waist.

Then they moved up along her ribs, the circle expanding to accommodate her feminine curves. Soon they would reach her breasts.

Chelsea stiffened. She had always felt inadequate when it came to her bosom which she perceived to be rather small. Michael had been the only man to ever express a like opinion when it came to her attributes or lack of them—at least in front of her.

And it seemed that Khalil, too, found them wanting, for the moment he grazed the lace and padding of her push-up bra, he halted and jerked back his hands.

"What's wrong?" she cried.

"The armor. Must you always wear it?"

Armor? What was he talking about? The only thing she had on under the dress was her bra. Then it dawned on her. Apparently the man had never before seen a woman's underwear.

"Here, let me show you," she offered, suppressing the urge to tease him in his ignorance. Sitting up, she drew her arms inside the dress and unhooked her bra, one arm emerging through a sleeve to drop the bit of flesh-colored lace and padding in his hand. "Not armor, Khalil," she said. "A brassiere."

"Bra-ssiere," he repeated, flipping the garment over in his hand, noting the thickness of it. With utter amazement he fingered the hook and eyes on the backstrap. "Most ingenious, you Americans," he commented; then he carefully set the undergarment aside. He looked at her longingly.

She couldn't explain it. It was as if an unnamed barrier loomed between them now, one neither knew quite how to breech. Her hand reached up, discovering the talisman still about her neck, knowing somehow it held the answer to the mystery.

Just where the courage came from, maybe the talisman, itself, Chelsea would never know for certain. Making up her mind, she withdrew her arm once more into the folds of her gown. Then without giving herself time to really think about what she was about to do, she drew the dress over her head, tossing it aside.

The air against her naked flesh was cool, for in their haste they had not taken the time to light a fire. Shivering slightly, she couldn't help it when her nipples puckered in response. As for Khalil, well, he wasn't making it any easier, just sitting there staring at her as if he'd never seen a nude woman before. What in God's name had come over her to even think about much less do what she'd done? God, she was literally throwing herself at a man, a stranger, an Arab sheikh who no doubt expected her to be sensual yet . . . virginal. And when he discovered that she wasn't. . . .

Instinctively she moved to cover her breasts and gather up her clothing, feeling inadequate in more ways than one.

"No," he murmured, brushing away her feeble attempt at modesty. "You are much too beautiful to hide."

"You are wrong. I am not beautiful," she replied matter-of-factly, wishing he would release her hands. "But then there are many things I am not."

"Such as."

"I am not a virgin," she blurted.

At that he honored her wish. He let go of her, sitting back as if displeased.

She lifted her chin in pride. God, this was the twentieth century. Few American women her age could truthfully claim to be innocent. And if he in his ignorant desert existence didn't find that to his liking, well . . . that was his problem.

"I suspected as much, but it does not matter." With the decisiveness of a swordsman's stroke, he pushed her back against the cushions. Following, he drew her close, pressing his mouth against her womanly flesh, claiming it as if he had every right. It was an exotic mixture of pleasure-pain she experienced at his eager fondling.

And yet, she knew she shouldn't be doing this. If she expected gentle wooing, then she was probably in for a big disappointment. But it was such an exquisite torture his mouth and tongue created, overriding each and every one of her reservations. This time, this time it would be different. Oh, God, please let it be different.

Giving herself up completely, she arched against the heated pleasure. She cradled his head in encouragement, and just as she'd hoped it would, the twisting rope of need grew more and more taut within her.

Lost in the lovemaking, in the wondrousness of it all, Chelsea was not quite sure just how it happened, but suddenly he was filling her, the flesh of his hips hot against her inner thighs, his rhythm sure and powerful as it carried her along on a plateau of sensations that was indeed most pleasurable, hinting at an unknown rapture, assuring her it was just within reach. If only she could strive a little harder, she could make it happen—this time.

But then it was as if her body shut down, turned on

her, mocked her—pointed out her inadequacies in a voice that sounded remarkably like her father's. That terrible something inside of her, fear perhaps, rose up, slammed into automatic pilot, dousing the promise of paradise attained in the arms of a man. It left her rigid with frustration, suddenly no longer a participant but an observer of what was taking place.

As devastating as the disappointment was, it was nothing new to Chelsea. The few times she had been with Michael, he had simply ignored her withdrawal, finishing the deed without her involvement. She anticipated the same from Khalil. If she couldn't find sensitivity from an educated man like Michael, how could she ever expect it in some primal desert nomad?

She braced herself to just endure, praying the ordeal would be over soon. That she could regain her dignity, get dressed, and get out as quickly as possible without further complications.

How had she gotten herself into this predicament? Had she really thought it would be any different? How could it be when she was obviously the problem? *Face it, Chelsea, old girl. Michael was right. You are frigid. Even the legendary Don Juan himself would be hard-pressed to break through the ice.*

"Chelsea? What is it? Have I done something to hurt you?"

She looked up through a veil of unshed tears into dark, demanding eyes. Could that be genuine concern she read in them? Most unlikely. She sniffed, struggling to maintain her composure. She didn't want to reveal too much about herself.

What was there to say? Not to worry? It had nothing to do with him? Better yet. If he was finished, would he just kindly get off her? That was what she had wanted to tell Michael and had been too afraid, too ashamed to say aloud.

"Please, just let me go," she pleaded, tempering her bitterness with the realization that she had only herself to blame for once again being used by a man. She pushed at his chest, ignoring the glorious feel of the crisp, dark mat of hair that cushioned her fingers.

Well, he had had his way with her. Gotten his jollies. What more could he want?

"Chelsea?"

Ignoring the undisguised surprise in his voice, she fought him, swinging at him with clenched fists, taking all of her frustration out on this man who in his masculine perfection represented everything that in her jaded opinion was wrong with men. It took him only a few moments to pin her wrists to the carpeting.

"Chelsea, just tell me. What have I done?" he demanded.

"What all men have done, since day one," she replied between gritted teeth. "Use women for your own gratification without once thinking about how we might feel or what we might need." Mindlessly she fought on, bucking to free herself of his weight, his dominance, his male sense of self-importance. She didn't give a damn about his precious ego. It was then she realized that they were still joined, man and woman, apparently his fulfillment as unattained as her own.

She grew perfectly still, her surprise manifesting itself in her harsh breathing. But that wasn't possible. Why would he stop when he didn't have to?

Was it only her imagination or was he looking at her and acting in a way that contradicted everything she had thought she'd known about men? She lifted her hips ever so slightly, just enough to confirm her suspicions. He met her thrust with a powerful one of his own, one that took her breath away and rekindled the desire. Yet when she didn't move again, he, too, remained motionless, breathing hard with the exertion it took to do nothing. Could it be he might truly care for what she was feeling?

Oh, God, what must he think of her and the way she had gone berserk.

"Khalil, I'm sorry. I didn't mean those things I said. It's just that I've never . . . I can't . . ."

"Shh. Shh." This time it was his mouth, so knowledgeable now in what pleased her, that cut off her awkward confession. "Yes, you can."

What happened next happened so quickly, she had no time to protest much less think about the strangeness of it all. Pulling away, he rolled her over on her stomach, his hands slipping beneath her and lifting her up on her knees. He slid one of the thick cushions under her hips.

"Khalil!" she expressed her surprise and trepidation even as he pressed himself against the curve of her backside, filling her once more. "I don't think . . ."

"Don't think, sweet Chelsea. Trust me. Give me a little of your precious credit. I can be a most enlightened teacher, if given the chance."

Enlightened didn't begin to describe what he did or the wonder of the sensations his lovemaking evoked, especially when his hand became intimately involved in the rhythm. Each time she came so close to achieving that unattainable goal and failed, he began it all again, kissing the line of her shoulder, her neck. His gentle, undaunted patience caused her to finally relax and let go of all of those preconceived notions she had harbored over a lifetime as to how it should be, what she should do, what he should do.

When it began to happen, she thought for sure that some cruel twist of fate would surely snatch the elusive ecstasy away at the very last moment. But there she was, standing on the brink, her heart gone still and near to bursting, her soul taking wing and departing her body. And then at the very final second, she lost her nerve. No, she didn't want to lose control this way, and she struggled to turn around and go back to the safety of the ledge.

But it was too late. The world fell away; the only thing tangible to cling to was the man who had brought her to the gates of paradise and now forced her ever so gently to go on through them. Surely she must be dying, her physical body being torn asunder, and yet she never wanted it to end.

How would she ever find her way back to reality? she wondered as she was flung into the heat of a blinding light and then into a cool darkness.

As if in answer, she once more became aware of all that was around her. The soft, deep piled carpet against the side of her face, the silkiness of the pillow on which her hips had been elevated, the snapping of the tent over-head, her own labored breathing, and her heart still racing like the wind. But most of all there was an overwhelming sense of peace and accomplishment that enveloped her, the likes of which she had never felt before, not on horse-back, or as a physician. Only as a woman.

Then the warmth of Khalil's mouth pressed against the sensitive skin on her nape, reminding her that this was not to be her victory alone. His powerful thrusts continued, and then she felt him tremble in his own moment of ecstasy. Yet he never forgot her, still stroking her gently, releasing every drop of pleasure her body had to give.

What she had experienced had been shared, had been his gift to her, a gift like no one had ever bestowed upon her before. How could she ever express her gratitude?

"You are my woman, brown shell of the sea. Mine. Forever and always, until the end of time and beyond," he murmured softly. Then he shifted so that he lay beside her. His arm remained possessively about her waist as he pulled her up against him.

Lying there with that great desert lord pressed against her naked back, it took her a moment to absorb what he said. Forever and always. Just what did he mean by such a statement? She was his until the end of time.

Nothing more than pillow talk, she assured herself. For surely no human being, not even one from the Middle East, could honestly think to own another.

But at the moment being owned, protected, and loved so thoroughly didn't sound so very bad.

Fourteen

"Please, Turki. I beg of you. Do not do this," a woman's voice pleaded.

The shouts that followed were those of a man.

Deep in a euphoric state, Khalil chose to turn a deaf ear to the commotion that erupted just outside the tent. Nothing would disturb his bliss, not if he could help it.

Not so Chelsea. She jerked in his arms.

"What was that?" she murmured, attempting to rise.

"Nothing to concern yourself about," he replied, savoring the feel of her back against his naked length, the smell of her hair, her skin so soft and white. Already he wanted her again. As his woman, he could have her whenever he pleased.

Ah, the glorious solitude, the freedom. Privacy was a luxury rarely afforded the Bedouin with families crowded in close quarters. He vowed then and there always to have a place to be alone with Chelsea. His hand moved up to cup her breast, small by some men's standards perhaps, but more than enough to fill his palm and his aching need.

"Khalil, stop." Chelsea brushed aside his ardent caress, managing to wiggle from his clasp. "How can you just ignore what is going on out there?" she demanded, tossing her hair out of her eyes.

It was easy enough with her naked breasts quivering so enticingly, just within reach.

Again she thwarted his advances, gaining her knees and then her feet. *Wallahi!* Would she ever learn to abide by the rules? Even as he asked himself that question, she located her dress and drew it over her head. If he didn't stop her, she would go out there and interfere in what was obviously a domestic dispute.

"Very well, Chelsea. Stay here," he ordered, snatching up his own clothing with a disgruntled air. "I will see what is happening."

Hastily pulling on his *thobe,* he emerged from the tent, his mood as black as a moonless desert night. Just as he had expected, the cries were indeed a woman's. He recognized her. The wife of Turki, one of his best warriors, the mother of the dead boy. Rakia was his cousin, the eldest daughter of Umm Taif.

"Turki, why do you disturb my solitude?" he thundered, not bothering to curb his misdirected anger.

"Ya ràyyis!" The young Bedouin, who stood over the kneeling, pleading woman, turned to bow his head with respect. "I was not aware that you had returned," he replied in obvious surprise. He dropped to one knee before his leader, the respectful posture taken to ask for a favor. "I seek to divorce my wife, oh, wise one."

"Divorce her?" He eyed the young woman, his own flesh and blood, and felt a twinge of pity for her. "That is your right if your cause is just."

"No, my lord," cried the woman, crawling on her knees close enough to grasp the edge of his *thobe.*

"Please, my cousin, I do not deserve such shame. I have done nothing wrong. I have been a faithful, obedient wife."

A crowd began to gather. He tried to pretend they were not there, but it left a bitter taste in his mouth to see his people thrive upon the misfortune of others, especially one of their own.

"What is your reason for wanting to cast aside this woman, Turki?" Khalil asked, ignoring both the onlookers and the crying, prostrate woman at his feet.

"My son is dead. His mother is responsible."

"How so?"

"If she had sought the healing powers of the *duktur* earlier, Nuri would be alive—just like your son," the man explained.

A father's love was something Khalil could understand; the loss, something he could sympathize with. And yet, he wondered why Turki did not think that he, too, was responsible for not taking the boy to the *duktur* sooner. Still, it was his place to remember a man's rights and remain impartial.

"Your wife is healthy. You can have another son."

"Begat of a child slayer? Never," the young warrior exclaimed. "The dishonor is too much for me to bear, my leader. I'd rather go heirless than to take the chance of her killing again."

At that the crowd gasped.

Khalil looked down at the accused woman, knowing her fate, once again feeling pity. But as harsh as the law might be, it was still the law.

"Very well, Turki, I give you my permission to—"

"Khalil, no! You can't mean to do this." He looked up. Chelsea stood at the entrance to the tent. Her un-

272

bound dress, as hastily donned as his own clothing, flapped about her bare legs and feet, her hair disheveled golden strands about her face. A sense of disbelief rose up inside of him, although Allah knew he should have expected something like this from her. When had the foolish woman ever done as she was told? To reveal herself here and now like this, before witnesses, obviously having been alone with him. . . .

"Chelsea, go back into the tent. This does not involve you."

"Yes, it does." In total disregard to his warning, she took several steps forward, pushing her way through the gathered, gawking throng. "That child's death is no more his mother's fault than it is yours," she declared, dropping down to throw a protective arm about the distraught woman and staring up at the faithless husband. "If you must blame someone other than yourself, Turki, then blame me. I was the boy's physician." Then she turned her sky blue gaze on him. "Khalil, please, don't condone this."

As reckless as her words were, they were not what concerned him the most. Instead it was the knowing looks that passed discreetly from Bedouin to Bedouin. They questioned their leader's conduct. Now, how would it influence his ability to make a wise decision?

The law was the law.

"Proceed, Turki," he instructed, never lifting his eyes from the woman whose look of betrayal tore his new-found heart asunder. Nonetheless he could never allow his personal feelings to change who and what he was, nor what he must do.

"I dismiss thee," Turki began in a loud, unemotional voice.

"No, don't do this." Chelsea rose up in protest. "Khalil, make him stop."

"I dismiss thee."

She flinched as if the words were spoken to her.

"I dismiss thee," Turki finished.

That simply, the deed was done. Terrible memories of doing the same welled up within Khalil. Only his wife had not cried like the poor, defeated female at his feet. He looked down at the woman, his cousin, feeling a kinship with her he would never express openly, but it was there nonetheless. Tuëma, like Turki, the proud Bedouin that he was, had turned and walked away, never once looking back. It had been the last time he had seen his wife.

"Barbarian!"

Khalil turned a cool, hardened gaze upon his accuser. Chelsea. His beautiful brown shell of the sea. Wild-eyed with anger, could she not see the error of her thinking? His behavior was not the unacceptable one, but hers. Already she garnered looks of disapproval, a resentment that would eventually be turned on him. Rather roughly he claimed her arm. There would be enough gossip as there was. Any more and the situation would get completely out of hand.

"Khalil, stop." She threw herself to her knees. He was not deceived. There was nothing submissive about her actions, just a method to make him halt.

Still the crowd watched them, no doubt coming to their own conclusion.

"Go on. Be gone with all of you," he shouted, turning on the people as if they were a pack of disreputable dogs.

They dispersed quickly enough, but he suspected they were still watching. There was no way to stop them short of drawing his sword and threatening them all with be-heading. Then Chelsea would be right. He would be bar-baric—or mad.

"What will become of her?"

"What does it matter to you?" Khalil stared down at her glorious pale beauty, searching for signs of contrition where he knew he would never find them. "What do you think will happen to her, Chelsea?" he demanded in ex-asperation. "Do you think I will just leave her in the desert to die?"

The look of accusation in her blue eyes confirmed his suspicions.

"But of course that is what you think, is it not?" He threw back his head and laughed, but it wasn't humor that prompted his reaction, rather bitter irony. For was that not what she had thought he had planned to do to her? Cast her out into the desert to the jackals? "Very well, Chelsea." He frowned down at her. "I will tell you what will happen. She will be returned to her family." He didn't remind her that family was his own.

"But in disgrace?"

"Yes, disgraced." Again he didn't tell her that as Rakia's protector he had no intentions of treating her any-thing but fair. If she did not already know that, then she knew little of him. Turki may have been within his rights to divorce her, but it had been a foolish decision. Still, a sheikh did not have the right to be swayed by personal opinion. It was simply his duty to carry out the law. "She failed in her duty to please her husband."

"Oh-h-h!" Chelsea gained her feet and threw up her hands. "Is that all you men ever care about? Your own pleasure?" she lashed out.

"I believe it was *your* pleasure I considered not so long ago. Or have you already forgotten?"

Her pale face turned such a bright shade of red that Khalil regretted his frank cruelty even if he spoke the truth.

"Chelsea, wait."

She ignored him, shouldering past him as if he were not there.

"Rakia," she said gently, kneeling to gather up the distraught woman. Only then did she shoot him a squelching look, turning away before he could reciprocate. "There is no shame in what you did." She stroked the woman's bare head with hands that had so lovingly caressed him not so long ago. "I promise you. No one will accuse you or mistreat you again. Not as long as I am here. Please, won't you come with me?"

It was only natural that Rakia would look to him, her appointed protector, for direction. Chelsea didn't seem to see it that way.

"Just give her your permission, will you please?" she demanded.

It wasn't that easy.

"Where do you plan to take her?"

"Back to the hospital, of course. But what concern is it of yours?" she replied flippantly.

As fast as a desert viper, he snatched her up by the arm, pulling her so close he watched her sky-dyed eyes dilate with undisguised fear.

"Everything about you concerns me, Chelsea. What you do. What you wear. What you eat." His gaze honed in on the curve of her beautiful mouth. "Where you sleep."

"You don't own me. And if you think to tuck me away

276

in some smelly tent, to spend the rest of my life rotting in idleness at your beck and call, well, you know nothing about me," she insisted. "I am a *duktur*. An American. Or have *you* conveniently forgotten that?"

"When it comes to you, Chelsea, I forget nothing. Not who you are, nor what you are, nor where you came from." But oh, he had forgotten, for just a little while. If only he could make her forget as well. Instead, he released her.

"Go with her, Rakia," he ordered, never once looking down at the groveling female. "Perhaps, cousin, you can teach her what it means to be a woman. Allah knows, I have tried and failed." He turned and marched away.

"I *am* a woman," Chelsea railed at his retreating back. "I am, damn you. And I'll do whatever I want. Do you hear me? Whatever *I* want."

Her pain and her anger stabbed at him like sharp daggers. He didn't turn around to confirm what he suspected. Like all women, Chelsea Browne knew how to cry.

Chelsea swept into the tent with the force of a gale wind, Rakia quietly trailing behind her like some grateful stray she had befriended.

"Jamal?" she shouted, surveying her surroundings. Nuri's bedroll was missing. Thank God. Rakia wouldn't have to see it and be reminded. She could hear the other boys with Muhammad. Apparently they were playing. "Ja-ma-a-l? Where are you?"

So he thought to teach her how to be a woman, did he? An image of Khalil's arrogant face rose up in front of her like a solid brick wall. Well, she didn't need him.

Let him strut like some egotistical desert jackass if he wanted, thinking he was Allah's gift to women. She didn't care. For almost twenty-seven years she'd gotten on just fine without his. . . .

She couldn't bring herself to call what had transpired between them lovemaking.

The reality of what she'd done struck her so hard, she sat down in the middle of the tent, pressing the heels of her hands to her temples. Oh, God, how could she have been so gullible? How could she have let him do those things to her? How could she have enjoyed them so much? She'd not even thought to protect herself. Not that a man like him would probably even know what protection was. And now, what was she going to do?

"Wallahi! Chel-sea. What happened to you?"

She looked up. Reflected in her assistant's dark eyes was the most disheveled creature she'd ever seen. Could that truly be her looking like some desert-made bedlamite? She realized then what she must do.

With a calmness she did not feel, she glanced about the tent. When she spied the water container, half-empty, hanging from a hook on a tent post, she rose, retrieving the still-unidentified animal part, and placed it in Rakia's hands.

"Would you get us some water, please?" she requested.

If the woman was surprised at the strange, unnecessary instructions, she said nothing, nodded and slipped out of the tent to do Chelsea's bidding.

The moment she was gone Chelsea spun around.

"The children? How are they doing?"

"Well enough, but we only have enough antibiotic injections for one more dose for each of them."

"No new patients?"

"No." He gave her a suspicious look.

"Good. In my opinion the epidemic is under control. Start packing, Jamal."

"What?" He frowned at her as if in truth she had lost her mind.

"I said start packing." Tripping over the hem of her enveloping gown, she rushed toward the pile of packs and, falling to her knees, began to sort through them in a frenzy. "We'll take only what we need right now. We can come back for the rest later." If they could ever find this godforsaken place again. If she'd ever want to. Torn between her personal desires and her professional duties, she paused and pressed trembling fingers to her forehead. "The more expensive, rare drugs. I suppose we shouldn't leave them behind."

Focusing once more on the task at hand, she returned to digging through the pile. "Food and water. We'll need lots of water. All we can carry." She came up with a couple of empty containers that could be filled and tossed them to the side.

"Chel-sea, where are we going?" Jamal knelt down beside her. Why did he continue to look at her that way? Was he dense?

"Back to the clinic, of course. Ad Dawadimi. We've done all that we can here. More than could be expected." She wasn't sure if she was trying to convince herself or him. "Where else do you think we would go?"

"Chel-sea, I don't think you realize how . . . difficult getting back might be."

"Difficult or not, we have to try. Don't you see? I cannot stay here any longer."

Jamal's gaze softened into what she dubbed pity. He

wasn't telling her something. She was more sure of that than ever.

"What is it, Jamal?" she asked, gripping his arm so tightly it hurt her own hand.

She could see him debate his choices. What was so awful that he was afraid to tell her? Her fingers recoiled. If it was that bad, maybe she didn't want to know, not if it would cause her to waver in her decision to leave. She had to get away. If she stayed here for another moment . . . well, she didn't want to think about what might happen if she stayed here.

"Look, Jamal. I'm going whether you come with me or not," she declared, thoroughly shaken by the effects a few moments in a man's arms was having upon her. She stood and began gathering up the supplies she planned to take with her. There was too much, more than even two could contend with, much less attempt to carry by herself. Ruthlessly she began discarding packs, the needles and syringes so hard to come by, one cold pack, and then the other.

"What do you plan to do, Chel-sea? Just walk out of here?" Jamal asked.

"No, I plan to demand to be taken back."

"Do you think Khalil will honor such a demand?"

In all honesty? No, she didn't.

"Well, then, if he's bull-headed, we won't even ask him; we'll take a couple of the horses and leave on our own."

"So you are going to steal horses?"

"Not steal, just borrow." Why was he giving her so much resistance?

"Do you even know which way to go?"

"I'll figure it out," she snapped, tired of his relentless

280

questions, especially when they pointed out the endless flaws in her plan.

"And what about her?"

Chelsea followed where Jamal's finger pointed. Rakia. Good God, how long had the Bedouin woman been standing there? By the look on her face she would say long enough. What was she going to do with her? She couldn't just leave her behind. She had promised to take care of her, to see that no one hurt her, or shamed her, again. To break that promise was unthinkable.

"No problem," she replied, the edges of her mouth lifting in a smile. "We will simply take her with us. Would you like that, Rakia, to go back to Ad Dawadimi with me. There no one will treat you shamefully." There was nothing to hold Rakia here—no child, no husband. In fact, the Arab woman's knowledge of the working of the encampment, her familiarity with the desert itself, would even be helpful to them.

"Umm Dawa, you must not do this," the woman pleaded, her gentle eyes filled with apprehension. "Even with a man to protect you." She cast a doubtful look at Jamal. "He is only one. I fear a terrible fate awaits you in the desert."

It was like dealing with a child certain that monsters lurked under her bed. That was how she had to reason with her—as if she were a frightened child.

"A worse one awaits us here. Think about it, Rakia," she offered. Hoping to convince the indecisive woman, she began to hand her things to carry. "There is even the possibility I could take you back to America with me. Wouldn't that be better than being returned to your family in shame?"

"Chel-sea, be careful of what you promise."

"It's not unreasonable to think I could take her back with me." She glanced over at her assistant. "I could sponsor her in the States and . . ." Her reasoning stumbled to a halt. There it was again. That ill-defined look he had given her before. "What's bugging you, Jamal?"

"Chel-sea. Haven't you wondered about all of the strange things that have happened to us in the last few days? Don't you wonder where we are?"

"We are in some remote Bedouin village. God knows, we've seen plenty of those." She filled Rakia's arms and began gathering up her own load. "I don't remember the name, but I distinctly remember someone mentioned it."

"Rakia, what is the name of this oasis?" Jamal never looked up at the silent, overloaded woman; instead his gaze held steady on Chelsea.

"Dir'iyyah."

"Yes, that's it. I remember," Chelsea chimed in.

"Doesn't that name mean anything to you?"

"No." Chelsea frowned. "Should it?"

"Dir'iyyah is an ancient ruin eleven kilometers northwest of Riyadh."

"The capital city? Do you mean we're only a few miles from civilization? Jamal, why didn't you tell me this before?" She rose, quite irate at her assistant's deliberate neglect. "We could reach there in just a few hours. We could have even transported the children to the hospital there. We might have saved Nuri. I don't understand why you kept this information from me."

"Chel-sea, didn't you hear what I said?" Jamal grasped her shoulders and shook her gently, nearly causing her to drop her booty. "Dir'iyyah is an *ancient ruin.* The old capital of the Al Saud."

"Well, you must be wrong." A spurt of nervous laughter bubbled up in Chelsea's throat. "I've seen no ruins about, and if these people are related to the royal family, why are they living like this? Without any kind of medical advancements? Without . . ." Her brows knitted. There was so much they were without.

"Without a single pickup truck," Jamal took up her line of thought and continued it for her. "Not one transistor radio. Have you seen any of the typical clutter—old tires, rusting tin cans, empty oil drums?"

"No, but . . . Jamal, what are you insinuating?"

"Rakia, what year is this?"

By this time the poor woman, trying to keep from dropping anything, was staring at them in total terror. Her mouth opened as if to answer, trembled, then snapped shut again.

"Jamal, enough of this nonsense," Chelsea insisted, placing herself between her assistant and her newfound friend. "You are scaring Rakia to death." If the truth be known, he was scaring her pretty bad, too.

"Rakia, what is the year?" Jamal asked again.

"The . . . the year of our prophet, 1002," the woman muttered.

"The Islamic calendar is so different from the Georgian. That means nothing."

"I figured it out, Chel-sea. According to your calendar, it is roughly somewhere in the fourteenth century."

"Jamal, that's crazy. I don't know why you are telling me this, or what you hope to accomplish. Khalil." Her eyes narrowed knowingly. "He put you up to this, didn't he? God, men must think all women are gullible. Did the two of you actually believe I would fall for such nonsense? People can't go back in time just like that." She stomped her foot, the only appendage free to stress her words. "The next thing you'll tell me is that we got here in the fourteenth century on a flying carpet." She lifted up a cold pack she held in her hand and shook it. "And that there is a jinni trapped in here ready to give me three wishes."

Regardless of her brave words, an underlying doubt chipped away at her logic. Time travel was something fiction novelists like Jules Verne wrote about. It couldn't really happen. But Jamal was right. Where were all the signs of Western invasion that invariably made their way into the villages they visited? Spurred on by a rising panic she tried hard to conquer, Chelsea stormed toward the exit.

"You can tell Sheikh Khalil I didn't buy into his little hoax," she cried.

By the time she reached the tent flap, Jamal had placed himself in front of it, an impassable barrier. Did he never quit?

"Chel-sea. What about this?" He fumbled to clutch the talisman suspended about her neck. "How do you explain its power?"

"I don't have to explain it." There was nothing magical about the pouch, and she would prove it. "It's just a piece of leather, nothing more." Struggling to free up a hand so that she could pull the damn thing off, she lost her grip on her armload of supplies. She scrambled to hang on to them along with her self-control. Suddenly she was shouting, saying terrible things, things about Jamal, Khalil, even about herself.

The outburst was followed by an embarrassing silence that almost seemed to pulsate with regret. Composing herself as best she could under the circumstances, she bent down to retrieve what she had dropped.

"Chel-sea."

"Look, Jamal." Close to tears, she glanced up more determined than ever to prove him wrong. "I'm going. Maybe you believe all this mumbo jumbo. God knows, it's easy enough to get caught up with these people. I don't blame you. But I know there is a logical explanation for what has happened. Eventually I will know what it is. I'll even laugh about it in years to come." For now, her throat tightened about a sob that stubbornly refused to go away and she would not allow to escape.

"Is there nothing I can do to convince you this is a mistake?"

She shook her head, fearing to speak.

Jamal sighed. "Very well, *ya Duktur*. I have no choice but to go with you."

"Thank you." A forced smile fluttered on her lips, and she unloaded part of her burden into his arms. "I knew I could depend on you, Jamal. We've been a team too long not to stick together now." But if the truth be known, even though she wasn't sure she could have managed on her own, she would have tried. "Come on, Rakia."

"No, Umm Dawn. I dare not."

"What do you mean? I can't just leave you. I made a promise."

"These are my people. Don't you see? I cannot leave them. Besides, someone must stay with the children."

The children. Chelsea darted a look across the tent. How could she have forgotten the three little boys? Even now she could hear them playing beyond the dividing curtain, oblivious to the adult's upraised voices. Of course Rakia was right. Although they were on the road to recovery, they still needed nursing and care. Who better than a mother who had tended her own sick child, had watched the procedures day in and day out and had even added little twists of her own with herbal remedies Chelsea had to admit had often worked? Rakia knew what needed to be done better than anyone else in the encampment.

But could they trust her not to reveal their escape plans? And if the woman did keep quiet, what would happen to her? Chelsea's concerns manifested themselves in a frown.

"Do not worry, Umm Dawa. I will tell them you were here when I fell asleep. By morning you will be far away."

"I cannot leave you to face certain punishment."

"No harm will come to me." She patted one of Chelsea's filled hands. "The sheikh, my cousin, will not harm me. I know this with all of my heart."

Still unconvinced, Chelsea held her ground.

"You must go, and I must stay, Umm Dawa. It is the will of Allah. Now, hurry."

"I will not forget you, Rakia. I will come back for you, Mother of The Most Generous Heart," she promised, torn but knowing the woman was right.

"You honor me." Tears welled in Rakia's dark, devoted eyes. "I will not forget your kindness, both to me and to my son. I will wait for your return." She looked away, at Jamal for only a moment, but said nothing even though it seemed like she wanted to.

It was the hardest thing Chelsea had ever done in her life, walking out of that tent and leaving Rakia, but it was something she had to do, for both of them. She would be back, she vowed. She would come with an army if she had to, but she would never give up until she had given that poor woman the chance to have even half the advantages she had had in her life. Rakia's ability to endure made Chelsea's look quite pale in comparison. Never again would she bemoan how unfair life had been to her.

With undisguised relief, Khalil watched the unwelcome band of Rashaad saddle up their horses and camels and ride out of Dir'iyyah without formality or incident, though they had taken much more time than Khalil had given them to be gone. If he never saw his most hated enemy again except in *harb,* on a field of battle, he wouldn't be upset in the least.

He suspected war was inevitable. Aziz ibn Sha'la was not a man to give up so easily on something he set his greedy eyes upon. The old sheikh wanted the woman *duktur* who could heal the incurable and would stop at nothing to get her. Already he had proven that by the bold attempt to snatch her out of the encampment.

Temptation to rival *ird.* An irresistible lure even to the lion-hearted. The woman's magic was a very powerful one to control. Khalil would never give her up.

Not to his enemy nor to fate. And not for the reasons the Rashaad might think. His were much more personal.

Once the dust of departure settled, he had no further excuse for lingering outside, for avoiding the inescapable. Turning his back to the dying sun, he reentered the tent. Silently making his way to the circle of men, he sat down at their head. He cast a level look on the council of elders gathered around the comfort of his fire, drinking coffee, making small talk among themselves—waiting for him.

It was the woman they came to discuss. Chelsea. The beautiful brown shell of the sea. He knew that without being told. Studying each of their faces, as familiar as the steppe that gave them life, he tried to decide how much of the truth they actually knew. How much they only suspected.

"We have the right to be told, *ya ràyyis*. What forces have you unleashed upon us?" Zayd ibn Ahmad was the oldest of the elders, a fine warrior in his youth, a close companion of Khalil's father during his long, successful reign. Lame now from a nearly fatal lance wound, he spent his days in contemplation.

The uncertainty reflected in his ancient eyes was repeated in all of the others. Such fear made for discord at the very least. If they no longer believed in his ability to lead, then they would refuse to follow.

"Tell me, Zayd. Are you afraid of the powers of a mere woman?"

"Fear them, never," the old man said with a snort. "But only a besotted fool would refuse to respect them. From where has this woman come? To whom does she give her allegiance? What *zakat* will we be forced to pay in return?" They all worried about the toll this woman would cost them.

They were fair questions, ones that deserved straightforward answers, for no Bedouin cared to be indebted, not even to a fellow member of his tribe much less some faraway sultanate.

"It is true she comes from across the great little water, from Persia, but it is not what you may think." He held up his hand to quell the skepticism, offering the facts as he interpreted them. "There will be no *zakat* imposed on us." As far as her allegiance, of that he could not be certain, but as for payment, the only sacrifice necessary would be a personal one for himself. Of that he would make sure. "Have you not heard of the medical school in Jundishapur?" Where else could such a great physician have studied?

"Of course we have heard of it, but that is a fortnight away, beyond even Baghdad. Would you have us believe that you rode all that way to retrieve this woman in one day?"

A great murmur of indignation circulated the gathering.

So they knew of his journey, if not the destination or the circumstances under which he had made his way.

"You are right, such a trip would be impossible, if not impractical. But that is not the case. I received knowledge that a great physician had come to Ad Dawadimi." Such traveling clinics were not unheard of although rare so far into the desert. "It was there that I found her and . . . convinced her to come back with me." Convinced was much too mild a word, he supposed, but he let it stand.

"Who ever heard of a woman *duktur?*"

"I, too, was surprised by that discovery." He shrugged "But who can account for Persian idiocy."

That statement earned a round of amused assent.

"This woman. What does she mean to you, *ya ràyyis?*" old Zayd asked.

So they had wind of the incident down by the *wadi* already, had they?

"I claim protectorship and responsibility for this woman," he announced.

"She, then, shall remain with us?"

"Her knowledge and abilities would be to our advantage. Is that not so?"

"And does she agree with this decision?"

How could she not, after what had transpired between them?

"Yes," he replied with confidence that she could not do otherwise—eventually. Once she calmed down and once she came to accept that she had no other choice.

"I hope you know what you are doing, Khalil." The old man sighed. "There will be no peace for any of us as long as she is among us."

"Are you suggesting I have no power to control my household?"

"Not at all, *ya ràyyis.*" The old man bowed his head with respect. "But surely you must realize that her presence among us will create great envy among our enemies, more than even our finest camels and horses."

"That could be, Zayd." He looked each and every man of the council in the eye, then settled his gaze on the old, crippled warrior. "But would you be willing to slaughter your prize mares in order to keep the enemy from raiding our herds?"

"No, of course not," the old man agreed. "There is no pride in such safety."

"Just imagine, Zayd, what your life might be like now if such a learned physician had resided among us when you fell victim to the enemy's lance."

Without a doubt, it was the right thing to say. By the way the old warrior's shoulders sagged, Khalil knew he had won, at least temporarily.

"Know this, all of you," he vowed, rising to his feet so that they had to look up at him. "As sheikh I will not lead our people into a danger we do not benefit from. The day I fail in my duties is the day I will step down."

"Very well, *ya ràyyis.* Your word is good enough. But

know this, we will not forget the vow you have made here today. We will expect you to honor it."

It was all Khalil could hope for, all he expected.

Fifteen

A half moon cast its eerie iridescence across the landscape. Chelsea was most grateful for the illumination, even though it left them somewhat vulnerable. If someone should happen to spot them. . . .

However, without the light she might not have so quickly unraveled the mystery of the unfamiliar saddles with the hand-forged buckles. Although crude in design, the workmanship could not be faulted. They were beautiful, she had to admit. She realized then that everything in the encampment was handmade, a treasure trove of antiques in mint condition that had to be worth a fortune. Antiques that looked brand new? People living without a single influence of modernization? What did it all mean?

No, she dared not allow her thoughts to take such a dangerous path. Instead she needed to concentrate on catching two of the horses from the vast, milling herd and saddling them as fast as possible.

Jamal was no help at all with the difficult task presented her. As knowledgeable as he was about many things, he knew absolutely nothing about horses. His distaste for them showed in the nervous way he acted around the unruly mare she managed to capture first. No wonder, she supposed. The nag, for that was what it truly was, had to be as old as Methuselah with the scars on its flea-bitten coat to prove it. Displaying a nasty disposition, the beast refused to stand still as Chelsea fumbled with the assortment of strange straps and buckles, and even kicked out once when she cinched the girth.

"Watch her and keep out of the way of her front hooves," she warned, handing poor Jamal the reins and turning her attention to capturing another mount.

The second wasn't much better than the first. It was a fine specimen of Arabian horseflesh, brown with a white blaze on its well-formed face and four white stockings. When the mare allowed her to just walk up and bridle it, that should have alerted Chelsea to be on guard. The moment she tried to lead the animal away from the rest of the herd, it suddenly reared, nearly pulling her off her feet.

However, she knew a trick or two herself when it came to horses. Soon she had the situation under control, at least for the moment, but she remained alert to whatever else the animal might try to pull.

If she didn't know better, she would swear these horses displayed an undeniable disdain for a woman handler.

Saddled and ready to go at last, she donned an *abaaya,* the concealing overdress that all Arab women wore in public. Quite restricting, she wouldn't have bothered if Rakia hadn't insisted she do so just before they had sneaked out of the tent.

"To protect yourself, Umm Dawa. With your unusual hair and coloring, you would never go unnoticed."

Regardless of the well-meaning warning, Chelsea

planned to discard the confining garment the moment she reached the first signs of civilization—a paved road, a pickup truck, anything to disavow Jamal's wild allegations that they had gone back in time.

She studied her assistant out of the corner of her eye, watching him contend with the old mare which seemed resigned to its fate now that it was saddled, but he was jumpy, making the horse fidgety as well. Why was he doing this to her? Chelsea wondered. What did he hope to accomplish by trying to scare her? She could come up with no logical explanation for his behavior other than he truly believed what he said.

"Jamal, once we get back, you'll see," she offered in reassurance.

That he understood what she was talking about made itself evident in the way he pressed his lips together yet remained silent, but she knew he was still unconvinced. She, too, said nothing more, and deciding he would be better off riding the older, more predictable mare, she helped him mount and arrange the reins for optimum control.

"You got it?" she asked, waiting for his assent before releasing the horse to his unsure hands.

"Give me a Land Rover any day over this," he muttered, then nodded.

Chelsea stepped back, and once she was certain the young Arab would be okay, she turned her attention to her own horse. When it came to mode of travel she didn't agree with Jamal, not in the least. Pulling herself up into the saddle, she collected her reins. Without question, she preferred the feel of the strips of leather in her hands over a cold, metal steering wheel, saddle to bucket seats. Besides, it was nice to once more have control of her own transportation not just be a passenger, restrained by cultural restrictions.

Taking the lead, she urged her mare into a trot, heading toward the ridge. Once they were past the rise and out of sight, then she would stop and get her bearing.

The fact they made it even that far without incident or being noticed quite frankly surprised her. She turned to check on Jamal. He looked like a corked bottle bobbing in the water, listing from one side of the saddle to the other. He did not bother to conceal his relief when she slowed.

"Which way?" she asked, wheeling her horse about to match the uneven gait of Jamal's mount. The old mare was doing its level best to make the trot as uncomfortable to the rider as possible. When the animal stopped abruptly, he almost flew over its head. Regaining his seat, Jamal pointed off into the distance.

There was nothing to see but barren steppe that went on forever and ever. Eleven kilometers might as well be a hundred, she reasoned pessimistically, suddenly feeling unsure of herself and her impulsiveness.

"If we do manage to get back, Chel-sea . . ."

She glanced over at her companion when he left his statement just dangling.

"No matter what. If something happens and I don't make it, promise me that you'll go on without me."

"What kind of morbid nonsense is that, Jamal?" she retorted. "Not only will we both make it back, but tomorrow we'll be laughing with the others at the clinic over the whole ordeal. Just wait until I tell them about your notion about going back in time. Do-do-do-do. Do-do-do-do," she imitated the theme song of "The Twilight Zone."

However, he didn't laugh—probably he didn't get it—instead just stared at her in that reserved way he had of late that made her feel as if she didn't really know him or understand his concerns.

Cultural differences. That was all. They were to be expected.

Undaunted, she took the lead once more, slowing the pace to a fast walk. It would take them forever at this rate, she suspected, but sensitized by Jamal's strangely uncharacteristic outburst, she figured it was better than never reaching home at all.

Tomorrow? Would she be laughing? she wondered, unable to shake the forlorn feeling that shrouded her as much as the black *abaaya* that covered her from head to foot.

Oddly enough she doubted laughing would be what she'd do. Already she missed that arrogant desert prince who had somehow managed to break down the barrier of her innocence of what being a woman was really all about, an ignorance that she had lived with throughout her entire life. But not anymore.

Even if she never saw him again, and most likely that would be the case, she would never forget him and what he had taught her about herself. Reaching up, she found comfort in the talisman suspended about her neck. She would never take it off, she vowed, wondering as she did what her mother and father would think, or worse, say when they saw the crude necklace.

Her father? God, what would he do if he ever found out that she had gotten involved with a man like Khalil? Then there was Michael. He would laugh and declare there had always been a bit of the masochist in her and she deserved what had happened to her.

Still, she clung to that talisman, feeling like a vanquished warrior returning from a war lost, unable to let go of superstitions that had gotten her through the battles and brushes with death alive.

The talisman.

If nothing else, that bit of leather possessed the uncanny power to make it so that she could never ignore the fact that being a woman had its up side after all.

Khalil sat by the fire, contemplating the bobbing, evasive flames, yet not really seeing them. He was very much aware of their ability to draw a man deep into his own thoughts, a dangerous pastime for a man of action like himself.

The color reminded him of Chelsea's hair; the heat, of her hand when she touched him, so shyly at first, then with a burning passion that demanded an equal response.

He had responded. Oh, how he had responded. What had his reward been? Loneliness, uncertainty, incrimination.

Like shields, he lifted his palms to the crackling blaze, to fend off the spell, to remember who he was, what he was, and what was expected of him.

Where, in the ways of this world, was there room for love? he asked a deity who possessed little sympathy for such human needs.

Reward comes after suffering.

He had suffered enough in his opinion. Apparently Allah didn't agree with him.

"Father."

Startled from his reverie, Khalil glanced up to find his young son standing just within the shadows of the otherwise empty tent. His heart welled with joy and, yes, love. How could he have so selfishly forgotten this greatest gift returned to him from the brink of death? His son. His most important possession.

"Muhammad, what are you doing here so late at night?" Actually it was early morning. The sun would rise in a short while. "Should you not be resting?" Still, he held out his hand in invitation.

"Am I disturbing you?"

"No, no." He sighed. "I have been alone for quite long enough. And you?"

The boy moved forward, dropping to his knees before his sire. "I was bored. Besides." He reached inside the fullness of his *thobe* and pulled out that infernal rodent he called a pet. "Saba was hungry. I thought Umm Taif might part with a few grains of rice."

Khalil watched in silence as the jerboa seemed quite content climbing one of the boy's hands, then on to the other, and back again, a never-ending staircase that led nowhere. Just like life.

"Your aunt is old and needs her sleep, boy, just as you do."

"But I am not old, and you are not asleep," he balked, looking up with a determination that stirred Khalil's parental pride.

"I have not been ill."

"I am well now."

"Yes. By all that is sacred, yes, you are." An unexplained desire to hug the boy to his heart slipped by the rugged, manly exterior. He resisted the urge, instead putting out his hand and allowing the rodent the opportunity to climb his fingers.

Saba hesitated, seemed to study him with eyes much

too intelligent for something meant only to be food for dogs. With a little encouragement from the boy—actually he was unceremoniously thrust into Khalil's large palm— the rodent began to explore the lines and ridges of character time had given his hand, finally discovering the sleeve of his *thobe*.

"The *duktur* will be mad at both of us should she discover you are missing."

"She will not." Muhammad shrugged.

Such a boastful statement for one so young.

"How can you be so sure?"

The rodent was becoming much too bold as well. Khalil lifted his arm and shook the little beast back down into his hand.

"The *duktur* is not here anymore."

"But, of course she is," Khalil insisted, sensing the note of jealousy in the boy's voice. A man's jealousy, perhaps? He smiled down at his small prodigy with renewed respect. Thinking back, he had not been much older when he had found interest in females. It was only natural. Perhaps it was time as a father to explain a few things to his son.

"I tell you, Father, she is gone," the boy reiterated on a note of exasperation.

A twinge of alarm caused Khalil to take pause. The boy was wrong. There was nowhere for Chelsea to go, and after the fiasco with the Rashaad, surely she would prefer to stay put. "You must be mistaken, Muhammad."

"No, I heard her leave. I'm sure of it. She and the *hadhar*, they left together."

"You and the other children were left alone?"

"No. Nuri's mother. She is there. Asleep. Is she old, too?"

Without answering the question, Khalil rose, dropping the jerboa into his son's hand and strapping on his scimitar.

"When you catch up with her, Father, what do you plan to do? Will you cut off her head?"

He looked down at the boy, reading the man's reasoning in the youthful eyes. In all honesty, it was a decision he had yet to make.

"How far do you think we have gone?" Impatient to reach their destination, Chelsea nonetheless brought her mare to a standstill and dismounted, waiting for her companion to catch up with her.

"My aching body says a hundred kilometers." Jamal groaned, sliding from the saddle and onto the ground when his knees gave out. "But I should say we are getting close, very close. *Wallahi!* I hope so."

"Don't worry." She looked down and smiled at him. "Your misery will be over soon." Automatically checking the saddle girths to make sure they were still tight, she stared off into the distance where Riyadh by all rights should be and squinted. "You would think we would see the glow of the city lights from here." She frowned. "Or at least have crossed one of the main highways."

Jamal's silence spoke as loud as a verbal I-told-you-so.

She glared down at him, then relented when struck with a twinge of pity as she watched him rub his aching calves. Hurting or not, he was wrong. They approached the city from a direction where the hills blocked their view, and luck would have it that there weren't any roads running through this part of the desert. Riyadh was out there, probably just over the next rise. Besides the sky was clear, already a hint of dawn brightening it. Any halo from artificial light would be hard to spot at this point.

But still, why hadn't they seen a single sign of civilization?

"Come on. Don't get too comfortable, Jamal," she insisted with renewed urgency.

Once they were on their way again, she approached the hills with the unflagging confidence that each would be the last one to be surmounted. Up and down. Up and down, the blowing sand beginning to get deeper, the horses tiring. Even they who were used to the desert wouldn't be able to continue on for much longer at such a grueling pace.

At long last her determination was rewarded.

There it was. Riyadh. She paused on the knoll and glanced out over the sleepy, little village that lay in the distance. Or was it Riyadh? Why, it looked more like Ad Dawadimi than the sprawling metropolis she knew the capital city to be.

When Jamal finally joined her on her vantage point, she turned to him.

"I don't understand it. Do you think we've gone the wrong way or veered off course?"

Judging by his expression, he didn't need to answer her. She already knew what he thought. Well, she refused to give his ridiculous theory credence.

Descending the hill, she urged her mount to muster one last burst of energy to race across the open flatland that lay between her and salvation.

"Chel-sea, wait!"

She ignored Jamal's cry, giving the mare its head, exhilarated with the sound of the pounding hooves beneath her, the wind ripping off her head covering and tearing at her unbound hair.

It didn't matter that they might not have found Riyadh. Whatever town they approached, it was large enough to have a medical clinic of some kind. There had to be other doctors who would know her identity and see to it that she and her assistant were returned safely to their own unit.

She didn't stop until she reached the edge of the village. Breathing as hard as her winded horse, she waited for Jamal to overtake her position in his slow, jaunting pace. By the time he got halfway there the sun crested the ridge they had come from, highlighting his valiant effort to hurry. Those efforts had to be commended, especially when he nearly careened from the saddle more than once.

She didn't mean to, but she started to laugh, not so much at him, but with the giddiness of success and relief. Quickly, she stripped off the ugly, black *abaaya,* wadding it up with the intention of tossing it away—forever.

"Please, Chel-sea." Clinging precariously to the horse's back and wheezing like broken bellows, Jamal frowned and snatched the garment from her hand before she could drop it. "Do not be foolish. We have no idea where we are or what kind of people we will find here."

"They will be normal people," she assured him, still laughing with elation. "People who live in real houses not tents. People with electricity and running water." Ah, yes, a bath. That was definitely one of the first things on her list to do. An honest-to-goodness soak in a tub of water, not just some dab and dip with a washcloth. Even as she made her plans, she found herself looking about. Her excitement began to wilt a little. Certain things were missing—like electric wires.

Big deal. So they didn't have electricity. It was common knowledge that some of the more remote medical stations had to generate their own power. There was no need for alarm.

"Put this back on." Jamal held out the hideous garment of feminine subjugation.

"I don't want to."

The words were no more out of her mouth than two of the most fierce-looking Arabs she had ever seen rode past them astride horses and sporting huge swords at their sides. Something in the way they looked at her made her shiver.

"All right." She snatched the despised shroud from his fingers and pulled it on over her head. "But just until we find someone to help us." Concealed once more from head to foot, she started to lead the way into the village.

"Why don't you follow me," Jamal suggested.

Follow him?

"At how many paces, *ya ràyyis?*" she mocked.

He shot her an angry look to match her own.

"Cover your face and keep your head down. I do not want anyone to see your eyes."

"Jamal, this is ridiculous."

"Just do it, Chel-sea."

Even as they debated, another group of riders filtered by. This time there was a woman among them, dressed as Chelsea was, only her eyes showing, dark and mysterious as they collided with her blue ones.

Chelsea covered the lower part of her face quickly. Just why she made the gesture, she wasn't sure, but she couldn't ignore the pounding of her heart when she felt

303

the masculine gazes slide over her with more than mere curiosity.

When at last they were alone again, she looked up, relieved to find the passersby had not stopped to question them as she feared they might.

"Okay, Chel-sea. Stay close behind me. No matter what, do not look up."

Overwhelmed by the strange feelings, Chelsea obeyed, allowing her tired mount to plod along behind Jamal's. Every time she had the urge to look up, which was quite often, she fought it down, forcing her gaze to remain leveled on the mare's lathered neck.

Although she tried to ignore them, she couldn't help but notice the warning signs, some subtle, some not, that all was not what it should be. Everywhere the few women they passed were shrouded and veiled, even the market vendors who ordinarily uncovered their faces while bickering with a customer in an open, aggressive manner. But now, the few she saw hurried to get their men when a question was asked of them.

Why did it all feel so . . . wrong and foreign to her? She'd seen plenty of marketplaces during her service in the Middle East, had become quite efficient in bartering, even with a language barrier. Now she could understand what was being said. But something just wasn't right. Oh, there were plenty of the customary stalls, among them the ones selling squawking chickens in cages or suspended by their feet, and the fruit and vegetable vendors whose stalls were encompassed in the cloying smell of overripeness and flies. But instead of the water barrels, cheap transistor radios, and spare truck parts that were always available in the *souq,* she saw only restive camels and horses being hawked.

Still, she refused to panic. There had to be a logical explanation.

Blocked by a herd of sheep crowding the narrow street, they were forced to a halt. Battling the urge to lift her head, she continued to search the marketplace out of the corners of her eyes, looking for something reassuring. A street urchin raced past, fell against the side of her horse, then scrambled beneath its legs before disappearing. Frightened, the animal bolted. Without thinking about it, she grabbed up the reins, expertly keeping her mount under control.

Jamal gave her a dark, warning look. Dropping her head once more she realized she had to be more careful. When the way finally cleared, they moved on. A little farther down, Jamal purposely stopped.

"Kind sir." Salaaming to a well-dressed merchant, he posed the question they both anxiously wanted an answer to. "Can you please tell me where to find the *dukturs?*"

"There is no *duktur* here," came the disheartening response. "But I will buy your brown horse and even the woman on its back if she is even half as beautiful as her eyes suggest."

She hadn't meant to look. Somehow it just happened. Mortified, she quickly lowered her face once more.

"I am not in the market to sell today, horses nor women," Jamal replied as if it were the most ordinary thing for him to say. "I seek information as to where I can find a *duktur.*"

"There is no *duktur* here in Riyadh." The merchant's dark, beady eyes continued to linger on Chelsea in a most disturbing way. "But there is one rumored to be in Dir'iyyah. A woman with blue eyes . . ." The marketer's voice trailed off. "If you change your mind about your horse or your female, you have only to come to Abdullah. I will give you a fair price . . ."

That was all she heard as they quickly moved away.

Panic didn't begin to describe what Chelsea felt at that moment. It was more like sheer terror.

Oh, God, what kind of nightmare was she trapped in? To be treated like marketplace merchandise? How would she ever escape?

"Jamal?" she ventured to whisper.

"Shh. Be quiet, Chel-sea." His voice remained steady, but his hand trembled where it clutched the headstall of her horse, leading her through the crowded marketplace.

Holding her tongue when she had a million questions that demanded answers was nearly impossible. But she managed, at least until they turned into a quiet alleyway. There, thinking they were alone, she jerked off the hideous, black covering from her face and head. It was suffocating her, and she couldn't stand it for another moment.

"Wallahi!" Jamal's dark eyes, focused on something directly behind her, widened with what she could only label horror.

"What's wrong?" She twisted in the saddle, just in time to glimpse a pair of hands coming toward her. They grasped her about the waist and pulled her from the back of the horse with a roughness that spoke of a lack of respect.

"Jamal! Jamal!" Hitting the ground, she screamed and rolled to avoid those same hands grabbing at her again. But there were even more now, tugging at her arms and legs, pinning her down until she couldn't move, could barely even breathe.

Immobilized on her stomach, she turned her head to

find herself surrounded by Arab men—two of whom she instantly recognized.

Mutt and Jeff.

What were they doing here? She took up her struggle once more, but little good it did her. Soon her arm was pushed so far up her back she thought for sure the bone would snap. Going limp, she couldn't stop her heart from racing, or her mind from trying to figure out how those two had gotten there and what they wanted.

Then there was no more time to think, only to feel, as a handful of her hair was grabbed and her head jerked back painfully.

"I told you it was the same woman," declared the tall man she remembered from before.

"How did she get here?" came an unidentified voice behind her.

"Does it matter?" Jeff said, smiling down at her in a way that made her shiver uncontrollably. "It is enough to know that our sheikh will be pleased, and will reward our quick thinking."

At that she was unceremoniously dragged to her feet.

"Let go of me," she cried. She kicked out, striking the leg of the man who held her. Spurred on by her success, she twisted from his grasp and began to run.

She didn't get far, a few steps at the most, before she was uncaringly knocked down again and dragged back into the circle of gawking men. Then her struggle was over when her hands and feet were quickly bound.

She screamed, dragged another breath into her lungs, and screamed again. That, too, came to an end when a foul-tasting rag was stuffed in her mouth and secured without thought of her comfort.

Trussed up like one of those poor chickens she had

passed in the marketplace, she had no choice but to await her doom with the same resignation.

"What about the other one?" she heard one of her abductors ask?

Jamal? Her heart took up racing once more. What had happened to her assistant, her friend?

She bucked in her bindings, trying to maneuver so that she could catch a glimpse of him, to reassure herself that he was unharmed.

"Just leave him. He's done for anyway."

She railed against her gag. No. No. That couldn't be true. Still she could see nothing.

Then she was picked up and laid on a carpet, soft and thick like those on the floors of her parents' home back in Georgia.

As soft as the one upon which Khalil had made such unforgettable love to her.

Khalil!

It was a cry she knew he would never hear, never respond to even if he could.

Then her world went black as she was rolled like a sausage into the tight, suffocating cocoon of the carpeting.

Sixteen

"I swear to you, oh, cousin, I was asleep. That is all I know. She was very upset. If she is gone, she did not mention her destination . . ." Rakia's eyes darted about and would not settle. "Only that she wanted to go home."

Khalil stood over the woman, who cowered at his feet like a beaten dog, but he had never touched her. Her reaction could have been a result of her husband's past mistreatment. The beating of one's wife. He did not approve of it, although it was an accepted way of life among the Bedouin.

When he made no move toward her, Rakia looked up. She still trembled, yet her eyes held as steady as his own. Never in all of his life had he felt such an urge to punish. He had every right, for she should have come to him immediately and told him all that she knew. However, he could not bring himself to strike even if she was withholding information, which he suspected she was.

"How could you have betrayed me so?" he demanded.

But he knew the answer. She was a woman, and like all women, betrayal was part of her very soul. Not one of them knew the meaning of loyalty, commitment . . . or love.

Chelsea. His heart twisted as if a dagger had been plunged into it. He should have expected and prepared for her betrayal, too.

Infuriated beyond words, he turned and stormed toward the tent opening.

"Ya ràyyis, what is to become of me?" cried Rakia.

He flinched in memory. Tuëma had asked him the very same question before he had sent her back to her family and eventual death. Always a woman thought only of herself when caught in a deception, he decided bitterly, expecting the man to forgive her.

"Better than you deserve." Better than all women deserved. "Gather up your possessions and return to your mother. I will feed you and clothe you as is my duty as your protector, but I do not want to know you exist, Rakia. If I should see your face again, my cousin, I swear I will cast it from my presence with little regard."

"No," she cried. She crawled across the tent to cling to the hem of his *thobe.* "Please, Khalil. I would rather die now than be forced into total seclusion."

"Then, tell me where she has gone."

"I do not know." The stubborn woman shook her head. "I swear, I do not know."

"So be it, then, foolish woman. You do not deserve the sweet rewards that come with death."

Callously he brushed her off and continued on his way. Her wails as unnerving as those of a trapped wolf-bitch followed him, but her pain could be no worse than his own.

Chelsea.

Outside, he stared out over the desert. Where was she?

Rakia had said she intended to go home. Had she figured out the secret to the talisman, how to evoke its power, by repeating the chant, the brown shell of the sea? If she had, would she only go back to Ad Dawadimi where he had found her—or beyond? To an unknown destiny—this America she spoke of so often? He wasn't even sure where to find America, or how to reach it if he discovered the way, if she had in truth returned to her own time.

She could have ridden off in any direction. Although he knew she had taken two of the horses, the tracks had long since been eradicated by the wind. He followed the line of the distant ridge with his eyes, seeking nonexistent answers, feeling helpless, frustrated, angry with both Allah and womanhood for leaving him with so few clues.

Chelsea.

Even accompanied by the *hadhar,* she was ill-equipped to face his world beyond the sheltered view he had allowed her to glimpse from the door of her tent.

Chelsea.

Allah save him. He loved her. To lose her would be worse than to sacrifice the most valuable of Bedouin possessions, his honor. But there was more than himself to think of.

What would his people say if he suddenly took off, abandoning them along with his responsibilities, to go on a quest that could very well last a lifetime. What would become of his family, his precious son? He could not turn his back on those who depended upon him, to follow after a woman who obviously did not even wish to be with him.

Chelsea!

It was a cry from his heart that would go unanswered.

A need unrequited. A love disdained. A bitterness that would forever remain with him.

The worst part, perhaps, was never learning what had become of her.

If only he knew. . . .

"Surely, oh, nephew, you did not think to keep her forever, did you?"

Startled to find himself no longer alone, he whirled to face the intruder, his aunt, Umm Taif.

"If you think to change my mind in regards to your unworthy daughter . . ."

"No, *ya ràyyis."* The woman lifted her hand to reassure him yet silence him. "I came only to thank you for allowing my Rakia to return to me."

"She asked for death instead."

"So I am told. A grieving woman knows not what is best for her. Given time, she will most likely come to appreciate your generosity."

"I wish that could be said of all women," he murmured. Then he turned his back to the wise old sorceress, not wishing to reveal too much of his inner feelings.

"To leave was most unappreciative. Is that what you think?"

"Quite frankly, I do not wish to discuss it, much less think about it."

"Only to brood upon it." Umm Taif snorted. "Well, it is time you thought about it, oh, nephew. Like all men, you do not stop to consider how we as women feel about the way you treat us, mere property to be acquired and discarded as the mood strikes you. You blame us for your failing; even the ills of the world rest on our shoulders. We are nothing if not what men have made us."

"Are women truly so unhappy with their lot in life?"

312

Frowning, he looked back at her. "Spoiled temptresses cared for and sheltered by men. You have only to be faithful and obedient. Why is that so difficult for a woman to do? Bah!" He waved her off and turned away. "What does any woman know of responsibility or self-sacrifice?"

"Just try to imagine, Khalil, what it is like to have no control over your own destiny. Then you will know what it is like to be a woman. What it was like for the brown shell of the sea to be snatched from everything familiar and forced into a life not of her own choosing."

"I had no intentions of keeping her."

"Did you not, oh, nephew? Is not that exactly what you set out to do when you seduced her?"

"Mind your vicious tongue, old woman."

"Can you not see that you gave her no choice except to submit to your will or run away?"

"I asked only that she trust me."

"Trust. A man's word that means submit without questioning. Tell me, nephew, when Allah asks that you trust him, do you obey?"

"It is not the same."

Ah, but it was. Especially in the way she presented the evidence. How had the wily old witch managed to twist the truth to her own advantage so easily?

"Are you suggesting I should simply resign myself to fate and let it go at that?"

"Have you truly heard nothing that I have attempted to tell you?" Umm Taif demanded, not bothering to disguise the disgust in her voice.

He stared at her blankly.

"I cannot understand how Allah in all his wisdom

313

could have chosen men to be in charge of this earth." She threw up her hands and turned to leave.

He could not allow that. She had not answered his question.

"Do you mock me, woman?" He grabbed her arm, forcing her to face him.

"It is not mockery you deserve, Khalil, only pity. You are determined to repeat your mistakes. A woman's loyalty and, yes, even trust is not something a man has a right to expect. He must earn it, like any other honor. He must prove himself worthy." She spat on the ground right next to his foot. "Only then does a man deserve a woman's love. Tell me, nephew, what of the talisman?"

"She still has it."

"Allah protect us," she whispered and turned away.

He watched her leave without asking permission, but did not try to stop her again, even though he could have—if he had chosen to. Crazy old woman. She had dallied too long with her spells and charms. Had they finally touched her feeble mind and left their indelible curse upon it?

Who better than he to know of loyalty and trust? And what of honor? Umm Taif had completely forgotten about that and the fact that he was responsible not only for his own, but that of his people, as well. Did she not see how much he gave up to defend them all?

What could women, so steeped in their deception, possibly know of honor except what a man forced upon them for their own good?

Not that he resigned himself to fate, not at all. He had simply made up his mind. There was a pattern to be seen here. Only a fool would not recognize it.

Chelsea reminded him of a stubborn mare he had once

owned as a boy, beautiful, spirited, a friend when with him, but the moment he turned his back, she had been determined to escape, no matter what it cost. Time after time he had tracked that mare into the desert, rescuing her from one disaster after another. It had been his father who had told him no horse was worth such bother. Let her go, let her face her own fate. That next spring he had found her bleached bones on the steppe.

Chelsea might expect him to repeatedly chase after her, like he had that horse. But having gone after her once, he would not do it again, and again. No woman was worth such sacrifice. Was that not what his father would say to him?

He started to turn his back on the rising sun and the woman somewhere out there who had so callously turned on him. But then he paused, unable to walk away that easily.

The talisman. What did old Umm Taif mean, Allah protect them? Would some terrible disaster befall them all if Chelsea should try to return to her own time by herself?

The next thing he knew he was running, not away from fate, but toward it. Allah help him, he would ride to the ends of the earth, to the end of his life if he must, to find the woman and stop her.

The end. That consequence may be very well what he would have to face.

Stiff, bruised over every inch of her body, unbearably hot, and gasping for even the most shallow of breaths, Chelsea prayed for an end to it all. For there in the confining cocoon of that carpet with nothing but her own

315

incriminating thoughts as company, she had come to a conclusion.

. Past, present, future . . . or hell. What did it matter where she was? She should have listened to Jamal, listened to her own instincts, and her assistant, her friend, might still be with her now, alive.

But at least his suffering was over. She wondered about her own. How much more would she have to endure before . . . before . . . Oh, God, what was to become of her?

Aware that something was different, she sniffed back a flood of tears. Had the horse, over which she had been tossed like a bedroll, truly come to a halt, or was it only her imagination? She strained to hear, but the voices beyond her dark world were nothing but a muffled murmur she could barely make out much less understand.

Then she was falling. She hit the ground and rolled, over and over and over.

The shocking brightness of the sun when it struck her full in the face nearly blinded her. Closing her eyes, she concentrated instead on taking one deep cleansing breath after another. Oh, she had never realized how sweet the air could be. Never again would she take it for granted. Cautiously she parted her lashes just enough to take in her surroundings.

The precious moment to regroup was short-lived. That she had been brought to some kind of temporary Bedouin encampment was obvious; that it was Khalil's, doubtful. There was something different about these men—harder, leaner, much crueler.

Then she was staring up into the face of an Arab she had seen before.

She knew not his name; nonetheless her heart thundered with fear, certain he was the same man who had been with Khalil, the rival sheikh, the Rashaad who had looked upon her so greedily.

He studied her in that identical way now, his dark eyes drifting over her thoroughly.

"Surely you can see that she is the same woman, Aziz?"

"What I see or do not see is for me to decide, Ibrahim," the old man stated. Then it appeared as if he were about to ask her a question. Instead he made a gesture, short and demanding.

His order was quickly obeyed. Lifted to her feet, legs unsteady from disuse, Chelsea barely managed to stay upright when her arms, still bound behind her back, were released. The gag, that foul-tasting rag, was removed as well.

"Is it true? I am told you studied medicine in Jundishapur," the old sheikh demanded.

Every medical student had heard of the ancient school of medicine in Persia that had produced such greats as Rhazes, Avicenna and Averroes, whose ancient writings were still the basis of much in modern medicine.

"Harvard, actually." She lifted her chin a notch with pride.

When that got no response, she tried again.

"United States of America."

But of course those names meant nothing to these desert thieves. Harvard, the United States, those places didn't even exist yet, which meant she didn't exist. She brushed aside such chilling thoughts and the panic they produced. It was important that she keep her wits about her, remain calm.

"Jundishapur." She nodded. "I am a student of those great teachers." In a roundabout way, that wasn't a lie.

Grunting, the old Rashaad nodded his approval and turned to walk away.

"Wait a minute," she cried in protest when she realized he had not disclosed his plans for her. "What are you going to do with me?"

"I shall give you the chance to prove your skills and worth—to me, to yourself. For your sake I hope they are all that I have been told that they are."

Spoken with a deceptive smile, his response left her shaken. She wished now she'd never asked the question.

How reckless of him, dashing off without a plan of action, without a single track to follow, with nothing but his instincts to guide him. He had behaved recklessly from the very beginning, Khalil supposed, from the moment he had gone after the *duktur* to save his son without thought of what could happen. He should have known better. A man could defy the laws of Allah for only so long before the consequences caught up with him, with them all.

Any moment the world as he knew it could very well cease to exist. Oddly enough, that prospect didn't frighten him as much as the thought of never seeing Chelsea again.

Chelsea. That mysterious brown shell of the sea. What power she held over him. He suspected that she did not know the magnitude of it. Having just found her, he wasn't ready to let her go, to never again cradle her in his arms and experience the sweetness of her release.

Just when his priorities had taken such a drastic

change of course was difficult to say. The first time he laid eyes on her he should have realized his downfall was inevitable. Men far greater than he had died fighting over women like Chelsea Browne.

And yet he rode on, willing to face his own shortcomings not only as a man, but a leader of men.

Hours later when he reached the edges of the little settlement known as Ad Dawadimi, he doubted he would find her there. They were a poor people, these fellow Bedouins, who at first mistook him for some kind of demon bearing down on them on his lathered black mare. But the hostile greeting turned to frightened apologies when they recognized him. Still, they had no idea why so distinguished a sheikh as Khalil ibn Mani al Muraidi would decide to visit them. They had nothing of value.

"Please, oh, great *Amir,* you are welcome to enter my humble tent." Without question, their leader invited him to dine, continuing to address him with a more respectful title than necessary because he feared so powerful a band as the Durra would swoop down on them and raid their herds, as meager as they were. Khalil couldn't help but notice the distressed look on the man's face when confronted with the prospects of butchering a young camel to feed even such an honored guest.

"No need, my friend," Khalil declined the sacrificial offer. "I have no taste for camel tonight."

To be sure, he was tired and hungry after his long ride. He began to eat the bowl of rice drenched in clarified butter an old woman brought him. Even then he wondered if others, women and children, would go without in order to feed him, but outright refusal of so miserly a meal would have been tantamount to an insult.

As the circle of men consumed their meal, an unvoiced

question burned as brightly as the fire, a question that by protocol could not be asked for three days. Why was he there?

"I am searching for a woman," he explained without prompting, noting that the uneaten portions in his bowl were carefully set aside and not thrown to the dogs. "A beautiful woman with blue eyes and pale hair."

"I am sorry, but we have seen no such woman, oh, great one," the other sheikh assured, "but should we, I would send a messenger to Dir'iyyah without delay."

And so, he had been right. Chelsea was not in Ad Dawadimi. There was no reason not to believe the old Bedouin. So, where did he go from here? He lifted his hands and warmed them in front of the fire as meager as the people crowded about it. She could be anywhere, have gone a thousand different directions. One infinitesimal grain of sand in the endless desert, impossible to find, even if he searched for a thousand years.

But find her, he must. Find her, he would. Even if he spent the rest of his life looking for her. It was his heart, once lost, that spoke now, without reason.

A bleak thought overtook his determination. Would he perhaps one day stumble upon her bleached bones in the sand?

If Allah would grant him only one wish, it would be that she be safe and alive, no matter where she had gone.

Chelsea's moment to prove her skills as a physician came almost immediately.

Wrapped in the inadequate protection of her *abaaya,* she huddled as close to the camp fire as allowed, seeking the little bit of warmth it afforded. How did all of these men manage to ignore the freezing gusts of wind?

Just like they ignored her. Laughing, they ate their food, never once offering her any. Finally she resigned herself to the discomforts, both the cold and the hunger, willing her eyelids closed. There, in that state between wakefulness and sleep, she heard the cries. It took her a few moments to realize they were real and not part of a dream. Someone was injured.

Rising with a calmness she did not feel on the inside, she waited, knowing her guard would never allow her to venture out of the glow of the camp fire. Wondering just what the emergency would be, she fought down the panic. Not that she couldn't handle almost any emergency under the proper circumstances. It was just that she didn't have anything to work with, not even a basic medical bag. All of the precious supplies she had brought with her had been lost in the struggle in Riyadh.

"What happened?" she demanded when her patient was carried in and dumped unceremoniously at her feet. A quick assessment showed no broken bones.

"He was guarding the horses. Snake bite."

"Where?"

"On his ankle."

Time was of the essence. With so little light it was hard to distinguish the tiny punctures, but at her insistence the men all moved back from the flickering fire to give her as much as possible. Once she located the twin marks, she laid them bare.

"Give me your knife," she said, sticking out her hand.

The man's friend would have obeyed without question if his leader had not caught his hand.

"What kind of deception is this, woman?" the old sheikh asked.

"No deception. I can save his life, unless you continue to interfere. But I must hurry if I am to extract the poison in time."

However her hand was not as confident as her voice. It shook as it accepted the heavy knife and quickly passed it through the flames to sterilize it. When she made the crude but necessary incisions on the man's ankle the audible gasps around her nearly made her hand slip.

Then when she put her mouth to the wounds and sucked out the poison, spitting it out on the ground, she knew her observers had no idea what to think.

Magic, no doubt, they would assume. Well, let them assume whatever they wanted.

She sat back, staring down at that dirty ankle she had just put against her lips. Unable to master the urge, she wiped her mouth with the back of her hand, but then her attention returned to her patient's needs. What she wouldn't give for a packet of adhesive bandaging about now. She had nothing, not even a clean strip of material to bind up the crisscross cuts, no antiseptic to cleanse them with. Even if he did survive the snake bite, he might die of an infection.

Picking up the knife again, she held it in the fire, until the handle became almost too hot to hang on to. Then she placed the flat of the broad blade against the wounds, cauterizing them.

The man screamed and then fainted. She presumed that was the drama the onlookers waited for. Their murmurs of approval filled the night air, and they drifted away, resuming their meal so abruptly abandoned.

No pain, no gain. Such was their Neanderthal motto, it seemed, she thought with disgust.

"He will live?" It was the sheikh's voice, devoid of emotion, that asked the question.

"He should."

"Good. Then so shall you," he stated as matter-of-factly as if he had given her the time of day. He, too, moved off.

No expression of gratitude. Not even an offer of payment.

Unless you considered the tasteless piece of unleavened bread that, as an afterthought, her guard tossed to her when the men finished eating. Only by sheer luck did she manage to catch it before it hit the ground. Starving as she was, she devoured every smidgeon as if it were a gourmet meal, even retrieving the crumbs that dropped down the front of her clothing.

God, it seemed she was becoming no better than these barbarians. Her gaze leveled on her captors with a loathing that included herself, keeping her mind alert and active.

Through the night she sat in silent vigilance, shivering in the cocoon of her black shroud, cursing her own stupidity, her selfishness. She felt dirty, abandoned, helpless, an utter fool. She had worked so hard to gain her freedom. Look where it had gotten her. Deeper in trouble than before. And Jamal. Oh, Jamal. The guilt of knowing she was responsible for what had happened to him as well overwhelmed her.

What was she going to do? What was she going to do? Hugging her knees, she rocked to the repetitious rhythm of her unanswered question.

At the moment she could do little but bide her time

and resign herself to fate. Hope, that positive outlook that had gotten her so far in life, seemed futile now. She could think of not one reasonable thing to hope for other than a quick and painless death.

For Khalil, the next morning brought no ready solution to his problem. He awoke, refused all but coffee from his host, and departed the poor settlement without a clue as to where he would go from there.

But as he rode out into the desert, Shiha made the choice for him. When the mare instinctively headed in the direction of home, he did not try to change its course. Instead he took the animal's actions as a sign from Allah.

At this point to continue an unorganized search made little sense. The logical thing to do was to return to Dir'iyyah. From there he could send out messengers in all directions, offering a reward for information leading to Chelsea. Someone somewhere had to have seen her. The enticement of payment more often than not unsealed even the most soldered, loyal lips.

His was a good plan, one that should have satisfied even those insatiable feelings of frustration that drove him to do whatever it took to find her. However, the dissatisfaction lingered.

Chelsea. Like a hot desert wind tearing at the fabric of who and what he was, the memories of her eyes, her touch, her laugh, left him breathless and suffering a pain that he knew would not release him until he held her in his arms once more.

Although obsessed, bewitched, vulnerable as no free Bedouin should be, he had never felt more alive. He had a need, wonderful yet frightening to a man accustomed to being in control. A need beyond his responsibilities, a need only for himself, a need to be fulfilled at any cost.

Urging the mare to a faster pace, he vowed never to rest until he found his woman and made her recognize that her own needs were as strong as the ones that possessed him. Whether she realized it or not, he had imprinted his mark upon her as indelibly as she had branded him. They were tied forever in a manner that no distance, time or circumstances could ever sever.

Dare he label this bond between them for what it was? The one emotion that frightened even the bravest of men. Love. Oh, destroyer of paladins and conquerors, annihilator of nations, why did it seek him out?

Allah help them both for succumbing to the human frailties of both body and soul when so much more than just themselves was at stake.

No glorious ride into the Rashaad winter encampment like when Khalil had carried her off from Ad Dawadimi, Chelsea was forced to walk, humbled and degraded. When she refused, they beat her, not merely threatened, without regard to the fact that she had just saved the life of one of their ranks the evening before.

Given no other viable choice, she walked. Often she stumbled, but she always picked herself up, refusing to cry out or to let these . . . men, if she could call them that, see that she suffered from their callous, cruel mistreatment. Suffering at the hands of men was nothing new to her. Still, this was different. This was life and death.

Cold, footsore, exhausted, hungry to the point of de-

325

lirium, she wilted into a black heap before the equally black tent, totally insensitive to the covert stares and comments her arrival caused. For the longest time no one bothered her, didn't even check to make sure she was still alive. She could have easily frozen to death, not that it was actually cold enough, for all that any of them seemed to care.

Then, at long last, someone roused her, none too gently, with a nudge in her ribcage.

"Get up."

She didn't want to and didn't bother to respond.

The nudge became sharp, repeated jabs that she couldn't continue to ignore.

"Leave me alone," she murmured with irritation.

"If given the choice, I would, but you are my responsibility now."

Chelsea looked up into the covered face of a woman. Old or young, she couldn't tell by the slits through which two dark, glossy eyes stared down at her.

"If you are hungry, I will feed you." There was nothing generous in the offer.

But hunger was a powerful master, one Chelsea couldn't combat. She rose, her legs, her entire body, stiff with prolonged abuse and then sudden inactivity.

The woman didn't bother to help her, just lifted the flap of the tent and stood there waiting for her to follow. A wave of what Chelsea could only describe as irresistible warmth, intense and wonderful in her state of cold, feathered the loose hairs about her face. The fire she could see glowing in the interior was an enticement she couldn't deny.

"Whose tent is this?" she asked, moving forward with an unsure gait.

326

"Sheikh Aziz ibn Sha'la. I am Umm Musaid, his first wife."

Once inside, she moved forward, hands outstretched to the flames. But the woman touched her arm, and when Chelsea looked at her, she shook her head.

"For the men only," the woman informed her. "This way."

Through a curtain.

The women's quarters, of course. She should have expected that. Then an overwhelming memory of her first, unforgettable encounter with the *hareem* of a sheikh caused her to pause. If the need should arise, she was in no condition to defend herself.

But she received only curious stares that quickly diverted when a well-picked-over platter of food was brought in. It was like watching dogs fighting over a pile of bones already stripped by buzzards. The women squabbled and squawked, their cries of indignation mingling with those of triumph. If eating meant acting like that. . . .

But it was Umm Musaid who ended the discord. She lifted her veil to reveal a face well lined with age and, most likely, misfortune. Taking up a bowl without argument from the others, she filled it from the platter with what looked like half-baked, mostly burnt rice cakes, and brought it along with a cup of water to Chelsea, who didn't miss the seditious looks she got for such special treatment.

At the moment she didn't particularly care what this pack of she-wolves thought of her. Guarding her bowl with her life if she must, she moved off into a corner and began to eat, blindly at first, just filling her mouth to assuage the discomfort in her stomach.

After the first few bites, she began to take note of the taste, the texture of the pasty concoction. Odd. It had a distinctive flavor that reminded her of spinach, but it was gritty, sometimes even crunchy. She reached into her mouth to remove one of those unidentified crispies. When she glanced down to inspect it, she felt the food she had just swallowed rise back up into her throat. What was that dubious-looking thing? A bug part? To be more specific, a grasshopper's hind leg?

Okay, so one little bug had gotten into the supply of flour, and she had just been unfortunate enough to get it. As hungry as she was, did it really matter? She ate peanut butter, and she'd heard the horror stories of what ended up in that.

She glanced suspiciously at the strange women all around her. Maybe they had given it to her on purpose, a joke of some kind. But no one seemed particularly interested in her anymore.

Then she stared down into the bowl, focusing on the limp dough patties. There was another leg and another, and that looked like a piece of a wing.

Horrified, she spat the mouthful of food back into the bowl and dropped it on the floor. She drank the water in one mighty gulp, trying to get rid of the lingering taste on her tongue.

Everyone looked at her.

"What's wrong?" Umm Musaid demanded, hurrying over to join her.

"Look." She pointed at the bowl, where she could see even more disgusting evidence.

The Arabian woman looked, too, but expressed not the slightest surprise.

"Surely you can't expect me to eat food with ground-up grasshoppers in it?" Chelsea asked with indignation.

The twitters of amusement all around her didn't go unnoticed. So this was some kind of cruel prank, and she stared back up at the woman to confirm it.

"Locust are better than nothing. Either you eat what I have given you, or you do not eat at all." Umm Musaid's expression, calm and unruffled, showed not the slightest sign of humor or of relenting.

She may have fallen to the lowest point in her life ever. But eating bugs? Never. She would rather starve to death than degrade herself in the most unimaginable way.

When the Arab woman picked up her bowl and marched away, not giving her the chance to change her mind, Chelsea realized that starving to death was probably where she was headed. So be it. At least she still had her dignity, if nothing else.

A commotion erupted across the tent, a messenger of some kind who went directly to Umm Musaid.

Then everyone was looking at her.

"What is it?" she asked in a small, uncertain voice.

"Our sheikh. He is demanding your company for this evening."

Chelsea glanced around at all the feminine faces which glared back at her with a mixture of hatred and jealousy. Who were they? The old sheikh's wives and concubines?

So what did that make her?

No doubt, his latest acquisition.

Her gaze darted about, looking for a means of escape.

Oh, God, just give her back the bugs. She would eat them if only that would save her from a fate far worse than death.

Seventeen

At the distant thunder of hooves, the startled hunting falcon took wing from Khalil's gauntleted fist. Overhead, the bird's mournful cry served as a warning to any who listened. Abandoning what had been a halfhearted attempt to train the young tiercel, he turned over his glove to the master falconer and made his way to an opening between the tents that would give him a clearer view of the ridge. Whoever approached, it could not possibly be one of his messengers returned, for they had only departed the encampment hours before. Still, he knew the commotion had something to do with Chelsea.

The horse, an old battle-scarred mare, came to a halt, its sides heaving with exhaustion as it lowered its head. The animal had been ridden too hard and too long. But what concerned him the most was the battered figure that slid from its back and landed in a heap at his feet.

The *hadhar.*

His heart skipped a beat as he scanned the full spectrum of the horizon in the direction from which the lone rider had come. Chelsea. Where was she? Why was she not with Jamal? What disaster had befallen her in the vast, unforgiving desert? The possibilities were endless and unthinkable.

Dropping to his knees, he rolled the young Arab over. Was he dead, the precious knowledge only he possessed forever silenced?

Khalil shook the blood-soaked figure, relieved to discover the chest rising and falling. When he didn't get an immediate response, he mercilessly jounced the injured man once more.

A moan. Then blood-crusted lashes fluttered and parted.

"Ya ràyyis, thank Allah I have found you," Jamal whispered through the obvious pain.

"Chelsea," he demanded. "Where is she?"

When it seemed the *hadhar* would faint again before answering, Khalil shook him harder.

It did him no good. Frustrated, he released the unconscious man, allowing him to drop back on the ground, unsure what to do when it came to caring for the injured. If Chelsea were here, she would know. He missed her more than ever.

"Yusaf. Find that useless, old physician right away and bring him to me," he ordered the gathering crowd. Then he scooped up Jamal's slight body and carried him into his own tent.

He did not argue when the women emerged from their quarters and took over, bathing the young man's bloodied face. However, he found it impossible to just stand there and watch. So he began to pace.

"Where is Yusaf?" he bellowed when the seconds turned into unbearable minutes. "I swear I will cut off his miserable head if he does not get here soon."

"Patience, oh, nephew. Ranting and raving will not

make his old legs move any faster. Nor will it bring the woman back to you."

Angrily, he stared at his aunt's restraining hand. Although he recognized the truth in what she said, it did not make the waiting any easier, nor did it alleviate the regrets for the way he had treated Chelsea.

The *hadhar* stirred and moaned incoherently. Kneeling beside him, Khalil reached out to shake him, but Umm Taif stopped him.

"It is best if he comes around on his own."

Oh, how he resented the interfering old woman, but he knew she was right.

"Ya ràyyis, you must go after her."

"Where, Jamal?" He grasped the injured man's shoulders. "Where is she?"

But the *hadhar* was gone again, and no amount of rousing would awaken him.

The front flap of the tent lifted. Khalil looked up, anticipating with impatience to see Yusaf shuffle inside, whining about his age and infirmities. Instead of the old physician, one of his trusted men entered.

"Well, where is Yusaf?" he demanded.

"It seems the old man has . . . disappeared."

"Disappeared? Where could he have gone?"

The man shook his head. "No one has seen him since yesterday."

Yusaf. Had the foolish man managed to fall into the *wadi* and drowned himself? It was the most logical explanation, for he never left camp on his own. Usually he was underfoot, making a whining nuisance of himself. Khalil thought back. Since Chelsea's arrival he had not seen that much of the physician, but admittedly had not considered it that important. Allah only knew what the crazy old coot had been up to during that period of time.

Nothing, of course. Yusaf had been loyal to Khalil since his arrival all those years before, the physician to a peevish mistress. Tuëma. He had never expressed a single sentiment when she had been sent away; in fact, he had seemed almost relieved to be rid of so cruel a mistress.

Time enough later to look for the lost old man.

Chelsea was out there somewhere. She needed him. Of that he was positive. If only he had a clue as to where to begin looking for her.

She could refuse to go with them, she supposed, analyzing the situation as if she had options. Chances were they would only drag her unwilling.

But then she looked and probably smelt so horrid, what man in his right mind would want her? It was a logic quickly dashed. She had to remember that she dealt with a people with the mentality of goats. They ate grasshoppers, didn't they? God only knew what else they did or didn't do. Personal hygiene probably was not high on their list of priorities.

What a contrast between these Rashaad and Khalil's people, who ate and dressed well by comparison and kept themselves clean.

She had thought desert people all the same. How very wrong she had been. Such an assumption could cost her dearly in the end. The end. Oh, God. By all indications, her end was close at hand.

Confronting such impossible odds, she couldn't begin to explain the feelings that welled inside of her, a sense of pride not only in herself, but in the fact that she represented a superior tribe. In truth that was what she was, a representative of the Durra. Whatever the Rashaad planned to do with her, she was determined to face it with dignity.

With an air of affected superiority, she rose, dusted herself off, and lifted her chin. Somehow she would find a way to convince this rival chieftain that she was far more valuable to him as a physician than—dare she even think it?—a concubine.

Oh, Khalil, Khalil. What have I done? This was what you tried to protect me from, wasn't it? My own ignorant folly.

Her questions went unanswered. No doubt, Khalil didn't know where she was. Even if he did, why would he care what became of her? She had run away from him, her troubles of her own making. Could she really blame him if he chose not to chase after her again? The fact remained, she had left not only herself open to attack, but him as well with her thoughtless actions.

What was she thinking? Had her brain fried in the intensity of the desert sun? How could she of all people validate such chauvinistic nonsense that a woman's actions reflected against the men she associated with?

Honor, she realized, or the lack of it, was what this was all about. The only reason the Rashaad chieftain would care to harm or debase her was because of her connection with Khalil.

They were enemies. Exactly why, she wasn't sure, but she sensed what lay between these two men went deeper than petty tribal rivalry.

Pushed from behind, she stumbled forward. Apparently she had stalled for as long as they were going to allow her to. Her escorts, both fierce-looking warriors, took her by the arms and marched her forward.

The sacrificial lamb led to slaughter, she thought, swallowing down an outrageous impulse to laugh at the irony of it all. How had she, Chelsea Browne of Atlanta, Georgia, gotten herself into such a fix?

But worse. As much as she despised herself for displaying typical female weakness, the only name she could think to call out in her moment of abject terror—Khalil. Brave and strong, a chauvinist through and through, he would never stand by and allow these men to harm her.

If he knew. If he cared.

Khalil, her heart cried out to him over and over.

She couldn't possibly expect an answer, or a knight in shining armor to come to her rescue, and yet she strained to catch the sound of his comforting baritone among the many masculine voices she could hear beyond the dividing curtain. What a relief to know the old sheikh was not alone. Surely, even he was not so crude as to try and have his way with her in front of a crowd. For the moment at least, she felt relatively safe.

"I swear to you, *ya ràyyis,* I have told you only the truth and all that I know. My loyalty is only to you. Always and forever. I will not fail you."

An unidentified figure cowered facedown in front of the Rashaad chieftain, who sat casually draped across a camel saddle, Bedouin style. Although her lip curled in dislike, her eyes were drawn back to the prostrate man. Odd. That high-pitched whine sounded vaguely familiar.

"I do not question your loyalty, old man, only your judgment. I find it hard to believe that . . ." Mid-sentence, the sheikh looked up. Spying Chelsea, he spread his weathered lips into a gap-toothed smile. "Ah, my beauty, here you are, at last. Come forward, come forward." He gyrated his hand in invitation.

She didn't move. She couldn't, for her gaze remained fixed on the face of the man kneeling before the Rashaad.

"Bring her here to me," the chieftain ordered.

The guards dragged her forward and deposited her at the sheikh's feet.

Face-to-face with Yusaf, the old physician from Khalil's encampment, she cast him a suspicious look. What was he doing here? Consorting with the enemy?

Never in his life had Khalil cared so much if another human being lived or died—other than his son. It was not compassion, but a driving, selfish need that kept him stationed day and night beside the still figure of the *hadhar*, willing him to come about, to just open his eyes long enough to tell him where he could locate Chelsea.

He even found himself ignoring the presence of Rakia, his cousin, whom he had banished from his sight. The woman tended to Jamal's every need with a tenderness that could not be mistaken. One of his with a *hadhar?* He would have to think about that, long and hard.

But that wasn't the only problem to consider. No sign of Yusaf had been found yet. If he had drowned, they would have discovered his bloated body floating in the *wadi* by now. Khalil assumed something else had happened to the old man.

A nagging concern festered like an old knife wound deep in his gut. Yusaf's strange disappearance somehow had something to do with Chelsea. But such a notion seemed so impossible that he refused to give it credence.

He stood and began to pace. Already there was a path worn in the carpeting on the floor of the tent from his constant walking. Rakia, who sat patiently replenishing cool compresses across her patient's hot forehead, watched him only for a moment before resuming her duties.

Never in his life had he felt so helpless and utterly useless. He felt like a woman, waiting, waiting.

Was that what love did to men, even the strongest of men, turned them into simpering females? No wonder the wise never succumbed to the siren's song of the heart.

Spinning on his heels, he marched toward the exit of the tent. He couldn't stand the inactivity for another moment. He must do anything to make it seem as if he were accomplishing something.

Outside, he sucked in a lungful of crisp night air. The sky was starless, moonless, a black void as vast as his own heart.

"Chelsea. Chelsea," he cried out, not caring who might hear his mournful plea.

In the distance, the scream of a desert wildcat answered just as forlorn. Did that beast call for its mate, too?

"Ya ràyyis? The hadhar."

He turned to discover Rakia standing before him. The fact she had spoken had taken great courage.

"Yes, yes. What is it, woman?"

Had she lost her tongue? Why didn't she speak? Had Jamal awoken . . . or had he died?

337

Khalil rushed back toward the tent, brushing the dumb-struck woman out of his way.

The questions on her tongue burned to be asked, but there was no opportunity. Throughout the ordeal she kept glancing at Yusaf from the corner of her eye, but she never once saw him look back at her. She could only assume they were in the same boat, both there unwillingly. To cooperate was their only option at the moment. Unlike the cowardly old man, she would never pledge an allegiance to the horrid Rashaad, whether truth or lie, not even to save her life.

To make such a pledge was never asked of her. In fact, she had no idea why she was there. No one spoke to her, or even seemed to notice her presence, except when another group of men was ushered into the tent and treated like honored guests. They looked at her all right, spoke in whispers she could not decipher, leaving her even more curious than before.

Ignored once more, she ever so slowly began to scoot closer to Yusaf. Soon she was only a few feet from where he sat, a part of the circle of men and yet far enough outside to not be noticed.

"What is going on?" she whispered, craning forward so that only the old physician could hear her, hopefully. The others were talking so loudly among themselves, she was pretty sure of success.

"Shh." He shot her the most incredulous look over his shoulder.

Surprised, she sat back to escape the intensity of his glare, but she wasn't willing to give up so easily. When he turned back around, she leaned toward him again.

"You cannot imagine how relieved I am to see you here," she said in all sincerity.

The withering look he gave her showed he did not reciprocate her feelings.

What was wrong with Yusaf? They had had their differences, but they were both on the same side now. He should be just as glad to see her as she was to see him. She studied the back of his head. There had been all of that business about him vowing loyalty to the Rashaad. Surely, he hadn't meant what he had said.

Did he plan to betray Khalil?

She frowned. Perhaps, he already had.

"Woman, I said come forward."

Jarred from her reverie, she looked up to find that everyone was staring at her, even old Yusaf, whose sour expression offered no encouragement at all. Like a schoolgirl caught napping, she scrambled to her feet. Chelsea made no other move to obey the sheikh's curt order, but when the guards started coming her way, she voluntarily threaded a path through the gathering of men.

She no more reached the center of the circle when she noticed the litter being carried into the tent from the outside. Instincts immediately took over, and she hurried to meet the entourage.

There were no words to describe the poor woman lying on her stomach on the makeshift stretcher. Even the strongest constitution was tested by the putrid smell, the oozing wound that ran the length of the spine. Cancer in the final stages, beyond help or even relief, at least here in this desert oasis.

She lifted her face to voice her opinion and realized what the looks of anticipation meant. Surely, they didn't

339

expect her to simply snap her fingers and heal this poor creature.

But it seemed that was exactly what they did expect.

Turning an imploring gaze on Yusaf, she found, if not sympathy there, then at least comprehension. Apparently he waited for her to fail.

She focused once more on the patient. Never in her life had she felt more helpless or inadequate. God, she didn't even have a bandage strip with her. Without her medical supplies and sophisticated equipment Chelsea Browne, physician, at least in the eyes of these people, was no more than a fraud.

She glanced out over the waiting crowd. What would they do to her when they came to that inevitable conclusion?

"Father! Father!"

Khalil turned from saddling his horse to watch his beloved son race toward him—alive, healthy once more, if still a little weak.

"Is it true that you go on a raid?" The boy's eyes, so like his mother's, stared up at him in expectation.

"Yes, it is true," he replied, resuming the task of preparation.

"Then, let me come with you. I am old enough to be blooded on *ghazzu.*" Muhammad thumped his small chest with pride.

"No." This was to be no normal raid to steal camels and horses. He went after a woman, a disreputable act to violate *hareem* seclusion. He did not want his one and only heir endangered or tainted by his dishonor.

340

"That is not fair, Father. You were no older than I when you went on your first raid."

That was true, but that was different, and he had almost been killed. He knew the boy would never understand.

"The answer is still no, Muhammad."

"But, Father."

Wallahi! This should be a moment of pride for him, of shared camaraderie between father and son, planning their strategy, not an argument. Frustrated, Khalil cinched the saddle girth a bit too forcefully. Shiha grunted a protest and danced away.

"There is to be no honor in this raid, my son. I promise I will make it up to you." He paused and looked down, trying to convey his regrets, but he knew it would never be quite the same for either of them.

"Then, it is to be war with my grandfather?" The boy's eyes widened with seriousness.

"That will be up to him." Khalil mounted his war mare, waiting for the others to follow suit.

"Chelsea?" Muhammad clutched his leg, staring up at him. "Is she to take the place of my mother?"

Only one so young would have asked so blunt a question. It deserved an honest answer.

"I do not know that, either, my son."

And then he turned and looked out over the unrelenting desert, accepting how very little he did know.

"I will be back," he said, looking down once more.

"You will be victorious."

Khalil smiled, and clasped hands with the boy in the age-old grip of brotherhood. Only a fool would discount the prophecy of one so innocent.

Then he put heels to horseflesh, leading the band of

well-seasoned raiders into the desert, confident his son was safe.

Physician, heal thyself.

Chelsea had always harbored disdain for that bit of ancient philosophy, until now. The wounds of inadequacy struck deep as she carefully examined the little girl, terribly thin, yet her belly bloated.

"Does she eat well?" she asked of the mother.

"Everything she can put in her mouth," the Arab woman replied from behind the cover of her veil, "and she's always hungry."

"Does she have the flux?"

The woman nodded.

Chelsea carefully prodded the child's stomach again, noting how hard it was.

"She probably has worms."

Oh, it was easy enough to make the diagnosis, but then came the hard part. If she'd had her medical supplies, there were pills she could have given the child to rid her of the infestation. But without the medication . . . she had no idea what to do.

While the mother waited expectantly, she could only stare back in silence.

Then just like with the old woman and the half dozen other patients she had been taken to see, Yusaf came up with the remedy.

Well, if not exactly the cure, at least a treatment that was far superior to what she could do, which was nothing. He made her look like a fool.

It seemed that was his intention all along.

Like all of the times before, he opened his camel-hair

satchel, extracting mortar and pestle in which he ground up a mixture of unidentified leaves, stems, and other plant parts. Again she succumbed to the urge to ask him what they were.

"Betony, serpentwood." He added a bit more out of one pouch. "A touch of garlic." Filling a small sack, he handed it to the woman. "Steep and give the drink to the child every day for a week," he directed.

Herbal medicine. She knew very little about it, and like most doctors tended to discount its validity.

"Surely that can't do much good," she scoffed.

"You would be surprised, *Duktur*, at its effectiveness." The old man scrutinized her, then shrugged. "Enough that I keep using it. I do not have any magic pills from the future. I must depend upon what is available to me."

The spoken truth stung along with his obvious dislike.

"Yusaf, why are you helping me when it is so apparent you do not . . . approve of me?"

"Perhaps where you come from it is not the custom to put the patient's interest first. But here . . . now, it is a physician's duty." He began to pack his bag. "My personal likes or approval have nothing to do with it." Undisguised bitterness tainted his voice.

"And what of the old woman with the cancer? Even you must admit the salve you gave her will do little good."

"Hassa?" He paused to stare at her. "She is the sister of the sheikh." He stashed away his mortar and pestle. "I have told Aziz there are some things no physician can do, and rightly so. Sometimes death is what is best, not only for the patient, but for all those around them." He gave her what could only be construed as a warning look. "He did not believe me. He will now."

343

"Is that why I was brought here by the Rashaad? To prove a point?"

The old man didn't answer, just closed up his satchel and slowly stood.

"Why am I here, Yusaf?" she demanded, following him to the tent entrance where they had a moment alone. Suddenly she sensed that it was more than sheer coincidence that the rival tribe leader had stumbled upon her in Riyadh.

"You should have stayed where you belong, woman, in your own time, your own place. Umm Taif, meddling old witch, should never have tampered with what should have been. The child's fate was sealed, and then you interfered. But now, with you out of the way, events can once again take their natural course."

"What are you saying?" A terrible fear ricocheted through her. "That Muhammad's illness was no accident?"

"Does it matter now? You saved him."

"But he had typhoid fever," she pressed, clinging to her skepticism. "Such disease cannot be conjured up from the thin air. There had to be a point of contamination. How and where, I've not yet figured out, but I have racked my brain to understand why only those four boys came down with such a contagious disease and no one else in the encampment."

"Anything, even death, can be bought in the *souq* of Riyadh."

"Yusaf, are you saying someone intentionally gave those little boys something to make them sick, to kill them? Why?" she demanded. "Who would want to do something so heinous?"

The why might not be clear, or even the how, but when

she looked into the old man's steady gaze, the who was only too obvious.

"You? Yusaf, why?"

"The fate of those children is not your concern, nor is it mine. There are far greater concerns that affect us all. You should just be thankful to have survived thus far, Chelsea Browne, woman *duktur.*" He snorted. "There are those who think killing you now would be in the best interest of all. But I say you possess a well of great knowledge to be siphoned off first." He leaned toward her, and put his hand on her shoulder, as if he had more to say and it was of vital importance.

What happened next would always be a blur in her mind.

That someone entered the tent from behind her was clear. The mother of the child screamed, and when Chelsea turned to investigate what upset the woman, she saw the glittering, curved blade of the scimitar descending toward her.

There was no time to duck, not even a moment to consider such evasive action. Odd. She was unbelievably calm as she contemplated death. In fact, it might even be a relief.

The *whoosh* of the blade rang in her ears, and it took her a few moments to realize she had not been touched. She spun back around and stared dumbfounded at the headless figure standing before her, whose hand still rested on her shoulder. The fingers clamped down hard, so much she flinched in pain, dislodging them.

Even as she watched, Yusaf's decapitated body crumpled toward the ground in surrealistic slow motion.

"Yusaf!" she screamed, reaching out to catch him. Trapped from behind, her arms mercilessly pinned to her back, she was dragged out of the tent. The last image she had of the dead man was his sightless eyes staring up at her from the ground in frozen terror.

Hustled across the Rashaad encampment, she was once more tossed at the feet of the old sheikh. He said nothing, merely sat there, drumming his fingers against his raised knee, contemplating her as she silently wept for an old man whose death should mean nothing to her. But it did. Even the fact he had been the enemy all along did nothing to alleviate her grief. No one should die like that.

She lifted her face to the Rashaad chieftain, his cool gaze raking her without a shred of emotion. She knew then who was behind Yusaf's actions, who wanted the boy dead, even if his reasons were not so clear.

Somehow she had to escape, had to make her way back to Khalil, to warn him. Not only for her own sake, but for Muhammad's, whose life might still be in imminent danger.

Eighteen

The guard posted outside the tent to watch over her was either a fool or an idiot. It was nothing more than a matter of waiting patiently until he settled down, his back to the door, and then slipping up behind him. Chelsea swung the piece of firewood she had fished from the flames in a wide arc, then diverted her eyes so that she didn't have to watch as she brought the makeshift weapon down on top of the poor man's unsuspecting head.

With a quiet grunt, he collapsed face forward in the sand, unconscious.

Thank goodness he was not a tall man, otherwise the hems of his *thobe* and *mishlah* when she put them on might have dragged along the ground and tripped her up. Adding his *keffiyeh* on her head and his wicked-looking scimitar at her side, she hoped to pass, at least at a quick glance in the night, as a male, one of the Rashaad. She prayed the disguise would be enough to get her by undetected.

When it came to a plan, Chelsea admitted she really didn't have one. Once before she had absconded with a horse. She banked on being able to do so again.

Without even a ribbon of moon to guide her, she groped her way in the darkness, darting from the concealment of one tent to another, as silently as a shadow. Once, she stumbled over a tent stake, fell facedown in the bits of rock and shard, biting her tongue to keep from crying out. The heels of her hands sticky with blood, she picked herself up and continued on her way, undaunted by the minor setback and more determined than ever.

She didn't even think about what she would do once she managed to catch a horse. Without any proper tack, just the hand-fashioned bridle she had hastily constructed from some strips of cloth she had ripped from a dividing curtain, to snag and mount one of the headstrong mares would be a feat in itself. Then she would have to figure out which way to go. Her only hope—to locate the mare she had taken from Khalil's encampment in the first place, unhobble her, and trust that she would make a beeline toward home.

It was not an unreasonable assumption. Horses had an uncanny sense of direction and an even stronger herding instinct. She just simply had to find that ornery mare and hope for the best. But no matter what happened, she had decided that taking her chances in the desert was far better than remaining at the mercy of such barbaric people. Faced with the unfavorable odds of getting back to Khalil and warning him of the danger his son was in, she continued on her way.

Once she passed the last cluster of tents, she released her pent-up breath, pausing to stare out over the wide open stretch between her and her objective.

The herd was out there, not far away; she could hear them, their hooves muffled in the sand as they hobbled

348

along on three legs, their soft snorts as they ferreted out every overlooked blade or leaf of edible vegetation.

Then they must have caught a whiff of her. Their nickers quickened with alarm to whinnies, mistaking her for some prowling predator. They began to mill about uneasily.

"Whoa," she called softly, clicking with her tongue until the herd grew calm once more. A three-legged stampede was the last thing she needed. Besides, there were the posted guards to be concerned about. She didn't want them to become suspicious and decide to check out what had stirred up the horses.

Hunkering down, she darted forward, her long strides carrying her quickly over the open space. Once again she almost fell on her face when she caught the hem of her masculine clothing with her toe. Without thought of modesty, she gathered the flying robes up over her bare knees and kept on running.

Knowing them to be curious beasts, she wasn't the least bit surprised when the horses gathered about the stranger in their midst, nosing her with dew-covered muzzles that left her face wet and no doubt dirty. Even as a little girl she had discovered this was a form of communication between themselves, alternately sniffing and blowing in each other's nostrils, a sign of nonaggression. Mimicking the ritual with each new investigator, soon she was accepted. Finally, ignored by all, she felt free to move amongst the herd that had once more returned to the serious business of grazing. During that time, her eyes had grown accustomed to the lack of light.

Now to find that one horse in hundreds. God, she prayed that the law of averages gave her a break just this once. Oh, there were plenty of dark horses, some with stockings and blazes, but none with the exact configuration of the mare she had taken from Khalil's encampment. At least she was fortunate enough that the stark whiteness of the markings stood out even in the relative darkness. Tenaciously she continued her search, weaving in and out of the great bodies with a confidence born of familiarity. She was safe from being trampled as long as they remained calm.

A suluki dog barked and then another. To her left the herd startled, creating a domino effect of nervous, unpredictable activity. The horse she had been inspecting stepped back, stomping down on her sandal. Pain shot throughout her trapped foot and up her leg. Chelsea somehow managed to choke back the cry of anguish that formed in her throat.

It took a few moments that seemed like hours to her tortured flesh to convince the confused animal to step forward again, releasing her. Unable to do more than limp, she managed to dodge several more hooves, making her way to a small outcrop of rocks that afforded her a little protection. Squatting down, she took just a moment to inspect her injured foot. It was not broken, but it would be swollen and bruised come morning. She prayed she wouldn't have to do any long-range walking anytime soon.

From her hiding place, she glanced out over the restless herd, wondering what had stirred them up. The dogs set to barking again, so very close, and then they grew suspiciously quiet.

Had she been discovered? If so, she was determined to fight with every ounce of strength she had to keep from being taken back into the Rashaad encampment.

Heart beating wildly, she waited to see what would occur next.

When nothing happened, and the animals around her began to calmly crop the short winter vegetation once more, she wasted no time venturing forward to continue her search.

She couldn't believe her fortune when she actually found the mare with the four matched stockings and off-center blaze.

"Whoa, girl." Double-checking to make sure she wasn't mistaken, she fastened the makeshift bridle to the horse's head before reaching down to release the hobble. Then, remembering how unruly the mare had been the first time she caught it, she decided instead to mount before giving the animal its freedom.

Clutching a fistful of mane, she gingerly swung up onto the horse's broad back, careful not to put too much weight on her injured foot. Comfortably astride, she tested her makeshift bridle that at best could only steer the mare, not stop her. But then once they were on their way she had no intention of trying to slow her down. As prepared as she could hope to be, she bent over to release the hobble strap.

The hands that grabbed her from behind about the waist dragged Chelsea from her seat as if she weighed no more than a feather. She started to scream, more in outright rage at being thwarted when she had been so close to success than in thoughts of sounding an alarm. The palm that clamped over her nose and mouth didn't give her the opportunity, as if it anticipated what she might do.

Remembering her vow not to go down without putting up a good fight, she began to struggle, reaching back to dig her claws into unprotected skin and lifting her good foot to kick behind her. The repeated grunts and curses of her captor left no doubt that she had inflicted as much pain as she'd received, but she refused to stop.

Then she felt the sharp blade press against her exposed throat. She weighed her options. Defeat was inevitable, death soon to follow, but she clung to every precious moment of life, unwilling to get it over with as quickly as possible.

"Do not struggle so, my young and foolish friend. I do not wish to harm you, but I will if I must. We have come only to raid, nothing more, then we will leave your encampment in relative peace."

Was it possible or was she only dreaming. She knew that voice. Khalil! Khalil!

She struggled against his restraining hand, trying to remove it so that she could speak out, trying to turn about in his arms to confront him.

He misinterpreted her actions for stubbornness and mercilessly clamped down on her face harder, cutting off her access to air. She felt the razor-sharp steel dig deeper into her neck.

Why was he doing this to her? she cried in indignant anguish. Then she remembered her hastily donned disguise. Of course he must think her one of the hated Rashaad.

She went limp against the familiar warmth of his broad chest. Staring up into his handsome face, glittering with the same hardness as the knife he held at her throat, she feared he intended to suffocate her, then slit her throat and never even realize it was her. When the world and his beloved face began to slip in and out of focus, she struggled one last time, attempting to speak, to make him see the terrible mistake he made.

Just before total blackness set in, she was sure she glimpsed recognition in his dark, piercing eyes. Or maybe it was only her willful, distorted imagination that conjured up hope where there wasn't any.

"Chelsea!"

Khalil caught her limp, feather-light body and lowered it gently to the ground. What was she doing here, all alone, dressed as a man? *Wallahi!* Why did she do such outrageous, unwomanly things? With only a tad more provocation, for his taste for vengeance against the Rashaad was strong, he might have unknowingly slit her slender throat and left her there to bleed to death.

He brushed the dirt and grime from her pale, beautiful face, and against his will his anger subsided into begrudging respect and, finally, full-blown pride. Never had he known a woman of such valor and strength, nor of such determination. Were all women from the future so . . . extraordinary, or had he been fortunate in his choosing?

The need to possess this most perfect of women, to cradle her to his heart and never let her go, surged up inside of him with such force that he had to remind himself who and where he was, and that only a weak man would allow himself to feel so much for any woman.

Then she opened her eyes. Their blueness, the color of a spring sky, never failed to amaze him, and he found himself wanting to crawl inside their lovely depths and forsake the harsh demands of the world all around him, to cast aside all caution.

In response to his runaway emotions, he could have sworn he saw a flash of something in her spellbinding gaze akin to feminine devotion; but then whatever it was disappeared, or maybe he only imagined it to begin with. She now looked at him with that cold distrust that was such a natural part of her.

"What are you doing here?" she demanded.

I have come to rescue you, my lady fair, he had an overwhelming urge to reply, but for reasons only too clear, he hesitated.

"Ghazzu," he said instead, concealing his emotions behind an unwavering look. "My men and I have come to raid the Rashaad herds. They have some fine mares that I have wanted for a long time."

"You just ride in here and take another man's horses? That's theft," she accused. "I thought you Moslems frowned on stealing."

"Raiding is the Bedouin way of life." He stared at her, uncomfortable with the way she put him on the defense. "What about you?" He grabbed her by her slender shoulders and shook her. "How do you explain your unexpected presence here among my enemy? Or did you tire of them just as you tired of me?"

And there it was. That something between them forever inhibiting the unfolding of their hearts to each other, the unrelenting distrust they both harbored and could not relinquish. It flashed in her eyes once more. Did she see the same thing when she looked at him? A suspicion, a fear of becoming too vulnerable, of being betrayed?

Then she averted her gaze and looked beyond him, scanning the selected group of men he had brought with him.

354

"Muhammad? Is the boy here with you now?" she asked fervently.

Perplexed, he frowned. Why this sudden, unexplained interest in his son's whereabouts?

"He is much too young to go on raid." That lie like all of the others came easily. "Besides, he is still too weak."

"Is he sick again?" Her eyes clouded with undisguised worry.

"No, of course not." He rose, dismissing the subject of his son, confident it was only a diversion on her part. "Come, Chelsea. We had best hurry if we wish to get out of here without being noticed. I do assume you were leaving." He turned his back, thinking she would follow him; then he noticed she just sat there. What was she waiting for, foolish woman, for him to help her up?

After a moment he realized that was exactly what she expected. Even more ridiculous, he considered giving her what she demanded. What would his men think of such catering to a woman's whims? Then he noticed that she struggled to gain her feet, wincing when she put weight on her left leg. Ignoring the sacrifice he undoubtedly made, he stuck out his hand, offering her assistance.

"What of your raid, Khalil?" She stared at his outstretched hand, then shot him an indignant look before managing to scramble to her feet on her own. "Surely you have not forgotten the *only* reason you came here."

Wallahi! Why did she push him so? Why did she make him feel this need to prove himself as much to himself as to her? He glanced around at the milling herd, spotting an exceptional specimen of horseflesh, as white as the sands of the *al rabba al khali,* the barren lands, and as difficult, for the mare snorted and backed away, displaying all of the uncontrollable characteristics he normally shunned in a mount and in a woman. Quite frankly, he should have known better.

"That one," he said, pointing. "She will do quite nicely for me." He started forward with the intention of catching the animal. "Each of you make your selection," he said to his men, "but be quick about it."

The first moment that horse gave him trouble, he should have abandoned his attempt to take her, but his reasons for wanting her became manyfold, if not foolish.

Least of all, Chelsea was watching him. Clearly she found his inability to master the beast most entertaining. He would not be laughed at by a woman. Then there was the mare, itself. No-four-legged nag would ever get the better of him. And finally, if his memory served him right, this particular horse was the Rashaad chieftain's favorite mount. To steal it would be striking a blow to his enemy.

There was only so much resistance a hobbled horse could offer, but that mare made the challenge most infuriating, especially under the circumstances. When he finally captured the animal and led it back to the waiting group, no one uttered a single word. They did not have to. The amusement dancing in Chelsea's eyes said it all.

"We have gotten what we came for. Now we ride," he ordered without acknowledging the looks.

He made no attempt to help the ungrateful woman mount her horse; instead he concentrated on keeping the vicious Rashaad mare from nipping Shiha on the rump. Forcing himself to stare straight ahead, he vaulted into the saddle and led the way out of the Rashaad encampment at a fast clip.

Moments later, when he felt certain no one was watching him, he glanced back over his shoulder to make sure Chelsea was with them.

He should have known. She rode like the wind. Ignoring protocol, she advanced to keep stride beside him, as if that were her place. Brazen woman.

If not for the mare he had taken and was determined to keep, the ride home could have turned into a race to prove just who was the best horseman. To be challenged at all was inconceivable to Khalil, but by a woman—intolerable. And yet, he suspected she would not have been an easy opponent to beat, even though he knew his mare to be faster than hers in the long run.

She rode as few men dared, without reservation or fear. Even when the agile mares jumped a small pile of stones, Chelsea never lost a beat, as if such challenges were everyday occurrences. By Allah, it was obvious she enjoyed the danger as much as he did, maybe even more.

Far ahead of the others now, he brought them to a halt, turning Shiha so that she cut off Chelsea's out-of-control mount. Her cheeks were flushed with vigor and excitement, so beautiful against the paleness of her face as she laughed, free as a desert spirit carried along by the wind. He joined in her gaiety, reveling in the uninhibited spontaneity. But that was what she did to him, lifted him up out his ordinary existence.

Then their eyes met, and he felt her waver, her confidence fading as she looked down, so unsure of herself.

He could not resist her or her enigmatic charm, so confusing to him, while most likely unintentional on her part. Did she not know that she was the most beautiful woman he had ever seen? Did she not sense that he wanted her like no other?

Reaching out without turning loose of the Rashaad

mare, he captured her fragile beauty, dragging her against his chest and pressing his mouth to her more luscious one. Her resistance was minimal and only initially. Soon she was kissing him back, her arms clinging to him as tightly as he clasped her.

To hold her so made him realize just how empty his arms and life had been for so very long, if not for always. Chelsea! Chelsea! He wanted her there forever.

Umm Taif's warning rang in his ears. *You cannot keep her.* But his aunt was wrong. He was Khalil ibn Mani al Muraidi, was he not? Who would stop him from doing whatever he pleased?

"Promise me, Chelsea. You will not run away from me again," he demanded against the soft curve of her gazellelike neck.

He felt her shiver. Was it with fear or indecision? Could he hope it was with desire?

"So you *did* come for me," she said, pulling back to study his face as if to find the confirmation she sought there.

But he held back, unwilling to give her what she looked for. Why was it so hard for him to admit that he cared?

"Khalil? I am right, am I not? It was me you wanted and not that mare," she pressed, her delicate brows knitting with consternation.

His moment of ambivalence came mercifully to an end before he had the chance to make a fool of himself. He turned his focus on the approaching riders whose thundering hooves could not be ignored. He set her aside just as he did his own desires, once again the leader of these men who expected so much from him.

He realized then that who he was limited him more

than had he been a pauper responsible only to himself. But could he give up all that he possessed for a woman? He glanced at Chelsea, so alluring and desirable, especially when she looked at him in that vulnerable pleading way.

Surely Allah in all of His wisdom would not ask such a sacrifice from any man.

Without ever answering her, he backed Shiha away and took his rightful place in the lead. Then he realized she, too, had never answered him, never promised to obey—to stay.

She would follow for now. There was no place else for her to go. But once they reached the encampment, he knew it would be a different story.

He would do whatever he had to do to keep her by his side. Confine her, put guards at her door, chain her if he must, but he would not let her go.

For even if he refused to admit it to her, he could not deny the truth to himself. She held him prisoner as surely as if she had bound him hand and foot.

Chelsea Browne, the brown shell of the sea, was his, by right and by design. But, Allah help him, he was possessed by her just as well.

Nineteen

Unquestionably, Chelsea realized she was once again a prisoner. There were men stationed in front of her tent, and she was never alone even for a moment. Either Umm Taif, whose ever-watchful eye left no doubt as to what purpose her presence served, was with her, or whenever the old crone left, she always sent a replacement, one of her daughters or other village women, to sit quietly in the corner, noting the *duktur's* every move and spoken word.

With every "changing of the guard," Chelsea sent an urgent message to Khalil that she needed to speak with him. In all of the confusion of their wild ride back to his encampment, there had been no time to inform him of Yusaf's death and shattering confession. She was worried about Muhammad and his safety, but refused to discuss the matter with anyone but Khalil. There was no way of being certain who the traitor among them might be, if in truth there was one at all.

That Khalil didn't trust her and saw to it she had no opportunity to escape her confinement, even to find him, didn't brighten her mood. Didn't he realize that should she want to run away, she had no place to go, nor anyone to go with her? For whether she particularly liked it or not, she had learned to accept that she was a female alone in a time and a place intolerant to a woman's right to do what she pleased. It was not safe to venture beyond the boundaries of his protection.

Under such self-imposed limitations she continued to send him messages that grew more and more curt each time he ignored them. She didn't dare mention the potential danger to Muhammad, for she was afraid to place her confidence in any courier.

There were other things to consider and keep her busy. To arrive and discover Jamal miraculously alive had swept away some of the guilt she felt for her impulsive flight in the first place. His injuries were serious. Several of his ribs were broken, but in time they would heal. She was especially worried about the large bruise on his lower back where he had been kicked repeatedly. She could only hope the abuse hadn't damaged his kidney. And so with caution and concern she doctored him, at the same time attempting to make up for her thoughtless mistakes that had caused him so much pain.

The one bright spot in all of this came from a surprising source. Rakia. At first Chelsea mistook her constant attendance as just another check on her activities. She welcomed the young woman, found her company and her assistance quite valuable, for Rakia had a real knack for nursing and a great knowledge of herbal remedies that Chelsea learned to appreciate.

But then it began to dawn on Chelsea. Rakia tended to Jamal as if he were the most important man in the world. And it seemed that in the young woman's world, which was more limited than Chelsea could ever imagine, he was just that and more. He was her salvation.

"I do not care that she has been divorced."

It was modern Western influence that spoke to her now, through her once traditional assistant's mouth. Chelsea chuckled to herself, but didn't say anything, just smiled down at the young Arab. A smile that didn't abate even when he winced as she carefully palpitated the bruise seeking signs of abnormal swelling.

"Of course you do not care, Jamal." She picked up his wrist and checked his pulse out of habit. "And you shouldn't," she emphasized her support. "Rakia is truly a wonderful person, so kind and giving." She glanced up at the woman in question, busy off in one corner of the tent. "She deserves your . . . loyalty." She couldn't bring herself to call it what it really was—unconditional love.

Then she stood back and let Rakia take over, her gentle caring the therapy that would put him on the road to a quick recovery. The Arab woman offered the one thing she, Chelsea, could never give him, or any man for that matter, and as hard as she tried she couldn't suppress the jealousy that rose up within her.

Love did not come out of a pill bottle or a medical book. It couldn't be detected under the most powerful microscope, or created in a test tube. Love, the strongest panacea to endure throughout the ages, and she was not privy to it, despite all of her years in training and practice.

She sighed, feeling more inadequate than ever. Why couldn't she experience its healing powers, even if for only a little while?

If the truth be known, if she needed someone to blame, the fault lay within her own inhibitions. Why couldn't

362

she just let go and learn to trust others, to be more specific, to trust a man for more than a moment? A horse, as independent and wary a creature as any other, still jumped fences blindly, depending on its rider to steer it on course. Oh, if only she had the courage to hurdle the never-ending barriers life put before her with such courage. Blind trust. It was like closing her eyes and leaping from a cliff, never doubting that someone would be at the bottom to catch her.

No one had ever been there for her before.

Until Khalil had come along. He had made a career out of rescuing her, even when she had thought his help was the last thing she wanted. He had also taught her a lot about herself, things perhaps she'd been better off never knowing.

That one night she had spent in his arms—she couldn't explain what had transpired. She didn't want to explain it; she didn't even want to think about it. And yet that was all she could think about.

Khalil ibn Mani al Muraidi. He was nothing like her image of what a man was supposed to be. Those sensitive men of the nineties. The nineteen nineties, she reminded herself, and almost choked on the overwhelming realization that the concept of manliness she'd grown up with didn't even exist yet except in her own mind. Open and communicative, able to express their feelings without embarrassment, a real man wasn't afraid to cry, or to commit, or to let a woman lead.

God, the last thing she could imagine was that stone-faced Bedouin shedding a single tear over anything or anyone much less expressing himself in other than a curt, direct order or a threat. And as far as letting a woman be in charge . . . inconceivable. No doubt, he would much rather be dead.

Yet in spite of his lack of textbook qualifications her willful heart beat faster whenever he entered the tent. In fact, her entire being experienced an uncontrollable quickening when she saw him, remembering the feel of his hands and body doing things to her that had created a communication between them beyond mere words.

The power of good sex, the so-called experts would say. That was all she had shared with him. But they were wrong. It was more, much more.

Still, the uncertainty was enough to make her hesitate, to question her own intuitions. Not so long ago, she had thought Michael to be the man of her dreams, hadn't she? Look how long it had taken her to figure out the truth about him.

Oh, he had been open and honest, all right, brutally so. He had made no bones about what upset him, nor failed to express his emotions and use them to get what he wanted. But none of that had changed who and what he was—a selfish, uncaring, manipulative man.

All men were the same. Selfish brutes, unwilling to give a woman her deserved due.

Such was her frame of mind when an answer to her messages at last arrived.

"You are to follow me, Umm Dawa." Even the title of respect did not disguise that it was a command not a request that she present herself before the almighty sheikh. His timing couldn't have been worse.

"You tell him if he wishes to see me, he can damn well come here and do it for himself."

The courier, blinking in surprise, no doubt hadn't an inkling as to what to think of her reply, or how to tell his master without incurring his wrath why he returned unaccompanied. Well, that was his problem, and she figured that would be the end of it.

How very wrong she was.

She was helping Rakia prepare a meager meal for the three of them when Khalil burst into the tent, a whirlwind of destruction to the tranquility they had carved out for themselves. Mr. Strong-and-Silent, true to his nature, said nothing, took her by the arm and marched her toward the exit.

"What did you mean by rejecting my generous invitation? You were the one who wanted to see me," he finally demanded once they were outside and alone. His grip on her upper arm was anything but generous; in fact, it was most painful, and down-right irritating.

"Quite frankly I don't care if I ever see you again. Believe me, if that's your idea of an invitation, then I am the queen of the Nile," she replied, not bothering to disguise her contempt or to restrain her struggle to disengage herself from his unwanted attention.

"Ah ha! So that is where your America is. Along the Nile." His angry look of false comprehension was so comical, she couldn't help the spurt of derisive laughter that burst past her lips.

"By Allah, how can anybody be so stupid?" She rolled her eyes in condescension. Prying his fingers from her arm, she turned to walk away.

Apparently he didn't find her attitude, her biting comment, or her lack of obedience the least bit funny. When he pulled her back around and up against his long, lean masculinity, his dark eyes raking her as if she were an object to be possessed not a person, she didn't consider his way of thinking particularly funny either.

"Let go of me." Low and deadly, her words served as a warning.

For all that he listened, she might as well have suggested he fly to the moon. He swept her up into his arms and carried her bucking, kicking, and cursing across the compound unmindful of secretive eyes that might be watching them.

"Put me down this instant, damn you."

That, too, went unheeded as did her attempts to lash out and strike him in any vulnerable spot she could reach. It was as if both his body and heart were made of stone.

When at last he deigned to release her, they were in the confines of his private pavilion pitched along the waterfront. Her hair had come unbound and fell into her eyes. Her dress was in no better shape. Breathing hard, as much in indignation as with physical exertion, she fingered the tear on one shoulder, then shot him an accusing glare.

"You're nothing but a brute."

His return look suggested he could have inflicted far more damage if he had wanted and there would have been little she could have done to stop him.

"And you are a woman to try any man's patience. You should be taught your place."

If that was his intention, why didn't he just get on with it?

"My place?" Close to tears, she couldn't stop her voice from trembling. "Well, it's not waiting on you hand and foot. I will be damned before I will give in to your ridiculous misconceptions of what a woman is entitled to." Straightening, she brushed the hair from her face, the fear from her heart, issuing what could only be interpreted as a dare.

He didn't waste any time picking up the symbolic gauntlet she threw down before him. Stepping forward, he grasped her under the chin, turning her face up to his, the battle continuing in silence now.

As much as she wanted to jerk away, to deny him, she couldn't. Nor did she close her eyes, even though the urge overwhelmed her, as his lips moved toward hers. Stronger was the desire to assuage the gnawing need he awoke within her with nothing more than a masterful look.

That his mouth, although demanding, was gentle surprised her. Only then, as his kiss sent a shock wave washing over her that left her stripped of the shell of anger and indignation that up until now had protected her vulnerable heart, did she lower her lashes. A tear slid silently down her cheek.

She began to struggle, fighting desperately to hang on to the scattered remnants of the shredded pride and self-esteem that had made her who she was for so very long. She couldn't give up; she couldn't give in.

But Sheikh Khalil ibn Mani al Muraidi, that arrogant-Arab prince of the desert, would not be denied his pleasure. Nor would that something deep inside her that craved to be a woman, complete and whole—his woman—that yearned to share every nuance of ecstasy his sensuous kiss promised, be thrust aside. To trust him, to obey him, God help her, to love him without reservation. To claim only what he could give her in return, the forbidden fruit of Eden, but she no longer possessed the strength necessary to resist.

Nor the will.

Her arms extended and curled about his neck, her fingers entwined in his long, dark hair. Brazenly she pulled him closer, committing her whole being, body and soul, to what would inevitably follow.

He took her capitulation in stride, simply accepting it, playing upon it with a confident domination that she knew was so much a part of who he was. Without hesitation, he made his lovemaking seem the most natural act, nothing to be ashamed of, nothing to be embarrassed about. Sitting her before him, he quickly stripped away her clothing and banished the last of her reservations to another time and place. Within that tent there was only him and her and now, his hands upon her flesh, his mouth creating, then fine-tuning, an intense passion the likes of which she had never known even existed.

Wanting to learn more about him as well, she started her own bold exploration. That, too, seemed only natural, at least to her. Plucking at the leather tie crisscrossed down the front of his *thobe,* she loosened the garment and ran her hands inside the gaped opening. His flesh was firm and warm like a wild animal in tip-top condition, no sign of softness or excess. There were scars, too, rough ridges beneath her fingertips, that spoke of a life of adventure. She could only imagine what it must be like to live such derring-do freedom.

Caught up in fantasies she evoked, it wasn't until her palm skimmed over the hard, flat plane of his stomach and lower that she realized he had grown perfectly still. He watched her with the strangest look on his face.

"What is it?" she asked, sensing she had done something to upset him.

"No woman has ever touched me that way before." He sucked in a ragged breath when her hand feathered over him again.

"Never?" She threaded her fingers through the soft

mat of dark chest hair, noting the way he shivered in response. "Why not?"

"It is not our way." Taking her hand, he removed it from the front of his *thobe,* pushing her back against the pile of cushions. Once more he assumed control.

"But it is mine," she insisted, leaning forward to trace the hair-surrounded nipple exposed by his open neckline with the tip of her tongue.

"You are a brazen witch, woman, who knows no bounds. I should punish you," he warned, pressing her down and pinning her arms to the soft carpet on which they lay.

"No more brazen than you," she replied, staring up into his handsome face without fear. "Pray tell, do you still wish to cut out my wicked tongue?"

"Never." He lowered his face and kissed her, engaging in swordplay just the way she had instructed him, but with a masterfulness she had never taught him. "Its wickedness gives me too much pleasure. Only a fool destroys what pleases him most." He took her lips once more.

"And when I no longer please you, or someone pleases you more . . . then what?" she demanded, turning her head away, biting her lips for their wayward outburst.

It wasn't as if she meant to ask for commitment, but once it was out, she waited, uncertain, unable to look at him for his reply.

"Chelsea."

Still she couldn't face him, but he forced her to.

"The true pleasures of life cannot be measured by endurance or time. I cannot say what will please me tomorrow. But you are likened to my right hand." He lifted his hand so that she could see it, flexing it into a fist, then opening it again so that the fine lines of fortune

369

were revealed. "I cannot live without this hand any more than I could live without you."

She realized that was as close to a confession of love as she would ever get from a man like Khalil. It was more than enough.

Eagerly she gave herself up to him, to the shared pleasure. At his patient insistence she quickly forgot the need to hold back. Why should she when there was nothing of him shielded from her any longer? That her dignity and freedom might be at stake only crossed her mind momentarily. His gentle generosity put those fears to rest.

They were man and woman in the purest form, doing what their bodies had been designed to do so well. What she had once in her life thought of as an invasion was now a glorious union. There wasn't anything she wouldn't do or give to him. He needn't even ask. In fact, he didn't. She just matched him caress for caress.

To her delight the more she gave, the more she received in return.

Flesh against flesh they scaled the steep mountain of passion reaching the apex with such lightning speed it took their breaths away. For Chelsea there was no time to think, to consider the outcome, to worry if she had what it took, if she would survive so daring a plunge.

Pushed from the brink before she had the chance to prepare, she found herself falling, falling, her heart racing out of control, reaching out to grasp anything that might save her, but it was too late to turn back. Closing her eyes she succumbed to ecstasy's storm as it engulfed her, buffeting her about as if she had no will of her own. At the moment, she didn't. She could only wonder what awaited her at the end of so long a thrilling descent.

What awaited her were Khalil's arms, securely about

her, keeping her from harm, his mouth kissing her, reassuring her that she was not alone, now or ever, as he joined her in the trembling afterglow of heightened senses.

Shamelessly, she clung to him, to the unspoken promise that he would be there for her—forever and always.

Always was a very long time. But here with Khalil time, both past and future, meant absolutely nothing.

That Chelsea could sleep so peacefully pleased Khalil, truly it did, yet left him feeling restless. Just like a woman with no worries or woes to keep them from succumbing to love's satiety. Wistfully he lay there, holding on to her tightly, wanting never to let her or the wonderful fulfillment go. Oh, to be like the wealthy Persian caliphs who spent their days idly exploring the never-ending mysteries and pleasures of a woman's body.

Alas, such a luxury was rarely afforded a beleaguered Bedouin sheikh like himself.

Reluctantly, he extracted himself from the willowy, pale arms of the woman who had captured his heart and his power to reason. Careful not to disturb her further, he bent and kissed one bared shoulder, the taste of her skin a lingering sweetness he would take with him for the rest of the day. Rising, he dressed, watching her the entire time. The way she moaned, seeking a more comfortable position. Then when her lips pursed, pink and inviting, he almost stripped off his *thobe* and rejoined her.

Responsibilities beckoned; duties demanded his attention. His household would be in an uproar by now. Umm Taif resented his exclusion of a part of his life that by time-honored tradition should have been her domain. Concubine, wife or ward, all of the women he gave protection to by right was under her jurisdiction. She couldn't understand his overwhelming need to be alone with Chelsea, sharing their scandalous pleasure without curious eyes to watch. Privacy was not the Bedouin way. Neither was their style of lovemaking.

But both were the way between himself and Chelsea, and he would keep it so.

He started to leave; then as an afterthought, he returned to cover up Chelsea's nakedness with a blanket, not only to keep her warm, but to shield her perfect beauty from eyes other than his own. That his aunt would eventually come looking for them, he did not doubt. However, he would do everything in his power to make certain that what she found would not be the subject of wagging female tongues throughout the encampment.

Then he sighed, acknowledging if not necessarily liking how much this one woman had changed his life and ambitions over the course of so few days. Whether she realized it or not, or had planned it to be that way, she wielded great influence over him.

It seemed the great Antar, the legendary Bedouin warrior and poet whose adventures were the subject of camp fire recounting from one generation to another, had been right after all when he had spoken of the power of love. "The eyelashes of the songstress from the corner of the veil are more cutting than the edges of the cleaving scimitars." He, too, must have known an extraordinary woman like Chelsea Browne, Khalil decided, with long, lethal lashes of shimmering gold.

With that conclusion he departed, determined to get

things done as quickly as possible so that he could return once more to his haven of paradise on earth.

Chelsea stirred at the melodic clatter of children laughing and playing outside the tent. The familiar sounds conjured up memories of her own childhood that floated about her in a dreamlike haze, making her feel warm and content. Suddenly wide awake, her heart slammed to a nauseating halt, and her eyes snapped open.

Muhammad. In the sweeping passion of the last few hours, she had somehow forgotten to tell Khalil about the possible danger to his son.

Rolling over, she thought to arouse him and spill forth her confession of neglect, only to discover that he was not there. Her disappointment at his desertion in the face of what they had shared only added to her sense of failure.

Then a strange sensation rolled down her spine. She was not alone. Sitting up, she scanned the tent and spied the dark, steady gaze of Umm Taif sitting next to the fire.

"I must see Khalil immediately," Chelsea announced with a regal haughtiness that stemmed from a resentment that Khalil still didn't trust her and would send his favorite watchdog to guard her.

"He is not here." The old woman's eyes, glistening in the firelight with disapproval, settled on Chelsea's exposed back.

Well, if Umm Taif didn't like what she saw, then she shouldn't have been there. Chelsea clung to her basic, God-given right of privacy.

"Then, I must find him right away." She searched the

cushions for her clothing, determined to dress and allow nothing to stop her this time.

The woman's continued intense scrutiny focused on Chelsea's barely concealed breasts. In modesty she pulled the edges of the blanket up to her collarbone and stared back with open hostility. As a physician she had thought about the naked human anatomy only in a clinical sense, but that was other people's bodies, not her own. And she was not used to being glared at accusingly as if she had four mangled arms or four unsightly eyes, as if she were an ugly scar on the face of humanity. Did it truly upset the old woman to discover that her healthy, virile nephew had an intimate relationship? Was she jealous? Anything was possible. How was she to know what a fourteenth century Arab mind thought?

"I should have never brought you here. You are a curse to us all with your strange ways." The woman rose and came toward her, with what purpose Chelsea could only imagine. "You are destroying my nephew and will destroy us all before you are done."

She didn't bother to remind Umm Taif she had never asked to be so rudely jerked from her own time and life and be carted off to the desert without consideration as to what it might do to her. Obviously, the old hag didn't care.

Thinking to protect herself and escape an unwarranted attack, she frantically snatched up her crumpled dress, and scrambling to her feet, she raced naked across the tent. An audible sound of disbelief followed.

Clutching the gown tightly, she turned to confront her opponent, who stood there staring in what Chelsea surmised as indecision. Taking the few moments afforded her, she pulled the dress over her head. But without the sash to wrap about her, the skirt hung long, dragging the ground. Even clothed, she still felt naked before the condemnation that she didn't fully understand.

Then before she could anticipate what she would do, the old woman took a swipe at her. Thinking she went for her hair to yank it or to claw at her eyes, Chelsea ducked, only to discover that it was the talisman, a permanent fixture at her throat, that Umm Taif lunged for. The gnarled hand grasped that bit of magic, tugging and pulling without thought of how painful the thong digging into the back of her neck had to be to Chelsea.

Indignantly she slapped at her adversary's cruel hand.

To her surprise, it slapped her back—hard across her unprotected face.

Stunned yet freed, Chelsea shielded the talisman as if it were the most precious of possessions. She would never forfeit her one link to the future where she truly belonged.

"Give it to me."

She shook her head which still rang with the force of the blow, unwilling to tell Umm Taif that she couldn't remove it either, even if she chose to.

"Then, I will take it, for it belongs to me."

The blade of the knife when Umm Taif whipped it out from the folds of her dress glistened in the light of the fire between them with an undeniable malice. Mesmerized, Chelsea took a step back and tripped over the dragging edge of her unbound gown. Breaking her fall by grabbing one of the tent's central poles, she saw the knife come toward her and knew it would strike before she could regain her balance and scramble out of its way. Against her neck the steel felt so cold; then it sliced through the thong that held the talisman in place.

"No," Chelsea cried, grabbing the leather pouch before the old woman could.

Umm Taif shrieked in rage, lunging for her again with the knife. This time it sought to kill.

But then the tent pole gave way beneath Chelsea's hand, and she was falling again, the black tent collapsing with her. She heard the old woman's angry scream of defeat even as they both were buried beneath the heavy woven fabric.

Disoriented, the air growing thin and uncomfortable, she couldn't decide which way to begin crawling. Then she caught a whiff of smoldering camel hair. Pushing at the heavy, suffocating tent, her movement released a billowing cloud of smoke that engulfed her. Coughing and gagging, she found it nearly impossible to catch her breath.

The fire that had burned between her and Umm Taif. She had forgotten all about it. Already she could detect the heat as it took hold of the cloth strips and burst into flames. Turning in the opposite direction, she dragged herself toward the edge of the collapsed tent.

Then she heard the horrible screams and knew who made them. She paused in her own struggle to escape, and heart beating wildly with fear, she turned back around.

"Umm Taif. Umm Taif," she cried out hoarsely, her throat raw with smoke.

The continued screams were her only answer.

Unsure what to do, she knew she could never live with herself if she thought only of herself and ignored another in pain. She started back along the path she had just come, praying to Allah that she would reach the other woman before it was too late.

* * *

"Look, *ya ràyyis,* one of them is headed back toward the flames."

Khalil stared down at the movement, only a few feet away from reaching freedom, and instinctively knew which one would be so foolish.

"Chelsea, no," he cried over the shrieks of his aunt whom others were working from the opposite side to reach. He continued to roll the heavy tent out of his way bit by what seemed ineffectual bit.

And then the silhouetted figure stopped, collapsed, and did not get up again.

Dropping to all fours, Khalil ignored the risk of possibly losing his own way and crawled beneath the heavy fabric. Groping his way through the stifling darkness, he at last stumbled upon her bare ankle. He cried out in relief. Thank Allah, he had found her. He prayed he had not arrived too late.

Reeling her in by one bare leg, he heard her moan softly and willed that she do it again, for it reassured him she was still alive. Then he had her in his arms and dragged them both back toward safety.

The heat was unbearable, the smoke so thick he could hardly breathe, and he could hear the hungry ring of fire crackling right behind them. A few more moments and it would overtake them. Then when he thought he could go no farther, he saw a flash of daylight just ahead even as he succumbed to the smoky darkness.

"Chelsea," he murmured as hands grasped him under the arms and dragged him forward. "Take her first."

"Not to worry, *ya ràyyis,* your woman is safe."

Lying on his back on the ground, he gasped for air

with lungs almost too raw to function. The he realized the screams that had been so predominant were silent now.

"Umm Taif?" he managed to ask in a painful whisper.

The moment of hesitation should have warned him of what was to come.

"I am sorry. We tried, but reached her too late."

Umm Taif. His beloved aunt. Could she truly be dead? She had been his friend and advisor for so long, he depended upon her for so much. . . .

He closed his eyes, resigning himself to the truth and the numbing grief. He would miss her terribly.

Chelsea. Chelsea. Allah forgive him, but he must find her and, no matter what he had been told, prove to himself that she had not met with the same horrible fate.

Pushing himself up with all the strength he possessed, he scanned the smoke-filled scenario. A short distance away he spied her lying on the ground, her beautiful pale face and hair darkened with soot. Her eyes were closed, but her chest rose and fell, proof of her survival. Making his way unnoticed to where she lay, he reached out and gathered up her hand, fisted even in her unconsciousness.

He pried open her fingers. To his surprise he discovered she clutched the talisman. The thong had been neatly severed.

Something had happened between Umm Taif and Chelsea, of that he was certain. Whatever it was, he claimed responsibility. He should have never left Chelsea alone even for a moment. As resentful as his aunt had been toward her, he should have realized she would confront the source. Had she even attempted to take back the talisman? Was that how the thong had gotten cut? Quite possibly.

And then he recalled the words of caution his aunt had once given him. The magic of the *baraka* was closely connected with the power of the fire. Tamper with the one, evoke the other.

Poor Umm Taif. How could she have failed to heed her own warning?

He stared back down at the unconscious woman. Chelsea. Did this mean she, too, was in danger of forfeiting her life? Picking her up in his arms, he held her close, rocking her as if she were a child.

No. Never. He would not give her up. He could make her happy, make her love him. Reaching out, he unwound the talisman from her fingers, hesitating only for a moment before slipping the thong of the leather pouch into his belt.

It was in his power to make it so that she could never leave him, even if she wanted to.

Twenty

When Chelsea regained consciousness, her lungs ached, her nose and throat burned, even her eyes stung as if she had gotten soap in them, but the debilitating pain refused to dissipate. With blurred vision she glanced around at the unfamiliar surroundings, not sure where she was or why she was there. She only knew she was besieged by an overwhelming terror of being alone and abandoned, but uncertain why she would feel that way.

Then her hand crept up in an automatic gesture. Her labored breathing paused as she blindly searched her neck for what should be there.

The talisman, so much a natural part of her now, was gone.

Memories came tumbling back, vivid memories of the fire and what had preceded it—Umm Taif slicing the leather thong of the charm, the struggle to possess it and the subsequent collapse of the tent. The horrible screams had followed. The sound of them still rang in Chelsea's ears even when she attempted to cover them.

She had tried, God how she had tried, to reach the woman in time to save her. Now she realized her failure may have cost her dearly, for she suspected Umm Taif had somehow managed to snatch the leather pouch away from her before . . . before. . . . She didn't want to think about what had happened then.

In spite of her conclusion, she frantically began to search for the missing *baraka*—in the blanket that covered her, in her smoke-saturated clothing, even between the pile of cushions on which she lay. She didn't find what she sought, but she did recall having the pouch clutched in her hand when she had been knocked down as the tent had caved in on her.

Therefore, in her confusion, *she* must have dropped the talisman in the fire. Did that mean she'd lost it forever? A fear more terrible than any she had ever experienced before assaulted her. Without its magic, she had no chance of ever getting back to her proper time and place. But just as frightening, without it, she probably couldn't communicate with those around her.

It was almost as if she'd landed back at square one with no hope of advancing.

Like geysers under pressure, the hot tears welled on their own, fighting their way through her soldered lashes and determination not to give in to the ever-rising panic. Winning the battle, they streamed silently down her face. Oddly enough a trite yet apropos expression came to mind that made her choke with bitter irony. The straw that broke the camel's back. That best described the effects of this latest defeat. What was she going to do now?

She knew what she couldn't do—turn to Khalil. He would never understand her carelessness with such a precious gift. God only knew what his reaction would be. With no hope of salvation, what was left for her? A forced existence as some nameless Bedouin woman, banished to seclusion behind a veil like poor Rakia just because she displeased a man?

No. No. She was Dr. Chelsea Browne of Atlanta, Georgia. She refused to give up her hard-earned identity or the place of authority she had so carefully carved out for herself.

Khalil. He must never discover her vulnerability, even if it meant maintaining complete and total silence on her part. Oh, God, how long could she keep up such a charade? Driven by the need to find the missing talisman before someone else did, she rose with the intention of searching the accident site. She had to find it, had to. . . .

Still dizzy from the effects of the smoke inhalation, she sat back down, forced, at least for the moment, to reconsider her plan of action. Perhaps she could devise something to replicate the talisman, something that at least at first glance would look like the little leather pouch, until she could locate the real one, if it still existed.

Until then she would say nothing, only pray inwardly that her crude plan would work.

Khalil offered no outward indication of how much he worried about Chelsea's recovery. He listened to the daily reports, his face blank, his questions delivered with no show of emotions, nothing that might be misconstrued as a weakness by those around him.

"Has she spoken today?" He carefully sipped his coffee from the cup his cousin handed him.

"Still she refuses," Rakia replied, with an audible sigh of frustration. "And since that morning she was discovered at the cleaned-up site of the fire, she has also refused to eat. I still cannot explain her strange actions. It's almost as if she has no purpose to continue living."

As he listened, his free hand kneaded the leather pouch he now kept with him at all times. He could explain Chelsea's odd behavior to the concerned woman, but chose not to. She had been searching for the talisman. Perhaps he should return it to her. His fingers continued the debate, definitively squeezing the precious possession. No. To do so would only offer her false hope when what she needed was to accept her place here, with him, forever and always.

Chelsea. The brown shell of the sea. Such a wild and unpredictable creature, but with time and patience he would tame her, just as he would the irascible Rashaad mare that he worked with, a task he immersed himself in every day. Yes, he was determined to master them both.

In the meantime, what havoc those two stirred up for him and his people.

The Rashaad, those devious sons of Satan, wasted no time avenging the Durra raid against them. Only three days later, they had swooped down on the once peaceful encampment. Khalil and his men were prepared for retaliation and had sent them packing with their tails tucked between their cowardly legs like the curs that they were.

From the ridge above, the old chieftain had turned to confront his pursuers, and raising his scimitar high in the air, he had issued a challenge and a threat that provided surprising answers to several heretofore unsolved mysteries.

"Your son," the Rashaad had vowed. "Only through his death am I released from the shackles of our blood ties."

383

So, just as he had feared, Yusaf's disappearance had been part of a plot to destroy Khalil and his people through his son. But it was the old physician's willing involvement that had left Khalil reeling with the shock of once again having been betrayed by those he thought to trust. The loyalty that Khalil had always taken for granted over the years had secretly remained with his previous master. It sickened him to think that his lack of intuition might have cost him Muhammad's life. The boy's near-fatal illness had been no accident either, and if it had not been for Umm Taif's magic and Chelsea's medicine the Rashaad chieftain would have finally been successful in destroying his most hated enemy.

But for now, the victory belonged to him, and the Rashaad had once again fled before his superior forces, empty-handed, the possession of both Chelsea and the white mare a symbol of Durra domination of the desert.

The mare. Khalil thought of the beast with an impatient sigh. So far, just like Chelsea, the beautiful horse had proven to be more difficult and obstinate than an ass. Just like Chelsea, in the beginning the mare had refused to eat, and he had feared losing it to starvation. But yesterday the horse had finally surrendered to its hunger just as Chelsea would in the end. Of that he felt certain. Chelsea was capable of many things, but martyrdom? She possessed too much of life's spirit to so foolishly sacrifice herself.

And so the two, horse and woman, merged into one and the same challenge to him. Progress with the first promised success with the second. But just as important, a defeat often indicated a like response from the other. Today he would make great strides with both.

He chose to begin the battle of wills with Chelsea. It

was time to remind her of who she was and what she was now, a beautiful woman of great worth among one of the most powerful tribes of the desert, the woman of Khalil ibn Mani al Muraidi, their undefeated leader. She should be proud of her privileged identity.

When he swept into the tent, unannounced, he could not be certain of what she was doing. Praying? She was kneeling, but he doubted it was for the sake of piety.

"Chelsea?"

Had not her slender shoulders twitched like a wayward child caught filching, he would have thought she had not heard him. Still, she offered no voluntary response—not even when he touched the top of her head with gentle concern—except to quickly bury beneath the cushions whatever it was she held in her hands.

She refused to look at him. Even so, he noted a new frailty about her, causing his heart, oh, traitorous beast, to worry that he underestimated her strength of will and determination. Before she would ever succumb to his protective domination, for his motive truly was to protect her, she would choose to perish from hunger—or perhaps she might even attempt suicide.

His keen vision darted to the place between the cushions where she had stuffed what she had been holding. Some kind of weapon, perhaps? A weapon she planned to use on herself? Before he left he would find out for himself.

Chelsea. Sweet Chelsea. His hand moved down to cup her shoulder, so well remembered in its soft paleness. The warmth of her flesh contrasted sharply with the ice of her reception. Dropping his hand, he continued to caress her, but with his eyes only.

Had she no inkling that his life would be empty without her? Why, oh, why, must she make this so difficult for both of them?

"Chelsea, look at me." Once again he summoned her attention. This time he did not bow to her refusal.

Forcing her to her feet, he turned her to face him. But then he was suddenly at a loss as to what to do when she stared at him blankly, no resistance but no joy either to find him there with her. He shook her. Her head merely lolled on the slender column of her neck.

He could think of only one way to reach her. Lowering his head, he kissed her, confident that would arouse her from her state of vapid passivity.

When his kiss evoked no response, even when he slipped his tongue into her mouth the way she had taught him, a chill of frustration and defeat raced through him. Could it be she no longer cared?

No. No. He would never accept her lack of interest as anything other than it was, a most ingenious, obstinate form of rebellion. His conclusion made him all the more determined to get his way.

With renewed vigor he deepened the kiss, dragging her to his chest with arms that could have crushed her if he had chosen to do so. The spark although infinitesimal, was nonetheless real. Recognizing it for what it was, he masterfully stoked it into an ember with the patience and power of a man possessed by love.

"No, I will not," she protested in a vehement whisper, twisting her face away and pushing at his chest with fisted hands.

Her lips, bruised red from his passion, puckered so invitingly. That she defied him meant nothing in comparison to the fact that she had at last broken her self-imposed vow of silence.

"You will not what, *ya araif?*" he asked, smiling down at her, knowing he had won a victory, at least for that day. The endearment, one of his own invention, meant a mare lost in a raid and recovered in a counter raid. It fit her perfectly, he decided, teasingly tracing the edges of her once more soldered mouth with his thumb.

"I will not be a party to your sexist lust, Khalil. Not ever again. I swear to you . . ."

"Enough of this." With a passion fanned to flames by regal impatience he silenced her unwarranted outburst—much of which remained meaningless even if the words themselves were very clear.

"How can this be? I understand you . . ." Her eyes widened in confusion, and her hand moved up to her throat as if seeking something, then to her mouth to cover her surprise. Did she look for the talisman which he now possessed?

At first, her frantic gestures made him smile broadly. Then the reality of the situation washed over him. The talisman. The fact that he now controlled it, not her. . . . How could they understand one another?

What new trickery was this? Determined to get to the bottom of the mystery, he grabbed her, his hand searching her unadorned neck for some new kind of magic. He found nothing.

Remembering that she had hurried to hide something when he had first arrived, he dragged her back over to the pile of cushions and forced her to her knees. He made no pretense of his purpose. Tossing pillows out of his way, it took him only a moment to find what he sought.

The uncompleted pouch looked nothing like the real

387

one, much larger, the leather coarse and stiff in comparison.

"Did you think to deceive me with this?" he demanded, shoving the forgery into her face.

"You are just as guilty as I am of deception," she declared with disdain, lashing out and knocking it from his hand. "Have you done something with the real one?"

"What does it matter? It is obvious by this conversation, you do not need it anymore."

"You have no right to decide what I need and do not need. I want to go home."

"You are wrong. I have every right. I have claimed you on raid. Therefore, you will stay with me. I have chosen you, Chelsea, over all others to be my woman, to hold a place of great honor among my people, especially for one who is not one of us."

"I do not want your place of honor. I want only to go home to my own kind. Please, Khalil, please, if you have the talisman, just tell me so I know I am not resigned to stay here, in this godforsaken time and place, forever."

They were kneeling face-to-face in the pile of scattered cushions, their wills and their needs of equal proportions. Surely his offer of commitment to honor and protect her, not easy for a man like him, would make her see that his way was the best for both of them. He would not necessarily lie to her, but he would not give her false hope.

"You must learn to accept fate and be happy."

"Learn? Never. I would rather die than accept that I must remain here, a prisoner and a pawn in your desert games of power and lust. I will find a way out. I promise you, I *will* find a way home."

That she spat upon his love, speaking of it as if it were

an inconsequential game, hurt him deeply. Admittedly so, Bedouin life was a lot like chess, a great game of strategy, one sheikh pitting his strength and wile against another. Only the strongest survived the harsh existence in the desert. But those who prevailed were free as no other people could claim to be.

Chelsea was wrong. Why could she not see that? She would be no pawn, but a great queen on the chessboard, wielding a power few women could ever hope to claim. That would be his gift to her.

In the meantime, he had to show her that resistance to his superior strength would get her naught. Only by giving in would his other gift, the most extraordinary of all, be hers for the asking. A great freedom only a man could give a woman when he took her in his arms.

Wordlessly, he set about to do just that, remind her of how wonderful their lovemaking could be, kissing her in the way he knew she liked best. Contrary to her vow, he swept her along on the desire they had cultivated and shared and would only make better each time they came together. Let her think her hurtful words would deter him from the path he knew was best for her—for both of them.

Without giving even a little, he allowed her to play out her strategy until she boxed herself into submission all on her own. Then, when she was kissing him back, only then did he relent, lifting his face from hers, allowing her to see the error of her way.

"Shah mat, Chelsea, your *shah* is dead," he announced the traditional Persian phrase of victory as he cornered her imaginary king on the game board of what she had so fallaciously called his lust. If it was lust that bound them, then it was her lust, too.

But more than lust kept him awake at night, worrying about her state of health when she refused to eat, to even speak. Sheer lust did not make him wish to give her everything she wanted—short of taking her back to a place and time he could never enter—to see her happy and content as a woman should be. Lust could not create a fear of losing her that drove him to want to forget all else, to risk so much to keep her.

No, it wasn't lust. It was love. She had only to open her spellbinding blue eyes and see the truth for herself. He could not do it for her.

And so he demonstrated this unspoken love in the only way he knew how. He would cherish her pleasure above even his own. Knowing her likes better perhaps than she knew them herself, he pressed her down into the soft cushions, stroking the dormant cords of the rapturous song that had been sung between men and women since the beginning of time and, no doubt, to the end of it.

Suddenly he paused, suspecting they were being watched. The evidence lay in the flutter of the dividing curtain behind which the women of his household lived. Rakia ruled where once her mother had, another concession he had made knowing it would make Chelsea happy—in the long run. And because he sensed the two women were truly friends, he depended upon his cousin to keep the curious at bay, but some things were impossible.

Under the circumstances, he pulled back, remembering the vow he had made to himself, to jealously guard their privacy at any cost. Never would he make love to Chelsea in the traditional Bedouin way. The act meant too much to him. But oh, how he yearned to thrust aside his hesitations, take her in his arms and lose himself in her soft, white skin and throaty cries of passion.

He would simply have to wait. They both would have to. At the moment, the fact he had ordered another tent to be constructed, just for Chelsea, did little to alleviate his desire. Need and impatience did not make the needle stitch faster. Such an undertaking, especially in the winter, took time.

Time. It seemed that one factor would forever be their unrelenting nemesis. Time and the stubborn way she clung to a reality that no longer existed.

"Khalil, tell me that you will help me. If you care for me at all, understand why I cannot stay here." Lying there beneath him, trusting him, she searched his face for a clue.

Dare he take the risk and tell her how much his love for her meant to him? That he would die without it? He realized then and there that to be without her would be the same as death. Would she only laugh at him for being so vulnerable, or worse, like Tuema, some day use such a confession against him?

"I must go now," he said, extricating himself from her clinging arms and her plea for help that he could not give her and remain the man that he was at least on the outside.

He slipped quickly out of the tent, knowing he had suffered the first defeat of the day.

The mare stood hobbled, trembling before him as pale and beautiful as the woman he had just left. It was as if its large, intelligent eyes spoke to him, saying the same thing Chelsea had said. *I want to go home. Please release me.*

That he could not do.

He edged toward the horse, bridle and saddle in his hand, accustomed to the task. The mare's mood turned hostile, just as Chelsea's had, the defiance shining like the blade of a sword. He preferred the anger to the pleading; it was much easier to counteract.

By Allah, he would ride the beast today if it was the last thing he did.

He did not care who might be watching. The war between himself and that mare was for all the world to see. Today he would win the battle.

With several pairs of hands to hold the still-shackled horse, it took him no time to saddle it and then mount. But the moment all impediments were removed, the mare went wild, twisting and bucking to rid itself of the unwelcome rider.

That he was good, one of the finest horsemen of the desert, no one dared deny, but in no time Khalil found himself sailing through the air. He landed facedown in the biting sand, more angry than hurt.

Spitting the grit out of his mouth, he rose, tossing aside his *keffiyeh,* already askew. Having had his fill of female audaciousness for one day, he confronted the equally maddened animal.

Moments later, he climbed into that saddle again. Before he could even begin to plan out his strategy, he hit the ground. Had he not rolled to the side, then rolled again, he would have been trampled by the slashing hooves aimed at his head.

Once more, he scrambled to his feet. If he had been wearing his scimitar, without a doubt that mare would have fallen victim to its sharp, curved blade. Such action would have been justified. Fortunately he was weaponless, so, snatching up the reins, he waved back his many helpers who rushed in to assist him, determined to do this on his own. He must master the beast, the symbol of resistance. Otherwise, his power and authority would be damaged in the eyes of his people. Round and round they went, until he managed to swing up.

For the longest moment they stood there, kindred spirits of the desert, the mare trembling in indecision, the man tensing with uncertainty as to what to expect. In that instant, he felt the eyes of disapproval settle upon him, and he looked up, knowing before he did, the source.

Chelsea. She stood there among his men, wrapped in the traditional *abaaya* that whipped about her like a black cloud of determination. It did nothing to hide the strength of the soul it shrouded, nothing to conceal the beauty and intelligence of the woman who wielded such power over his heart, and yes, Allah help him, the very way he viewed his life.

Where her sympathies lay, with the mare, marked the slant of those devastatingly blue eyes. So blue. So different. So unchangeable.

She did not belong. His dreams of possessing such a woman were nothing more than a fool's delusion, a mirage, one that no matter how hard he tried to grasp it, would always remain just out of his reach. No. No. He refused to accept such a truth. Fate had given her to him. He would keep her, no matter the cost or consequences.

In that moment when he thought to dismount, pursue and dominate the real challenge in his life, the mare made its decision. Wheeling about, it took off, running for its freedom or just as likely death, he decided, whichever came first. Just like Chelsea. So much like the woman of indomitable pride and strength willing to race headlong into danger rather than be bound to a life that did not suit her.

He allowed the crazed beast to have its head, willing to let the mare exhaust itself, to a point. Then he would rein in, bring the horse to its knees if he must to stop it, becoming the conqueror if not yet truly master.

He suspected he would never really vanquish either of them, woman or horse. He could only hope to break their spirits. And then what would he have? Mere shadows of the majestic grandeur that had made them so desirable.

Would that be enough? Was it worse to have nothing of them at all?

Chelsea watched them ride away, man and horse, white on white, the billowing *thobe* giving the illusion of wings. To have seen them take off from the ridge when they crested it and fly magically through the air wouldn't have surprised her, not in the least. This was the famed desert of the Arabian Nights, after all. Ali Babba and Aladdin. They were out there somewhere, having their adventures, as real as her own. She laughed. Maybe even more real.

A most sobering thought. In fact, it scared the hell out of her. Would she, too, simply turn up in some fable, a character forever lost in the annals of history. If so, she would gain the notoriety she had always sought, if not exactly in the way she thought to attain it.

Foolish notions, she told herself. Probably, she already had become nothing but another name written off as lost—to inexperience and bad decisions. A victim to forces stronger than her own, easily replaced by another as naive who harbored grand illusions of saving the world.

And yet, through it all she had obtained the one thing she had thought to never have, to know what it meant to be a woman in the purest form. However, she wasn't sure the sacrifice necessary to hang on to so glorious—if momentary—ascent to total femininity was truly worth it.

At times like this she fervently wished Khalil had never opened the doors to her sensuality, never shown her what she had been missing all of her life. How much easier it would be if he hadn't, if he had remained the distant barbarian she could never understand.

How blind not to see that hers had been a fantasy just waiting to happen. Had she just used her subconscious power to make it all come true? She had no one but herself to blame.

Not long after such self-revelation, she caught a glimpse of motion on the desert, white on white, moving slowly. Lifting up on tiptoes, she strained to make out what she saw, to be certain.

Yes, it was them all right. Khalil and that beautiful white mare. They were both walking, the man in the lead. As they came closer, she realized the horse, head hung low in defeat and exhaustion, was limping.

As a lover of all animals, especially horses, Chelsea felt a sense of righteous anger well within her. So, he had done exactly what he had set out to do. Decimate anything and anyone who dared to resist him, who tried to achieve independence in an effort to be true to their nature.

She started running, that mare somehow a symbol of

her own predicament and eventual fate. Halfway to the ridge she met them, her heart pounding, her lungs pumping, her eyes searching Khalil's face for what she feared she would find there—a lack of any sense of regret. His hardened, unwavering gaze said more than any words.

"No," she cried, lunging for the reins as if they were lifelines. "I will not let you."

"It cannot be helped, Chelsea." He held them out of her reach. "She has to be destroyed."

"You are wrong." She cast about for a way, a logic to use to stop him. "As a healer, maybe I can do something." She darted around him and knelt beside the horse, which stood quietly as she ran her hands along the cannon bone of the injured leg.

"Chelsea, are you crazy? The mare is possessed with an uncontrollable lust to kill." He jerked her back, standing between her and the horse.

What did he think he was being? Heroic? More likely, he thought of her, too, only as valuable property to be protected as long as it had worth.

"Life means nothing to you, does it?" She pulled away from him, rubbing the spots on her arm where his fingers had clamped about her flesh. "Not hers." She flung out her arm, pointing at the mare, now passive, but only because it was tired and hurting. "Not even mine. You think only of yourself, how best our existence can serve your needs and your insatiable ego. And when it ceases to please, you . . . you destroy it just like that." She snapped her fingers in his face.

"That is not true." He spoke quietly.

She should have recognized his restraint for the warning it was.

"Oh, really," she accused recklessly, not caring that

she might be running headlong into disaster. "Then, what possessed you to ride this horse, or any horse for that matter, with so little regard?"

"Our ways have been our ways for a long time. Spirit is to be admired, but obedience is expected, beast to man, man to Allah."

"And women? Pray tell, just where do we fit into your grand scheme of things? I suppose we are no better than the lowliest beast. What is the life of one horse or one woman compared with your universal law. The world will simply come to an end if you are disobeyed. Is that how it is, oh, great master?" She rolled her eyes contemptuously. Testing her brave words, she attempted to brush past him.

It was as if fire and ice came together, creating a sizzling steam.

He grabbed her so forcefully, she gasped aloud, his hard body like running headlong into a boulder of granite.

"Shut up, Chelsea."

"Make me." Her chin shot up in defiance, even as her heart raced with fear.

His knuckles whitened in contrast to his dark, desert complexion.

This was it, she had finally pushed him too far. She swallowed her trepidation. Well, at least she would go with her pride in tact. Staring back into his dark determination, she calmly awaited her fate.

She couldn't believe it when he released her and stepped back. What had made him change his mind?

Still shaking, she took advantage of the moment, kneeling once more beside the horse. Feeling along the injured leg, she prayed it wasn't broken and truly beyond salvation.

A long silence followed in the wake of that unresolved confrontation. He stood over her, staring down, his gaze boring a hole into the top of her head.

"Can she be saved?" he asked at long last.

"I don't know." Chelsea looked up at him, searching his face for a reason for his uncharacteristic retreat. It couldn't be that he might care. "If you will give me the chance, I will try."

Without offering her an answer, one way or the other, he once more thrust her out of his way. Taking a firm hold on the reins, he led the tired, limping horse toward the outlying tents.

Chelsea followed and held her breath. Only when he tied the mare to the trunk of a palm tree, walked away, and did not return with the means to destroy it did she finally let the stale air out of her aching lungs and truly believe that he'd agreed to give her the small reprieve she'd asked for.

All alone, she set to work immediately, racking her imagination to come up with a plan of attack. First, she tore strips from the hem of the *abaaya* she wore. Simply wrapping the leg wouldn't be enough; she needed something to help reduce the swelling.

Instantly she thought of Rakia and her vast knowledge of herbal medicines. Did the Arab woman know of something that might work? She rose with the intent of finding her friend. To her relief she spied the familiar black-clad figure making her way toward them.

They looked at each other, the unspoken bond of the shared sisterhood as strong as ever.

"What can I do?" Rakia asked.

"I need something to help alleviate the swelling."

With a quick nod, the woman disappeared, returning in only a few moments with a poultice made from ingredients Chelsea couldn't begin to identify, but the strong smell remarkably reminded her of remedies her trainer used to use. Without question as to the preparation's effectiveness, she dipped her hand into the thickened mass and began smearing it over the swollen leg, knee to fetlock.

The mare lifted its hoof several times, nickering nervously.

"It's all right, girl," Chelsea cooed reassuringly, patiently rewrapping the leg. She knew the mare had to feel the strange tingling, almost burning sensation, just as she had when she had dipped her own fingers into the poultice.

Wraps secured in place with what she liked to call "Red Cross" knots, she sat back to admire her handiwork. She glanced at Rakia. *Their* handiwork, she corrected herself. Didn't they make quite a team, and without magic pills or commercial potions?

Reaching out, she squeezed her associate's hand.

"Will it work?" Rakia asked.

"It has to," she assured—both of them. She stood and gently rubbed the soft velvety nose that nuzzled her gently with what she interpreted as trust. Khalil was wrong. This mare was no killer. The horse had simply been frightened by unfamiliar surroundings and handling. Just as she, herself, was fearful of the unknown and the strange, uncontrollable whirlwind that had swept into her life.

She did not question that she would return to her own time and place if given the opportunity. But until then, if the opportunity ever presented itself at all, she had better learn to make the best of it—or else end up like this mare, nearly destroyed by her own inflexibility.

"Teach me, Rakia," she said softly, her request twofold. "Not only about your way of life, but about the herbs. How to use them to heal, where to find and identify them. I want—no, I need to learn."

"Of course." Her friend reached up and grasped her hand. "Come spring, I will show you all of my secret caches and teach you how to prepare them."

Come spring. Such a long way off, a lifetime, in fact. Chelsea prepared herself to still be there, forever and always.

Twenty-one

Day after day, Khalil observed the healing process, keeping his distance, wanting more than anything to participate. Chelsea never asked for him, did not seem to miss him; therefore, he did not press her. Even so his heart grew closer and closer to hers, despite the fact that the feeling remained one-sided. He watched her tend that lame mare, the one he had ruined with his recklessness and then considered a loss. Experiencing her moments of joy and accomplishment, he admonished himself for his own shortsightedness.

The end results were yet to be seen, but if anyone could make that horse sound again, it would be Chelsea. Who had ever heard of such a thing—to doctor an injured animal as one would a human? But then, there was much he could learn from Chelsea. Much to be gained by accepting her way of doing things. Much to be admired in her ability to handle such an unruly beast as the Rashaad mare.

Perhaps the future and those who made it held more promise than he had ever given any of them credit for.

In the meantime he would continue to observe her,

looking for a sign. Of what, he was not certain, but he knew he would recognize it when he saw it and know then what he must do.

Each day marked a new level of success in the healing of the mare if not of their severed relationship. He recalled the moment when Chelsea unwrapped the bandaged leg. Waiting anxiously from afar to see, he wished to join her but dared not. The mare meant a lot to him, as well, even if he had been the one to nearly destroy it with his determination to break it. He regretted his thoughtlessness more times than he could count.

That the injury looked healed was deceptive. The mare might still be lame. Chelsea led her patient around, slowly at first, observing the way the mare moved with more than casual interest. Now and then she stopped to examine the leg with her hands. It was almost as if she were as knowledgeable about horses as he. But who ever heard of a woman with such skills?

He had never seen anything like it. That docile mare followed her around, not a trace of the wild untamable beast he knew it to be. And watching Chelsea be so tolerant and gentle, he could only wish she would lavish the same attention on him. He, too, might be so receptive.

Contrary female or not, he came to respect her abilities and knowledge of horses and love her that much more. Not even the best of his trainers could compare with her. Her methods—so nontraditional—produced amazing results and controversy that became the focus of fireside debate.

Like today. He stood by quietly, out of sight, watching as she worked with that mare as if it were the most natural thing in the world for her to do, as if she had done it all of her life. On a long line, she ran the mare round and round in circles. Neither he, nor any of the others who paused to observe, could see the point in such futile exercise. Then it dawned on him that it gave her the perfect opportunity to study how the animal moved, which proved to be with no residual effect of the injury. However, until the mare was mounted and ridden, its soundness could not be certain.

No sooner did he think it than it happened.

"Chelsea, no." In his anxiety he revealed himself as she climbed on the mare's bare back. Remembering his own perilous experience, he only knew he must stop her before it was too late.

To his surprise, the mare just stood there, seemingly relaxed, waiting for direction from its rider. However, the minute the mare spied him racing toward them, it pinned back its ears, snorted a warning, and began to prance nervously.

"Come no closer, Khalil." A hostile look accompanied Chelsea's curt warning. Before he could respond, she wheeled the mare about, and the pair trotted off as if he were not even there.

He weighed his options and found them sorely lacking. To march out there and demand she dismount, which was what he wanted to do, would accomplish nothing. He would never truly master them, neither horse nor woman. But to concede? It went against his very nature to allow a woman or a horse to get the better of him.

"Damn you, Chelsea," he muttered, agitated by his inability to control the situation. Seething, he watched her put the mare smoothly through its paces. Like only the finest of horsemen, she rode from the leg, a part of the horse. They were beautiful. They belonged together.

They would not be ruled by him. Love was much like

403

leadership, he begrudgingly realized. A sheikh could only lead his people where they chose to go. Sadly enough he had to accept that the same could be said of a woman's heart.

By all that was sacred, he missed her, the feel of her in his arms, the taste of her sweet lips. Would the moment ever come when he could claim her again?

He doubted it. If it did come, it would only be fleeting and temporary, an illusion that would never give him or her true satisfaction.

And so he knew what he must do. Let them go. Both of them, the mare and the woman, for neither would ever truly belong to him.

Exalted after the long, thorough workout, Chelsea felt more at home here in the desert than she ever had since her arrival in the Middle East. God, she remembered that day well, stepping off the plane filled with naive wonder and the grand delusion of making her mark on universal society.

To think she'd found it necessary to travel halfway around the world and then back into time to rediscover what it was that truly gave her a sense of accomplishment. Horses.

"Shamaal. Yes, I will name you after the powerful desert wind that brought me here." Confident now that the mare's injuries were completely healed, she patted the perfectly arched neck, truly believing this to be the finest mount she'd ever had the pleasure of riding. What a prize to take back to Georgia. She laughed. That would be like trying to steal that elusive wind. If she were to show up

with such a mare, no papers, no traceable lineage, and yet so utterly perfect, her father would be flabbergasted.

Since she couldn't take Shamaal home, then she would simply train her here. She glanced out over the level area she now envisioned as an arena. Over there she must construct a line of jumps, maybe a few cavalletti as well.

Yes, yes. She would get started tomorrow.

Finishing up the thorough rubdown, she led the mare back to the herd and turned it loose, hobbled of course, to graze for the rest of the day.

As she made her way back to the encampment Chelsea surprised herself by whistling. Could it be she might actually find happiness giving up her identity and remaining in the desert?

One could never predict the unexpected twists that life often took.

She looked around wondering where Khalil had gone, suddenly wanting to share her newfound discovery, not just with anyone, only with him.

"Have you told Chel-sea yet, *ya ràyyis?*"

"Not until the time is right." Khalil stared at the young Arab, Jamal, with whom he shared a pot of coffee, trying to decide his tribe of origins. Ruala, perhaps, taking into account his slenderness, even delicateness for a man, or perhaps Shammar from the coastal areas. That would account for the wide set of his eyes.

"Are you sure this is what she desires?"

"I am sure."

"Has she told you this?"

Khalil bristled, abandoning his cup. Why did the *hadhar* persist in his annoying line of questioning?

"This is how it is to be, Jamal."

"But of course, great one," Jamal conceded, burying his face in his cup. "Am I expected to go as well?"

"Expected? I suppose not. But it is your right."

"And if I should decide to stay?"

"That, too, is your right, my friend." Surprised, Khalil took in the younger man's demeanor. To look at him one would never suspect he did not belong, here and now. "You are welcome, of course, but may I ask why?"

Jamal glanced at him nervously.

"What is it?"

"I fear you will not approve."

"Approve?" And then it struck Khalil. "Ah. I see. Does this have something to do with my cousin, Rakia?"

Jamal looked up hopefully, his dark eyes steady with true Bedouin pride.

"What are your intentions?"

"To marry her, if she will have me, and if you will give us your blessing."

"And how do you plan to provide for a wife? I fear you will never make much of a herdsman."

"Trust me, oh, great one." Jamal leaned back comfortably against a saddle, suddenly quite sure of himself. "The camel and the horse mean little to the future of Arabia. It is what is found beneath the sand that will make a man, a tribe, a nation rich."

"Beneath the sand?" Khalil leaned forward, most interested.

Jamal only smiled.

"So you plan to become a *kuhlan.*" Jamal a soothsayer, he mused. "You are very shrewd for a townsman. What man would not pay well to know the future and how to insure that generations of his people will be well provided for? Tell me. What will you charge for such . . . insight?"

"For you, *ya ràyyis,* I will be most generous. After the customary dowry of a tent and all household necessities . . . my fee will be a small one indeed. Merely a few head of camel, say fifty or so, to be tended by your herdsmen, of course. After all, we will be family."

"A most convenient arrangement." Khalil threw back his head and laughed. "Very well, my cousin." He retrieved his coffee cup and lifted it in a salute. "With your help, perhaps, those who carry on the name of Khalil ibn Mani al Muraidi will be wealthy beyond imagination."

"Not perhaps, *ya ràyyis.* Guaranteed." Jamal raised his cup in reciprocation. "You have only to follow my advice."

The bargain was made and sealed.

Still, that did not solve the question of Chelsea Browne.

Chelsea was humming softly in her solitude only mildly concerned with the whereabouts of the other women. Not even Rakia was present, an oddity indeed, but being alone was such a rare thing, she decided to just enjoy the reprieve.

Busy drawing up her plans for the hunter course she wished to construct, she was wondering how she might approach Khalil and convince him to give her six . . .

No. Quickly she adjusted her sketch. She needed more like seven or eight of the precious supply of extra tent poles to make a decent course.

It was then, still singing under her breath, that she realized she was no longer by herself.

Growing silent, she looked up to find him standing there, almost as if he had been drawn to her by thoughts alone. But of course that was silly, wasn't it?

"What do you want?" she demanded, returning to her drawings. She should be nicer, she supposed, considering that she wanted something from him. When he didn't answer her, she readjusted her attitude. "Look, I am quite busy here. If you could just tell me what you need . . ." She lifted her gaze and came up against a most intense scrutiny; in fact, it made her quite uncomfortable.

Could his need be the same as the one that she continually repressed? She refused to give credence to something so unacceptable as a desire to surrender herself wholly, body and soul, to this man who was anything but good for her. Yes, there it was, that look, almost a hunger, even if it had only been fleeting; there was no denying he felt it, too. If nothing else, she had to commend him for his efforts to control himself.

Quite an accomplishment for a self-centered man like Khalil, accustomed to getting what he wanted, when he wanted it.

"You will come with me."

If she hadn't had her own reasons for wanting to talk to him, she probably would have refused to yield to such an outright demand, if for no other reason than to see him puff up like a silly, old toad.

"Very well," she said, stifling a chuckle. Setting aside her sketches, she rose to stand beside him, his towering height and imposing demeanor making her feel safe and secure.

He seemed taken aback at her easy compliance, but

he said nothing more, just took her by the arm and led her out of the tent and across the encampment. To her surprise she discovered both his black mare and her white one saddled and readied for what appeared to be a long trip.

"Just where are we going, Khalil?" she asked, tugging at his restraining hand, but with very little effort he continued to propel her forward.

"Mount your horse."

Was this some kind of test? Or better yet, a challenge, perhaps?

"And if I should refuse?" It pleased her to see the white mare begin to fidget at the sight of the man who made her just as uneasy.

"Rest assured, that you will not do." He smiled down arrogantly from his superior height, waiting. Just waiting. For what? For her curiosity to get the better of her?

She might have turned then and marched away if only to prove that he could not so easily anticipate her every move. Then she spied a familiar leather pouch encircling his tan neck.

"The talisman!" she gasped, lunging for what she felt rightfully belonged to her. "Where did you find it?"

Something in the way he blocked her hand and stared at her so calmly. . . .

"You had it all along," she accused, eyes narrowing. By the way his sensual mouth tightened she knew she spoke the truth. "Damn you," she cried, not caring that she cursed him before a quickly growing crowd. Forming fists, she swung at him.

With little effort he fended off her unbridled attack.

"How could you do that, Khalil? How could you so callously take away my hope of ever getting back . . . ?"

"I had hopes of my own, Chelsea." He lowered his voice so that only she could hear. "Hopes that you would learn to be happy here with me, perhaps come to care even just a little. But you are like that accursed Rashaad mare—wild, headstrong . . . hopeless. I rue the day I captured her. It was a mistake."

"And me? Am I a mistake, as well?" she asked, finding that her heart beat so rapidly she thought it would burst with the pain.

His silence served as a very clear answer.

"So now what, Khalil? Now that you have decided you made a big mistake, how do you plan to rectify it? By taking me back?" God help her to understand the irrational feeling of rejection that jolted her. It was one thing for her not to want him, but for him not to care. . . .

Men were all the same. His reaction was no more than she should have expected.

Wordlessly, she turned away and walked calmly—at least outwardly—toward her mount. It was then that she spied Jamal and Rakia standing off to one side.

She could never leave without her assistant. And, oh, how she would miss Rakia and her gentle ways. Should she offer to take her with her? No. Rakia had said it once before. This was her home. These were her people. Oh, how she envied the woman.

"Jamal, you must make preparations to leave. Knowing Khalil," she warned, shooting the silent Arab a frosty look, "he won't wait long for you to get ready."

"Chel-sea, I am not returning with you."

"But, of course you are." She laughed; then when she thought about it, she whirled about with the intent of confronting Khalil and demanding to know just who he thought he was to keep Jamal from returning home. "If he thinks he can keep you here against your will . . ."

"Chel-sea, no one is preventing me from leaving except myself. I don't want to go. I want to stay here."

"Why?" she demanded. But the answer was clear in the way her young assistant reached out and grasped Rakia's hand. "Oh, I see," she murmured.

She should say something to them, congratulate them, but all she could do was stand there and stare, her tongue stubbornly cleaved to the roof of her mouth.

It took Rakia to make the first move. The woman, her friend, probably the best, most undemanding friend Chelsea would ever have, reached out and put her arms around her.

"Come spring, I will think of you. I will miss you so very much."

"Oh, Rakia, I am so happy for you, truly I am."

"I know. I know. Should I be happy for you, too?"

"Yes," Chelsea replied, making up her mind that this was truly what she wanted. "I am going home."

They squeezed each other, neither willing to be the first to let go. Chelsea couldn't help the flood of tears that welled in her eyes.

"Jamal." Releasing the woman, she turned to her assistant, her friend. "Take good care of her . . . and of yourself." *I envy you,* she wanted to say, but didn't.

It wasn't fair. She had finally come to feel a part of these people, a Bedouin at heart. She didn't want to leave. And Shamaal? What would happen to the mare once she was no longer there to care for her?

Somehow she had to convince Khalil he would be better off by returning Shamaal to her rightful owner. Surely, if he was so eager to be rid of a difficult woman, he would not miss an unruly horse, either.

She shot him a furtive look, plotting what she would say just before they parted. But nothing seemed adequate. Then her heart skipped a beat when she thought about the inevitable moment of separation. No, she couldn't think about that now. Climbing into the saddle, she reined the mare toward the distant ridge.

"I am ready," she announced, feeling more like a condemned prisoner on the way to the gallows than a woman joyously returning home.

With no words of apology, not even a few simple ones of explanation or encouragement, Khalil commanded the lead. They rode to the ridge and headed west. Chelsea made no attempt to overtake the black horse and rider, even though she was confident Shamaal could have outdistanced them easily.

Alone, she confronted her confusion. Why did she feel so reluctant to go home when all she had dreamed of so long was just such an opportunity? Why this change of heart?

No, she adamantly refused to accept that her lack of enthusiasm had anything to do with the state of her heart. She could not love a man like Khalil, for it was obvious, he chose not to love her.

On they rode, the late afternoon sun a beacon to follow. And then the sky began to darken as a haze gathered, an eerie shroud that made the air feel heavy, almost unbreatheable.

She tried hard to think back to that night when Khalil had swept into the clinic, demanding to see the doctor. With his glittering eyes and jeweled sword, she had thought him the most fierce-looking Arab she had ever seen. Had she known then what was in store for her, would she have balked at going with him? Even if she had, she doubted he would have accepted her refusal.

Of the ride itself, she remembered little, except that it had been so dark already, there was no way to recall if the strange phenomenon that was happening now had occurred then as well.

Nor would she have ever surmised that a man so frightening to behold would become the gentlest of lovers, the one to help her finally shed her lifelong inhibitions, to show her what it meant to love. . . .

No, it wasn't love. It couldn't be. It must only be wild infatuation with a fantasy come true, nothing more. Once she was back where she belonged, and that would be soon, those nights of abandonment would be reduced to memories of bygone dreams. Truly an adventure, it would be no more believable than the other thousand and one.

As if the earth chose at that moment to agree with her logic, a great wind began to whirl the sands beneath them, the air all around them. In a matter of moments it began to moan and howl, tearing at her hair, her clothing, her eyes.

Shamaal shrieked like the wind after which she was named and reared. Chelsea clung to her back, finally calming the frightened horse, but for how long, she could only guess.

"We cannot go on," she cried, covering her face and head as best as she could with the black *abaaya* she wore.

"We must," Khalil shouted back, his own face concealed behind the edges of his *keffiyeh* as he fought to keep his own mount, which knew what lay ahead, under control.

"Khalil." She almost told him then and there she didn't wish to continue, that she wanted to go back, to stay here with him, and not just because of what she must face to return to her own time, but because . . . because. . . .

His look, as hard as mirrored glass as it raked over her, offered no encouragement.

Regardless of how she might feel, if he no longer wanted her, what choice did that give her? Only one, for she was much too proud to ever throw herself at the feet of a merciless man.

"Give me the talisman," she demanded instead, wanting only to be free of him as quickly and painlessly as possible, before she broke down and made an utter fool of herself. "I can make my own way from here."

"No. I brought you here. It is my sworn duty to take you back." With that vow he moved on ahead, once more taking the lead.

Obviously, he either didn't trust her to go on alone, or more likely, he did not wish to part with the precious talisman. It couldn't be that he cared.

Bowing her head in defeat, to the elements and to the truth once again that men knew only how to think of themselves, she followed him and focused on keeping the increasingly nervous mare moving forward one difficult step at a time.

She heard the crackling of the fire long before she actually saw it, felt the heat that was like a hot breath of wind sweeping down on them, a warning of what was to come. Her heart pounding, she brought her mount to a halt and looked up.

There it was. The awesome ring of fire, alive and spinning like some circus trick from the netherworld, coming toward them, so fast. It had nearly killed Jamal because he had not been next to the talisman.

The talisman.

"Khalil," she called out, panic-stricken. Unable to see him in the darkness and the whirling sand, she feared her position left her vulnerable. Had he changed his mind and deserted her? She glanced overhead again. Should she stay where she was, attempt to move forward, or flee from where she had come? No matter what she did, her actions could be fatal.

"Chelsea. Chelsea. Get down." He was there, pulling her from the saddle, his great cloak enveloping her before her feet landed. His strong arms, brooking no resistance, threw her to the ground.

"The horses," she cried over the awful wailing of the wind, struggling to get up. Thinking of the unfortunate camel with the fuzzy feet, she couldn't forsake Shamaal.

"There is not time, Chelsea. They must fend for themselves."

Shielded by his wide masculine body, the talisman pressed between their wildly racing hearts, she could hear Shamaal's terrified shrieks. With fear or pain? She couldn't be certain. Choking back a sob, she buried her face against his shoulder, knowing he was right. There was nothing more they could do.

She only knew Khalil had chosen to protect her when he could have as easily deserted her. She clung to him, closing her eyes, wishing she could do the same with her heart, wanting never to let go, wanting never to leave him.

"The brown shell of the sea," he chanted. She found herself saying it with him.

In that moment of transition, she knew not from where she gathered the courage, but she lifted her face to find his just above hers. She kissed him, passionately, thoroughly, so lovingly, losing herself to the whirling sensations that seemed to turn everything into black and white within the circle of flames.

"I love you, Khalil, I love you," she murmured. Or had she only thought she had said it aloud?

Either way she could swear he reacted, returning the caress with equal fervor.

And then the moment ended as quickly as it had overtaken them. Once more he stared down at her with that stone-hard expression that she could never decipher. It tore at her heart, ripping it to shreds, leaving her battered and bleeding—and determined to go on the best that she could.

Still trapped in Khalil's arms, she listened to the desert around them. Was it only her imagination, or did it sound somehow different? That distant hum. What was it? Curious, she peeked around his shoulder.

And the sky. The colors of the sunset. Was it only her imagination or were they not as brilliant as the ones she had witnessed from the door of Khalil's tent? But that was impossible. A sky was a sky.

And an airplane was an airplane.

She rubbed her eyes. Yes, that was definitely a jet in the distance streaking across the sky.

Home. Truly she was home.

"You can get off me now." She pushed at Khalil's chest. At first, she thought he would deny her request, but then he rose up off her, staring down at her with a look of longing. But then a soft nicker caused them both to glance away.

"Shamaal!"

The two mares were standing only a few feet away. Chelsea scrambled to her knees and quickly inspected them for injury, relieved to find none. Without questioning the miracle that had brought them all through the fire safe and sound, she sat back on her heels and glanced at Khalil.

There was no sense delaying the inevitable. The time had come to go their separate ways. Gathering up the trailing reins, she stood and led the horses to Khalil, placing the strips of braided leather into his hands.

"Point me in the right direction, and I will make my way from here," she announced, lifting her chin to denote a courage she wasn't too sure existed.

"No. You would only get lost." His gaze slid over her in that contemptuous way it often did when he assessed her as if she were property of questionable value. "We still have a long way to ride." Handing her back the reins to Shamaal, he mounted his black mare and started off.

Given no other choice, she scrambled into the saddle and trailed after him.

He had not exaggerated. It was a long distance indeed that they rode. Hours before, the sun had set. Guided only by a thin strip of moonlight, they finally came across a modern highway. The road sign staked in the sand along side said: "Ad Dawadimi, 9 km."

Dismounting, she ran her hands along the concrete as if it were a monument made of solid gold.

"Chelsea. This is as far as I go."

At the sound of her name and the words of departure so softly spoken, she lifted her head in dread. He did not dismount—but then what did she expect? Him to vow his love at the very last moment? To demand that she return with him? To offer to stay with her? He just sat atop his coal black mare, dressed in black himself, calm, not one emotion to be found on his hard-planed face. Tall and regal in every sense of the word, if ever there were a man who deserved the title of prince, it was Khalil.

She knew then not only would she miss him, but her life, that meager, unimportant existence that she clung to, would never be the same, never be complete without him. Leading Shamaal forward, she offered up the reins to the man who had managed to master her heart and then trample it with nary a flicker in his eyes.

Glancing down at her hand, he shook his head, his dark glaze flicking over her so quickly that she longed for it to linger. But it didn't.

"The mare is yours, *ya Duktur.* Payment for saving the life of my son."

Before she could thank him or plead with him not to go, he wheeled his dark horse about and took off across the sand, leaving nothing behind but footprints to assure her he had been there.

A ragged sob caught in her throat as she stood there, waiting, watching, hoping. After a half an hour she accepted she waited in vain.

He had not even looked back, not even once, not even to say goodbye.

Wrapped in the warmth of her *abaaya,* Chelsea allowed the mare to pick its own speed as they rode along the side of the highway. A pickup truck, red of course, passed them, slowing down at the sight of the lone horse-woman.

Someone asked her if she would like a ride into town. She declined with a shake of her covered head.

The truck and its rowdy occupants zoomed ahead.

Alone again, they plodded on, avoiding the trash along the highway.

From a small rise, she spied the lights of the village. It was like some kind of dream, those lights. They seemed to weave in and out of focus. Urging the mare to a lazy canter, they entered the outskirts of Ad Dawadimi.

The streets were quiet, not a soul to be seen. But then, that wasn't all that unusual. Automatically she made her way to the clinic, navigating a garbage-strewn alleyway and crossing through the vacant lot across the street from the rear of the clinic just as Khalil had done that evening when he had led them on that merry chase.

Wallahi, it seemed like only yesterday that she and Jamal had jumped into the Land Rover and sped out of the village in pursuit of a stranger on horseback.

Behind the clinic, Chelsea paused. To her surprise she discovered the Land Rover sitting in its customary parking spot in the alley. Quickly she dismounted and went over to it, placing her face against the glass of the rear window.

It was well stocked, ready to leave at a moment's notice for any kind of emergency—just like that night not so long ago.

She tied Shamaal's reins to the door handle.

"It's all right, girl. I'll be back," she reassured, patting the mare's arched neck.

To be frank, she didn't expect to find anyone at the clinic at so late an hour, but it had seemed the logical place for her to come, anyway. Actually, she expected to find the back door locked, but to her surprise it wasn't.

She opened the door to the sound of . . . was it some kind of party? Automatically, she pulled the edges of her *abaaya* tightly about her face for the sake of modesty.

On silent feet she walked down the familiar hallway. The laughter was coming from the large waiting room in the front of the building. Rounding the corner, she thought she must have made a mistake, for the people were so strangely dressed, as if all of the pages of history had collided.

Wallahi! It was some kind of nightmare. There was a cowboy, an Indian, an Egyptian Pharaoh, a court jester, a demon from hell.

"Happy New Year," someone shouted. Horns started blasting; confetti flew into the air as all the strange figures began to hug and kiss.

"Where am I?" she cried, drawing her hood tighter about her face and covering her ears with her hands.

The noise and the celebration stopped. Everyone turned to stare at her. No one said a word.

"Who are you?" she demanded, stopping in the middle of the room which suddenly began to sway, tilt drunkenly, then spin wildly.

"Jesus Christ. How did one of the locals get in here? What is she babbling about? God, we're in big trouble now."

That voice. She knew it even if she didn't recognize the demonic face so close to her own.

"Joe? Dr. Joe Huff?" she murmured.

Her knees turned to jelly, and she felt the floor come

420

toward her. She was grateful for the arms that caught her just in time.

"Chelsea? Yes, I'm sure. No, I don't know how she got here."

The *abaaya* was peeled away from her face. She tried to smile, but wasn't sure she succeeded.

"Good God, look at her. Somebody hurry. Get me my medical bag."

Twenty-two

"Jamal!"

Jerked from a chaotic dream of her assistant lying in the desert, calling to her, Chelsea opened her eyes. Her heart slammed as if she'd been running. She glanced about, not recognizing exactly where she was, but instinctively knew it was a hospital room. She spied the white-clad figure coming toward her.

"Jamal," she repeated. "I left him in the desert. I have to find him."

The nurse, no one she recognized, ignored her, looking past her.

"She's at it again, Doctor."

"Chelsea. Chelsea."

She turned her head at the sharp command, discovering her friend, her fellow physician, Joe Huff, standing next to her bed.

"Joe. I have to find him," she began again, clutching his arm.

"Look, Chelsea." He sat down on the edge of the bed beside her and took her hand gently in his large, very white ones, patting it. "If you want me to understand you, you simply must speak English."

Speak English? But that was what she was doing. Wasn't it?

"Joe, you don't understand—" His hand over her mouth stopped her mid-sentence.

"English." He smiled with encouragement.

Chelsea cleared her confused mind and started again.

"Joe. It is Jamal." The words, and they were English, came out so slowly. She looked up to make sure.

Joe nodded his understanding.

"I left him. In the desert."

"It's okay, Chelsea. We know. He was found four days ago."

"Then, he is here?" she blurted.

"Ah." He lifted a finger admonishing her. "English."

Her hands were trembling so violently, she clutched them to her chest to control them.

"Where is he?" she asked slowly.

Joe didn't answer, but his expression frightened her.

"Joe, what is it?"

"Look, Chelsea, I'm not sure you're up to this, but I think keeping the truth from you would be wrong. Jamal was found with the Land Rover. He had been burned severely . . ."

"Are you saying he's dead?"

Joe gave her a steady look.

"No." She laughed to cover her confusion. "You don't understand. The burns healed. I doctored them myself. Only yesterday I left him in a tent, with an Arab woman. . . . You don't believe me."

"Do you believe it?"

"It's the truth."

"Of course it is." He patted her hand once more, then carefully placed it on the crisp, white sheet. "We'll talk

423

about this later. Right now, I want you to concentrate on rehydration and rebuilding your strength."

"Joe. Joe. I was there. I saw him. There was a man. A handsome desert sheikh. He came to the clinic in need of a doctor."

But Joe wasn't listening. He was only shaking his head.

"English, Chelsea. English." He looked over her head at the nurse, who stared at her in wide-eyed curiosity. "Keep an eye on her, Miss O'Neal. Make sure she has plenty of fluids."

Oh, God. She glanced from one sympathetic face to the other. They both thought she'd lost her mind.

Perhaps they weren't too far from the truth.

"Chelsea? Chelsea Marie? Is that really you?" The telephone crackled, breaking up the familiar, faraway voice.

"Mother. Stop crying," Chelsea said over the loud, racking sobs from the other end. "I'm all right. Truly I am."

"Chelsea. Your father wants to speak with you."

"Mother, no. Don't put Daddy on the—"

"Chelsea, girl."

"Hi, Daddy," she replied with a resigned sigh, knowing exactly what was coming. He would proceed to tell her what to do, just like he always did, deciding her life contrary to what she really wanted. But that was her father, inclined to tell everyone what to do and expecting them to obey.

"I don't want any argument from you this time. You get on the next plane home. Do you hear me?"

"I hear you, Daddy, but—"

"No buts, little lady. I'll make the reservations on this end. You just show up at the airport."

"Daddy, I don't want you to make reservations for me. When I'm ready to come home, I'll call you and tell you my plans."

Except for the crackling, the line remained silent, but she knew it wouldn't remain that way for long.

"Goodbye, Daddy."

"Why, you ungrateful little bitch . . ."

Chelsea put down the receiver, trying to block out the abusive language loud enough to be heard by everyone in the room.

"Are you okay, Chelsea?" Joe's steady gaze conveyed his genuine concern.

"Yes, I am." She forced her lips to smile, to reassure him and convince herself. "Probably for the first time in my life. Now," she said, picking up her medical chart and plopping it into his hands, "if you would just kindly release me, Dr. Huff, I would like to get back to work."

From the very first day Chelsea walked back into that clinic, everything was different, especially her attitude. She couldn't quite explain it, but she found herself attuned to not only the physical needs of her patients, but more importantly, to their psychological ones.

She understood the Arab mind and found herself sympathizing with it. The fact that she now spoke the language quite fluently, even if a bit archaically at times, helped tremendously. She didn't try to explain how she'd obtained the skill in little over two weeks—modern time, for more than two weeks had passed for her in the desert. She couldn't explain that either and didn't try. Every time she started to talk about the experience, she received polite but sympathetic looks. No one else might care to believe her, but she knew where she had been, if not exactly how she'd gotten there. They couldn't convince her that Khalil was only a delusion brought on by exposure, or that she had spent the last few weeks roaming aimlessly, lost in the desert.

Fatima, the cleaning lady, had been the only one who had seen Khalil except Jamal and herself. But the old woman had apparently disappeared the next day. Not that that was so unusual. The locals often came and went like the seasons, and upon learning that she had been threatened by some crazed Bedouin, her husband had probably refused to let her come back to work and had whisked his family away.

As for Jamal. Well, let them think what they wanted. She knew the truth. He was happy and no doubt in ecstasy wrapped in Rakia's loving arms.

The other physicians she worked with often as not gave her a wide berth, thinking her crazy. Even Joe gave her odd looks now and then, especially when she unconsciously began to mumble to herself in Arabic, or when she donned the traditional *abaaya* whenever she went out in public.

She couldn't explain the strange compulsion, except that she didn't feel comfortable dressed otherwise.

It was inevitable, she supposed, that her popularity among the people would grow. They came day after day, seeking umm Dawa, the Mother of Medicine. Most preferred to wait for hours to see her even when other doctors were available.

426

And so, walking through the *souq* of Ad Dawadimi on her way home always dropping by the small shed where she boarded Shamaal, it wasn't unusual for the locals to call out to her and for her to respond in kind, knowing many of them by name.

That particular day started out no diffcrent from so many. She had seen at least three dozen patients with every imaginable ailment. Tired, after being on her feet for so many hours, she made her way slowly home via the stable.

Finding the white mare well fed but restless from the days of confinement it seemed never to get used to, Chelsea spent a few moments brushing Shamaal out and making promises.

"Sunday," she vowed. "We will take a long ride then. Be patient, Shamaal, this will be over soon."

That was being optimistic, she chided herself, as she walked the few blocks to her small apartment.

She didn't see the magnificent Rolls Royce parked in front of her building until she practically ran headlong into it, banging her knee on the bumper.

Rubbing what she knew would be a giant bruise come morning, she limped past the gathered crowd and up the stairs to her apartment, forced to push her way past those congregated even there.

She knew the man was important, if not by his ostentatious dress—although garbed in traditional Arab clothing, he wore an expensive gold Rolex watch, sunglasses that cost a fortune, at least by her standards, and he sported a diamond ring that could feed the entire planet for a week—then by his equally showy mannerisms. Probably some wealthy oil baron who wanted her to examine his ailing wife.

"Duktur Chel-sea Browne?" he asked. He dipped his head in deference, but he did not bother to take off his sunglasses.

The way he said her name reminded her of Jamal. The way he looked reminded her of Khalil. The blood began to roar in her ears. It was the clothing, she assured herself, and her out-of-control heart, nothing more.

"Yes. But unless it is a dire emergency, could you please bring the patient to the clinic first thing in the morning. I promise to see you then." She started to brush past him.

He stopped her.

"You do not understand. I am here by royal decree."

"By what?" she asked.

"From the king." Extracting a scrolled document, gilded and banded with a solid gold ring, from the folds of his *thobe,* he placed it in her hand.

"I don't understand." She peered up at the Arab.

"I have not read it personally, madam, but I suspect it is an invitation from His Highness to visit the palace in Riyadh. *Majlis,* a royal audience, is a rare honor for anyone, but especially for a woman. You must have done the royal family a great service, Duktur Browne." He bowed his head once more.

For the life of her, Chelsea couldn't imagine what she could have done for the king of Saudi Arabia.

Although nervous as hell, Chelsea tried hard not to show it. The black limousine sped along the Mecca Road, a four-lane freeway between the two great cities. Ad Dawadimi just happened to be on it. She clutched the gilded royal invitation in her hand, still unable to believe the last twenty-four hours were real.

What did one say to a king? Discussing the weather somehow just didn't seem appropriate. Whatever she did, she had to make sure she didn't slip into one of her strange stories about Khalil.

And not just for her own reputation, but the fact was she represented the entire United States. She had spent the morning with diplomats and deputy ambassadors who had coached her thoroughly on what she could and could not say. By mid-morning her head was spinning, and she was so nauseated she'd had to lie down for a few moments.

Why her? Chelsea dropped her head against the expensive leather seat, still not feeling well. She'd never asked for this . . . honor.

Apparently that was exactly how the diplomats had felt as well. Nonetheless, they were determined to take full advantage of the opportunity to improve relationships with the Saudi government, no matter how it had come about.

The superhighway crossed over the Wadi Hanifah. It made her think of the small pavilion she had shared with Khalil. The vehicle slowed once they entered the city. Brushing away a longing that would forever remain in her memory, Chelsea sat up and stared out the window.

Riyadh. The huge modern city was nothing like she recalled. What she remembered was a little village where she had been captured by the Rashaad and rolled in a carpet. Up ahead she spied the Royal Palace.

Suddenly she changed her mind. She didn't want to go through with this—*majlis,* royal interview, no matter what its purpose. All she wanted to do was go home, back to Atlanta, Georgia.

"Allah, get me through this day, and I promise . . ." She closed her eyes. "I swear on my professional reputation, I'll get on the first plane back to the United States. I'll stay in Georgia for the rest of my life and be satisfied."

In the driveway, the chauffeur sat patiently, the limousine idling until a pair of wrought-iron gates opened of their own accord to admit them. She wished her nerves were so composed. Before the Royal Palace with crowstep crenellations along the roofline and round minarets, its spectacular domes and cupolas, its sculptured gardens and fountains, she discovered her curiosity overrode her terror. Odd, but for reasons she didn't quite understand, she felt at home here.

"Duktur Browne, welcome."

At that official greeting by a man she assumed to be some kind of minister, she gathered her *abaaya* about her and stepped from the open car door and followed the stranger. Everyone she passed, some servants, others official, acknowledged her with a respectful bow.

By the way these people were acting one would think she had saved the life of somebody important. She thought back on all of the patients she had seen over the last few days. None of them stood out as particularly impressive, mostly poor nomads and villagers from around Ad Dawadimi.

Warned by the American diplomats, she prepared to be ushered into some kind of waiting room and then wait, for hours most likely, until one of the king's minor ministers chose to join her and tell her whatever it was they wanted from her.

430

What if it was something beyond her skills? Her nervousness returned, her knees began to knock, her stomach to knot. She made her way to a small overstuffed couch against one wall and sat down, clutching her middle.

She had been told to stand until asked to sit, but she didn't feel well.

Now she was beginning to sweat.

"Perhaps, madam, a drink of water would help."

Without looking up, she nodded. A few seconds later a glass was placed in her hand, and she swallowed the water in several giant gulps.

Empty, the glass was removed from her trembling hand.

"Better?"

"Much," she replied, wiping her mouth on the back of her hand. "Thank you. I don't know what came over me." She glanced up, expecting to see a servant.

Instead, the man standing over her, as tall and regal as any she had ever seen, was without a doubt a prince. It had to be her crazy imagination that made him look so much like Khalil.

"I'm sorry." Pulling her *abaaya* closely about her face, she scrambled to her feet and stayed that way, unsure how long she could remain standing with her legs feeling so shaky.

"I did not mean to frighten you, Duktur Browne." His smile was genuine and so very familiar. It made her feel comfortable. He made her feel safe. *Wallahi,* it scared her to death.

"You didn't, not really." Pulling the covering tighter about her face, she looked down, fearing if she continued to stare at him she would do something foolish like blurt out Khalil's name. "I'm sorry. I didn't catch your name."

431

"I am Prince Saud."

"Oh, Your Highness." For the life of her, Chelsea couldn't remember what she was supposed to do. Curtsey? Drop to her knees? Just standing there staring at this royal prince wasn't it.

"Come. Sit." He took her arm and pressed her back down on the couch. He joined her, and then to her utter surprise, he reached out and brushed back her head covering. "This is forward of me, I know. I hope you do not mind."

"Mind? No, of course not." However, her entire body was shaking. She wanted to ask him what he was looking for, but couldn't, even when his dark eyes lingered on her hair in utter fascination.

"So, madam, I hear you have had a great adventure in the desert. Tell me about it."

What had he heard? What did he know? What was she going to say? Chelsea's heart picked up speed like a runaway car down a steep hill. She felt compelled to tell him the truth, yet she hesitated. He would be the same as all of the rest. He would think she had lost her mind.

"It's true, Your Highness, I was lost in the desert for a few days."

"And did you meet anyone?"

"Well, yes. There were these nomads, Bedouins." Dare she say more? "They fed me." Knowing he expected more, she stared at him in silence.

"I see." He lifted his hand and snapped his fingers. "I have something I would like to show you."

A servant came running in with a small, bejeweled chest and set it on the table before the prince and just as quickly disappeared.

Taking a key from the sash at his waist, he leaned over and unlocked the casket. He took out several scrolls.

"These are very ancient writings, Duktur Browne. Very important to my family, as were the people who wrote them. Am I to understand that you can read Arabic?"

"I'm not sure." She looked at him with doubt.

He smiled reassuringly, then placed the brittle parchments in her hands, which trembled at his touch.

Unrolling the first, she studied the florid script.

"Breeze-flowing tents I prefer to ponderous halls," she read aloud. "And desert dress to diaphanous veils. A crust I'd eat in the awning's shade, not rolls." She glanced up to find the handsome prince's eyes misted with an emotion she couldn't quite identify. Happiness, relief?

"Please, madam, continue."

"And watched by a dog that barks, not a cat that smiles, I'd sleep to the wind's tune, not to the tambourine. A youth's impetuous sword, not a husband's wiles, uncouth slim tribesmen I love, not corpulent men." Finished, she allowed the scroll to curl back up. "That is beautiful," she whispered, swiping at a wayward tear, the words making her think about Khalil. Oh, God, how she missed him. She should never have come back here. She no longer belonged.

"Especially when read by the one who wrote them."

"I didn't write this." Jarred back to the moment, she frowned. Why would this man, a stranger she forced herself to remember, say something so bizarre?

"Are you sure?" He looked perplexed, then tapped one of the other scrolls. "Please read this one."

Filled with apprehension, Chelsea flattened the one he indicated across her knees.

433

"Across all barriers unknown to man she came to me, her hair shimmering with gold, her eyes like pieces of the sky. My beautiful brown shell of the sea. Oh, how I miss her now that she has left me." It was signed Sheikh Khalil ibn Mani al Muraidi.

"Impossible." She let go of the scroll, watching it snap back into a tube, as if it had shocked her. In truth what she read had.

"Is it, madam?" He reached down and retrieved the ancient writing. "Perhaps now you wish to tell me what you are so afraid to reveal to others. I will believe you."

The story came tumbling out, of its own accord, and in its own way. Every time she paused to judge the prince's reaction, she found him listening, taking in every word with a seriousness she had thought never to find.

"And the child, Muhammad. You saved him."

"Yes, but his life was still in danger when I left. I forgot to tell Khalil." She stood, trying to figure out a way to correct so drastic an oversight. "How could I have forgotten to tell him?"

At that, the prince laughed. Again, he reminded her of Khalil—so much she ached to be held in his strong arms. "Not to worry, madam. Don't you see. He survived any future attempt on his young life . . . for I and my entire family are living proof. I wish to thank you for that. I also would like to repay you. Your wish is my command."

Repay her? Chelsea sat down again. It was all so much to absorb, to accept. But if it were so, then she had fulfilled what she had set out to do—to make her mark upon the world. But it would always leave its mark upon her. There was nothing to repay.

"You are peaked, Chel-sea, perhaps another glass of water."

"No." She lifted her hand, and then her face, staring into his dark eyes, so like Khalil's. He had said her wish was his command. If only that were true, if only he were a magic *jinni* who could wave his hand and give her back the one and only thing she wanted—the precious love she had so foolishly forsaken. But he was no *jinni*, nor was he Khalil, and no amount of wishing would make him so.

That part of her life was over, gone. Forever and always. She simply had to let go of it and go on.

"There is one thing you can do."

"Anything, madam, just name it," he agreed without even knowing what it was.

Shamaal. The mare was so unhappy confined to that tiny stall. She needed so much more than Chelsea could ever give her. Her dreams of taking the horse to America some day . . . well, they were unrealistic. If the confinement of transportation didn't kill her wild, desert spirit, the months of quarantine would.

"I have a mare I brought back with me . . ."

"From America?"

"No, from your ancestors. Actually she was taken in raid against the Rashaad."

"Ah, *ghazzu*." The prince's intelligent eyes glittered with envy. Khalil would be proud of this man of his blood. "That is an experience I will never know. Tell me. Were you there? What was it like?"

She tried to describe it as best she could, conjuring up details that had seemed so unimportant at the time. They talked on for hours, about so many things. When she happened to glance out of the window, she realized it was getting dark.

"I should go." She popped up from her seat.

"Must you?"

"Yes. I have a full day at the clinic ahead of me tomorrow." Then she colored, belatedly remembering it was not her place to end a royal audience. How could she have forgotten that this man was a Saudi prince and she merely a woman.

"Your wish is my command." The prince rose. "I will call for your limousine."

"And Shamaal?" she asked.

"I personally will pick her up and see that she is settled in the royal stables outside the city. Whatever price you ask for her will be transferred to your account anywhere in the world."

"I don't want money for her. What I want . . ."

No, Chelsea, remember. What you want you can never have.

"What I want is for you to take that money and put it toward a concentrated effort by your government to see that every child in the Middle East receives their vaccinations."

"That, madam, is a tall order."

"When you see Shamaal," she replied with a confident smile, "you will realize she is worth every *riyal.*"

"You are truly what the people say you are. Umm Dawa. Mother of Medicine." He dipped his head with respect. "I will personally see that your request is carried out."

Chelsea left, knowing she should feel good about the day, but all she felt was an emptiness she suspected she would carry with her for the rest of her life.

"Chelsea, what is it?"

"Nothing, Joe. Just all of the excitement of the last few days, the long hours—you know. I'll be okay in a few moments. I have to be okay. Already the waiting room is filled to capacity." Chelsea propped herself against the edge of the laboratory table and closed her eyes.

It was the same thing every morning. She felt like hell for a few hours, and then it went away.

"Chelsea, how long has this been going on?"

"Not long. A few weeks." That was a stretch. "I'll get over it."

"All right, Dr. Browne. You know better than that. Come with me. You need a thorough examination."

"Joe, this is *not* necessary. I'll be all right in a moment. At least wait until the end of the day."

But he would have none of it.

Moments later Chelsea found herself on the examination table, giving samples under protest and then waiting.

God, the waiting was the worst part.

When at last her colleague returned, the look on his face alarmed her.

"Well, what is it?"

When he didn't instantly reply, she felt her stomach knot with apprehension, her mind going over all of the possibilities in textbook style.

"Whatever it is, I can handle it. Just tell me. What's wrong with me?"

"You're pregnant."

"But that's impossible." She glared at him, ready to

demand another test. But it wasn't impossible. Khalil. It was more than likely.

"Look, Chelsea. I wouldn't ask you how this happened, or who the father is; but I'm in charge of this clinic, and its welfare has to come first."

"Joe, what are you saying?"

"I'm sorry, Dr. Browne, but under the circumstances, an unmarried woman pregnant in a Moslem country—I have to terminate your contract."

"Joe, please. Don't do this."

"I have no choice. If I don't, others will, and they will be much more public about it." He quietly closed the manila file folder and walked out of the room.

And so her father got his way. She was going home, and he had made the necessary reservations.

Chelsea listlessly packed the last of her stuff and placed the pile of suitcases at the front door of the apartment.

She was leaving Saudi Arabia forever. For always she would have Khalil's child. She still hadn't told her parents, thinking it would be easier to explain her condition in person. Protectively, she cupped her belly, still flat and firm, beneath her Shantung traveling suit, then nervously checked her watch for the time.

From the window she saw the taxi pull up and stop in front of her building. If it seemed odd to the native driver that an obvious foreigner spoke Arabic so fluently, he didn't comment as they haggled over the fare and came to an agreement. In no time her bags were loaded and she was on her way.

Home.

Atlanta, Georgia, didn't feel like home anymore. Instead it was as if she were leaving everything near and dear behind. Everything except. . . . She cupped her midsection once more, sat back and closed her eyes, preparing as best she could for the long trip ahead of her.

She supposed she must have drifted off to sleep, for when she awoke in what seemed like only a few seconds, she checked her watch to find that over an hour had passed.

Sitting up, she cleared the fog from her brain and glanced out the window, spying smoke billowing in the distance. She never recalled seeing that before.

"Excuse me," she said to the driver in Arabic. "Do you know what the smoke is from?"

"The refineries are in that direction." He shrugged. "Maybe one of them has caught fire."

A fire. Already it blackened the horizon. It made her think of Kuwait and what it must have looked like during the terrible fires after the Desert Storm campaign.

She sat back in the seat and tried to ignore it, but her eyes and her imagination kept being drawn to the disaster.

"How far away are we from there?"

"Five or six kilometers."

She settled in once more.

Just forget about it, Chelsea. She glanced at the black smoke, then forced her eyes back into the cab. *It doesn't involve you. You have a plane to catch.*

Call it her Hippocratic oath or a commitment to these people, call it foolishness, or perhaps the deafening roar of the explosion. Whatever the reason, she couldn't just drive on and pretend nothing was going on.

"Driver," she said, leaning forward. "I want you to take me to that fire."

"Lady, are you crazy?" he declared in broken English.

Perhaps. In more ways than one.

"Look, I'm a *duktur*. Now do as I tell you."

"It will cost you more."

"I don't give a damn how much it costs. Just get me there as fast as you can."

Unsure how, she knew her presence was of vital importance.

"Look, lady, you can't stay here."

She pushed past the insistent American, urging the cab driver to open the trunk of the car as quickly as possible. From her baggage she dug out her black medical bag.

"I'm a doctor. I can help."

"Why didn't you say so in the first place?"

She followed the man through the gated area, running to keep up with his longer strides.

A scene from hell greeted her.

Injured were scattered everywhere and in every imaginable state. Quickly she assessed the situation.

"Where are the other doctors?"

"You're the first to arrive. They should be here any minute."

"A company medic, anything?"

He pointed at three young men racing from victim to victim.

Triage, the sorting of the injured by priority, was not Chelsea's specialty, but she'd served her time in emergency rooms. Clutching her bag, she raced into the melee.

What struck her as the strangest thing about the entire scenario was the hot, roaring wind that swept over them like a desert *shamaal*. But fire made a terrific wind, she knew that. Still it made the hairs on her arm bristle.

She had work to do, and she set about it with efficiency organizing the medics and the uninjured to sorting as best they could while she scurried around double checking, trying to keep as many alive until the emergency units could arrive from Riyadh.

The victims were a mixture of Americans and Arabs. She treated them one and the same, feeling utterly helpless in many cases and hoping she gave extra minutes to others.

Moments later she heard the sirens. Accepting another injured man from an Arab she couldn't see clearly through all the smoke, she laid her patient down and checked his vital signs. Using the last of her emergency supply of gauze, she staunched the blood flowing from the gash on his leg. He was conscious, so she placed his hand on the wad.

"Hold it there until I can get back."

And then there were more people being dragged across the compound, but there was now a team of trained emergency professionals swarming over the area as well.

Exhausted, Chelsea dropped back against a parked Jeep. She was coughing so hard from the smoke that she was having trouble catching her breath. With blurred vision, she watched the Arab who had been pulling people from the fire and bringing them to her as he dragged another victim to the end of the long line of injured.

He looked up, and for a moment she thought her mind must have at last completely snapped.

"Khalil."

Before she could see his face again and reassure herself that she was wrong, he was gone, disappearing into the black haze.

She stood there, straining to see through the smoke, waiting for the man to return. The seconds ticked by, turning into minutes. Oh, God, whoever he was, he wasn't coming out.

It was crazy. Chelsea couldn't explain her reasoning. She didn't stop to try. Suddenly she was running, running toward a burst of flames. The heat, the wind, she felt none of it.

She only knew she was doing what she had to do.

Khalil saw her coming toward him, her hair as bright and alive as the circle of flames surrounding him.

"No, Chelsea. Go back," he shouted over the loud crackling, but if she heard him, she chose to ignore him.

What was she doing here? She was supposed to be on her way home to America.

"Khalil. Oh, God, Khalil. I know you're here. I don't know how . . . but I know it is you. Tell me, it's you." She was crying.

By Allah, he never could stand it when she cried.

"Chelsea. I want you to go back."

"No. Not without you."

Searching the inferno all around him, he looked for an opening. There was not one. He would simply have to make one, or die trying. He had to get Chelsea out of danger.

Covering his face which was already blackened by the fire with the end of his *keffiyeh* he lifted his arm to block the flames as best he could. Then he darted forward, trying to ignore the unbearable heat.

The pain was excruciating, but not even the fires of hell could stop him from reaching Chelsea. Then she was in his arms, holding on to him, the curtain of fire all around them. There was nothing but Chelsea and the fire.

Looking up, he saw it coming toward them.

He did the only thing he knew to do. Throwing her to the ground, he covered her with his own body.

Protect her. Protect her. It was and always would be the foremost mission of his life.

"The brown shell of the sea," he cried and gave up to the flames.

Epilogue

From the ridge overlooking Dir'iyyah, Chelsea hugged the parchment to her heart and watched the people tearing down the tents, packing them, preparing to depart from the winter encampment. Already the spring grasses were lush, the herds impatient to reach new pastures.

Halfway down the hill Muhammad and a group of his friends played with a litter of puppies a little too roughly, tumbling them as if they were stones.

"Be gentler, Muhammad," she called out.

The other boys looked up at her, defiance marring their youthful faces until Khalil's son took charge.

"Gentler," he commanded, echoing her sentiments. "Or I shall cut off your heads."

It was the best she could hope for from a Bedouin.

"What are you doing, wife, besides trying to break my son like one of your horses?"

Startled, she looked up to find that Khalil had sneaked up on her again. She smiled secretively.

"I am writing a poem. Would you like to read it?"

"Tonight, when we reach new pastures and we are

alone, you may read it to me if you would like. But for now, we must hurry."

He put out his hand and clasped hers, helping her rise. Big with child, it was not an easy feat, not at all.

Wallahi! She felt like a duck, waddling, following him down the incline.

"Have you ever seen a duck?" she asked.

Shaking his head, he looked at her quite strangely. He did that a lot lately.

"Well," she said, placing her hand in the middle of her back to keep herself from falling over, "you have now."

"Then, a duck is beautiful," he said, taking her in his arms and holding her as if she were truly pretty and slender again.

She placed her arms about his neck, staring up into his handsome face.

It had been many months since their return home, but they had never really spoken about it. Perhaps it was time.

"Khalil, you never told me. What were you doing there at that oil refinery."

"I was working."

"Why?" She dropped her head against his heart, just listening, knowing it would be there forever and always.

"If I could not have you here with me, I wanted to be as close to you as possible. Every weekend I traveled to Ad Dawadimi and watched you ride that mare."

"I never knew." She lifted her face and reached up to caress the craggy lines of his cheek.

"I did not want you to see me. I thought my presence would upset you. I thought . . . when I learned you were going home, back to America . . . I thought . . ."

445

"Oh, Khalil, how could you think that? Do you not know how it is between us?"

"I know now, my love." He gently kissed the top of her *abaaya*-covered head. "Forever and always."

Yes, forever and always, until the end of time.